ACROSS OCEANS

~

Kelsey Gietl

Purple Mask Publishing
St. Charles, Missouri

Quotations within this book are sourced from the following public domain works:
The New Websterian Dictionary - 1912 edition
Alice's Adventures in Wonderland by Lewis Carroll
The Time Machine by H.G. Wells

ISBN-13: 978-0-9991105-0-8
ebook ISBN: 978-0-9991105-1-5
Library of Congress Control Number: 2017946464
First Edition

*For all those who see how rough the ocean can be
and choose to cross it anyway.*

ACKNOWLEDGMENTS

FIRST, TO MY READERS, including my incredible international support group of family and friends. Of the millions of novels you could choose from, you picked mine, and that means the world.

To my husband, Scott, and our children. Our family is my greatest dream come true. Thank you for making this novel a wonderful second. No matter how wide the ocean, or how rough the sea, I would cross every one for you.

To my parents, Ken and Ruth, for a lifetime of love and encouragement. You read everything I ever wrote, even the bad parts, and never allowed me to forget my goals, even when I forgot how to get there. I love you more than all the words.

To my in-laws, Mark and Sharon, for providing draft feedback, becoming my mini marketing team, and especially by always believing in me. Your outpouring of support these past fifteen years continues to amaze me.

To my critique partner, Susan, for late night outlining sessions, parking lot brainstorming after book club, pondering my many questions, and analyzing my manuscript with a fine-toothed comb.

To my godmother and critique partner, Mary, for hours discussing storylines, speculating over which characters would end up together, and listening to me spout random historical anecdotes.

To my beta readers: Ann, Helen, Katherine, and Kimberly. You found errors I may never have noticed, and asked questions I may never have thought of. Thank you.

To the St. Charles City-County Library, St. Louis County Library, and the many amazing online libraries for the substantial research they provide an author on a limited budget.

And lastly, to every teacher I ever had. Saying thank you will never be thanks enough.

~ ~ ~

REUBEN ASSISTED THE UNDERTAKER with his younger sister's body before the sun had barely even kissed the sky. He settled Mira's modest thirteen-year-old form inside an oak hewn coffin and fled to the town square. That was where the Radford family should have been on May Day, not mourning at a funeral.

The ten-foot maypole rose before him on the green, more akin to a lumber beam than an actual pole, the vibrant ribbons tied down with twine. Reuben loosed the knot, releasing the strips of fabric to flutter in the wind—sapphire, scarlet, emerald, gold. He shut his eyes, lest his emotions get the better of him, only Mira's image slipped under his lids all the same.

There lay the soft smile beneath the same signature russet locks and coffee-colored eyes all Radfords shared. Bouncing as she wove between the other school children around the maypole, a crown of purple and white blossoms in her hair. All white crisply laundered and pressed dress, stockings, and shoes. Clean, pure, perfect. Innocent.

The same clothing held her body now, lying cold and stiff upon their parlor table, awaiting burial. Her death was unexpected, barely two days passing between then and now. There was no need for extended waiting before burial, nor did the Radfords desire it. Seeing the train crash was harsh enough, but witnessing the

1

aftermath was worse: swollen cheeks, crushed legs, a pattern of sutures across Mira's brow, neck, and arms. For his mother to accept something so atrocious was once her baby girl ... it would be easier to pardon Frankenstein's monster.

So Reuben prepared the body. Mira had been Florence and Harris's only daughter, the child they prayed for two years after his birth to make their family complete. As their only son, it was his duty to ensure their angel was remembered only in beauty.

The sun broke over the eastern tree line of Fontaine, just another town lost on the rail line between London and Southampton. With the sun came heat, unusually warm for the first of May. Giving a swipe to his brow, Reuben shrugged off his memories and allowed his heavy heart to lead him to St. James's cemetery.

Alongside the fence, eight carriages lay in wait behind the curtained funeral coach. He recognized the second carriage immediately, even before the dark-clothed figures of his lanky father and petite mother emerged. Behind the Radfords' was another familiar carriage from which stepped a substantial fair-haired man, Karl Kisch, and his eldest, significantly trimmer, dishwater-blond son, and Reuben's best mate, Charles.

From the remaining carriages filed a few men Reuben recognized from the *Fontaine Gazette*, where his father served as chief editor. The rest were unfamiliar faces—no doubt attendees out of politeness for his father.

Reuben joined his parents, his stomach clenching at the sight of their distressed expressions. Florence's tear-streaked cheeks were visible even through her mourning veil, her chest swelling as the undertaker opened the back doors to reveal the little coffin inside. He slid the end to where he and Reuben could each lift a side. Charles offered a grim nod as he and his father shouldered the opposite end.

"Mama and the others send their sympathies," Charles whispered in his thick German accent, as they hoisted the coffin through the gate and down the packed cemetery path.

"Thank you for being here," Reuben whispered back. The two boys had been closer than brothers for six years; he doubted he could survive this without Charles by his side.

As they laid the coffin in the waiting grave, Reuben knew what he needed to do. Once the pastor extended the final blessing, Reuben shrugged off the interminable heat and stole the shovel from the gravedigger's hands. Burying Mira's body wouldn't clear his conscience, but it was a start.

"Blimey, son, are you sure you want to do that?" asked the grave-digger. "Your father paid me to take care of things."

"And well paid at that," Harris noted. He gestured for Reuben to hand over the shovel. "Stop this nonsense."

Reuben merely grunted as he unleashed a tirade of dirt into the hole before him. Sweat beaded across his brow and trickled down his neck where the shirt's moist fabric chafed against his skin. Giving in, Harris dismissed the other mourners and stood silently by; Florence, Charles, and Karl being the only others to remain. Sooner than expected, the little coffin was hidden from sight.

Reuben cast the shovel to the ground and bitterly crossed his arms at Mira's final resting place. Such an ugly remembrance to a beautiful person.

Harris rested a hand on Reuben's shoulder. "Time to go, son."

Reuben didn't move. "Not yet. You go ahead."

"But the luncheon, Reuben ...," said Florence quietly. "Everyone will expect you to be there."

"I'm not hungry. You go."

"Reuben," scolded Harris. "What more can you do here?"

"I need to be alone with her."

"To what end?" spat his father.

"Harris," soothed Florence, stealing her husband's hand from Reuben's arm. "Leave him be." She raised her crisp mourning veil to kiss Reuben's cheek. "Hurry home, sweetheart."

Their departure elicited a gentle embrace around Reuben's

shoulders from Karl Kisch. "My condolences, Reuben," said Karl. "Mira was a joy. Her absence will be noticed by all of us."

"Thank you, Mr. Kisch. No one understands that more than me."

"Do not linger too long, Reuben." With a final sympathetic glance, Karl released Reuben and took to his carriage.

"Do not blame yourself for this too," Charles said, his voice level despite the deep furrows etched upon his brow.

Reuben continued to stare at the ground. The mound of dirt baked under the sun, burning away at the uprooted grass until the edges wilted. Pink earthworms and slimy yellow maggots slid through the muck, fleeing from the same fate. Most burrowed into the ground. A few didn't make it. Reuben crushed one under his shoe, leaving the sole imprint in the mud.

Charles ran a defeated hand through his hair. "I can allow you to take responsibility for the fight, but not what occurred before or afterwards. You can only control your actions, not anyone else's. And you certainly could not have foreseen this ending."

Mira would have said all the same assurances if she was here. For this, he knew he wasn't responsible. Her death was an accident, fate stepping in where it shouldn't belong. Unfortunately, there were other secrets worse than losing one's life. Stains you scrubbed at until you began to lose yourself. With Mira's death, he lost the chance to ever make it right.

"It's May Day," said Reuben. "You should be with your family."

"You should too."

"As soon as I say goodbye."

Charles nodded in resignation. They'd had enough similar conversations for him to know Reuben wouldn't be swayed. Only the clatter of the gate and departing hoof beats signaled his departure.

Reuben sank, knees and knuckles buried in the soil, and wept until he was certain there was nothing left inside him. Knowing, no matter how long he stayed there, he could never say goodbye.

That was the thing about time. Some say to wait but an hour or a day and it can heal all wounds. But the truth was true happiness lasted but a moment. A single poor decision, however, ... Now *that* could torture you for a lifetime.

PART ONE

~~~

Safe Harbor

ONE

MAGGIE ARCHER LOATHED HER MOTHER. And she hated being seventeen.

That morning she bounded from bed, throwing back the window curtains to the warm sun on her face and nary a cloud in the sky. The weather promised perfect conditions for May Day, traditionally celebrating new life, romance, and the promise that summer was near at hand. Unofficially, the holiday also served as a reminder of her sister, Tena's, lifelong companionship.

"We celebrate Mothering Sunday, but there's no day for sisters," Tena reckoned ten years ago. "May Day will be our day."

And so it was declared; on May Day, the Archer sisters were inseparable. Weeks were spent planning the day, practicing their performance around the maypole, and giggling loudly, much to their mother's chagrin and their father's delight. Their anticipation of the day's festivities expanded to every corner of the house until even Maggie's sleep was interrupted by thoughts of the merriment to come.

Until this year. This year everything had changed.

With a grimace, Maggie swept the curtains closed, falling back onto her bed with a soft bounce. Most girls her age anticipated their coming season as a year-long parade of gorgeous gowns and extravagant cotillions, alongside doting suitors and frivolous attentions, all to see which girl earned the best proposal.

Maggie viewed her season as she suspected the servants might—an entire year of hair-pulling, tantrums, and tears.

A quick rap sounded at the door and opened without waiting for Maggie's reply. The housemaid, Olivia, scurried in with a quick "Morning, Miss," opened the curtains once more, and retrieved Maggie's undergarments and ivory tea gown from the wardrobe. She laid them out across the half of the bed where Maggie wasn't sprawled. "Will you require assistance this morning, Miss?"

"No need, Olivia. I will assist her this morning."

Tena flounced into the room resembling a sketch from *Gimbel's* fashion magazine. Half her honey-nut waves cascaded over her shoulders, the crown interwoven with peach and white flowers. Her white tea gown hit just above the ankle, flowing around her curves in deep layers accented with beading the same color as her amber eyes. "Get up, sister dear," she crooned, yanking Maggie up by the arm with a groan.

"You are too cruel," Maggie complained, shooing at her sister in the same manner she would a pesky fly.

Tena waited while Maggie changed out of her nightgown and slipped into her undergarments, straightening up to hook the corset around her ribcage. She stepped into the ankle-length tea gown, allowing Tena to fasten the row of little buttons down the back, and examined her appearance in the looking glass. Even she would admit her mother had chosen well when selecting their dresses. The cerulean lace trim accentuated Maggie's eyes, deepening their usual blue-grey to a vivid indigo, while the cream lace overlay intensified her already dark russet waves.

Despite the striking difference in hair and eye color, there was no denying that Maggie and Tena were sisters. Their close age— only ten months apart—gave them all the same privileges of twins. Same year in school, shared friends, same potential suitors, shared seasons. Yet their internal differences were so strong Maggie wondered how they could still maintain so many other similarities.

"There. Perfect," Tena smiled. "All the boys will want to dance with you."

"How depressing a thought." Maggie smoothed the front of her skirt, embarrassed that Tena's face shone with such delight while her lips hung like withered stems.

Tena caught her sister's eye. "You're not even a bit curious about your escort? He's sure to be loads better than the last one— what was his name?"

"As if it mattered?" Maggie grunted. She swept her hair across her shoulder, tying a heather headband to reign in her unruly locks. "Mother chooses husbands like a Jane Austen novel. It doesn't matter if he's as dull as Mr. Collins, so long as his pocketbook belongs to Bingley. Choose me a pair of earrings." Maggie threw the last words over her shoulder on her way to the wardrobe. She slipped into a pair of sensible cream colored shoes with a low heel, perfect for fleeing from obnoxious suitors.

Tena rummaged through Maggie's jewelry chest, selecting a pair of sapphire teardrops. "Oh, Maggie, you take everything so personally. Mother's only acting how any mother would."

"You may feel differently when you're on the receiving end."

"Oh, how I wish I were!" Tena huffed. "You're the one they throw real celebrations for. My birthday was little more than a glamorous tea party."

It was true. Tena, although the one who longed for their parents' attention, was all too often forgotten by the curse of youngest daughter. Last June, their parents planned an enormous hurrah for Maggie's seventeenth birthday which, in Maggie's opinion, had been simply torturous. They invited every eligible man between the ages of eighteen and eternity, which delighted Tena and irritated Maggie. Each one feigned personal interest, always inquiring to her desires while superficially striving to uncover her family's financial assets. While the Archers would never reside in Hampshire's estates, neither were they peddling flowers along London's streets. There were many advantages to marrying a banker's daughter, comforts no man would thumb his nose at. Maggie spent every second concocting excuses to escape their annoying questions, all the while wondering if it would be terribly inappropriate to sneak off to the kitchen with the hired help.

By the time April arrived, and Tena rolled from sixteen to seventeen, their dual coming-of-age had long since sent their mother into a tizzy. Two eligible ladies in the household meant twice the pressure. With May Day less than one week after Tena's birthday, there was no extra time to host a second sensational affair. There were two new gowns to purchase for the festival, two wealthy escorts to obtain, and double the time their mother spent keeping a watchful eye on her daughters which culminated in twice the strain on Maggie's parents' already overwrought marriage. Between the bickering and the scolding, the senseless blaming and all-out fights, their relationship gave Maggie daily headaches.

"The best is always saved for last," Maggie reassured Tena. She nestled one of her own ivory and lavender rose combs amidst Tena's curls. "This is your season too. By year's end, you will have caught at least one man's eye."

A deep blush spread across Tena's cheeks. "Even one man feels like a pipe dream to me."

Maggie swung Tena around, dragging her from the room, both girls laughing. "How would you know what pipe dreams feel like? You never flow upstream!"

"Thank goodness for that!" Tena giggled.

The girls raced through the kitchen, retrieving their festival baskets completed with Olivia's final sprucing that morning. Last night they'd spent hours baking treats to share at the festival, although Maggie undoubtedly had sampled more than actually baked. Tena was the ample cook, the detailed seamstress, and the sweet schoolgirl with perfect penmanship and eidetic memory. If she still failed to attract a man after being presented this year, then all men were blind dolts, simple as that.

"Finally, there you are!" their mother clamored upon the girls' entrance to the parlor. Having married Laurence Archer at eighteen, Beatrix was still very much a societal beauty at thirty-six, all perfectly pinned raven hair, striking blue-grey eyes, and straight lined day suits. Maggie cursed that she'd been born sharing both her mother's physical traits and fierce resolve.

Tena, in comparison, was blessed to inherit their father's quiet introspection along with his brown sugar locks and eyes the color of candlelight. Laurence peered over that morning's edition of the *Fontaine Gazette* with a sly smile while his wife fretted over the girls' appearances, smoothing a crease here and securing a strand of hair there.

"There," said Beatrix. "You are both exquisite. These dresses are exactly as I'd hoped." She picked at Tena's hair, clucking at the borrowed comb which was not part of her planned ensemble. It remained only at Tena's insistence. "Now," Beatrix continued sternly, "please do not do anything to embarrass yourselves today." Her look pointed at Maggie as she said this.

"Yes girls," piped their father's voice. "It is very important for you to give these men a chance." He folded his paper, laying it across the sofa, and rose to meet them. Clasping their hands, nostalgia played across his features. "My girls. Already arrived at your seasons. You've grown up before I learned how to be a father."

Tena stood on toe to kiss her father's cheek. "You've done wonderfully, Father. With Maggie too."

Laurence released a boisterous laugh, not shared by his wife. He squeezed Maggie's hand. "Do you think so, little girl?"

Maggie stepped closer to bring her lips to his other cheek. "If I am a disgrace, it is not your doing. You are splendid."

Beatrix gave them all an uncharacteristically satisfied grin.

"Maggie, I promise after today you will disgrace us no longer."

Tena rolled her eyes. "How can you stop the rain from falling?"

"Not helping," Maggie hissed at her sister.

Beatrix draped an arm around each of her daughters and steered them from the room. "Oh, I think you'll discover all sorts of unexpected surprises today."

As Maggie would soon discover, truer words were never said.

TWO

THE WORLD WAS AN ODD SARDONIC thing. Unpredictable, erratic, able to change directions with the wind's passing. And yet, Reuben knew there was always one constant—inconsistency. That was the irony.

For instance, when he woke that morning, he expected his father to already be at the newspaper, managing what could still be controlled. Lost to his editorship for the last three years, Harris's attention could only be coerced through Reuben's articles, dealing in pure fact instead of anything resembling emotions. Likewise, Reuben anticipated his mother's weak reception when he joined the breakfast table. Florence spoke minimally since that cruel day, her heart having hardened against the pain. To Reuben's parents, it seemed little else pained them more now than the loss of a perfect daughter while their troubled son continued existence.

The smell of the cherry trees in bloom along the lane, the sound of the sparrows flitting through the trees, the harsh lines of Mira Radford's name within the cold cemetery stone. These things were understood. Predictable.

Reuben ran his fingers through his unkempt hair, took a deep calming breath, and nudged open the cemetery gate. Originally built in 1402, St. James Church's stacked stone exterior had suffered damage during the Civil War. They restructured the south wall in 1644, leaving her face like patched pottery—restored, but never quite the same. Her steeple rose on the north end, the bell within clanging out the same hour shown on the timepiece molded into the brickwork. On the path to his sister's grave, freshly dug plots intermingled with aging gravestones containing names rubbed away and no longer remembered. Above them wrapped the extensive arms of yew trees older than the churchyard itself.

In a life full of so many questions, it gave him comfort to know that this one place would never change.

But therein lay the irony. Just when you become comfortable, everything is flipped upside down and turned over by one chance encounter.

"Today is too pretty to sit alone weeping."

Reuben whirled, immediately on the defense against whoever was so rude to disrupt him from his grief. He barely managed to swallow the series of ill-advised language hovering over his tongue as he took in the visage of the girl before him. "Mira?" he croaked, and forced himself to perform a double take. The sun wrapped around her like a halo, highlighting the silhouette of a slender dark-haired maiden. Reuben raised his hand as a shield, revealing striking blue-grey eyes far removed from his sister's brown irises. This girl was perhaps only a year younger than Reuben's eighteen, but her posture was as poised as someone decades older.

"Hello," she said, holding up a basket of cookies, sweets, and flowers. "My sister and I were on our way to the festival when we saw you alone out here. It seemed a terrible sadness for someone to grieve on such a happy occasion."

Lost in the monotony of days, Reuben had forgotten what today was. May Day again—three years to the day since he'd buried his sister.

Mira loved May Day. Every year she helped their mother craft baskets similar to the one this girl carried full of treats to deliver to their friends. They would grow all a flutter, twittering around the house like little birds preparing for the anticipated day. Afterwards, they would trickle home from the festival exhausted from their merriment. But that was before Mira died. Their father had a new May Day philosophy now, one not involving flowers, laughter, or even mutually discussed memories. For the Radfords, today time simply stopped.

"Perhaps frivolity keeps us from remembering our true purpose," Reuben said.

The mysterious girl lighted her fingers across the smooth stone surface of Mira's grave. "Perhaps being among the dead is the best place to think about life."

"They're dead," Reuben shot back. "They know nothing of life."

"Of course they do!" she cried. "All these people lived once, didn't they? Each of their lives had a story. You haven't ever wondered who they were?"

In truth Reuben tried not to think about the other people at all. When he considered that he was surrounded by a field of corpses, it only increased his angst.

"Never," Reuben stated. "I didn't know them."

The girl wove her way between the gravestones, examining the engravings while she spoke. "All the more reason to give them a story—what if they have no family? Someone should remember them." She bent to squint at a stone half buried in mud. "Jonathan Cumberland. Forty-two years. Shall I tell you his tale?"

Reuben sensed a lengthy conversation in the making and wasn't in the mood. After three years of isolation in this place, he was miffed to share it with someone else. He had a growing desire to tell her off and kick her out on her derriere.

He stood, flicking away the dirt that clung to his pant legs. "I appreciate your concern for my welfare, but would much prefer to be left in peace."

"You'll have plenty of peace when you're dead," she affirmed. "Now sit down and listen to Maggie Archer's story time."

Reuben remained standing. "Is that your name?" Maggie

seemed too sweet a name to be attached to so forward a lady.

"It is. Does that displease you?"

Reuben shrugged. "No. It just doesn't seem to suit your, ah ... demeanor."

"Is your name any better?"

"Reuben Radford."

"Well, I suppose it is." Maggie flipped her hair over her shoulder and leaned against Mr. Cumberland's tombstone. Reuben's jaw dropped. "Oh close your mouth, Mr. Radford. The dead have better things to do than be incensed about my seating preference. If you're expecting politeness, may I direct you to my sister, Tena? Never a toe out of line. She refused to even say hello to you. I said it was rude not to; she said you might be a ruffian out to murder me."

Reuben's lip twitched. Maggie intrigued him, he'd give her that. It wasn't every day, or even on a semi-frequent basis, he encountered a girl his age so lacking in vocal filters. He would play her game. "Tena sounds delightful. Where can I find her?"

"Number seven, Union Street. Go forth." Maggie tapped her finger on her chin thoughtfully, slowly making her way back to where he stood. "Or, if you stay, I could tell you how Mr. Cumberland was actually a brilliant scientist much beloved by London society."

Reuben grinned. He knew the ending to this novel. It was only one of a few hundred he'd read over the years. "Until he was shunned by that society, forcing him to manufacturer monstrous creatures on a far-away island."

"That's absurd," Maggie muttered. "At the very least make up a believable story." She rummaged through her basket to retrieve a cloth bundle secured with blue ribbon. With a flourish, she untied the knot to reveal a mix of chocolate chip and sugar cookies. She offered them to Reuben then took two for herself.

He bit into the cookie, savoring the taste of sweet butter and chocolate on his tongue. "These are incredible! Our cook could take a few lessons from yours."

"Actually they're Tena's." Maggie laughed in between bites.

Reuben grabbed two more, popping them into his mouth in quick succession. "I'm surprised your parents allow you in the kitchen at all. Why haven't you hired someone?"

"We have, but Tena fancied her hand at it, and Father sided with her. It was one of the only arguments he ever won against Mother. He said there are certain skills even proper ladies may be wise to learn." Maggie finished her cookie, and brushed the crumbs from her fingers. "Would you like to invent a story this time?"

Reuben pointed to the stone of Jacob Simmons, aged fifty-two years. "I'll bet he battled invasive outer space creatures. And that woman—" Reuben pointed at the next one excitedly. "Isabella Sweet. She lived among the Morlocks for years until one day she returned to Fontaine to live in the present instead of the future."

"What are you on about?" asked Maggie.

Reuben sat flummoxed. "Don't you read?"

Maggie swiped crumbs from her fingers. "Of course I read ... occasionally. I just don't read whatever nonsense you're spouting."

"But, it's Wells!" Reuben sputtered. "I've read *The Time Machine* two dozen times. It makes me realize there's something bigger out there than myself. That maybe sometimes impossible things can happen."

"Father read to us every night when Tena and I were children. *My* favorite was Jules Verne's *Journey to the Center of the Earth*." Maggie scratched a pebble out of the dirt with her toe. She kicked it, scattering a gathering of blackbirds into the sky. "Mother's wrath eventually ruined it. She never had much regard for academics—books were in the way of important skills like pouring tea and not being a constant disgrace to the family. You know, everything that makes us ladies worth keeping."

Maggie glanced at the dates carved into Mira's grave and did a quick calculation in her head. "Your younger sister?" Reuben nodded and she gave a bright smile straight into those sparkling blue eyes. He would never understand how, when she reached for his hand, he allowed himself to accept her gentle grasp. It had been years since anyone came near enough to hold his hand or embrace him, not his father nor his mother, and certainly not an unfamiliar woman.

"Mira has a beautiful story," said Maggie. "Years from now people will talk about the amazing life she led. Only thirteen years old. She was a perfect child to be taken so young. Constantly laughing, of course. Never a bad word to say about anyone. And now she dwells with the fairies in the grotto of the—'"

Reuben threw off her grip, now shaking with emotion. His words punctuated every gasp. "That is my sister you speak of, not a fairytale. Fairies and grottos? Her death was horrible! I was there. I saw it happen! How can you speak so lightly when you don't even know?"

Reuben didn't need her telling him the kind of girl Mira was or the magic that died when she did. He was constantly reminded of Mira's absence every night when he went home. The house was akin to a cellar without her in it.

"I meant no disrespect," Maggie said evenly. The two of them locked stares, neither backing down or saying a word, but all the while a strange fire grew within Maggie. Reuben saw it simmering, afraid what madness it would bring, while also craving it. Eventually, "Please understand this is how I deal with an uncomfortable situation."

"How is that?" Reuben demanded.

Maggie grinned. "I don't."

Without warning, they were running across the cemetery. She pulled him along, encouraging him to run faster. And Reuben was baffled as to why he was actually listening.

They tiptoed inside the church, closing the door quietly behind them. No one was within now, not even the pastor. Thin rays of light permeated the darkness through colorful stained glass windows. Dust danced in the beams, giving the room an ethereal quality.

"What are we doing?" Reuben whispered, his heart pounding, from the run or his emotions he wasn't certain.

Maggie squeezed his hand, leading him up the rear staircase to the choir loft. "You need to do something impulsive," she whispered back, "something you would never do if I wasn't here right now."

"Why do I need to do that?" Reuben demanded.

"Because you're sad about your sister, and I don't like sad people. Time to have some fun." She opened the door for the bell tower, gesturing to the thick rope hanging down from the rafters. "Gentlemen first, I insist."

Reuben hesitated. "Only those appointed by the pastor can ring the bells and only at specified times."

"Oh please!" she scoffed, her volume rising, "This is a crime for children. No one will even notice."

"We're not supposed to be here," he tried again. "How will it look to everyone if someone catches us here together? ... Alone?" It would definitely not leave a good impression of their character, especially not hers.

Maggie leaned against the doorframe and shrugged, "Who cares what people think?"

"My parents do. I do. You should too."

"I have never been one to follow many rules. My *mother* can attest to that." Her emphasis on the word *mother* was not at all polite. "But my sister *likes* rules. So if that is your forte, number seven, Union Street is only a few blocks down the road. The two of you can wile away the hours deciding if it's boorish to prop your feet on the furniture."

Reuben gave her a look. Maggie scowled right back at him. And that was how they stood for a solid five minutes looking from each other to the rope and back again. At some point they must have reached an understanding because Maggie slammed the door and left the church. Reuben trailed out behind her.

He stood silent while she gathered her things, relieved she hadn't forced him to break out of his comfort zone and yet feeling equally pathetic.

Maggie packed the remaining items into her basket, carefully attempting to arrange them so it would appear as though they hadn't eaten any. "Take this," she said, handing him the basket. "For your parents."

Reuben hesitated only a second before accepting her offering. "Thank you. I suppose you'll be heading to the festival?"

Maggie nodded.

"May I escort you?" He hated the thought of saying goodbye so soon. Being alone with Mira's grave did not seem a peaceable thought right now.

Maggie frowned. "No, I don't think that's such a good idea, however—" She stepped back, hands on hips, sizing him up. "Yes, yes, I think that will work perfectly. You must make me a promise."

Reuben folded his arms through the basket handle. "I'm too old for a girl to make demands of me."

"Wait until you're married. My mother makes nothing but demands of my father. *My* request only requires a simple yes or no response."

"If your request is for me to marry you, that isn't happening," Reuben stated resolutely.

Maggie's eyes hit the sky. "Ha, ha. On that we agree, Mr. Radford. Now take my hand."

"What for?"

"For heaven's sake, just do it."

Reuben hesitantly did as she asked.

Maggie's next words were spoken very low, very serious, and sounded very ridiculous. "I've deduced you need an escape from your life and, heaven knows, I would prefer never to return to mine. Promise we'll meet back here next year, and each subsequent year thereafter, until we are either driven from this land or meet some terrible fate."

Reuben's free hand moved to conceal a smirk. "Have a flair for the theatrical?"

Maggie poked him in the sternum. "Shut up. I am deathly serious. The dead will not look favorably upon you if you refuse to take this oath." She gave another winning smile. "We all deserve a good story do we not? This can be ours."

Warmth emanated where Maggie's fingers met with his. This girl was nothing like the other girls he'd met. She seemed adventurous and impetuous, which was far reached from the life he lived right now. Maggie was exactly the sort of distraction he needed.

And a very eye-catching distraction at that. Time spent in the cemetery wouldn't be nearly as depressing with her around.

Reuben repeated slowly, only with far less dramatic flair, "I promise we'll meet back here next year, and each year thereafter, until we are either driven from this land or meet some terrible fate. And I'll receive more of Tena's supremely fashioned baked goods."

"Only if Tena brings them to you herself. I am not a courier." Maggie's grin radiated straight into her eyes. "Until next year then, Mr. Radford."

"Until next year."

And that was it.

The gate swung closed and the familiar feeling of despair instantly squashed any amusement Reuben had at his random encounter with a stranger. He could try to ignore the reality of the situation again when he met Maggie next year—if he met her next year. It had made sense when she'd said it, but now that he was alone ... the thought of meeting a lady in a cemetery seemed a bit crass.

Eh, that was a year away. He'd deal with it when it came.

Until then, it was back to the pit of darkness that was his world now.

What would Mira think if she was here?

She'd likely cock her head to the side, raise an eyebrow, and smirk.

Who was that? she would ask.

"Just some girl."

A bit eccentric, don't you think?

Reuben picked a pebble out of the mud and tossed it through a break in the trees. "She seemed harmless enough."

As harmless as the folks in the sanatorium once were. Mira would give him her most serious stare and, for a solid two minutes, he would be completely fooled into believing Maggie deserved to be committed. Eventually Mira would smile and he'd know she was only teasing. He'd always been so gullible when it came to his sister.

Reuben sat with his back to the gravestone and pulled his knees into himself. His chin weighed heavy on his knee. "I miss you, Mira," he confessed.

The wind whistled at him through the trees, conveying a series of hazy messages across the clearing. Reuben strained to fine tune the multitudes of indistinct sounds until with perfect clarity he recognized the one specific voice he longed to hear.

~ ~ ~

Maggie raced down the street towards the festival, unable to distract her mind from the boy in the cemetery. It was one year until they would see each other again, 364 days under her mother's scrutiny. All for one glorious day of freedom with a near-stranger. One day with those simmering hot chocolate eyes and shy smile, not to speak of the topics she could now discuss without reprimand!

Normally, when conversing with other men her age, she would press every issue, her only intention to drive them away with her incessant questioning and haughty opinions. With Reuben she had no such need. Unlike every other man in the whole of society, he had no expectations of her. There was no need to ward him off as their once-a-year friendship would never achieve fruition.

Maggie raised her face to the sun's warmth. Reuben was the perfect distraction. Even if she made a blunder, he was sure to overlook it by the following year. And if not? Well, she wouldn't be any worse off than before.

Yes, she decided. This could be the best friendship she would ever have. Or her worst mistake. There was a very fine line between the two.

THREE

LAURENCE ARCHER STEPPED FROM the Double Brougham covered carriage, his dress shoes squelching against the lightly falling snow. He offered his hand to his wife and youngest daughter in turn, pausing as he took his eldest daughter's hand with a reassuring smile. "Nothing must be decided tonight, little girl." He brushed the wet flakes from Maggie's elegantly coiffured hair. "It's Christmas Eve. Try to enjoy yourself."

Maggie ceased his worries with a wave of her gloved fingers as the door opened into the Winchesters' brightly lit entryway. "Oh, Father, why must you even mention it when a decision is still months away?" She busied herself with unbuttoning her winter coat as much to put her father off as to calm her own nerves. Cinched into an emerald and silver ball gown of her mother's choosing, Maggie didn't need to be reminded why she was the catch of the night.

"Alas, here's the reason now," she muttered, handing her coat to the footman.

"Oi, Maggie!" In a rush of identical rustling mauve satin, cream lace, and faultless fair curls, she was set upon by two wildly giggling twin girls. Suppressing the urge to violently strike them both, Maggie returned their friendly kisses and plastered whatever might pass for pleasant on her face.

26

"Good evening, Edith, Bianca. Another lovely party." Her eyes roamed up the main staircase to the gallery beyond, where nearly every inch of dark woodwork was adorned with holly and evergreen mixed with a smattering of elaborate red ribbons and silver baubles. "Everything looks magical."

Bianca patted her updo as though it were she, and not the host of servants, who had manufactured such an event. "I insisted Papa take every pain this year. Three new pieces in the band and every worthy man from here to Farnborough!" She exchanged a sly grin with Edith. "At least all the inviting ones."

Edith returned her cheeky grin, revealing two dance cards from behind her back with a flourish. "Ta da! Your husbands await, ladies!"

Tena snatched her dance card, eyes hungrily scanning the lines. "So many dances!" she exclaimed. Her irises shone brighter than the iridescent lavender of her dress.

"Let me see that." Maggie took her dance card from Edith, scowl lines digging a trough across her forehead. "Fifteen?" she cried. "Why so many?"

"This is our season too, Maggie," Bianca puffed, blowing wayward hairs from her eyes. "I intend to have my taste of as many men as I can. However will I decide who to settle down with otherwise?"

"You won't settle down even then," Edith quipped.

Bianca bit her lip and giggled. "Don't tell the boys my secret." Tena hid her smile behind her gloved fingers and steered Maggie towards the ballroom, leaving Bianca and Edith to follow in a cloud of flirtatious laughter.

"Who will ask us to dance first, I wonder?" breathed Tena. Her head swiveled over the expansive room, chattering guests, and continued festive holiday decor. An eight piece band filled the area farthest from the floor-to-ceiling windows framed on either side by nine foot embellished Christmas trees.

Maggie stared at fifteen empty lines on her dance card in need of a signature. Fifteen men whom she would be forced to tell the same tiresome stories about herself over and over again. Fifteen men who would decide if she was worth dealing with for all of eternity.

She didn't want fifteen men. Heavens, she didn't even want one. All that marriage nonsense was for someone else, someone who wanted a mess of emotions and a complicated life. If it wasn't for Edith and Bianca and a stupid May Day tradition, she might very well have avoided marriage altogether. Her parents would have been upset, but eventually they would have accepted it.

As if on cue, Tena linked her arm with Maggie's, "I do hope Reuben will be here," she whispered. "You can introduce us."

Maggie's eyes shot to her sister's face. "Brilliant. He'll be the perfect husband for you."

Tena erupted into fits of giggles. "Hardly, sister dear. The way you've gone on about him these past seven months, I wouldn't dream of interfering!"

"What utter rubbish," Maggie admonished. "You mention him twice as much as I do." Tena hadn't shut up about Reuben since Maggie told her about their meeting, and was now deeply sorry she had. Even if Maggie's thoughts *did* spend their fair share of time imagining those tortured-soul eyes he wore so well, she was never falling for such romantic rubbish.

Maybe if she hid in the toilet everyone would forget about her.

She held her card out to Tena. "I'll be right back," she lied.

"Oh, no you won't!" Bianca gleefully swiped Maggie's dance card and wrote a name down. She gestured to a man of thirty now standing before them. *Where did he come from?* Maggie wondered. "Maggie, this is John Tennant," Bianca said cheerily. "He's in law and travels all over the world." She gave a high-pitched giggle. "How delightful!"

Maggie gave a quick nod. "Pleasure, Mr. Tennant. I suppose I will join you for the—" Maggie glanced down at her dance card. "—third dance of the evening."

"It seems so, Miss Archer." John Tennant smiled, his mouth far too large for his face, overwhelmingly so. Maggie had a mere minute to dread the third dance before Edith pulled her in another direction, Bianca quick on their heels and poor Tena left behind in the crowd. Maggie threw a withering look over her shoulder, catching the disappointment lurking behind Tena's eyes. Maggie would never understand why her sister wanted a part of this lunacy. Bianca and Edith passed her between them like two children playing hot potato, and Maggie with no say as to whose hands she was thrown into.

"Maggie, this is William Capaldi," Edith said, marking another spot on Maggie's dance card.

"Paul and Patrick Baker. They're twins like us!"

"Sylvester Davison. His family owns a shipyard!"

"Peter McCoy. His dancing is divine!"

Names and faces flew by in a rush. Tom Eccleston, Peter McGann, David Pertwee, Matthew Troughton, Friedrich Kisch, Christopher Hartnell. Maggie wasn't sure she would be able to keep any of them straight without the safety net of the card attached to her wrist. None of them had particularly memorable faces. They were all handsome and charming and knew all the proper things to say. But none of them enticed her to choose them over something more appealing, say a stiff drink or a soft blow to the head. Either of those seemed equally lovely at this point.

"Maggie, let me introduce Colin Smith." Bianca forced Maggie's hand into that of a silver-haired gentleman easily pushing past seventy. Despite requiring the assistance of a cane, Bianca had still assigned him to a dance!

"How desperate do you think I am?" Maggie hissed once Mr. Smith was out of earshot, which probably didn't need to be very far given his age. "You can't honestly think I'm going to fall for a man old enough to be my grandfather!"

"He's the wealthiest unmarried man at this party. Why wouldn't you fall for him?"

Maggie rounded on her. "Maybe because I don't even want to be here! And yet, here I am with you parading me around like a prize winning sheep at the fair!" Maggie shoved her dance card into Bianca's hands. "I wouldn't even be in this mess if it wasn't for you and Edith. My dance card would have only been half full and it would have been a halfway enjoyable party."

"We only did it to help you!" Bianca threw the card back at Maggie. "Don't you know what everyone will say if you don't give up this spinster routine? Rumors about you mean rumors about your parents, about your upbringing. Edith and I changed that." Bianca looked squarely at Maggie like she was a disobedient child. "Don't be so stupid, Maggie. They all want you. For goodness sake, let *one* of them have you."

"I'll thank you to not do me any more favors," Maggie said gruffly, wishing she could relive last May Day. That day the twins' co-conspiring minds—and their daddy's pocketbook no doubt—had landed Maggie in her current predicament.

After she left Reuben in the cemetery, Maggie hurried off to the festival, arriving out of breath and slightly sweaty, only to be immediately rushed by her giggling sister, her exasperated mother, and her amused father.

"Where did you disappear to?" asked Beatrix. Her gaze swept suspiciously over Maggie's disheveled appearance.

"Oh, Maggie, look!" Tena cried, whisking Maggie away to where a crowd anxiously waited before a raised podium. "They're about to announce the May Queen!" Never before had Maggie been so grateful to have a sister. Tena's quick thinking allowed her time to concoct an excuse for why she inexplicably disappeared for hours.

Tena jabbed Maggie in the ribs. "Were you with him all that time? Tell me everything!"

"There's nothing to tell." Maggie threw a glance over her shoulder. Good, their parents were exactly where they left them.

The crowd drew silent as the festival chairman took his place at the podium. A girl of around ten stood beside him holding the may crown as though the delicate white hawthorn, daisy, and myrtle blossoms were made of glass. Tena bounced on the balls of her feet. "When will I meet him?" she whispered.

"Never," Maggie hissed. "You had your chance at the cemetery."

"That's not fair! I'm your sister—I have to judge if he's acceptable."

"Acceptable for *what*?"

"Well because if you were with him for so long he *must* fancy you."

Maggie removed herself from her sister's grasp. "He doesn't. Mind your own affairs, Tena."

"But—"

"Listen, if you shut up about it now, I promise to give you more details at home." Tena's eyes lit up, but she remained silent and Maggie instantly regretted the offer. Tena was sure to be a fountain of inquiries.

"And our May Queen for 1910 is ..."

With her ridiculous desire to marry young and make a brood of babies, Tena was the perfect candidate to be May Queen. She was the correct age—16 to 20. She'd been presented to polite society. She was charming and courteous and could find her way around a kitchen to boot—all talents Maggie severely lacked. That frivolous crown of flowers would catapult her to a new level of prosperity on some well-bred man's arm. It was no wonder then that it was considered one of the highest honors a young woman could receive.

As if Maggie cared about any of that. She would rather run through the streets, burning wedding gowns and screaming "Oi marriage! To the gallows with you!"

Well, not really. She didn't use words like "oi."

Heads turned from all directions to stare at Maggie including Tena's. For an incredibly long minute there was complete silence, and Maggie wondered if she'd spoken her tirade out loud. Had she uttered sharp resentment for the institution of marriage? If so, that was embarrassing even by her standards.

"Is Miss Archer present?" asked the chairman.

"Oh good," Maggie breathed. "Tena, you won!"

Tena's hand pressed the small of Maggie's back, pushing her forward. "No, Maggie, they chose *you.*"

Now Maggie understood why everyone was inexplicably silent. No one could believe Maggie was deserving of this honor because, simply put, she wasn't. She was the last person who wanted it. Someone was playing a cruel joke.

She planted her feet, willing them to root her to the soil. If she didn't move, maybe they would call on someone else. Edith and Bianca appeared out of nowhere, dragging her off by both arms while their raucous laughter filled the air.

Maggie jerked forward unsteadily to the podium, eyes on her from every direction. She caught a glimpse of her parents standing nearby. Her father's face beamed with pride. Her mother smiled and patted tears from her eyes. They knew what it meant to be named May Queen, and few things could make them happier.

Her heart swelled, a smile forming on her lips in spite of herself. It was so rare that she was able to please her parents, especially her mother. Perhaps everything was well. Perhaps she didn't need to worry.

"Congratulations, Miss Archer." A bouquet of pale pink peonies and ivory may lilies appeared in her arms. They smelled beautiful, and felt like a tiny slice of sunshine in her hands. Maggie sought out Tena in the crowd as she felt the ring of flowers entangle in her hair. Her sister hopped from foot to foot, giddy with excitement. She didn't seem to care at all that she hadn't been crowned—there was always next year for her. Maggie tried to keep her focus on that happiness instead of what was later destined for her. If she could accomplish that, then maybe she could fool herself into accepting the inevitable. With those thoughts in mind, she found it surprisingly simple to smile as she cast her gaze out among the crowd.

Even from across the green, she found Reuben's face.

Maggie squeezed her eyes closed and shook her head. Her mind was playing tricks on her. Reuben hadn't been there that day.

"Maggie, are you well?" Bianca asked. Maggie opened her eyes, and returned to the ballroom, her vision of May Day pushed to the recesses of her memory.

Bianca stared at her with concern and repeated her question. Maggie nodded. "Yes, I ... I thought I saw someone ..." Her voice trailed off when she realized her mind hadn't been playing tricks on her. Reuben was really here.

His appearance had altered from the last time she saw him. Then he had been so casual, not bothering to wear his jacket, tie loose and sleeves rolled up. Now he was decked out in full black dress, all the i's dotted and the t's crossed, complete with cufflinks and shined shoes. Only seven months had passed, but boy, had he grown up nicely.

Confound it, Maggie, pull yourself together. Just go talk to him.

"Where are you *going*? Your card isn't full yet."

Ignoring Bianca's irritation, Maggie strode across the room, dodging party goers and skirting around another beautifully decorated Christmas tree. She was only five paces away when she collided with Friedrich Kisch.

Friedrich regarded her with annoyance and rearranged his skewed spectacles. They were a tad too small for his eyes, making him look like a well-dressed eighteen-year-old insect. His words came out in a burst of haughty German accent. "Ladies should not rush, Miss Archer."

"My apologies, Mr. Kisch."

"Where were you headed in such a hurry?" He removed his spectacles again, holding them up to the light with a squint. He began polishing the lenses furiously with a handkerchief from his breast pocket.

"I saw someone ..." Maggie strained to peer around his erratic spectacle cleaning, but Reuben had disappeared in the ten seconds she'd wasted talking. *Confound you, Friedrich!* she silently cursed.

Seemingly satisfied, Friedrich perched his spectacles back on his nose.

The band began playing a lively piece and couples passed by to take their places on the dance floor. Friedrich extended his hand. "This dance is mine, Miss Archer."

"Yes, yes, if we must," Maggie sighed and mentally marked him off her list.

One down, fourteen to go.

FOUR

REUBEN WAS COMPLETELY OUT of his element. Ironically his last party was this same one, hosted by the Winchesters, four years past. He was only fifteen then, Mira barely thirteen, and he stuck to her side like sap to a tree. As a consequence, proper ballroom etiquette was as foreign as a conversation with the Russian czar.

He wouldn't even be here now if it wasn't for Maggie. Whenever his footsteps led him to the cemetery, his thoughts wandered to their unusual meeting. Such memories turned to wondering whether she would keep her promise after a year apart. And those thoughts inevitably led him to a list of possible chance encounters where they might meet again before May. Nothing so obvious as church—he already knew she sat in the third pew from the front every week, and he carefully kept to the shadows to avoid her parents. And nothing so outlandish as loitering outside the ladies' shops on East Elm—what reason would he give for being there? To show up unannounced at her house was out of the question without a declaration of courtship.

So he had succumbed to awkward social gatherings. Five parties since May: four of which he actually managed to get through the front door before turning tail. Two of those four, he had inquired if Miss Archer was on the guest list before fleeing, and one he'd been tossed out at the stoop for "suspicious activity."

Tonight he convinced his father for the first time in years to attend as a family. "It's Christmas!" Reuben cried with false bravado. "We haven't celebrated in years! Just think how thrilled Mother will be to dance again. A party may bring her out of things."

Reuben should have felt guilty using his parents' insecurities to potentially see a girl he'd known all of a few hours. Until his mother touched his cheek with her gloved hand, eyes glistening above lipstick and rouge not worn for nigh on a year, and said, "Reuben, you are a dear for suggesting this. Your sister would have loved a celebration."

He was hopelessly in over his head, and he knew it.

~ ~ ~

After brief niceties with several colleagues from the *Gazette*, Reuben declined invitations to dance and returned back to the front hall, only to receive a firm smack in the face with the most dignified food imaginable—a sausage. Granted, it was one link and not the entire strand, but no man wants to have one thrown in his face. Two strikingly fair and very familiar children doubled over with laughter on the upstairs gallery. The fourteen-year-old boy held a slingshot, while his nine-year-old sister guarded a basket of various edible ammunition.

Reuben rolled his eyes at the pair. "Causing trouble already, Emil?"

"Oi, Reuben!" Emil shouted in an accent Reuben could only dub Anglo-Germanic—an odd mixture of German and English dialects so muddled it could no longer be attributed fully to either region. As Charles Kisch's youngest brother, Emil was only five when they emigrated, allowing him to take on English mannerisms far easier than his brothers. Likewise, their little sister, Winnie, barely one when they arrived, now passed for full-fledged English.

The Kisch brothers had always been close despite their personality differences, and if you found one the other two usually weren't far behind. Which meant Charles and Friedrich were somewhere in this house. And if Charles was here, even if Maggie wasn't, the remainder of the party wouldn't be so tiresome.

"Watch yourself!"

Reuben ducked as Emil launched a cluster of grapes down the stairs. They flew past him, slapping a footman in the back. Reuben stifled a laugh inside a cough.

"I'm so sorry, sir," Reuben apologized. The footman smoothed his lapels and walked away in irritated silence. Another round of giggles erupted from the gallery.

Winnie bounded down the stairs while her brother chose the faster route of sliding along the banister. Reuben swallowed the little girl in a hug before slapping Emil good-naturedly across the face. Logically Emil found that an invitation to punch Reuben, but Reuben, still bigger than Emil for now, grabbed his fist and pulled it behind his back. The younger boy struggled to no avail.

"Codswallop, Reuben! I surrender!"

"If I release you, will you behave?"

"'Course. How could you not trust me?" Emil shrugged out of Reuben's grasp to immediately reload his slingshot. A well-aimed piece of cheese sailed through the ballroom door.

Reuben chuckled. "You're right. How could I not trust you?"

Winnie looked at Reuben expectantly. "Reuben, may I attend the party?"

"What did your parents say?" Reuben knew this childhood game. He and Mira played it many times.

"They said no!" Emil expounded. "I'm fourteen! Why do I need to stay upstairs with the babies?"

"I'm not a baby!" Winnie exclaimed. "And you're not allowed because Mama and Papa know you'll cause mischief."

Emil gave a smirk. "Well, they're right ... and you're still a baby," he muttered.

Winnie turned back to Reuben. "If I can't go, then will you play with us upstairs? They have checkers!"

"'Course he doesn't, Winnie," Emil said as he sifted through

Winnie's basket for more ammunition. "He'd miss the party."

"That would be a tragedy, wouldn't it, Mr. Radford?"

Edith Winchester approached from the ballroom, gloved hand extended. He'd met the Winchesters officially only once at that last Christmas party, but he'd remember their flirtatious daughters anywhere.

Edith rubbed her thumb along Reuben's knuckle in small circles, her face contrite as she batted her long lashes. "Please forgive my rudeness for not finding you earlier." She smiled shyly. "I lament not yet claiming you for my dance card."

"You can claim *me* for your dance card," Emil said, wriggling his eyebrows in what, Reuben assumed, he thought was a seductive manner. It wasn't.

"No one else has claimed you yet, has she?" Edith asked Reuben, completely ignoring Emil. He plopped on the bottom stair in a huff and took back to the basket of food, no doubt hoping to pelt Edith with rotten fruit. Reuben shook his head and Edith's face lit up. "Oh good! My next dance is unaccounted for."

"I suppose you want me to take possession of it." Reuben didn't say it as an offer, but Edith slipped her arm through his and sighed. Winnie giggled. Emil snorted derisively.

Edith scanned the party guests from the doorway. "We must find my sister, Bianca. I believe she has an open spot on her card as well."

Something soft and wet squelched into Reuben's back. From over his shoulder, Emil and Winnie sat doubled over on the staircase. Emil braced the slingshot against his knee to load another orange. There was a time in Reuben's life when that might have been him and Mira. What Reuben wouldn't give to be a few years younger and a lot less responsible.

"Oh, there she is!" Edith cried, pointing across the dance floor. A girl with features identical to Edith waved vigorously and started to make her way through the sea of black jackets and embellished gowns.

"You will simply adore my sister," Edith told him. "We are both excellent dancers. Papa hired an instructor from London. Have you been to London, Mr. Radford?"

"No, although my father has been many times."

"A man your age and never to London!" Edith pressed a hand to her brow. "It is unheard of, Mr. Radford! I do insist you allow Daddy to have you at our home there a weekend soon."

"You would certainly not be the first man my sister has entertained," cut in Bianca.

"I have not had nearly so many suitors as you, Miss Bianca."

Bianca gave a shrill giggle. "Oh, too true!"

While the girls continued to banter over the number of their great many previous male companions—Reuben was up to eight for Edith and twelve for Bianca—he finally found what he'd been searching for all evening. Even the prospect of these two glamorous, obviously easy catches could not derail himself from tracing Maggie's movements.

Every inch of her was mesmerizing. Her dress flowed around her ankles as she waltzed, and hugged the rest of her in all the best places. Her lips pouted as though she was bored of the entire affair—a goddess who tired of being forced to mingle with mere mortals. She was beautiful amongst the gravestones, but here surrounded by the illumination of a gilded ballroom ... here she was stunning.

Edith followed his eyes, then exchanged an incensed look with her sister.

"Don't even bother trying with that one," Bianca snapped. "She's already taken."

Reuben mind slammed back to attention. "She is?"

"Well ... no ... not officially, but she will be. We've seen to that." Edith fluffed her hair with a little pout. "She's not exactly easy to work with though, if you understand my meaning."

"Some women, like Maggie, don't notice when a man is interested in her." Bianca ran one finger along Reuben's cheekbone and batted her eyes flirtatiously. "Some women, like us, do."

Edith laced her fingers through his right hand. "My next two dances are free. Won't you dance with me?"

"Or we could find a cozy couch and ... er ... talk?" Bianca suggested, taking his other hand. Both girls laced him with withering stares.

"Uh ..." Reuben stammered. He glanced back towards the ballroom.

Bianca snapped her fingers in front of his face. "Don't waste your time with that prude," she said in disgust.

Reuben decided he really didn't like Bianca.

Edith fluffed her already perfectly pinned hair. "She's not worth the trouble."

Reuben seriously doubted if sticking with these two could result in anything except trouble. "Perhaps," he said. "I'll take my chances though, thanks."

FIVE

REUBEN JOSTLED HIS WAY through the crowd surrounding the ballroom door, ignoring outraged cries as he elbowed his way past. He scoured the room for a full thirty minutes, rejecting dances with half a dozen pretty girls in his pursuit of the elusive Maggie Archer. He knew little more about that girl than any of the other women at this party; what was it then that had burned her into his thoughts these last months?

It wasn't until he sleuthed in rooms off-limits to partygoers did he finally discover where she was hidden. Reuben lingered in the doorway to Mr. Winchester's upstairs study, a sweaty palm clasped upon the knob, formulating words to say. Trussed up in her decadent emerald gown, Maggie sat curled in the window seat, legs pulled under her dress, and hands clasped around her knees. Her bare toes stuck out beneath the hem. Her thoughts must have been outside with the falling snow as she didn't even give notice to his entrance.

Reuben cleared his throat, his stomach turning over as their eyes met. Maggie frantically slid off the bench on a wild grab for her shoes.

"Why are you hiding?" he asked, joining her at the window.

Maggie blew the hair out of her eyes. "Ten dances with hardly a break in between. And all those men—" Maggie wrinkled up her nose, and Reuben found it an adorable gesture. "Ugh, I have yet to meet one—just *one!*—who has something halfway intelligent to say."

"The women are no better!" Reuben countered. "I met your friends, Edith and Bianca. I feel quite sorry for the men who land those two."

Maggie pretended to gag. "Those two are the worst! Stay away from them or you'll find yourself at the end of one of their tricks. Their father thinks they're angelic, but the truth is they've seduced every man at this party."

"Well, not *every* man." Reuben wasn't comfortable discussing this topic, of all things, with Maggie. He still didn't know what their friendship really was or had the potential to be and, blast it all if her ability to be downright gorgeous right now wasn't helping.

Maggie regarded him with a mixture of surprise and, was that ... relief? Then she frowned as though she had only just noticed him there. "What are you doing up here anyhow?"

"Searching for you. Seeing as we're both anxious to escape this madhouse, would you care to explore the gardens?"

"It's freezing out there."

Reuben held up two coats draped over his arm. He'd swiped hers from the valet's care with a little monetary persuasion. No one would think to search for them in a barren garden on a bitter winter's night.

"You stole my coat?" Maggie said, astounded.

"And now I'm returning it." Reuben stretched his arms into his own coat sleeves. "Always come prepared for a date with a lady."

"This is not a date." She gave a crooked scowl and pressed her lips together. "But the gardens here *are* lovely, even in the winter. Fine. I'll give you a tour." She tugged on her coat and closed each silver button.

"You visit the Winchesters often?" Reuben asked as they maneuvered down the back servants' stairs, moving in the

42

direction allowing the least detection from partygoers. The kitchen staff stopped to watch them pass by, lips pursed against comments too illicit to speak without repercussions.

"Mmm, my mother and Mrs. Winchester have been friends since we were little girls." Maggie swiped a raspberry tart from the tray of a passing footman, leaving Reuben to mumble an apology and follow her outside.

A beaten gravel walk wound around the house's exterior opening through a break in the garden hedge to reveal a raised portico overlooking the rest of the grounds. Both electrical lights and candlelit lanterns flickered across the patio's stone railing. Torches lit the pathway into the gardens, accentuating the winterberry trees and barren flower beds surrounding a frozen lily fountain at its center. Over it all lay the palest dusting of snow radiating with the moon's soft glow. Their feet crunched into the wintry silence.

Two paths led through the gardens, one already occupied by a solitary set of lady's prints. They steered in the opposite direction past the barren rose bushes with their thorny wires.

"So what do I need to know?" asked Reuben.

"Sorry?"

"The gardens," Reuben gestured. "You promised me a tour."

"Of course." Maggie pointed to the nearest rose bed. "There are four rose varieties. Darcey Bussell, Princess Anne, Graham Thomas, and Queen of Sweden. They're all lovely in the summer, although I think I like the Princess Anne best."

Reuben nodded. "And what do I need to know about you?"

"Excuse me?" Maggie asked again.

"We don't know much about each other yet. There must be something I should know."

"My favorite food is fish. I think it's deplorable to keep animals in the house. And I enjoy long walks in the park and meaningful conversation," she finished with a smirk.

"How clever," said Reuben. "Now tell me something real."

Maggie tapped her finger on her chin thoughtfully. "Well, if you asked my father, he would say you can decipher someone by asking them three questions. But they have to be the right questions."

"What exactly *are* the questions?"

Maggie hopped onto the ledge of the frozen fountain, arms outstretched, carefully balancing step for step along the four inch stonework. "Father would never tell me. He said I had to decide for myself. He did say, however, one question he always asks is 'If you could redo any one day in your life, when would it be?'"

"I don't like that question, but I can tell you the answer. It's the day Mira died. I'd bring her back and saving her would make up for everything else."

Maggie glanced over at him, nearly losing her balance. "What else?"

Reuben gave a jerky shrug. He wasn't about to get into his past now or ever. "Did I get the answer right?"

"I don't know. I never have. Father asks me that question all the time. He says it's the only question that, in his opinion, has a black and white answer." Maggie hopped down from the ledge, burying her dainty shoes in the snow. Reuben would never understand how women thought those things were considered acceptable winter footwear.

"Which answer do you usually give?"

"Every day," Maggie admitted. "Not a day goes by that I don't fail them."

Reuben plucked a twig from the nearest winterberry tree and offered it to Maggie. She twirled it between her fingers, watching the crimson berries blur against the snowy backdrop. "I think you're perfect," he said.

Even in the shadows, Maggie's embarrassment was apparent. She tossed the berries into the snow. "I think we've talked about me quite long enough. Tell me about you."

"There's not much you need to know about me."

"Why are you so antisocial?"

"Who said I'm antisocial?"

Maggie checked the list off on her fingers. "No friends. You like to frequent cemeteries. You read those awful penny magazines." She motioned to his coat pocket where the top of a booklet peeked over the fabric. Filled with exciting, and often gruesome, stories of intrigue, penny dreadfuls were nearly a thing of the past now, replaced by more socially acceptable publications. Reuben's father grew up reading the weekly serials and passed them all along to Reuben. After *The Time Machine*, Reuben had read each issue a dozen times.

"One of those things does not influence the existence of the others," Reuben argued, tucking the magazine farther into his pocket. "I have one friend, Charles, and his brothers, and they are all I need." He retrieved a cigar from his inside coat pocket, cut the end, and secured it between his teeth. He flicked his lighter, sparking it to life.

"Cigars?" Maggie coughed, waving the smoke away.

"Courtesy of Charles." Reuben offered her the cigar. "Care to try?"

"Heavens, no," Maggie cringed. "The smell is foul enough to drive any woman away. So tell me, where *are* all your lady friends? I know far more than my preferred share of young men and each one has three or four ladies clamoring to win him over." She sized him up and whispered, "Or are you more of an Oscar Wilde type?"

Reuben blew smoke in her face. "Definitely not."

"Blimey, my apologies," Maggie muttered, rubbing her eyes. Although slightly affronted, Reuben didn't blame her for her assumption. He'd already reached his nineteenth year without any current prospects. The question wasn't unfair, just way off the mark.

"Tell me about your sister. Tena, was it?"

Maggie dug her toe into the snow. "She's the only person who knows about you."

Reuben eyed her inquisitively. "The *only* person?"

"Yes."

"You must be very close."

"We are. She's one of the few people I trust completely."

"I believe you tried to offer her to me when last we met."

Maggie shrugged dispassionately. "I still maintain you would make a fair couple, likely to share opinions on the disreputable ladies who show a bit of ankle."

Reuben gave her a coy smile. "I enjoy a lady's ankle as much as the next man. Especially if she's disreputable." An unbidden laugh escaped his chest with a snort.

"You're making fun of me!" Maggie reproached. She squatted to the ground, pulling her dress up in an effort to create a snow ball with her free hand. With a single swipe, Reuben formed a wet mass between his hands, flinging it at her down-turned neck. Maggie straightened up, bouncing on her toes to shake the frigid water from her back. Her ammunition landed far left of Reuben's current location.

"You are in so much trouble!" she yelled, kicking haphazard waves of snow in Reuben's direction. He leapt out of the way, pelting her another half dozen times until the front of Maggie's coat was spotted with dark watermarks.

Her eyes flashed, only adding to Reuben's opinion of her overall attractiveness. He snatched her hand, spinning her around to face him. "Dance with me."

Maggie extricated her waterlogged dance card from her wrist. "Sorry, Mr. Radford. There aren't any free dances. Not that I would even give you one."

"Let me see." Reuben yanked the card from her fingers before she could respond and held it out of her reach, reading the now streaked writing. Sure enough, all the spots were assigned except for the last one which was still several dances away. Maggie grabbed at his arm, trying to pull it down to her level.

"Give it back. I need to know who my next partner is."

Reuben analyzed the card, pretending to mull it over. "What jolly good news! It's me!" Reuben tossed the paper behind a snowy rose bush. "I promise my waltz is only slightly less horrible than my two step. Although really either one could be used as a productive form of torture."

Maggie removed her sodden gloves, breathing onto her frozen fingers. "I'm sending Bianca to teach you a lesson."

Reuben stumbled as though he'd been shot. "Such ugly threats from such a pretty face. Have you no shame, Miss Archer?"

"None at all, Mr. Radford." Maggie stooped to collect more snow, and smiled mischievously. "You should know better than to trust a pretty face."

Maggie smashed the snowball on his head with a maniacal squeal.

"*Reuben?*" echoed a voice from across the garden.

He stared hard into the darkness. Slush ran down Reuben's face as another batch of snow pelted against his ear, and he barely heard Maggie's snigger. Someone else was with them. Silent. Watching them.

He held out an arm against Maggie. "Wait," he whispered to her then called out, "Who's there?"

"Reuben?" came the voice again. "Is your sister with you?"

"Mother?" Reuben wiped his face with his coat sleeve and squinted. Slowly Florence Radford appeared on the dark path. She was alone, in nothing more than her sapphire gown and gloves, cheeks flushed and lips blue from the cold. Her greying hair was pinned, but only just; strips stuck out haphazardly, matted by the falling snow. She clutched Mira's locket around her neck and toddled around the frozen beds to meet them.

Reuben lowered his arm. "Mother! What are you doing out here?"

"Walking. Wondering where your sister had gotten off to. I see you found her."

Reuben glanced between his mother and Maggie. "Mother?

That's not Mira."

Florence glared at her son. "Of course it is. I laid out those silver shoes this evening." Maggie shuffled to hide her shoes in the snow.

Reuben stepped between the women. "This is Maggie Archer, Mother. She sent us that basket last May."

"I'm so sorry about your daughter, Mrs. Radford," Maggie said. "Reuben told me what a wonderful person she was."

Very slowly, his mother swam back to the surface. The glaze disappeared from her eyes only to be replaced by repugnance. She pointed a long jagged nail over Reuben's shoulder. "Who is *this*? You're replacing Mira with some little harlot!"

"Mother!" Reuben exclaimed. "You cannot speak to her like that."

"Your sister is coming back." Florence told him matter of fact, hands to her hips. "Goodness knows where she is, but she'll return eventually, and you need to be ready."

The pounding turned to a roar in Reuben's ears. He'd known this was coming. The doctor explained it many months ago. He'd seen it all before. Sometimes when the grief was too much, the patient went into a kind of psychosis to escape. It was only a matter of time before they lost all sense. But still Reuben had hoped ...

"Mother, please," he implored. "Mira's gone. She can't come back."

Reuben's cheek burned before he could comprehend that his mother had struck him. He stared agape, astounded. His mind couldn't believe it. It wasn't possible. His mother was one of the gentlest people he knew, that everyone knew for that matter.

Reuben fought tears down his throat. Crying was for babies and school yard sissies. He was neither. Thank goodness his father was inside. If he was here, the situation would be ten times worse.

Florence's eyes swept over Reuben in disgust, as though she would like to spit on him and throw him into the snow. "You did this," she spat then strode inside without a second glance at her only living child.

Reuben couldn't even apologize to Maggie. All he could feel was the weight of his mother's accusations and the handprint on his face. His gaze lingered on the bare branches over Maggie's head so he didn't have to meet her eyes. He knew she'd be able to tell in an instant how deep his mother's wound had gone and he was embarrassed to share those emotions with her.

What if he lost it too? He missed Mira. His chest physically ached with the thought of her. He didn't even have a photograph to remember her by. It didn't seem like such a far leap between fixating on his sister's grave and his mother's version of reality. If he wasn't careful, he could become as waylaid as she was.

Maggie's icy fingers laced with his. "How about that dance?"

Reuben squeezed her hand. "I would be honored."

~ ~ ~

Maggie's presence in the ballroom was intoxicating, the winter garden a faint memory with her in his arms. It also helped that Edith and Bianca stared open mouthed as Reuben tripped her across the parquet.

As promised, his stunning dance technique sent them with repeated frequency into other couples until Maggie's heel crushed Miss Wild's toes and they were not so politely asked to remove themselves from the dance floor. Even so, Maggie laughed right along with him as they spun out of the ballroom, across the hall, and into the parlor next door.

"You are the worst dancer I have ever been with," Maggie jested, trying to catch her breath.

"I warned you," Reuben said. "What about the words *form of torture* suggested a delightful exchange of pleasantries?"

"I thought you were joking!"

"I would never joke about something so serious as the art of dance."

"No, that would be a crime," Maggie mocked. Her eyes were

like the ocean, changing colors with the weather. They were an intense blue now without a speck of grey. For once the sea was calm.

"Would you have ever thought this morning you'd be on a tryst with some bloke like me?"

"I wouldn't call it a tryst." Maggie lowered her eyes. "Although I am glad you're here."

If Maggie recognized how close they stood, or how her words might be misinterpreted, she didn't acknowledge it. But Reuben noticed. He stood completely still, barely daring to breathe. Even if her words meant nothing, he didn't want to ruin this moment.

"Miss Archer, I believe the next dance is mine?"

Maggie burst apart from Reuben like exploding shrapnel. Her face beat crimson. Reuben swore inwardly and frowned at the man who had interrupted them. Wasn't he intelligent enough to know when two people were holding a private conversation?

Maggie quickly regained her composure and smiled at the interloper. "Yes, quite so, Mr. Capaldi. You are number twelve."

Reuben rolled his eyes. "Please excuse us, sir." He pulled Maggie to the side and lowered his voice. He now remembered why he always hated these parties. "Ditch this guy, Maggie. The whole lot of them. The pond is frozen solid now—I was there a few days ago. Let's go skating. Bring your sister."

Maggie startled. "Tena? You've never met her."

"But I'd like to," Reuben said seriously. "Come on, Maggie, where's the harm in it?"

Maggie appeared to want to agree, but was spinning all the reasons in her mind why she shouldn't. He couldn't think of a single good excuse, but he also wasn't in her head. He didn't know the thoughts she might have hidden away.

"Reuben, we must maintain boundaries or this agreement cannot continue."

"I thought we were *friends*," Reuben countered. "You make this sound like a legal contract."

Maggie's eyes narrowed. "We *are* friends, but our friendship helps us escape from reality, Reuben, not complicate it. Do not complicate it now."

"I want to go skating. Friends go skating. How am I complicating it?" Reuben realized he sounded like a whiny child and was beginning not to care.

"I do not wish to intrude," Mr. Capaldi spoke up, "Only the next dance is beginning."

Maggie and Reuben stood arm's width apart and glared at each other. "Three dances and I'll be back," She said then pasted a warm smile on her face for Mr. Capaldi and took his hand. With one simple gesture, she transformed from a carefree girl to a poised woman from a world he wasn't allowed to be a part of.

Mr. Capaldi swept her across the dance floor as Reuben had been so incapable of doing. She was graceful and so made for this life. Only there was another side of her too—the contemplative girl in the window seat—that he saw when they were alone. She lived two lives—one in the real world and one in Reuben's world—but what would happen if they completely collided? She said he freed her from reality, but what was it she was so afraid of?

The music switched to a two step and Maggie exchanged dance partners. Reuben remembered when his father twirled his mother around the house until she would fall down dizzy. Then he would kiss her until she blushed and whisper secrets in her ear that made her giggle. Reuben always wanted to be with someone like his mother, someone who he could make that happy. But that was also long ago, before Mira's death ruined what his parents had.

He knew why Maggie was so afraid of reality. It was why his mother was what she was now. Reality was where the monsters lived. If you lived in reality for too long, like his mother, it would drive you mad.

SIX

"WOULD YOU SIGN FOR ONE of my dances, sir?"

Reuben scowled at the girl who'd interrupted his line of vision with the dance floor and his general aura of self-loathing and despair. He took one long look down her figure and groaned inwardly. Of course this creature was beautiful. The twinkling lights of the Christmas tree reflected off her violet dress and sparkled straight through her enchanting features. A deep magical blend of phoenix flames, her irises smiled back at him like the sun's warm glow.

She ran her teeth across her bottom lip. "You see, I've only had four dances all night, and you're standing alone so I hoped ..."

"I'm not dancing with you."

"No, no, of course." She blushed. "Forgive me. I was too forward."

"It's not that." This girl was distracting. He was losing his senses, just like he did with Maggie. Where was Maggie anyway? That girl had disappeared yet again.

"Do you have an aversion to ladies?"

"What?" Reuben nearly burst out laughing. Maggie had asked him the same question.

The girl's fingers flew across her beet face. "Forgive me, sir, again! I meant nothing by it! Please don't tell my mother of my grievous insult."

This time Reuben did laugh. "No apologies necessary. I'm not dancing because I'm a right awful dancer. Already tried tonight and failed." She lowered her fingers an inch. Reuben smiled. "Trust me. I would very much enjoy spinning you out there if my clumsy feet allowed it."

Relief crossed her face. "Splendid. If neither of us are dancing, would you care to sit? I'm afraid there are few others worth talking to." She sat on the sofa beside the Christmas tree, pulled a twig off, and picked the fine needles one by one. "Who have you danced with tonight?" She rolled her eyes. "Please say not Edith or Bianca."

Reuben sat on the other end of the sofa. "I would rather spend the night with this tree."

The girl laughed, the sound ringing even in the crowded room. "Quite so! The tree is less annoying than both of them combined."

She tossed the barren twig back into the tree and set to work on destroying another. "I don't mind being here alone," she said somberly. "Edith and Bianca flirt with everyone in pants, my sister is led around by a host of different suitors, and I'm fine on my own. My sister says I'm lucky. Better alone than like our parents. Father's hiding out in the billiard room, while Mother is off somewhere gossiping. Heaven knows they wouldn't be with each other."

Reuben nodded. What else could he even say to that?

"She's exactly right," the girl continued. Her eyes were on the dancing couples. "My sister may have a plethora of prospects—that she doesn't want—and I have none, but it matters little. I am perfectly capable of being alone." She crushed the pine needles and threw them to the floor. Reuben doubted if she had actually been talking to him.

It was then Maggie glided past with Mr. Hartnell, capturing both of their attention. She gracefully transferred to Mr. Pertwee and reintroduced herself with a tight smile. One more dance to go.

"That's her," Reuben pointed. "My first and last dance of the night."

"*Her?*" the girl cried. Reuben thought he might blister under her steaming gaze. "You're one of the fifteen? Well doesn't that just figure all!" The girl sprang from her seat, and Reuben jumped up to block her hasty retreat.

"Fifteen what?" he asked.

"Dance partners!" She threw her hands up. "Everyone wants my sister, Maggie Archer: the May Queen!"

Reuben choked. "You're Tena?"

Now it was Tena's turn to appear startled. "How do you know that?"

Of course, he saw the resemblance now. The same eye shape, the same build, even their hair was styled similarly. It was so obvious Reuben wanted to kick himself for not making the connection sooner.

"Blimey, you look just like Maggie."

Tena rolled her eyes to the ceiling and sighed in disgust. "It didn't win *me* any awards. Who are you anyway?"

"Forgive my lack of manners, Miss Archer." Reuben extended his hand. "I'm Reuben Radford."

Tena almost fell over the sofa.

"It's *you!*" she yelped, all propriety forgotten. Everyone near them glanced sideways at her outburst. Only the music concealed her proclamation from the rest of the room.

Tena drew in a breath to regain her composure. She ushered him back to the couch beside her and lowered her tone to a slightly softer pitch than what dogs could hear. "You're the boy from the cemetery! Tell me everything, Mr. Radford! For all Maggie's arguments, I just knew someone would tame my wild sister!"

Reuben held up his hands in protest. "Oh no, no, you are mistaken. There are no romantic entanglements between myself and your sister." Tena nodded, unconvinced. Her eyebrows had nearly hit her hairline.

"She speaks of you often," Tena commented casually, although she threw him a sly look Reuben didn't know what to make of. She carried the same mischievous glint in her eyes that her sister did.

"Does she?" Reuben asked, surprised and, he had to admit, a bit flattered too.

Tena laughed, "Oh yes, although I must admit she left out all the best parts. You made quite the impression on her, and believe me when I say few men do." She smiled wickedly as heat crept into Reuben's cheeks. He tried to hide it by pulling at his collar, but knew the damage had already been done.

"My apologies, Mr. Radford," Tena said, obviously not sorry at all. "I seem to have overstepped my bounds yet again." Reuben was finding it more and more difficult to believe this was the same stodgy girl Maggie described to him, especially when she said, "If I have not given too grave an insult, perhaps you might change your mind about a dance?"

"You risk your life by dancing with me."

"I shall accept your challenge, Mr. Radford." Tena gave a cheeky grin, clearly up to something more compelling than the boring life her sister claimed she loved so much. "You will need skills slightly more adequate in order to woo my sister."

Reuben leaned in as if sharing some engaging secret. "You're far lovelier. It's a shame every man here is too loathsome to notice."

Tena blushed. "Although I thank you for the compliment, you cannot dodge the issue with flattery, Mr. Radford. Now about that dance—"

"Radford!"

Charles dropped into the empty chair beside Reuben. With frantic movements, he brushed his dishwater-blond hair back and adjusted his chair away from the dance floor. "Help me escape Miss Winchester!"

Reuben grinned. It was refreshing to finally see one of his favorite faces. "Woah, slow down, Kisch. I haven't seen you in weeks and don't even get so much as a how-de-do before you throw me into your troubles?"

Charles nodded at Reuben. "Yes, yes, good evening Radford. Jolly good to see you ole' chap."

"You do know that continually using stock English phrases still won't make you sound like a native?" Along with six extra inches in height over the last few years, Charles had also gained a ridiculous need to prove he fit in with the English despite his pronounced non-English accent.

Charles frowned, ignoring Reuben's question. "Will you please agree to distract Miss Winchester? I have endured four dances with her and I can take no more."

"What's the matter, Kisch?" asked Reuben. "Not finding her to your liking?"

Charles sighed. "She refuses to leave me be. And her licentious sister too. Their behavior seems to indicate they have no one else on their dance cards."

"Impossible," Tena muttered. Charles rewarded her with his full attention, eliciting another scarlet flush to her cheeks.

"Are you with Reuben?" he asked, casting Reuben a hopeful glance.

Reuben spoke up. "Sorry to disappoint, Kisch. I'm as pathetically single as ever. This is Tena Archer. Miss Archer, may I introduce my good friend, Charles Kisch."

Charles's brows shot up. "Archer? Maggie's sister?"

"One in the same," Reuben verified.

"Do you know her too?" asked Tena.

Charles shook his head. "I have only heard stories."

Tena laughed. "How refreshing to finally meet someone who is not captured by my sister's unjustly won charms!"

Charles returned her smile, revealing a row of dazzling straight teeth. "I must admit I am more interested in yourself, Miss Archer. Might you engage me for the next dance?"

"Me?" Tena squeaked. "Yes, of course!" She offered her hand to Charles, and he turned it upward to gently kiss her fingers. A deep blush flooded her face, about to float her away in the radiating warmth.

The band struck up the *Emperor's Waltz,* a favorite in the Winchester household. A dozen more couples vacated their seats to join those already on the dance floor. "Ah, it is a waltz," Charles acknowledged. "What I enjoy most about this dance is a waltz is still a waltz in every country."

Tena jerked her hand from Charles's. "Where are you from?"

"Originally? Bayern. Why do you ask?"

Tena looked like she wanted to cry. Or possibly throw something. Reuben contemplated moving out of range. "Then I'm afraid I must decline, Mr. Kisch. I was foolish not to recognize your accent before. My mother has strict rules against fraternizing with Germans."

Charles regarded her as though he had heard this complaint many times over. Which he had. "Fraternize is a harsh word, Miss Archer. I am merely requesting one dance."

Tena hesitated, looking to Reuben. He shook his head somberly. "Your mother has every right to worry. Kisch dances like a Russian ballerina." He cracked up on the last word, soliciting a deep scowl from Charles. Reuben nudged his friend's shoulder. "Oh, lighten up. All that bad German blood has turned you sour."

"I do *not* dance like a ballerina."

Reuben chortled. "Watch out, Tena. Those Bavarians get all inebriated. You see in late September they have this festival. Sixteen days of straight drunken debauchery. Not so easy to dance when one sloshes as they walk. Kisch is probably still recovering from this year's festivities."

"*Für gottes willen,* Reuben!"

Reuben punched the air victoriously. In the last few years, Charles had become adamant about only speaking English, so naturally Reuben constantly attempted to make him relapse.

Charles glowered at him. Reuben smirked.

"I suppose there's no harm in *one* dance," said Tena.

Charles folded his arms across his chest. "Your mother will not object?"

"She will never know." Tena rose to her feet, those startling eyes focused only on Charles. It seemed all prior promises of a dance with Reuben were now forgotten. He sighed. Alas, such was the story of his life it seemed.

Charles rose to his full height, over a foot taller than his new dance partner. Tena gave a nervous laugh as she slipped her arm through his. "Perhaps you can teach me more of your language while we dance?"

"What would you like to know?"

"What does 'four goddess villain' mean?" she asked, thoroughly butchering the pronunciation.

Charles chuckled. "*Für gottes willen.* Roughly translated, it means 'for goodness sake.'" He led Tena into the waltz, circling the floor with perfect steps, never once removing his gaze from hers.

Reuben couldn't hear their conversation and was dreadful at reading lips, so he hadn't the foggiest idea where the language lesson went from there. He could only assume they were hitting it off brilliantly. *That would figure*, he thought. *Charles meets one of the Archer daughters and she's smitten in minutes. I meet both daughters and neither one will give me the time of day. Must be the foreign accent. Every girl loves that.*

Reuben decided he needed to find some ugly, clumsy friends who were British-to-the-bone. Spending all his time with Charles would never land him a girl.

As they glided past a second time, with Tena's expression lit by more than the ballroom chandeliers, Reuben shrugged off his jealousy. If this worked out for Charles, Reuben wouldn't be anything but happy about it.

When the piece came to an end, Charles didn't release Tena. Instead, he kissed her. Normally that would have been cause for surprise and intense questioning of his friend. Unfortunately, it was also about the same moment Reuben spied Maggie.

SEVEN

REUBEN'S BLOOD MIGHT AS WELL have boiled straight through his skin.

This was the last dance—the fifteenth dance—the one Maggie didn't have an assigned partner for. She was supposed to skip this dance and meet back with Reuben. He wove his way along the edge of the ballroom, waiting impatiently a few yards from where She conversed with a group of giggly girls and their escorts. Bianca and Edith each hooked her by an arm and gestured for another man to join them.

And that's when Reuben wanted to enter into all-out battle.

Maggie was escorted onto the dance floor by a man Reuben hadn't talked to in years, and up until now had managed to carefully avoid. Roguish in appearance as well as personality, he was the only person whom Reuben could say he honestly hated. The mere thought of the man brought the taste of bile to his mouth, and Reuben cracked his knuckles, longing to permanently rearrange the other man's face.

With sleek sandy hair and dressed in a double-breasted tuxedo, Lloyd Halverson had both the appearance and the funds required to run his father's successful shipping line and a top-tier household of his own someday. He topped it off with the same venomous smirk Reuben received last time they were at a stand off.

This man and all his lousy money should be buried six feet under. Four years ago, death was a judgment Reuben would have gladly doled, but that was a side of himself he wished to never see again. Especially not here, not in front of Maggie. What would happen if Lloyd said something? What if he reminded Reuben of the boys they used to be? What would Reuben do then?

He didn't wait to find out. He fled from the ballroom like a bloody coward.

"Where exactly do you think you're going?"

Reuben rounded at the familiar voice, and his breath smashed from his lungs harder than the summer Charles hit him in the gut with a cricket ball. He simultaneously rubbed his eyes and his midsection as the night became infinitely stranger.

Mira stood on the fifth stair above him, contempt hardly an appropriate descriptor for the disgust flung across her movements.

"Mira?"

Mira extended a slender arm towards the ballroom. "What are you doing? Get back in there and face him. Don't be such a gutless little girl."

Reuben took a step up the stairs. "Mira?" he repeated. "Are you real?"

Mira raised her eyes to the roof and grunted. In thirteen years, Reuben couldn't recall her ever emitting such a boorish sound. "The question isn't am I real, Reuben. It's do I seem real to *you*?"

Reuben moved another step upward, now eye level to this unexpected girl. Her appearance was identical to Mira from the soft dark hair to the dimple in her chin. Her malachite green dress was the same style Mira wore at that party so many years ago. Smudges of dirt traced the hem, from some ill approved romp in the garden no doubt. A golden locket hung around her neck, the same one Reuben's mother now wore. Their parents gave it to Mira for her thirteenth birthday, the last birthday of her life.

This person *seemed* all too real. Only she couldn't be—that was impossible. This was just a crazy messed up daydream. His mother's words were souring his thoughts.

"No," Reuben determined. "I remember my sister. I remember the last time we were here at this same party together. Four years ago. You can't be her."

"Is that so?" Mira laughed. "How did that night go exactly?"

Awful, thought Reuben. *Awful, and all my fault.*

Reuben found Mira alone on the stairs that night, untwisting the ribbons from her braid with shaking fingers as tears streamed from her eyes.

"They said I shouldn't wear them," she sniffed. "They said I'm an ugly girl, and I don't deserve to look pretty."

"Bollocks." Reuben slid down beside her and gently wiped her cheeks. "You're beautiful. The most beautiful girl I'll ever know."

"You shouldn't say words like bollocks. You'll get the switch."

Reuben shrugged. "Father doesn't scare me."

"He frightens *me*. Lots of things frighten me now." She sniffed again. "I have nightmares."

Reuben wrapped his arm around his sister. Mira buried her face in his shoulder. "That's why I'm here."

Fresh tears rolled down her cheeks. "You won't always be! Those boys—they said you have the devil's hands. They want you strung up in the yard for what you did. I don't want them to hurt you!"

"Mira ..."

Mira shook her head forcefully. "I told them they were wrong. I tried to tell them the truth. Why won't they believe us!" Her little eyes went wide as saucers, a doe about to be shot in the woods.

"Mira, shhh, everything will be fine," Reuben asserted. "I'll protect you."

Back on the staircase, Reuben now stared up at this peculiar nightmare that stood before him, less than a ghost, more than a memory. Was this the same phantom his mother saw in the garden? A layer of the mind unable to separate delusion from reality?

"I shouldn't have stopped you that day," Mira said flatly. "Lloyd would have deserved it."

This was the exact worry Reuben had flipped over in his mind time and time again. He rubbed his knuckles where just visible white lines beckoned him to remember their cause. This was why he tried to keep those memories suffocated.

Mira's darkened eyes filled with heartless fury. "You should have killed him."

Reuben retreated backward. She may look like his sister, but this was something very different from the Mira he had known.

Stopping only for a moment to gather his overcoat, Reuben barreled out the front door, slipping in the fresh snow upon the stairs. Chauffeurs and cabbies struggled to clear carriages and motorcars before the guests exited the party. Sliding his fingers into his gloves, Reuben passed his own by. He would leave it for his parents. Returning to the house to phone another taxi risked being sidelined by any number of people including whatever that thing was he'd left on the stairs. Walking was the easiest solution to ridding himself quickly of this formidable night.

"Son, can you come here for a moment?" one of the drivers called out to him. "Can you help me push her out? She seems to be stuck in the ice."

"No, sir, I can't," Reuben snapped. "I'm in a bit of a rush."

"Please, sir, the master and mistress will have my head if the coach isn't ready when they are."

Reuben groaned. This man was not to fault for his unfortunate night. He retraced his steps, helping the man clear the carriage wheels in minutes.

"Thank you, sir! I could never have accomplished it on my own." He offered Reuben a warm smile and a firm handshake. "Good night and a happy Christmas."

Reuben nodded. "And to you, sir." The driver slapped the reins, directing the horse-drawn carriage to meet his charges at the door.

"Reuben?"

Maggie emerged from the darkness near Reuben's own carriage. He squinted down the drive to the front door. Good. She was alone. "Is something wrong?" she asked, her teeth chattering as she spoke. She held her arms tight to her chest and shivered in the cold.

"Why didn't you bring your coat?" Reuben removed his overcoat to wrap it around her shoulders. She shrugged at the loose fabric until he clamped her arms to her body through the coat.

"Take it. You don't even have sleeves—you'll freeze."

"Thank you." Maggie shuffled her feet in the snow, scraping the flakes into a pile between her dainty shoes. "Is anything wrong? You left so suddenly. I thought maybe your mother said something else—"

"I'm fine," Reuben snapped. He held his hand out. "On second thought, give me my coat back. Go inside to the fire. I'm heading home."

Maggie only tightened her hold on the fabric. "Are you angry with me? I'm sorry I didn't return right away. Mr. Halverson requested a dance and it seemed impolite to refuse."

Reuben's jaw tensed. "You didn't mind slighting Matthew Troughton to dance with me. I read your dance card before I threw it away. I know you also skipped out on another dance with Mr. Davison while we were in the garden. So what then is so special about Halverson?"

Maggie stepped back against the door of the carriage. Reuben realized his face must be revealing more than he'd intended. "There's *nothing* special about him. I only just met him. Why does it even matter to you anyhow?"

He doesn't matter, thought Reuben. *He's filth. Haven't you heard the stories, Maggie? No, you wouldn't have. Lloyd's father*

63

squelched those rumors before they traveled too far. Oh, you'd like to know? It was nothing. We had a disagreement. I contemplated permanently removing him from existence. Pretty typical Thursday afternoon.

Reuben forced the foul memories away before they could fully climb to the surface. Before his repressed anger became too much to bear. Before Mira, or whatever apparition had been on the Winchesters' staircase, returned to berate him for promises broken and mistakes long made. "It doesn't," Reuben muttered. "Do whatever you like. I'll see you in May."

"What aren't you telling me?"

Why *did* he care what she thought? Maggie was only one day out of a whole year of his life—well two days now. Her presence in his life was miniscule compared to everything else. She shouldn't matter. Maggie was so quick to shut him out—to choose *Halverson* over him— why wasn't Reuben capable of the same?

"If I tell you a secret of mine, will you tell me yours?" she asked.

Maggie inhaled, her story flooding in a rush of words, not waiting for his assent. "After I met you in the cemetery, I went to the festival. They named me May Queen." She paused, waiting for her declaration to sink in. It didn't have to go very deep.

"That's not a secret. Tena told me. The entire town probably knows."

Maggie slipped in the snow, her hand clasping the carriage handle before she could go down into the drifts. "You met my sister? When?"

He flicked his wrist towards the house. "While you were gallivanting with your future husbands. Maybe you'll think about sharing with her next time. You hurt her feelings."

"*Her* feelings?" Maggie cried. "I'm the one forced to choose a husband now!"

"Congratulations," he said coldly. "You have fifteen choices waiting inside for you."

"Are you angry?"

"No." Reuben ran a hand over his eyes. He needed sleep.

"It's your turn now," Maggie insisted. "What's your secret?"

Reuben hesitated. This May Day was their last. Reuben had understood that the second Tena mentioned her sister's newest title. If he wanted one more day with Maggie—and he was suddenly aware that he wanted it very badly—then he couldn't tell her the truth. Everything would change soon enough anyway. Why rush the inevitable? "No. I'm sorry, but I can't. Please hand me my coat."

"Excuse me?" Maggie gasped. "You agreed!"

"Listen, Miss Archer," he shot back. "I never agreed to anything more than one day with you. I believe you told me not to complicate it. So this is me not complicating it."

Maggie thrust his coat at him. He knew she also wanted to throw a well-spoken rebuttal and if she had, she probably would have made it a good one. He wished she would have; he would have deserved it.

Reuben shrugged his coat on. "I'll see you in May. Happy Christmas."

"Yes, indeed" Maggie mumbled. "Happy Christmas."

Then he walked straight into the darkness, leaving her alone in the falling snow.

~ ~ ~

Reuben lay awake all night. He welcomed the darkness. But even alone in his bed, he was unable to dispel the taunting of his sister's memory or the fear of what lay in wait for him from his mother's hands. Not until the sun's golden ascension burned his vision did he manage to drag himself from the safety of his bed.

He approached his parents in the dining room, pins and needles tingling his fingertips. Except his mother acted as if nothing unusual happened the previous night, and his father had no reason to suspect. Florence sipped her tea. Harris searched for his employees' incompetence in that morning's *Gazette*. So Reuben took his place between them and stared at his sister's empty seat in silence, wishing his mother could be right about Mira, longing for a life where she really would come back and fix everything.

EIGHT

SUNLIGHT FILTERED THROUGH THE draperies, warm and delightful, basking in the glory of another May Day morning. Maggie scowled at her reflection in the looking glass. How had four months passed already? Time sure flew when you were avoiding social obligations.

Seven gentlemen vied for her hand after Christmas, only three meeting her father's rigorous expectations. All three were intelligent men of exceptional position and good family background. Any of them would be an excellent choice.

And Maggie *would* be expected to choose.

How she despised this stupid town, its archaic traditions, and Edith and Bianca for throwing her into the fire. But as much as she wanted to kick them both, Bianca had been correct about one thing. To delay her decision any longer, or worse reject all three, would reflect poorly on her father's ability to raise a dutiful daughter.

The rap at her door interrupted her last moment of solitude. Pinning her hair into a messy nest, she smeared an extra layer of color on her lips. She'd hear no end from her mother if she didn't at least appear to be trying.

"Speak of the devil," she muttered as she opened the door to her mother's petulant stare.

"Behave yourself," Beatrix snapped.

"I haven't done anything."

"But you will. Now, I have secured you an escort for today. Be polite."

Maggie sighed. "Three proposals were not enough? Add a few more and I can have a husband for every day of the week."

Beatrix wagged a finger, "Listen to your mother when I tell you one husband is more than enough to deal with. Sometimes even one is too many."

My thoughts exactly, thought Maggie, but remained quiet. She knew her father would suffer the brunt of her mother's anger if she argued. She tried to press past her mother, but Beatrix held firm.

"No spiteful remark?"

"None I wish to share," Maggie shot back. Downstairs the front bell rang followed shortly by Olivia greeting their guests at the door. "Please excuse me, Mother. As I was only just now made aware of his existence, I need a few minutes to look perfect for our guest."

Beatrix's face was marred with suspicion. "Very well. Please do not tarry too long."

As soon as her mother was out of sight, Maggie hurried down the hall in the opposite direction. Her plan was to sneak down the back stairs, through the kitchen, and out the rear door, which would have worked if Tena hadn't been blocking the top of the stairs.

"Where are you off to?" she asked. "Wouldn't you care to meet your escort?"

Maggie tossed her a look. "Thank you, but no. He's all yours."

Tena threw her hands up emphatically. "I wish he were."

"What does that mean?"

Tena picked at a crease in the wallpaper. "It's nothing. I think you should meet him though."

"Why?"

"I just think you should. Maybe you shouldn't discredit him so quickly. He seems like a genuinely thoughtful man. If you put in a little effort, you would see it too."

"Ugh, Tena, why are you pressing this?"

Tena stamped her foot. "Because this time you're wrong."

"That's your opinion," Maggie argued. "Move out of the way."

Tena braced herself against the wall. "You're not leaving me here alone."

"Well, I'm certainly not staying. You can either give me leave or come with me."

"Fair enough." Tena snatched Maggie's hand and dragged her down the hall, sufficiently silencing any additional arguments.

Tena rapped twice on their father's door, sneaking inside when there was no reply. If he was already at breakfast, there were only minutes before Olivia arrived to clean the upstairs rooms.

"What are we doing, Tena?" Maggie whispered. They hadn't been allowed in this room since they were little girls. Their mother would go berserk if she found them in here.

Tena slid open the top dresser drawer, shuffling through articles of their father's clothing Maggie would rather not see, and removed a small wooden box. Inside contained a thick wad of one and five notes and a full coin purse. Tena counted the money, took a generous amount, and returned the rest to the drawer.

Although the house had a safe, their father preferred to keep some additional funds in a few other hiding places where their mother wouldn't find it. Tena must have learned about this particular one at an age when their father assumed she wouldn't remember.

"Please don't look at me like that," Tena pleaded. Maggie hadn't intended to give her sister any particular expression, but her astonishment must have been written all over her face. She hadn't lied to Reuben when she said Tena was the prime example of obedience. When Tena was ten, she hated to play outside lest she dirty her dress and upset their mother. At fourteen, she accidentally ripped a page in one of Father's favorite volumes and cried for hours. Theft was the last thing Maggie thought her capable.

"You're the good daughter," Maggie asserted. "I'm the disappointment. Why are you doing this?"

Tena's eyes suddenly filled with tears. She stared at the ceiling rather than allow them to streak down her precisely powdered cheeks. "It's Sister's Day. Our day to spend *together*. I lost you to Reuben last year and not long from now one or both of us will marry and I'll lose you for good. If this is our last day together, I want it to be spectacular. I don't have the ferocity to be impulsive on my own. You know me better than anyone—it's not who I am."

"You're also not a thief, Tena."

Footsteps sounded in the hallway. Both girls tensed, listening intently, and the steps passed by. Tena gripped Maggie's forearms. Her eyes held renewed determination. "I hate stealing from Father too, but this is not a time we can simply ask him for money. Will you do this for me?"

Maggie considered her sister before replying. Tena was right. Who knew where life would take them? Even if Maggie managed to weasel her way out of a union, Tena's eventual marriage was a certainty. She would leave the house, maybe even leave Fontaine. Their time together as it was would end.

This realization had, at least for today, morphed Tena into an unabashed, disobedient, thieving woman—in short, nothing close to the sister Maggie grew up with.

And Maggie thought it was nothing short of incredible.

She nodded excitedly. "You know I will."

Tena clapped her hands together and threw her arms around Maggie. "Thank you! I promise, my plan is completely brilliant. Just come down to breakfast and you'll see."

The girls exited the room as quietly as they had entered and snuck down the back stairs towards the dining room. Maggie reached for the door stopping just short of entering. One of Tena's comments snuck back into her mind, overlooked in the midst of all her other words.

"What did you mean when you said soon one *or both* of us would be married? Have you received a proposal too?"

Tena's face went redder than Maggie had ever seen it. She felt her cheek as if checking her temperature. "Oh no, but I'm eighteen now—I could find the perfect person any day."

Tena was clearly hiding something which was, again, not at all like her sister. What strange power had taken hold of Tena today? Maggie wanted to ask, except her desire to see how far Tena would take things won out over her curiosity.

"What of your plans with Mr. Radford?" Tena asked.

After Maggie's argument with Reuben at Christmas, she had decided to break off their agreement. The promise she'd requested last May was a mistake at its best, a disaster at its worst. She'd intended to give him one final day together—a last hurrah before she was possibly shackled to some other man for eternity. Now she didn't see how she could manage to sneak away from Tena for even the few minutes a quick explanation would take.

One day, Maggie, she reminded herself. *He's only one day.*

Reuben was a grown man. He'd figure it out easily enough without her clarifications and apologies.

"I'm not meeting Reuben," Maggie asserted. "Our friendship is over anyway."

Tena's expression lost all of its brazenness. Her voice was little more than a squeaky whisper. "Please don't hate me."

"Why would I—" Maggie's words were staunched by the sight of their breakfast guests. Her parents occupied their usual places at the heads of the table. A freakishly tall gentleman with light wavy hair greeted her with a formal bow. Maggie's ears barely registered his introduction as Charles Kisch in an annoying German accent. Under normal circumstances, his voice alone would have convinced her to tell him to shove off.

Of course, that was if Tena's escort didn't have the same face and annoyingly sly smile of one, Mr. Reuben Radford.

NINE

AFTER LAURENCE ARCHER COMPLETED the formal introductions, they all sat down for a hearty breakfast. It had been so long since Reuben enjoyed anything resembling a proper family meal that he couldn't help but be grateful for the opportunity, no matter how unconventionally he may have arrived at it.

He chatted politely with Laurence about writing for the *Gazette,* and Laurence responded with tidbits about management at First Bank and Trust. He even noted if Reuben ever felt so inclined to switch careers, the bank was always looking for "bright young minds" as he put it. It was only after the third or fourth witticism between the two men that Maggie released a loud sigh and moved the focus to Charles.

Charles shared how easily his family had adapted to the English culture over the last ten years, using his standard half a dozen stock phrases. Tena seemed to find it all quite endearing, while Beatrix's scowl turned so far down Reuben expected it to drill a hole clear through the table. Probably knowing full well where his wife's mannerisms could lead, Laurence quickly switched to a discussion of festival events with Tena.

Reuben seized the opportunity to elicit Maggie's attention from across the table. *Why so cross? Aren't you glad to see me?* he mouthed.

Maggie attempted to shoot daggers from her eyes, and Reuben blocked them with what he hoped passed for an endearing grin. *Why are you here?* Maggie mouthed back.

Reuben thumbed at Charles. *He asked me.*

Why?

Reuben discretely pointed at Tena. *For her.*

No!

Why not? he challenged.

Maggie threw an enraged glance at Charles and noticed everyone else silently watching their exchange. She began to enthusiastically shovel fruit into her mouth.

Laurence's gaze moved between Maggie and Reuben. His upper lip twitched. "It appears you two are already acquainted?"

"We danced at the Christmas party," Reuben supplied. If Laurence maintained a good opinion of him now, it might not continue when he discovered how they'd really met.

"He was abysmal," Maggie mumbled.

Reuben rested his chin on his palm and smirked. "Once I received your instruction, my dance skills have since become nothing short of greatness. You know you're dying to give it another go."

"What? I—uh—no! I certainly am not!" Maggie spluttered. "You embarrassed me!"

Reuben laughed. "If by embarrassed, you mean caused to have a wonderful time, then sure, I embarrassed you." Tena snorted into her tea, resulting in Maggie throwing her heel into Tena's shin in retaliation. Tena dropped her teacup, the brown liquid spilling across the tablecloth. She and Reuben both jumped up with napkins at the ready to mop up the mess, and in their haste sent the entire tray of biscuits rolling underneath the table.

He chanced a glance at Tena from beneath the table cloth, certain she'd be mortified. Instead he was surprised to discover her succumbing to silent fits of laughter. He pressed a finger to his lips, and they reemerged together, completely composed. Tena calmly set her biscuits on the tray Reuben held out.

"I do believe Mr. Radford is correct," Tena replied, picking the conversation back up where they'd left it. "Maggie had a most delightful time at the Christmas party. Perhaps we should switch escorts?"

"What a sensible idea, Miss Archer," Charles spoke up, all heads turning in his direction.

"Enough!" Beatrix exclaimed and struck her palms on the table. Four sets of eyes swiveled back to the other end of the table, while Charles affixed his own on his plate where they remained for the duration of the meal. Beatrix stood up, hovering over them all. Her face grew a shade of purple Reuben had rarely seen before in nature.

"Now cease this, all of you. There will be no switching of partners. We invited Mr. Kisch here for Maggie." She narrowed her eyes first at Charles, then Tena. "And only for Maggie. As for Mr. Radford, I'm not entirely certain why you are here. We chose a far more acceptable escort for Tena who was to meet her at the festival, but I suppose all is for naught. We cannot very well cast you out now. My husband finds such behavior *rude*." Her expression, however, said if it were up to her, she wouldn't so much as trust Reuben over the threshold.

Reuben remained silent, any rebuttal left sitting in the back of his throat for the remainder of the meal. Any energy he might have had for arguments was used up long before he even left his house that morning.

He had just slipped on his shoes when he heard a gentle knock outside his bedroom, followed by his mother's voice, "Darling, are you awake?"

"Yes, Mother," he called. "Out in a minute."

Reuben drew on his jacket and ventured into the hall, catching a glimpse of his mother as she disappeared into Mira's bedroom. He edged cautiously down the hall; no one had entered that space for four years.

"What a beautiful day, my darling," Florence's cheery voice wafted out to him. Reuben stopped just outside the door, drew a breath, and counted to three. She only sounded that pleased when she was having one of her flashbacks.

Florence stood at the dresser, pulling out undergarments, one of Mira's school dresses draped over her arm. She laid everything on the bed, smoothing the wrinkles from the material. Then she tied the curtains back at the window. The sunlight streamed into the room to magnify every dust-covered surface, the effect like peering into a forgotten crypt.

"Mother?"

Florence bustled about the room without response, first to pick out a pair of Mira's shoes, then carefully folding the quilt back on the bed. Reuben sneezed when a cloud of dust billowed up with it, and Florence turned towards him with glossy eyes.

"Mother?" he tried again. "Come to breakfast. It won't help you being in here."

"Mrs. Butaine!" She called out the name of their childhood housemaid. "Please come quick! We haven't all day to wait!" She returned to the bed, and spoke directly to the pillow. "Mira, dear, you have slept awfully late this morning. There will be little time for breakfast before school."

Violent tremors seized his hands as he approached his mother. Her ferocity with him last winter may have been the first time she ever struck him, but it was by no means the last. Her delusions grew stronger every day since then, sending Reuben to the refuge of the cemetery more than any psychoanalyst would consider healthy. Especially not with the inner conversations he so often held of his own design.

He really didn't want to set her off again today.

Unfortunately, luck was never with him. The moment his hand touched her shoulder, Florence focused him with a stare so piercing Reuben stumbled backward towards the door. He held his hand out like one would try to calm a wild dog. "Mother, we told you many times. Mira isn't here any more."

Florence stared at the empty bed. Her fists slowly balled at her sides as she took a step towards her son that he matched in reverse. "What have you done with her?" she hissed then screamed, "What have you done with her!" Surprisingly fast, she lunged with hands outstretched into claws, attacking much quicker than she ever had before.

Reuben managed to grab one of her wrists, but was too slow to stop the other before her nails raked across the side of his neck. "You killed her!" Florence howled, blindly clawing at him. He spun her around, wrestling her arms to pin both hands behind her back. She continued to stamp her feet and scream mercilessly, struggling to pull free, but his grip was still stronger. He shoved her into the room and simultaneously backed out the door, locking it before she could chase after him.

Reuben fell against the wall and listened to his mother throw things and curse his name from inside the room. He wanted to run far away from this house and his parents and all the devastation of his life. Leave Fontaine and never look back. But he knew he couldn't. Come hell or high water, they were his family. His sense of duty wouldn't allow him to abandon them completely.

Hadn't Maggie said May Day was their one day to escape from the world? Then that's what he would do. After today, she would be gone too and he would have to resign himself to endless days and nights in this house ... but today? Today he would pretend he hadn't just locked his insane mother in his dead sister's bedroom.

His father met him in the entryway and glanced up at the noises from the floor above. "Your mother is unwell this morning."

"Unwell is an understatement. I found her in Mira's bedroom."

Unbridled astonishment fell across Harris's face. "What was she doing there?"

"Waking Mira. I reminded her that Mira's gone and she so eloquently blamed me, yet again." Reuben moved past his father, but stopped when Harris placed a hand on the door. There was a plea in his eyes.

"It isn't your fault, Reuben," Harris said gently. "Please tell me you understand that. What happened to our family—it isn't your fault."

Reuben gave his father a dead stare. "That's hard to believe when I'm reminded of the opposite every day."

"Please son, I know life has been trying since your sister left us. I have seen the toll it has taken upon you." Harris placed his hands on Reuben's shoulders. "I know I have not always been the father you needed, but I see now I am all you have. Don't you give up on me too."

Would his father still feel the same if he knew how Reuben was sliding down the same slippery slope as his mother? What would he say if Reuben announced the truth of the matter—that he was literally haunted by the memory of what happened years ago? How almost every night before he fell asleep he held imagined conversations with his sister and wished part of them was real.

"Please son," Harris pleaded again. "Let the veil of doubt be removed between us. Your sister would want that. We will figure out a way to make this family whole again."

Reuben saw the desperation in his father's eyes. Maybe there was no hope for their family as Reuben believed, but he wouldn't be the one to convince his father of it.

One last day and then he would come back to reality. One last day with Maggie, and he could be everything his father asked.

Reuben stood straighter, hoping his face held nothing but conviction. He wasn't sure he was dead set on what he was about to say, but somehow he would have to be. Whatever it took to get their lives back to normal. "Tomorrow I will be the son you want. Teach me to walk in your stride at the paper. Find me a wife. Enlist me to the military for all I care. Or send me to university. I'll become a doctor and save Mother if that's what you want. I'll be whoever you ask me to be tomorrow. Just please give me today."

Reuben knew that his father was balancing the effects of refusing to comply. Then his chest sagged a bit and he squeezed Reuben's shoulder lightly. "I do not understand you, my son, but I love you and I think that's all you need to hear right now."

"Thank you." Then Reuben did something he hadn't done in over four years. He hugged his father.

TEN

"WHERE EXACTLY ARE YOU taking us?" Maggie complained for the tenth time during their walk from the Archer home. Tena audibly released the sigh Reuben was feeling. After dealing first with his mother and then Beatrix Archer, Maggie's poor attitude now was grating on his last nerve.

After the conclusion of breakfast, Laurence suggested the four youngsters take their leave for the festival alone. "It's difficult enough getting to know one another without your old parents along," he told them. "Have some fun."

Tena threw her arms around her father with a girlish giggle. "Thank you, Father. We'll have such a delightful time together, won't we, Maggie?" Maggie had shrugged in silence only to be impossibly annoying the entire way to ... well, wherever it was they were headed. After leaving the Archers, Tena turned in the opposite direction of the festival, not once explaining her end goal. Reuben, satisfied merely to be out of his house and spending another day with Maggie even if she wasn't pleased to see him, hadn't questioned anything.

Until now. Now he was about to lose his breakfast all over the street. Tena's excursion had dropped them at one of the places he least wanted to be—the Fontaine railway station.

"Radford?"

Charles held a ticket out while the girls waited on the platform behind him. Overshadowing them was the imposing figure of a deep maroon passenger car, windows reflecting the late morning sun, and steam rising above her engine. After what happened to Mira, Reuben could not force his legs to take him on that train.

He grabbed his friend's arm to steady his nerves. "Charles, you know I don't want to be here. This place ... Shouldn't we go to the festival as planned?"

Charles glanced at Reuben's knuckles gripping his coat sleeve then back at Reuben's face sympathetically. "I understand your worries, Reuben, but the chances of an accident are remote. The odds—"

Reuben shook his head feverishly. His throat was tight. His chest hurt and he couldn't breathe. The world started swirling. He should sit down before he blacked out across the platform.

Charles took his arm. "You must breathe, Reuben." He smirked playfully. "It is understandable for you to swoon in the presence of two beautiful women, but truly, Radford, you must regain control."

Reuben gave a coughing laugh, surprised to find Charles's comment had actually lightened his distress. His forced breathing slowed. He could do this.

"Are you mentally unhinged?" Mira asked, stepping out from behind Charles, and looking very cross. She wore the same green dress from the Winchesters' Christmas party, the same one she always appeared in.

Reuben stepped around Charles, Mira's question repeating like a broken record. *Are you mentally unhinged?* Yes, seeing his dead sister was a clear indication. He should leave his friends to whatever scheme Tena was planning. They didn't need a crazy person knocking all the fun.

"I think maybe I am ill."

Maggie gave a shrug. "How terrible, I guess you should leave."

Tena pushed her sister out of the way. "Oh dear! It came on

quickly, didn't it?"

"He is not ill," Charles cut in. "He is embarrassed at his inability to properly escort a beautiful woman. Radford fails in that area time and again I am afraid."

"Quite true," said Maggie.

Tena turned on her heel and roughly escorted Maggie up the stairs to the train car, whispering reprimands the entire way. Maggie gave a huff and disappeared.

Tena returned with a knowing smile. "Ignore my sister. She's simply jealous because you're *my* escort, and she missed her chance with you. As for you, Mr. Radford, you're not going anywhere. We need you with us. Maggie will come around, you'll see."

Charles pressed the ticket into Reuben's palm. "Onto the train, Radford."

Reuben buried his hands in his jacket pockets and attempted a lighthearted smile. "Never argue with a stubborn woman, right?"

"How wise a man you are, Mr. Radford." Tena glanced coyly at Charles. "If only all men were so clever."

Charles entered the train car first, heading in the direction Maggie had taken, and Tena ascended the steps after him. Perhaps sensing Reuben might take flight when her back was turned, Tena turned back to offer her hand down to him.

"I'm capable of climbing three stairs alone."

"I know you are." Tena playfully wiggled her fingers. "Now, shall we?"

He waited for the paralyzing fear to grip him and released the world's longest sigh when it didn't. Clutching Tena's hand, he pulled himself up beside her on the landing. "Look at that. I did it, thanks to you."

"Well, I couldn't be left on May Day without an escort, could I?" Tena's eyes sparkled in the spring sunlight, her cheeks flushed. "I assume you've never left Fontaine either then?"

"I haven't," Reuben acknowledged. Until Mira died, there

hadn't seemed to be any reason to ever go. His family was in Fontaine—why would he need to be anywhere else?

Now he anticipated the adventure. What would he find away from this town? Would whatever he discovered make him wish he didn't have to return home to deal with his father's disappointment and his mother's empty mind? Was there a chance he could leave even his own past behind? His mother may be trapped, but what if Reuben's own delusions only stretched as far as the edge of this small town? Something unexpected leapt in his chest at the thought.

"May I share something with you?" Reuben asked. "The real reason why I lost myself back there?"

Tena watched him expectantly.

"Charles knows why, but he also knows it's not something I want to relive." Reuben lay a hand against the train's exterior, fully aware of the power this mammoth machine could hold. The train whistle gave a shrill blast, compounding all those horrible memories from years ago.

"My sister, Mira, was on her way home from school in a lumber wagon with three other students. There was an accident.

"We heard the train whistle from our home down the street. My mother was out front with a neighbor when it happened. Even from the far end of the road, she knew someone had been struck, although she couldn't make out who it was. We ran to the tracks, only it was too late. Debris everywhere. Blood everywhere. Mira and two of the other children were dead. Thankfully, the driver and the remaining child, his son, survived. I never found out their names—*my* sister was dead, so at the time I didn't care about anyone else."

Reuben's breath caught. "My mother screamed, terrible agonizing wails. I'll never forget the sound. It was the most awful moment of my life, a horror I pray you never have to endure. Since that day even the mere sight of the tracks causes me more nervousness than it should. I never wanted to set foot on a train again." He caught her gaze. "And yet, what power do *you* have that you could change my mind?"

Lips pulled into a thin line, Tena studied him. Reuben couldn't imagine what she might be thinking at a story so awful as the one he'd just told. In a life so steady as hers, so normal with a living sister and without hallucinations or unreturned romantic interests, how could she possibly relate to a loss like his? Despite what Maggie said that first day about him and Tena being alike, Reuben couldn't think of two other people who were more different. How then could Tena so easily convince him to rethink the impossible?

Finally she offered a nervous half-smile, her eyes sliding to someplace near his left lapel. "I wish I could say I understand how you feel," she said. "I wish I even knew what to say. Only I don't. 'I'm sorry' would never be enough."

The metal of the train's exterior lay warm beneath his hand, nearly as warm as the skin of Tena's fingers against his own. Two elements both the same temperature, one holding passengers and the other holding emotional strength. Warm, strong, secure. Alike and yet so different. Just like Reuben and Tena were.

He lifted his palm from the train car where the cool air reached his skin, and covered Tena's hand between both of his. "It is though. Having you here, Miss Archer, you having made me do this ... Whatever your reasons are, it is enough."

With a settling breath and courage from her hand in his, Reuben led Tena onto the train.

ELEVEN

"So, Southampton?" Reuben said, reading his ticket when the attendant handed it back to him. Their conversation outside ended just as the train shoved off from the station, leaving Reuben and Tena to snatch the first empty compartment. They would locate Charles and Maggie when the train paused for passengers in Alresford.

Tena shrugged. "It was a logical choice. We can easily return to Fontaine by nightfall." She handed Reuben her own ticket and he tucked both into his jacket pocket. They certainly wouldn't be thrown off the train because his clumsy fingers lost their proof of passage.

Outside the windows, miles of countryside passed by. Hills, trees, even an occasional town approached and disappeared again in a blur. Nothing much different than Fontaine. Hopefully the city would prove more satisfying.

"Do you think Southampton will have a festival today?" Tena asked, then answered her own thought. "Of course they will. What sort of town doesn't celebrate May Day?"

"There must be a hundred other places to see in Southampton," noted Reuben, "and *that's* what you want to do? We could have done that at home."

Tena tucked a stray curl behind her ear. "I know it must sound silly, but May Day has always been somewhat of an exciting tradition for Maggie and I. Flowers in our hair, dancing around the maypole, hoping to be crowned May Queen and finding the perfect husband ... Or at least I always hoped so." Tena's voice took on a slight bitter edge. "I don't know what happened to Maggie over the last two years. She's become so aloof, so cynical about it all now. She's my own sister and sometimes I feel like I don't know her at all. Do you know what I mean?"

Reuben knew exactly how it felt to live under the same roof as someone you'd known your entire life and have no idea who they were. He'd lost his mother, and he doubted she could ever come back again. Reuben nodded. "After my sister died, my mother was never the same."

"I know. Maggie told me."

"She did?" Reuben said, his voice harsher than he'd intended it. "What else did she tell you?"

Tena studied her hands. "Pretty well everything."

"I see. Well, that's wonderful, it is." Reuben crossed his arms and slid down the seat to lean against the window. He wasn't angry Tena knew, not really. Embarrassed was a more accurate descriptor. No normal person brandished that their mother was a nutcase. In hindsight, it was really himself he should be furious with for not begging Maggie's silence.

They sat in awkward quiet then, pretending to look out the window, only to meet eyes at the same moments.

"Oh confound it," Tena finally exclaimed. "This is ridiculous. Are you upset that I know?"

"No."

"Then quit sulking. If I tell you something about me, can we call it square?"

Reuben straightened up some. "I suppose."

Tena made a cursory glance around the car and scooted closer. "Charles and I have been courting since Christmas. No one knows, not even Maggie. You won't tell her, will you? Please, Reuben."

Reuben crossed his arms again, feeling a twinge of annoyance return. "Why haven't *you* told her? You two seem to share everything else."

Tena matched his heated stance. "That's not fair. I didn't tell her everything about Christmas, only that I met you. Maggie doesn't know it was you who introduced me to Charles or how you're pining for her—"

"I am *not* pining—"

"Maggie wouldn't understand," Tena continued. "She thinks the whole notion is stupid, and I need to be certain Charles is truly who I want. If not, or if he tires of me, well, Maggie would ensure I knew what an awful mistake I made. And frankly, I have no desire to listen to it."

"Why tell me then?"

"I know I can trust you. We have similar problems, you and I."

Reuben frowned. "And that would be?"

Tena laughed. "Maggie, of course."

Before Reuben could refute Tena yet again, Maggie's face appeared above the seat, making them both jump. Her eyes narrowed as if she'd caught them canoodling in a dark corner. "What are you two doing? I heard my name."

Tena waved her away. "You did. We're talking about you. If we wanted you to know what we were saying, we would have included you."

"That's rather impolite." She rested her chin on Tena's shoulder and softened her voice. "Tena, that man is dull as tombs. It's so uncomfortable. He refuses to make even a hint of small talk, and then randomly mutters something in German."

Reuben choked down a laugh which sounded more like an elephant was escaping from his throat. Both women looked at him. "Sorry, ladies. Maggie, why don't you take my place?" Maggie didn't even protest. She plopped down the second Reuben vacated the seat.

Charles barely glanced over as Reuben landed in the seat

opposite and kicked his feet up on the bench. Charles studied the landscape rushing past the window, tapping his fingers absently on his knee.

"Trouble with the lady, my German comrade?" Reuben smirked. He raised his hand to his forehead in salute.

Charles pushed Reuben's feet off the bench. "I have no troubles with my lady. *Your* woman on the other hand is a relentless bore."

"Woah," Reuben threw up his hands in protest. "She is *not* my woman."

"She's insufferable."

"Right you are." Reuben leaned into the window corner so he could stretch his legs across the bench. "So, what exactly is between you and Tena?" Reuben asked, attempting to sound aloof and succeeding in only being painfully obvious.

Charles scowled. "She told you."

"Aw, don't be angry with her, mate. You both know you can trust me." Reuben tapped above his ear. "Like a steel trap. Or a bank vault! Nothing escapes."

"*Radford!*" Charles exclaimed. "She probably told her sister too. It's only a matter of time before her parents find out."

"You need to calm down," Reuben told him. "I assure you no one else knows. You need to have more faith in the woman you're with."

Charles glared at him. "This is your fault, Radford."

Reuben balked. "How did this turn back on *me*?"

"I have you to thank and curse. You introduced me to the most incredible woman and ruined my life in the same night."

Reuben gave a wide grin. "That's how I am. Reuben Radford—ruining lives since 1891."

Charles's scowl grew even deeper. "This is not a joke. Her mother hates Germans."

"And ..."

"*Für gottes willen*, Reuben. *I'm* German!"

Reuben tipped his head back and closed his eyes. "Bah! Forget about her mother, man. If you want to be with her, make it happen."

"That is easy for you to say. You're unattached."

Thanks for reminding me, Reuben thought bitterly. If only things with Maggie were a bit less complicated.

Talk in town had been proliferous lately, with everyone discussing how the girl most likely to never marry won the marriage lottery. As another May Day approached, Reuben found himself growing unnaturally anxious. He often lay awake at night arguing with Mira who she would choose. His feelings were absurd. She wasn't his and couldn't be.

That morning, Reuben had marched straight to the Archer house, determined to look Maggie square in the eye and ask her if she was engaged. If she said yes, he would return home and immediately begin whatever life his father planned for him. If not? He hadn't even gotten that far in his thoughts.

When Reuben arrived, he found a petrified Charles waiting outside. His face was so green, Reuben wondered if he should insist Charles carry a bucket under his chin.

"Are you here for Tena?" he'd asked.

"*Nein,*" Charles said. "I am here for her sister."

Reuben grabbed the fence as his knees buckled. His stomach crawled through his throat. He wished he had that bucket for himself. "Maggie picked *you?*" This could not be happening.

Charles looked confused. "No. Her mother did."

"But—but—" Reuben stammered.

Charles seized Reuben's lapels in a very uncharacteristically Charles gesture. "Radford, you have to be Tena's escort today while I'm with Maggie."

Reuben shrugged Charles off. He had an overwhelming desire to tackle his friend. "Escort her yourself."

"I can't."

"Why not?"

"Mr. Kisch?" A stern woman, who he assumed was Beatrix Archer, stood in the doorway, arms crossed with a scowl knitting her eyebrows into one straight line. "Are you planning to join us or spend the morning creeping along our path?"

Charles waved limply and looked at Reuben with pleading eyes. "Please, Reuben. Just for today. I don't trust anyone else."

Reuben followed Charles and Beatrix into the house, forfeiting his chance to ask for any more details.

Now, on the train, his curiosity had peaked again. There were a few things that just didn't make sense.

"Wait." Reuben held up a hand. "If her mother hates Germans, why would she think you're a good match for Maggie?"

"Exactly, Radford! It does not make any sense to me either. Perhaps she is not as strict with her elder daughter's suitors? Maybe her husband convinced her? How am I to know? Tena assured me her mother's leniency would not extend to our situation."

"But if Mrs. Archer thinks you're interested in Maggie, it takes the suspicion off of your relationship with Tena, doesn't it?" Reuben stated.

"That was what Tena believed, yes."

"What about Maggie?" asked Reuben. "Were you just going to dump her after today? What if she actually fancied you? Wouldn't it make things a little embarrassing when you revealed you're really in love with her sister?"

Charles looked like the thought never crossed his mind. "*Meine güte*, Reuben. I do not know." He ran his fingers absently through his hair, sighed, and switched to German. "Tena's different from any of the girls in school. Words are lost when I try to describe how much I adore her."

Reuben looked thoughtfully at his friend. He'd never seen Charles like this before. "Careful, Charles, your German is leaking. You must really fancy her to be so agitated."

Charles gave a wane smile. "*Ja*, and that is the problem. I may love her, but I will always be German. She may love me, but she also wants to please her parents. I cannot ask her to give up her family. How then can there be a future for us?"

Reuben didn't have an answer. That seemed to be the case a lot these days.

TWELVE

FOR AS OFTEN AS HER PARENTS spoke of the years they lived in London, Maggie was woefully undereducated about city life. She entered the bustle of the Southampton railway station with an immense sensation only to be described as overwhelmed and underprepared.

One street offered more shops than she could look through in a single day, and a single city block boasted enough restaurants, taverns, and inns to supply their entire town. Charles, being the only one of the four with any "big city" experience, assured her the abundance was simply a result of being so near the pier, but the reasoning didn't make it any less impressive.

"How fascinating to live in London," Tena quipped.

"It may have been if I were not ten years younger at the time, twelve inches shorter, and unable to speak a lick of English," Charles amended.

Tena, being Tena, managed to inquire from a local shopkeeper the direction of the city's May Day festival. Thankfully, the distance was easily manageable by foot proving no need to pay a taxi. Maggie's apprehension mounted with the acknowledgement that Tena had provided no further details on their misadventure and no way to determine how much money they would need. Better to be frugal than to end up stranded miles from home. The last thing they needed was for their parents to panic and send the police after them.

Eventually unease gave way to the familiarity of May Day. Southampton's festival put Fontaine's attendance numbers to shame. Multicolored flowers, ribbons, and banners decorated the city park. Children wove intricate patterns around the maypole, couples danced before a twelve-piece band, and the heavenly floral scents enclosed them like a cloud.

"We are also expected to dance then, yes?"

Maggie spun at Charles's request, ignored it, and sought out Tena instead. To Maggie's dismay, Reuben led her sister in a poorly executed waltz. As she'd suspected, his boasts at breakfast were all for show. Tena was brave to succumb to Reuben's clumsy donkey trot. At least she seemed to be having an amusing time of it.

Reluctantly, Maggie accepted Charles's hand. "Very well, Mr. Kisch. *One* dance." *If Tena can risk broken toes, I can too.*

Only one dance led to another, and soon they were switching partners back and forth and joining in when the crowd came together as a group. It didn't matter if they didn't always know the steps. The spirit of the day swept over them, hours passing in a haze of laughter and gaiety. Charles didn't appear quite so tiresome, and Maggie quickly forgot she was supposed to be annoyed with Reuben. There wasn't a time in her recent recollection when she'd had such fun.

"This was a wonderful idea," Maggie told Tena. "We should do this every year."

Tena swung Maggie around, laughing with each step. "Here's to Sister's Day!"

When the music stopped, Charles and Reuben left to fetch refreshments from across the green while the girls staked out space in the shade. Maggie pulled at her blouse where sweat plastered the fabric to her skin, and Tena fanned herself in an attempt to escape her own damp wardrobe. Even so, the warmth wasn't enough to hinder couples from joining in when the band next struck up a hearty rag.

Tena glanced sideways at her sister. "Have you decided on a man yet?

"No," Maggie frowned. "Thank you so much for reminding me though." Nothing sobers you more than reality sinking back in on a happy day.

Tena bit her lip, her eyes drifting where Charles and Reuben talked over their lemonade. Reuben drained his and asked for another one, elbowing Charles when he returned an inaudible, but obviously sarcastic comment.

"You have other options, you know," said Tena.

"What options?" asked Maggie. Tena slid her gaze back to the drink table with a perfunctory nod. Maggie rolled her eyes and released an audible sigh. "Reuben? He's not interested. Nor am I."

"But I've seen how he looks at you. I know that look."

"This conversation is ludicrous," Maggie argued. "If he fancied me, as you so claim, he would be more upfront with his thoughts. Do *you* know what he's hiding?"

"No, but I—"

"Exactly!" Maggie turned Tena to meet her gaze, ignoring her sister's continued protests. She pointed across the lawn. "You think he looks at me a certain way? It's a look of distrust you see. That's the face of a liar."

"You must really care to be so twisted up over him."

"Your *mind* is twisted."

"So, say we leave Reuben out of the mix," Tena conceded, "Winning May Queen still isn't a death sentence. You don't have to marry anyone. Take a position in a shop, be a seamstress, or a governess—"

"A governess?" Maggie snorted. "Can you see me with children? I'm not even wanting any of my own."

Tena sighed. "All I'm saying is there are other choices. Father will be happy with whatever you decide."

"And mother? How useful is father's opinion if mother sides against him?"

"There may be a chance to change her mind."

"You're no more able to offer a glass of water to those in hell than you are to please our mother."

"Then don't worry about her opinion and follow your own mind!"

"Easy for you to say. I'd like to see how you react when mother disapproves of something you want. As if that would ever happen."

Tena recoiled, cheeks flaming. She rubbed them absently, her eyes cast upward as though holding back tears. What did Tena have to be upset about? Maggie wondered. Her life was nearly perfect.

Charles and Reuben returned with glasses of fresh lemonade, ceasing any opportunity to ask further questions. Tena downed hers in one gulp.

"Thirsty?" Charles asked. "Shall I retrieve another, Miss Archer?"

Tena nodded. "Yes, thank you, Mr. Kisch."

"Perhaps you should accompany him, Miss Archer," Reuben handed Tena several coins. "Buy some food and meet us down at the pier."

Tena took the money and locked eyes with Reuben a second too long for Maggie's liking. Maggie looked from Reuben to Tena to Charles and back again. "What is going on?" she asked.

Reuben jumped in, taking Maggie's elbow to steer her across the green to the street. Tena and Charles headed in the opposite direction. "Don't ask what you don't really want to know," he said, quickening his pace away from the festival crowds. He edged around a number of boys sporting cricket bats and turned abruptly down a side alley, emerging onto another unfamiliar street.

Maggie ripped her arm from his grasp. "I do want to know. Are you interested in my sister?"

Reuben stopped walking. "Why on earth would I send her away

with my best mate if *I* wanted her? That's absolutely mental."

"Then what was your intent with that long lingering stare back there?"

"Tena and I have an understanding." Reuben continued walking, leaving Maggie falling over a flower cart in order to catch up.

"What kind of understanding? Tena told me this morning that she might meet the right person any day now. She's always talking about you. I think she likes you."

"Good grief, Maggie, she's alone with *Charles* right now," Reuben repeated. "That doesn't give me any chance at all does it?" He nodded like he'd told a riddle and expected her to answer it. Maggie just wanted him to give her a yes or no answer, not play a game.

"What are you on about?" Maggie asked impatiently. "Do you fancy Tena or not?"

Reuben abandoned his empty lemonade glass on a crate. He stripped off his jacket and rolled his shirt sleeves up to the elbows. Only then did he finally answer. "No, Maggie, your sister's not who I'm interested in."

"Good. Was that truly so difficult to say?"

With a thin shake of his head, Reuben threw his jacket over his shoulder and continued walking. Maggie had the sinking suspicion she still didn't understand the joke.

A refreshing breeze swept in as they drew nearer the harbor. Their arrival scattered a flock of seagulls directly into the path of a group of very irritated fishermen. The resulting murderous glares and foul-mouthed remarks caused Reuben to return a number of equally obscene comments instructing the men where they could relocate their fishing poles. Rather than come to blows over it, Maggie quickly apologized and ushered Reuben farther down the pier towards the tugs and steamers.

Thankfully that was all it took to distract Reuben from their confrontation. The tallest building in Fontaine stood at a mere three stories, nowhere near the height of the multi-deck three funnel creation before her. Rising in smooth grey steel, it could hold every person in their small town and three neighboring villages. Maggie expected something so massive should make her feel insignificant and pitiful in comparison, but it was exactly the opposite. Something so powerful made her think again on what Tena said about her having options.

"Tena doesn't want to lie to you, you know," said Reuben.

Maggie stared at him. "What?" It was easy to forget that another person's inner monologue continued even when you stopped speaking to them.

"Tena," Reuben repeated. "She wants to tell you, but she's afraid of you."

"Of *me*?" Maggie said, leaning away affronted.

Reuben smoothed his hair back to cool his face, wiping the excess moisture on his pant leg. "Blimey, she has reasons. You're not an easy woman to talk to, let alone share anything with. There are things I'd like to tell you, but—"

"Then tell me." Maggie had grown tired of this back and forth of his at Christmas. It was the entire reason why she'd decided not to meet him today. Confound Tena for changing the rules! Maggie was supposed to be the wild card, not Tena. Her sister wasn't allowed to call the shots.

"Charles is in love with Tena," Reuben said. "They've been together since Christmas."

Maggie didn't believe for an instant that his big secret involved a love story. Reuben, a closet romantic? Please. Maggie suspected Reuben's real story, whatever it was, wasn't one for sunny days strolling along the pier by calm waters. His story would only be revealed when the seas were choppy and the ship was already halfway under. Well, that was one ship Maggie wouldn't step onto, much less go down with. She would have to be completely mad to do so.

Speaking of completely mad, Reuben's admission finally caught up to Maggie's sprinting thoughts. "Is Tena insane?" Maggie asked. "Charles is German!"

"And the best guy I know," Reuben stated. "I've known him since we were ten. We met his first day at school. He didn't know English. I didn't know German. We became friends despite our differences. And he's never left me, not even after all these years."

"It'll never work," Maggie scoffed.

Reuben's gaze fell over the open ocean. "Your mother doesn't know what she doesn't know. Not all Germans are bad. Not all the English are good. But Charles will never hurt Tena. I would wager my own life on it."

"Say that's true; I still don't see how two people could love each other for their whole lives. Stay with each other, sure. But actually love them? Want to be with them? I haven't seen it yet." The thought was so foreign, Maggie felt her facial muscles scrunching up under the strain of imagining it.

Reuben smiled. "You don't need to worry about Charles. He'll be good to Tena."

"For now."

"You've known your parents your entire life. Do you think you'll ever stop loving them?"

"I have to love them. They're my parents."

Reuben stepped in her line of vision, successfully derailing her train of thought. "We're not forced to love anyone. We choose to love them."

Maggie frowned. "You're saying I have yet another choice to make?"

"Some choices are more difficult than others," Reuben said seriously. "Who we choose to love shouldn't be."

Maggie's parents expected her to choose a husband, but there was an enormous difference between choosing to tolerate one and choosing to love him. And there was no guarantee he would ever love her back. Or that she would even want him to. Maggie swallowed hard. "Sometimes it's easier not to choose."

Silence fell between them. Maggie knew she shouldn't have brought any of this up—it was completely inappropriate conversation—but she didn't have anyone else. Reuben's opinion was the only one that didn't matter. She could unload her emotional baggage without fear of what he thought tomorrow. For them, there was no tomorrow.

Maggie turned her attention again to the crew bustling across the decks of the massive steamship. Officers made their rounds on the upper decks while crewmen lugged crates of supplies, passenger cases, and wardrobe trunks up the gangplank. *What if I ran up there right now and stowed away with the cargo?* Maggie wondered. *I'm tiny enough to hide in a shipping crate.*

"You're not serious, are you?" Reuben gawked.

Maggie flushed. "Did I say that out loud?"

Reuben nodded. "Sure did. Glad I'm not the only crazy one here."

"Well, I'm not going to do it. I mean … I don't know. I would like to. Don't you ever want to run away?"

"Of course. But we can't just run from life."

"I know." Maggie looked at the ship longingly.

"Where would you go if you could?" Reuben asked.

A dozen locations popped into Maggie's head simultaneously, each one seemingly more impossible than the next. She wasn't destined to reach any of those places … not if her parents had their way. Even if they didn't and she sought employment as Tena suggested, her limited wages wouldn't get her anywhere. Maggie shrugged, trying to push the notion away. "London? That's at least a realistic possibility."

Reuben gestured thumbs-down. "Wrong. Boring. Choose again."

There was that word again. *Choose.* How she longed to strike it from the English language! If she could go anywhere, where *would* she go?

"Iceland," Maggie said firmly.

Reuben raised an eyebrow. "Iceland? You can go anywhere and you choose Iceland?"

"*Journey to the Center of the Earth*. That's where the entrance is."

"'Course." Reuben nodded like Iceland was a trip people decided to take regularly. "Why, Miss Archer, where do you plan to go on holiday this year?"

"I am so pleased you asked, Mr. Radford," Maggie replied in similar fashion. "We heard there was a delightful entrance to the depths of the world in Iceland. Seems to be all the rage this year." They both laughed then, from the absurdity or some deeper feelings she couldn't tell, but it continued until they both wiped tears from their eyes.

"Then see Iceland you shall," Reuben said, releasing a final chuckle.

"How?" Maggie scoffed. "Are you going to take me?"

"Sure. I'm always up for an adventure."

Maggie snorted. "Since when?"

Reuben stabbed his finger into her shoulder. "How dare you doubt me! If there is one thing Radford men are, it is determined. And I promise I will personally find a way to take you there."

Maggie couldn't hide her smile, even then. What he proposed, albeit unlikely, was also the most well-meaning proposal of any she'd received.

THIRTEEN

"WE'LL HAVE TO LEASE A FEW rooms here for the night."

"Impossible. Father will summon the police if neither one of us returns."

"We can't possibly take her on the train in this state."

"We have to, Reuben. Perhaps no one will notice."

"Not likely. They'll arrest Maggie for public intoxication, and your father will flay Charles and I alive."

There was a long pause while Reuben and Tena stood at the crossroads of their current predicament. Finally Tena nodded. "I will go home. Reuben, you will stay with Maggie."

"You're about ten pence shy of a shilling if you think that," Reuben shot back. "There is a line and I will not step over it. She's *your* sister, Tena; *you* stay with her."

"I told you, if Maggie and I are both gone in the morning, Father will lose his head. If I go home now, there's a chance I can divert them from noticing Maggie isn't with me. You'll ensure her safe return. Charles will tell your parents you are staying at his house after drinking too much at the festival."

"Getting sloshed isn't my standard," Reuben sighed. "Plus, he detests the festival. He won't believe it."

"Would you rather we told him the truth?"

"You make a fair point."

"In between arguments, did either of you notice when Maggie left?" asked Charles. Tena and Reuben's heads whipped towards the door as it bounced shut.

"Cor blimey!" Reuben yelled and raced off down the street.

He still didn't understand where everything went wrong. He and Maggie were having such wonderful conversation on the pier; it seemed they'd even put their Christmas argument behind them. They joked about pushing those rude fishermen into the harbor. They discussed the latest books they'd each read—*Around the World in 80 Days* and *Alice's Adventures in Wonderland* for Maggie and Reuben respectively. No, *Alice* was not a children's book, Reuben chided when Maggie jested of his reading selection. Just about the time Reuben checked his watch—now past five o'clock—Tena and Charles finally appeared and shattered the illusion. Maggie became so aloof towards him it was almost as if nothing happened between them at all.

"'Bout time you two turned up," Maggie scolded. "Where have you been? And where is our food? It's past tea and nearly dinner!"

"Sorry, we forgot," Tena apologized. "But the day is still young! We can procure dinner before we head home."

"Brilliant! I'm starved!" Reuben agreed at the same time Charles said, "The hour is late. Your mother—"

Tena's eyes flashed. "My mother?" she spat, her demeanor flipping in an instant. She pointed her finger at Charles. "You think I'm safe, don't you, Charles Kisch? And you—" She rounded on Maggie who stepped back, dumbstruck. "You think I'm a pawn in mother's pocket. Move more than one space—I wouldn't dream of it!"

"Actually, you can move a pawn more than one space," said Reuben. "Your opening move—"

"Agh, Reuben!" Tena exclaimed.

Reuben winked. "My ability to be annoyingly helpful knows no boundaries."

"No, that's just your ability to be annoying," muttered Maggie.

"No one asked for your input," Reuben shot back.

"No one asked for yours."

"Stop it!" Tena stepped between the two as if they were bickering children. "Can you focus on me for once? Now here's what we're going to do." She pointed to a squat Tudor-style building labeled the Goshawk Inn and Tavern. "There. Let's go."

Charles chafed in a manner suggesting he'd been asked to commit capital crime. "To a tavern?"

"We are all different people back home," Tena reasoned. "For tonight we forget them. We can do whatever we want, no matter the risk."

Charles folded his arms with a frown. "Miss Archer, a tavern is no place for a lady."

Tena threw her hands up. "Confound it, Charles. Call me Tena. They both already know! Reuben, I know you told her." Reuben couldn't even pretend to look sorry. Or conceal his smirk.

"Tena—" Maggie was silenced with the stamp of Tena's shoe. "No, Maggie! Back home everything we do is scrutinized. No one here knows us. Let's be who we want to be because tomorrow everything changes. We only have today. Isn't that what you always say?" The words left her mouth sounding far more desperate than she'd probably intended them, but they made her point loud and clear. "Now, I am doing this. So you can all go in or you can all go home. Don't get in my way."

Charles spluttered incoherently and gave up by crossing his arms and expressing his frustration in German, none of his comments appropriate enough for Reuben to translate. Maggie stood stock still in disbelief, probably wondering who in the world stood in front of her. This wasn't the sister she'd told Reuben about when they first met—Reuben didn't know who this woman was.

Maggie gently touched her sister's arm. "Tena, why are you doing this? You don't have to prove anything to me."

Tena elbowed Maggie away. "I know I don't. I have to prove it to myself." She looked to Reuben, the only one who hadn't spoken yet.

Normally, Reuben would have soothed her into reason like he'd tried to do with Maggie in the bell tower the year prior. Instead Tena's words spurred him into action, evoking a deviant side of him he found strangely alluring. He promised his father he would behave himself tomorrow. But he never promised today.

A mischievous smile parted his lips as he offered Tena his hand. "Reuben, what are you doing?" Maggie asked shrilly.

"What Tena said. Proving something," Reuben replied. Maggie didn't believe her sister's rebellious act, but Reuben knew this might be the most incredible thing Tena would ever do. If it stuck, none of them would ever underestimate her again. And maybe, just maybe, neither would her mother. Perhaps he could help give Tena and Charles their happy ending after all.

"Shall we, m'lady?" he whispered in her ear, before pulling her in the direction of the tavern, both of them high on the thrill. Tena's grin lit her eyes with the fire of two radiant suns.

Reuben wasn't sure what it felt like to be possessed by demons, but perhaps it felt like this. Because if they listened to Beatrix Archer, everything they planned to do tonight would send them straight to hell.

Four hours later, their wickedly brilliant spontaneity didn't seem as brilliant as it was wicked. Reuben stooped to catch his breath after sprinting two city blocks to where Maggie stared up at the steamships with glossy-eyed fascination.

"It's after nightfall. Reckon we could sneak aboard now?" she asked him.

"What I *reckon*," Reuben gasped, "is we need to get you off the street—"

"Maggie, you cannot be out here like this," Tena cried, running up beside them. Charles was just behind her.

"Your sister is out of hand!" Charles asserted. "What if the police arrive?"

"Calm down, Charles. I'll handle this." Tena offered Maggie some bills from her handbag.

Reuben grabbed them first and shoved the money in his pocket. "I'm not relying on *her* to ensure we make it home."

"I am well within my senses, thank you!" Maggie squawked. "I know who I am and where I am and I do not need a nanny." Maggie linked her arm through Reuben's and pointed down the road. "Now lead on! To the station!"

Reuben shot Tena a silent plea, begging her to relieve him of his duty. Nothing good would come of this; he was certain of it. Tena shook her head stubbornly. Reuben balled his hands to keep from screaming at her. Impossible girls! Both of them—completely impossible!

"Tena, I think you should stay," Charles tried. "I will speak with your parents."

"You are *not* talking to my parents." Tena glowered.

"Then Charles stays," Reuben offered. "And I'll—"

She laced him with the same icy stare. "You're not talking to them either."

"Fine! Then we all stay!" Reuben threw himself down on the nearest bench. "You're the captain of this voyage, Tena. If we're going down, you're coming with us."

Charles wrapped a protective arm around Tena. "Maggie's the deviant. Why should Tena be punished?"

"Ha!" spat Reuben, "This was Tena's idea! If you could control your woman—"

"You encouraged her!" argued Charles. "Maybe if you paid less attention to my woman and more to your own—"

Reuben sprang to his feet. "She. Is. Not. My. Woman!"

"Gentlemen!" Tena cried. "Reuben, may I speak with you alone?"

Clutching his sleeve, Tena dragged him down the pier, releasing him just short of rounding the street corner. She leaned against the fence overlooking the harbor and sighed, breathing in the salty air as she shook out the plait down her back. The strands rustled in the ocean breeze, the street lamps accenting the warm highlights. Unlike Maggie, who seemed so completely unbreakable, Tena's gentle features softened all her edges. It reminded Reuben of Mira before her face played the leading role in his nightmares.

If Reuben and Tena had entered that tavern looking to prove something about themselves, they had certainly succeeded. They'd shown their rebellious nature to only extend until common sense kicked in to keep them from doing anything stupid. Unlike Maggie, whose common sense ended at a bottle of scotch, a deck of cards, and an overwhelming desire to one-up her friends.

Reuben tossed his jacket over the rail, near enough that their forearms brushed when he rested against the rail beside her, close enough that they couldn't be overheard. "What do you want from me, Tena?" He asked softly. "You can't expect me to stay here with Maggie."

Tena returned her attention from the ocean waves. "She says you have secrets. They must be worth keeping if only Charles knows."

Reuben flinched. "Did he tell you?"

"No, he didn't. And I'm not asking you to tell me either."

"You don't want to know?" A woman who didn't need to hear every strand of gossip? Reuben found that unlikely.

"No, I do," Tena said just as he suspected. Then she said something he wouldn't have predicted. "And I guarantee this will not be the last time I wonder what you're hiding, however it's yours to hide or reveal as you wish. I only hope one day you will be able to trust someone enough to tell."

He thought about telling her. He bit the words back so hard blood percolated across his tongue.

Tena's voice held an edge of nervousness. "No matter your

secrets though, I trust you, Reuben. I know you will keep my sister from any more idiotic decisions."

"*Why* do you trust me?" Reuben asked incredulously. "I could have slaughtered an entire village before I met you."

Tena didn't even blink twice. "Did they deserve it?"

"Well, I don't like to talk about it, but they definitely had it coming."

Tena nodded in Maggie and Charles's direction. They stood a good ten feet apart, staring at opposite ends of the pier. "Do you see that man over there?" Reuben nodded. "I think I've fallen for him. Desperately. It's difficult to remember a time when I was not so very much in love."

"He feels the same about you."

Tena smiled softly. "I hope so. After the Christmas party, we said goodbye. Nothing fancy. Just … goodbye. I assumed I would never see him again. Then not even two days later, a messenger arrived. *'I will never forget our dance together. For you are both goddess and villain to my heart.'* From that moment, I knew I couldn't lose him." Tena's eyes focused on Charles, the curve of her lips raised in pure bliss. Reuben wondered how it would feel for someone to see him the way Tena saw Charles.

"Why are you telling me this?" he asked.

Tena returned her focus to Reuben. "You asked me why I trust you? Because I love Charles—silly weak-minded girl that I am— and Charles trusts you. What kind of person would I be if I didn't have faith in the man I love?"

After those words all sense left him; he would have happily followed Tena off the end of the pier if she asked. She gave the dictionary definition of a perfect answer. He was horribly envious of Charles's good fortune, simultaneously wanting to shake Charles's hand and punch him in the teeth. He could search the world and no woman would ever believe in him the way Tena believed in Charles, no matter how much said woman claimed to love him.

Compared to Tena, the best he could hope for in a woman was adequacy.

That wasn't how he viewed Maggie, was it?

He sighed. Maybe it was.

And maybe that's why Reuben liked Maggie so much.

He wasn't worthy of someone exemplary like Tena. He belonged with someone like himself—a woman with her own secrets to hide—and Maggie had plenty of those it seemed.

That was why Reuben would settle for adequacy.

Because adequacy was all he deserved.

FOURTEEN

"THIS IS IT." REUBEN DIRECTED Maggie to the second of six rooms above the Goshawk Inn and Tavern.

Maggie tapped her finger to the tip of his nose. "One room?" she asked, the scent of alcohol still rank on her breath. "Why Mr. Radford, how presumptuous of you."

Joint sleeping arrangements certainly hadn't been Reuben's first choice; however, given the need to purchase return rail fare, he didn't want to risk drying their funds. No one here was familiar with them anyway; there was no chance the night's events would be relayed home.

Maggie braced her body against the door so he would have to reach around her to unlock it. "What makes you think I would allow you to have me when those other men couldn't?"

"What other men?"

Maggie snapped her fingers. "Keep up, Mr. Radford. The three men who asked Father to marry me."

"Wait," Reuben sputtered, "you were proposed to *three* times since Christmas? Someone should have told me that before I agreed to this! If your father doesn't kill me after tonight, one of them will!" Reuben could feel his temper rising. Tena must have known when she asked him to stay, and knew exactly how he would react.

Of course Maggie had suitors. Just because an engagement hadn't been publicly announced didn't mean she wasn't being pursued. Why hadn't he asked straight away as he'd intended? What an idiot he was!

"No one will kill you," Maggie replied calmly. "I'll protect you."

"With what?" Reuben asked. "Do you also carry a pistol I failed to hear about?"

"Of course not. The pistol is locked in father's study." She threw an exaggerated eye roll implying the depths of his daftness. "I'll probably have to marry one of the poor sods instead."

"Well, you're not marrying anyone tonight." It was now after midnight and the day's exploits were wearing. "We're going to bed."

"You're serious?" Maggie flushed crimson, and Reuben immediately knew his words had come out all wrong. Even so, she slid closer until her only her hands on his chest lay between them. "I mean, do you think we should? I never have before."

He followed her fingers as they traced a path over the folds of his shirt and a sudden painful awareness rushed in of how very alone they were. How the dimly lit walls pushed them together. How no one would ever know what took place save the two of them. Maggie's eyes admitted she was toying with the same idea. Her dress's thin material couldn't conceal her heart's mad beating that mirrored the pounding of his own.

Reuben desperately desired to do something he would later regret. Maggie was the most beautiful, frustrating, incredible woman he knew. Even knowing she would belong to someone else—or perhaps because he knew it—he still wanted to. Their meetings ended tomorrow. He could literally seize the night and walk away in the morning. And, oh, how he really wanted to. He was a horrible person for even thinking it, but he did. In her current state she wouldn't stop him. Could it maybe even change her mind about him?

Reuben searched his pocket for the key now fitted within the bills from Tena. Maggie's eyes grew wide on sight of the money seconds before her palm slapped his hand. The bills fluttered across the carpeted hallway.

"I am not a prostitute!" Maggie exclaimed. She ripped the key from Reuben's other hand and unlocked the door. "I will take the room alone. Good night, Mr. Radford!"

The slamming door was just the ticket Reuben needed to regain his senses. He retrieved the fallen currency, seething at himself. "Life, why do you test me so?"

"Because you're a baseless fool," Mira laughed in his head.

"Oh shove off."

Reuben descended the stairs with a resounding breath, glad fate hadn't allowed him to be anything less than a gentleman.

FIFTEEN

MAGGIE WOKE IN AN UNFAMILIAR bed in an unfamiliar room considering which parts of her hazy memories could be trusted. What she *could* recall went something like this:

Somehow her sister—*Her sister!* It was still astounding to believe—bought Maggie a hearty drink of scotch then persuaded them all to join a group of ruffians for cards. Maggie had had no prior experience with either scotch nor gambling before, and unfortunately discovered she took to both far too easily. The hours after descended into a colorful blend of bad decisions.

Maggie splashed cold water on her face from the washbasin, praying her memories were actually an oddly vivid yet blurry nightmare. She had matched the other men drink for drink, proceeded to gamble away most of her money, and then surprisingly won half of it back. Despite her protests, Reuben maintained a growing suspicion that the other men went easier on her with each additional scotch she consumed, hoping she would pay them *special* attention before the night was through. Tena and Charles disappeared from the table around nine o'clock, or it might have been earlier; Maggie's head throbbed trying to remember the exact moment she noticed their absence. After that, Reuben refused to leave her side as long as she was playing.

It was the fisherman who led to her demise. Sporting a missing tooth and a scraggly beard, he handed her a vile liquid tasting of a combination of shoe polish and goat dung. Everything was a muddled haze from then on. Tena and Charles went home. She stayed with Reuben ... and then what?

Maggie patted her face dry and redirected her gaze in the looking glass, breathing a sigh of relief when she verified only one side of the bed was mussed. Thankfully it appeared they hadn't shared a bed last night, or she prayed anything more for that matter. She did not need another rash decision hanging over her.

When she ventured downstairs, Reuben was reading on the lone couch of the inn's modest parlor. She returned her room key and cautiously made her way to where he sat with that morning's *Southern Daily Echo,* absently stirring a cup of coffee on the side. He raised his eyes with great difficulty at her approach.

"Did you sleep well?" he asked.

"Not really. Did you?"

"I slept on this couch," Reuben said sourly. "How would you presume I slept?"

"I would presume not well."

Reuben returned his attention to the *Echo*, leaving Maggie to debate between sitting or hovering over him like a bird. In the end, the high ground was usually best for delivering conversations that may require a quick exit.

"Um, Reuben? Whatever I may have said or didn't say or did last night ... The truth is I can't remember it fully." Maggie bit her lip, picking at her thumb nail rather than look at him. "Did we, well, do anything together that I should know about?"

Reuben continued to scowl behind his newspaper. He flipped the page so hard the corner tore off in his hand. "No."

"Oh, good. That's certainly a relief."

Reuben laid the *Echo* aside and smoothed both hands through his tousled hair. "Listen, Maggie, about last night—"

"Miss Archer!"

Without warning, a pair of well-built male arms encased

Maggie between a slick charcoal suit and a dashing smile.

"Mr. Halverson! Why are you here?" *Curses!* thought Maggie. *Of all the people I could fall folly to so far from home, why him?*

Lloyd released her, twirling his hat between his palms. He tipped his head in the direction of an older gentlemen involved in discussion at the front desk. "My father and I are returning from business in New York. If you told me you were here, I would have arranged a private dinner."

Maggie changed a glance at Reuben. His sullen glare settled on Lloyd's before returning to the newspaper. Another sheet ripped in his haste. She returned her attention to Lloyd. "It was an unexpected venture."

"I see," Lloyd said although his eyes remained on Reuben. "Then your decision has been made? It's surprising your father sent no notice."

"I have decided nothing. I may not decide at all."

It wasn't that Lloyd hadn't tried to win her over. He had many times. Since their first meeting at Christmas, he made every attempt to charm Maggie with gifts, outings, and compliments. At first she'd lavished in the attention. As the arm decor of a shipping heir, she became the envy of all her friends and her mother's most favored daughter. It was the unaffectionate proposal, sent by courier one unassuming Tuesday afternoon in early April, that set Maggie's euphoric mind to rights. She'd dismissed his every invitation since then.

"Who will escort you home?" Lloyd asked.

"May a woman not travel alone?" countered Maggie.

"She may. But you're not alone, are you?" Lloyd turned his back on Reuben and lowered his voice. "Miss Archer, do not dismiss me lightly. It would be unfortunate if word of your ... indiscretions ... made its way home. Quite the scandal for your father. Wouldn't you agree?"

Lloyd stroked Maggie's hair, fighting knots as his fingers passed through the strands. The top half was still haphazardly pinned up from the day before; the rest fell in tangled waves down her back. Dreadful wrinkles patterned her dress from last night's sleep. This situation must look quite unseemly to an outsider. She may as well have been caught with her bloomers around her ankles.

A cold leer filled Lloyd's eyes. "For your father's sake, I hope you choose wisely."

Maggie blinked away unshed tears, digging her fingernails into her palms to stifle her anger. He had her trapped. For once, she, the always vocal Maggie Archer, had no idea what to say. Only much later, after he was gone, would she berate herself for not once defending her own honor.

"We will see each other soon, Miss Archer." Lloyd circled Maggie to face Reuben who had dropped all pretenses of reading.

Reuben gave a jerky nod towards the other man. "Halverson."

"Radford. Do give my regards to your sister won't you?" With a touch to his hat and a sneer, Lloyd joined his father at the front desk. Minutes later, the two men collected their cases and exited the inn.

Maggie sank onto the chair opposite Reuben. "Mr. Halverson doesn't know what happened to Mira?"

"Of course he knows." Reuben folded up the newspaper. And by *folded* was to say he crumpled it into a baseball sized wad and threw it across the room in disgust. "That louse proposed to you, didn't he?"

"I haven't made a decision yet," Maggie stated quickly. She paused, thinking of Lloyd's blatant threats against her father. "Would he truly ruin my father if I refuse him?"

"Yes. He would." Reuben's hands twitched uncomfortably in the space between them. "You *can't* choose him, Maggie. No matter what he says. He's *not* a good person."

"How do you know?"

"Trust me," he murmured. "I *know*."

And then Reuben did take her hands in his, locking fingers until their knuckles turned white and Maggie's fingertips began to tingle.

The air around them stood serious as a thunderstorm, about to strike lightening to a tree. Clearly something terrible occurred between the two men to bring about such odious feelings.

Reuben's lack of explanation only left Maggie as puzzled as she had been at Christmas, wondering what he was hiding. Her eyes lingered on their clasped fingers. Left alone, the entire mess was sure to drive her to madness. The question sat just behind her teeth like a caged animal snarling to be set free, but for once that's where she left it.

SIXTEEN

ONE SILENT TRAIN RIDE LATER, Maggie slipped into her bedroom, easing the door closed with nary a sound. An hour delay switching tracks had placed her home at a quarter past one. She would need to hurry or risk missing tea with the Winchesters at four o'clock. That wouldn't be any great loss to Maggie's day, although it would be a pretty poor way to repay her sister's trust after Tena covered for her last night.

Maggie dropped her distressed May Day dress on the floor and shimmied into a fresh tea gown of pale pink embroidery. Unable to unravel her hair to an acceptable sheen, she tucked the poorly pinned knots under a close-fitted cap then spent extra time reapplying her makeup. Finally satisfied her reflection could tamp her mother's suspicions, she descended the front staircase.

"Maggie!"

She caught Tena's word of warning in the same instant Maggie's back was shoved against the front door. A well-manicured nail jabbed against her sternum.

"How dare you!" Beatrix shrieked, peppering Maggie's face with saliva. "Such disrespect!"

From over her mother's shoulder, Maggie noted the presence of a police officer exiting the parlor with her father. "Why are the police here?"

Beatrix shifted, forcing the door handle sharply into Maggie's back. "Where were you? No lies. I already know you were with that Radford boy. Tena told me that much."

Tena rushed to Maggie's side, her eyes damp and puffy. "I'm sorry, Maggie! You should have been home hours ago. I was so afraid something happened to you."

Maggie stifled the betrayal filling her chest. It wasn't her sister's fault. If Tena were late returning home after a night out with a man she barely knew, Maggie would have ripped the town apart to locate her. There was no point to lie about her whereabouts to her parents, but she could save Tena from any further embarrassment.

"Tena had nothing to do with this," Maggie said evenly. "Mr. Radford and I went to Southampton alone. It started as a lark until—" She stopped as she remembered the police officer standing only feet away, and decided not to mention her overindulgence the night before. Better to not be arrested on top of everything else. "We missed the final train home, and needed to stay the night."

The entire house went silent. Complete devastation flooded her mother's pale features. Her father's held uncertainty. The officer raised a hand to hide his smile. "Ah, well, this matter seems well in hand. Good luck with that girl, Mr. Archer. Excuse me, ladies."

Beatrix released Maggie and thrust her arm at the officer. "Wait, Officer! You need to arrest that Radford boy."

The officer peered down at her. "On what grounds? No crime has been committed so far as I can tell."

"He defiled my daughter!"

"Oh Mother, stop it!" Maggie removed her mother's hand from the officer. "My apologies, Officer. Thank you for your assistance."

Two seconds after the door closed, Beatrix reeled on Maggie again. "What were you thinking?" she hissed. "Traveling with a man you are not promised to? Spending the *night* with him? And a man we met only yesterday! Do you wish to ruin us all?"

Laurence stepped in to lay a hand on his wife's shoulder. "Tena told me about Maggie's arrangement with this boy. Maggie may be headstrong, but we should not worry yet. The boy seemed quite acceptable at breakfast. Allow her to explain."

Beatrix shrugged her husband off. "You are too generous with your daughters. To this day I wish we were given sons."

"Silence!" shot Laurence. "You need to learn your place." Beatrix began to protest, but her husband cut her off with a wave of his other hand. "No, Beatrix. You have said more than your share for today."

Spurned, she gave a "hmph," and walked away muttering to herself about injustices. Inwardly, Maggie cheered at the rare gumption her father had finally mustered.

"Now," said Laurence. He planted a kiss on Tena's forehead. "I'm proud of you. You did the right thing, sweetheart."

"Thank you, Father. I don't feel like I did though."

Maggie clasped her sister's hand and gave a gentle squeeze. "Wait for me in your room? I have stories for you."

Tena nodded and hurried up the stairs. Her door clicked into place a minute later.

Guiding Maggie into his study by the elbow. Laurence locked the door behind them and directed her to take a seat near the fireplace. Sinking onto the opposite sofa, Laurence laced his fingers, two raised against his lips, and peered at his daughter thoughtfully.

"Mr. Radford and I did *not* spend the night together!" Maggie burst out, nearly slipping off the front of her chair in her haste to speak. "I promise he was nothing if not a gentleman."

Laurence remained silent while he searched for the truth within her words. Of her parents, her father had always been the one to believe her. It pained her to think she had broken that trust.

She rounded the coffee table to join him on the sofa. "I'm so sorry."

One minute passed, then two ... then three. Laurence's emotional palate remained static, and Maggie thought she would go mad, not knowing if she'd ruined his good opinion.

"Do you believe me?" asked Maggie, releasing a breath she hadn't realized she was holding in.

Laurence dismissed her concern with a wave of his hand. "You may be impetuous, but I know when you are lying. And you are not."

Relief flooded through her and left in the same instant. Even if her father believed her, it didn't mean anyone else would.

"Tell me, little girl," he continued, "you and Tena are both eighteen. So close in age, yet so dissimilar. Your sister speaks of marriage and yearns for children. Yet for you that is not so."

"Oh, father, you've never been able to make me an obedient daughter. How could anyone keep me as a wife?" The smile faded from Maggie's lips, however, when her father's expression did not match the joke.

Laurence held her gaze with eyes unexpectedly rimmed in sadness. Her father's sudden change in emotion left Maggie unnerved. It was rare indeed to see a man cry. Sorrow always increased one's appearance by no less than ten years.

"I know your mother does not love me. No, do not say otherwise," he said, holding up his hand to cease her arguments. His voice remained steady despite the grief behind its tone. "I have known since the day we married. Alas I have always loved her. That is why I stay. I cannot leave her to find her own way; she would not survive. This world is not made for people like your mother to live alone. You know that to be true."

Since nearly the day Maggie was old enough to understand the difference between boys and girls, Maggie knew her parents' marriage was void of mutual love. Her mother's actions spoke volumes. Still, it was difficult to hear the truth from her father's own lips.

"It's not fair though," Maggie argued. "You deserve much more."

Laurence smiled then, a genuine smile with no sadness in it.

"Your mother is wrong. Having my daughters is worth everything. You bring me such joy, despite the frustration you cause." He chuckled. "Or perhaps because of it."

He fixed his eyes on the window. The warm spring afternoon breeze rustled the trees in the yard and sent blossoms floating on the air. "I believe marriage is a sacred thing and should not be entered lightly. If you truly do not want it, then you are right to run from it."

"What are you saying?" Her heart leapt. Was he actually releasing her from her obligation to choose a husband?

Laurence gripped her hands. His stare bored into hers. "Mr. Radford is waiting for you, Maggie. It is the only explanation for his agreement to this illogical association you have with him."

Maggie's head spun. All the wishful thinking of his previous statement withered with this new announcement. "That can't be. We only see each other one day a year and then go back to our normal lives."

Laurence's brow furrowed. "One day with the person you care about and 364 days alone? Is that what you want for him?"

Maggie left her biting words unspoken in her open mouth. She stood, pacing before the window as though it would help to move her limbs. Even with the open breeze, the air was still stifling. She ripped off her hat, wringing it between her hands.

Her father's words had struck with the depth of her ignorance. He was right, and she had been blind not to notice Reuben's attentions before. They had always been there.

Reuben wanted a wife. He wanted children. Love. All the things she could never give him. If he waited for her, he would always be waiting.

"What do you want me to do?"

"Your mother has a friend in London in need of a lady's maid. It does not pay much, but you would have a room within their home, and one day off per week. It is the perfect position for a young woman who does not wish to marry." There was such struggle in his voice Maggie knew the considerable pain it must bring him to suggest losing his eldest daughter. He wouldn't suggest it if he didn't think it was the only way.

A few hours ago, Lloyd trapped her between choosing a husband she didn't want or disgracing her family. Now her father offered a third option. It was common for girls in compromising situations to be sent away. Even if Lloyd followed through on his threat, her father could use her unseemly behavior as an excuse for her quick departure.

The answer was so clear. So simple. She could avoid marriage and save her father's reputation. And she had the power to give Reuben the freedom he wouldn't give himself.

SEVENTEEN

AUGUST 10, 1911 –
THREE MONTHS LATER

REUBEN'S FATHER WAS TRUE TO HIS WORD. Life changed after their conversation. Harris didn't question his son when Reuben walked in on the second of May without a word as to his actual whereabouts. His father no longer acted ashamed of his eccentric wife or embarrassed when rumors of his son's erroneous behavior with the eldest Archer daughter seeped into so many conversations around town.

His father never asked him if the gossip was true, but defended his son as if he had complete proof of Reuben's innocence. It was an unexpected gesture of faith Reuben had difficulty accepting at first. Harris was usually so critical of his son, both in and out of the workplace.

Reuben received many a slap on the back from the boys at the *Gazette*, soliciting him for all the grimy details of how he roped in an unruly lady such as Maggie. When their wives visited, they threw him reproving looks, tsking loudly, and shaming him for taking advantage of "that poor girl." He had, of course, denied all the accusations, which, of course, no one believed, but he doubted rumors would sway those seeking Maggie's hand.

When talk first circulated, Reuben absorbed himself between work and time with Charles. His attempts to focus on anything but Maggie were difficult with Tena also spending so much time at the

Kisch house. She agreed that Lloyd must be the source of the rumors. The only thing curtailing Reuben's fury against Lloyd was the fact that Laurence Archer had not submitted a formal engagement to the newspaper, implying Maggie had not yet decided.

It was that same missing engagement announcement that woke Reuben on his twentieth birthday finally ready to change his life.

~~~

Nearly an hour of breathless apprehension passed while Reuben watched the formidable Archer residence. It wasn't until Laurence Archer met him at the gate that he contemplated the full effect of what he was doing and his stomach reeled, kicking up acid and general anxiety. His plan now simultaneously thrilled and nauseated him.

Laurence laced him with a hard, inquisitive stare. "Mr. Radford? My daughters are not home." He raised an eyebrow. "Nor is it May."

"You know about that?"

"I do."

Knowing Laurence understood the truth about his relationship with Maggie eliminated Reuben's hesitation. He had debated this decision with himself and argued about it with Mira for the last three months. Mira demanded he turn and flee, but right now his hand was wrapped around the watch in his pocket and he could only feel the possibility of lost time cold against his fingers.

"I would like your permission to court Maggie."

Laurence gripped Reuben by the arm and dragged him around the corner out of the house's sightlines. "Mr. Radford, if my wife knew why you are here—no, if she even knew we were speaking— she would find an excuse to have you arrested."

"Mr. Archer, sir, I understand your concerns," Reuben said evenly. "And I understand why. But I can also assure you my intentions are sincere."

Laurence's gaze remained unrelenting. "Mr. Radford, I cannot give you my blessing and you should be wise enough not to want it. Despite our most desperate attempts to mold Maggie into a dutiful wife, she wants no part of it. My girls are all I have in this life, and I fear I will lose her if I do not yield on this matter. My wife disagrees, however I must allow Maggie to choose her own path. If it means a life alone, then I will give her that."

"But, sir—"

Laurence cocked his head in earnest. "If you care for my daughter, as you say, why would you force a life on her she does not desire?"

"Thank you, sir," Reuben said, "but you will understand if I cannot fully trust you as her father to be honest in this matter. I need to ask her for myself." He tried to pull free from Laurence's grip, but the older man held firm.

"My daughter has taken a post in London," Laurence told him. "I do not know when, or if, she plans to return. It would be advised for you to forget this matter."

Reuben stifled his astonishment. He'd seen Tena at least every other week for three months. Why hadn't she said anything about her sister leaving? If Maggie left the city and rejected all of her suitors, perhaps her father's words were true.

Reuben simply nodded and disengaged himself from Laurence's grip. He was only a few paces away when Laurence's voice stopped him. He appeared as apologetic as he sounded. "Despite my misgivings about your friendship with my daughter, I believe you must be a good man. I am sorry I cannot give you what you seek."

Reuben left with no reply, heading into town to find Tena. He needed to know the truth and, short of asking Maggie herself, there was no one he trusted more than her sister to provide it.

EIGHTEEN

LOCATING SOMEONE IS A TIME-consuming process, unless you remember that most days said person is exactly where you'd expect to find them. If Reuben had realized that, he could have saved himself approximately two hours wandering around town. Instead, he ended up in an unpleasant forty-minute conversation with Edith and Bianca Winchester and arrived at the Kischs for his birthday dinner right on time.

"Hello?" he called, simultaneously knocking and opening the front door. Unlocked as always. After ten years, it had become Reuben's standard to show up unannounced and enter as he pleased.

"In the kitchen!" came the return call. Reuben made his way down the row house hall to the compact kitchen with windows overlooking the slight garden beyond. Tena and Mrs. Kisch were in the midst of meal preparation; Tena bent over a cook pot on the stove while Mrs. Kisch scrubbed pans already emptied into covered serving bowls.

Having "adopted" Reuben into their family long ago, Elsa Kisch could not be more opposite from the mother waiting for him back home. Elsa was as tall, perfectly plump, and fair as Florence Radford was petite, slender, and brunette. She also didn't have senile delusions or hold him responsible for the death of loved ones. When Reuben wasn't at the cemetery or at the newspaper, her warm smile and flawless affection were a welcome relief.

Elsa wiped her hands on her apron and swayed over to press Reuben's face against her round cheek. "Wonderful to see you, dear. Miss Tena and I have been running like mules this morning."

"Happy birthday, Reuben," Tena smiled and threw a little simper in Elsa's direction. "Mrs. Kisch forbade me from saying it until today, so I think I'll say it twice. Happy birthday."

Elsa frowned. "It is the very worst luck to say it before. *Alles Gute zum Geburtstag,* Reuben. Happy birthday. Twentieth is it?"

"Yes, thank you, Mrs. Kisch. It's really only another day though."

"Reuben!" Winnie cried as she ran into the kitchen. She dropped her school books on the table and threw her tiny arms around Reuben. "Did Tena show you? She made it special!"

Tena slid a pie from the oven, stepping around the other two to place it on the table to cool and tossed the warm mitts down beside it. Reuben extracted himself from Winnie to peer over Tena's shoulder. "So, what'd you make me?"

"This one's peach—"

"Peach?" Reuben gagged. Peach was Charles's favorite, not his.

Tena slapped him with a towel. "Don't be obnoxious. The other one is strawberry rhubarb."

"Is there enough—"

"There's plenty," Tena shot back. She flitted about the kitchen, moving serving platters from cabinet to table. "Don't think I forgot what you told me the last time. 'Not enough rhubarb. There's never enough rhubarb.'" She pointed a menacing finger at Reuben. "That was the first and last time you will ever insult my baking, good sir." Extracting a serving spoon from the nearest drawer, she dug into the center of the crust and offered it to Reuben. "Taste it."

Steam rose from the oozing pie. "I'll scorch my mouth off."

"It'll teach you to not bite the hand that feeds you." Tena motioned again to the pie then turned her attention to slicing a dark pumpernickel loaf.

"Can I have some?" asked Winnie.

"May I," Elsa corrected, "And no, you may not before the meal. Now out back with you. There's laundry on the line." With a groan and a lot of muttering, Winnie stamped her foot one final time, retrieved the laundry basket, and clopped down the back steps.

Reuben blew across his fork, wrapped his lips around the tines, and groaned. It was both extremely hot and ridiculously delicious. "Wow, that's amazing."

"Well?" asked Tena. "Is your mouth too '*scorched*'?"

Reuben grinned. "Yup. Totally worth it."

Tena took his fork with a smirk and flounced back to the counter.

With an uproarious commotion only three grown men could cause, Karl, Charles, and Fred poured through the kitchen door, followed by the pounding of feet on the stairs and Emil sliding into the kitchen. Their hair had been bleached by the summer's rays, leaving Charles and Fred with vibrant highlights and Emil's already florescent locks nearly white.

Karl kissed his wife and peered into the oven for a smell. Emil and Fred stole apples from the table basket while Charles leaned close to whisper in Tena's ear, eliciting her delightful giggle.

Elsa slammed the oven door, swiped both her sons' apples, and dragged Charles away from Tena by the collar. "Oh no," she scolded. "The women are not finished here. Get out. The lot of you. Charles, set the dining table please. Emil, Friedrich?"

Emil swiped another apple and ran for the back door, "Cricket, Freddie? Come on!" The boys were outside before their mother could do more than call their names. "Those boys!" she huffed, shuffling back to the stove.

Reuben followed Charles into the dining room, and removed a stack of plates from the oak hutch. Charles made certain the door had closed fully behind them. "I have news to share, Reuben."

"Let's hear it." Reuben said, divvying plates along the table.

Charles mirrored him on the opposite site.

"Our family is moving to the States."

Reuben paused mid-plate. "America? Why?"

"Many of Papa's friends from the fatherland have already gone. They established their own businesses, and are thriving. Papa believes the same for us."

"Another move? Is that what *you* really want?"

"I think it is a smart decision."

"When would you leave?"

"Papa can have everything ready by the first of the year." Charles retrieved the silver box from the hutch, handing Reuben a stack of forks. "He will sail the family over and I will finalize our assets here. I will go soon after."

Reuben set the silver around the table. First Maggie. Now Charles. He hoped all his birthday presents weren't this exciting.

Tena bustled in with a vegetable bowl and set it in the middle of the table. She smiled and bustled back out.

"And Tena?" Reuben asked. "What does she think about it?"

Charles lined up the remaining silver, knife beside spoon opposite fork. His eyes slid to the door Tena had departed through. "I have not told her."

"She needs to know!"

"How can I?" Charles hissed. He gave another glance at the kitchen door. "Did you know her sister left?"

"Yes, I ran into Mr. Archer this morning."

"Then you understand why I cannot add more burden to her. Maggie will not reply to her letters. Tena does not even know why she left."

"She doesn't?"

"No. Tena thinks she is to blame."

The dining room door flipped open with Tena's return entrance into dead silence. "What's the matter?" she asked. She set a second covered serving bowl on the opposite end of the table. "Were you talking about me?"

Charles gave a forced laugh. "Men do not speak of women nearly so often as women think we do."

"If you say so." Tena retrieved the water pitcher from the hutch and made for the kitchen.

Reuben gestured at her exit. "How can you keep this a secret from her? What about the rest of your family?"

"I've asked them not to say anything."

"What happens when it's February or March or April and you're packing your trunks? Will you tell her then?"

"I do not know!" Charles strode across the hall and out the front door, Reuben hot on his heels.

"Tena's not an idiot, Charles! Why are you treating her like one?"

"I know that!" Charles ran a palm over his eyes. "I love her, Reuben, and I do not know what to do. I want the world for her even if it is a world without me in it. Can you understand that?"

Reuben stopped. *A world without me in it.* So *that* was why Maggie left. To get away, be alone. She hadn't told anyone because she didn't want anyone to follow her. Including Reuben.

Hoof beats summoned a dust cloud on the street. A four passenger carriage clopped past without a glance their way. The plump woman from the house opposite shook out a rug on the porch while her toddler sons ran circles on the walk. Across the street life went on. Quiet. Plain. Happy.

"I do understand," Reuben said. "Telling Tena now would devastate her. So don't tell her yet. Not until you have to. But when you do tell her, you have to marry her."

Charles folded his arms with a grimace. "That is my only choice? I have to marry her? No matter if she wants it or if her parents never approve?"

"You found someone who wants you, Charles, which is more than I can say for myself. If you let her go, you're an idiot." Reuben directed Charles's attention across the street. The neighbor woman bent to scoop her son into her arms, smoothing his hair back to plant a kiss upon the child's crown. "Not everyone wants love or a family, Charles. But you do. And so does Tena. So you had better marry her. Or there's a good chance I will."

NINETEEN

REUBEN STRODE ONTO THE RAILWAY platform, fueled by adrenaline and fury rather than logic and reason. Months of repressed emotions drove him onto the train car and only his desire to finish his quest fought down Mira's rants.

What would he say to Maggie when he saw her? What *could* he say that would make an ounce of difference? She hadn't uttered even one word to any of them in ten months. How could she remain silent while their lives were upended? She had gone too far this time.

It was easy to find the house from the directions that the station master provided. The substantial blanched brick Victorian lay on London's edge, a neighbor to other equally extensive estates, each with their own luxurious gardens and arched front walkways. Although the Radfords were financially blessed, Reuben was quite out of place in his current surroundings; transplanted here, even the Winchesters' home would be utterly demure. Even in the countryside's currently frozen state, its extravagance was intimidating.

Reuben handed his full fare to the taxi driver. "Please wait here. I will not be long."

As the motorcar's door opened, the February wind hit him full in the face, and it was no better under the cover of the stone entryway. Reuben clasped his coat's collar tightly against his neck until finally a footman answered the door. Reuben spoke before the young man had a chance.

"Is your lady's maid at home? Maggie Archer?"

"Her day off is Tuesday." The footman began to close the door. "You may return then."

Reuben slid his foot in the gap. "Please, it's important. I won't stay long enough for her absence to be noticed."

"Are you family?"

"No."

The other man narrowed his eyes. "A suitor then?"

"Not even close," spat Reuben. "And I'm not here to collect a debt or accuse her of high treason either. Now may I see her or not?"

The man opened the door with a slight nod. "Of course, sir. Who shall I say is calling?"

"No one. It's my message that's important. Not me."

"Very well, sir." The footman ushered him through the drafty foyer and into the library. Four walls of floor to ceiling leather and fabric bound books stared back at Reuben surrounding a grand fireplace, piano, and an array of floral upholstered sofas and chairs. Lest he become distracted, Reuben ignored everything, and drew his attention instead to the windows overlooking the barren garden.

Voices wafting in from the stairwell. "A visitor?" asked Maggie. "I am not expecting anyone."

"A young gentleman," replied the footman. "He does not seem pleased to be here and refused to give a name. Shall I send him away?"

"No, I will take care of it. Thank you, Derby."

Quick footsteps descended the stairs and stopped abruptly in the doorway. Reuben turned to see her standing there, utter bewilderment on her face, fingertips against the doorframe.

"Reuben?" Maggie asked breathlessly. "What happened? Is someone hurt? Why are you here?"

He hadn't seen her in ten months, a horribly long ten months. He was absolutely furious with her, yet the moment she spoke, his anger abated. Her face seemed exactly as it had always been, perfect and smooth and unscathed yet by time. Her eyes were still the stormy blue-grey pools that glistened in the sunlight from the windows. Not even the characteristic obsidian lady's maid ensemble and rigid bun she wore could detract from the beauty he always noticed.

He cleared the distance between them in three strides and pulled her into a fierce hug. "Maggie. I missed you."

Maggie shoved him away. "Why are you here?" she asked again, throwing a glance towards the stairs. "You shouldn't be here." Her rigid stance brought Reuben's mind back into stark focus.

Before him stood the creature Reuben spent almost two years trying to decipher. And now he had. There wasn't any mystery left to solve. The real mystery was how he fooled himself into believing he wanted to change their friendship into something it could never be. Laurence Archer had been right.

This isn't the woman you thought she was. Remember why you're here.

His anger returned full force, both at Maggie and himself. "You abandoned Tena. You ignored her when she needed you to be there."

Maggie blinked. "What in the heavens are you speaking of?"

"Did you or did you not leave without so much as a word to your sister?"

"Yes, but I—"

Reuben raised his hand to cut off the start of what he assumed would be a meaningless tirade. "I don't want to hear excuses. I can accept you were not there when my parents died—one day a year was our agreement after all—however I cannot accept that you stayed away from your *own* father's funeral." His face was inches from hers, his breath heavy with his heightened temper. *"That* is unforgivable."

Maggie's expression contorted as though her mind held a hundred thoughts and her face couldn't decide which emotion to convey. "I'm ending our agreement," he finished coldly. "You won't see me again."

He strode from the house, ignoring Maggie's calls for him to stop. He jumped in the waiting taxi and slammed the door against her futile pleading.

Maggie pressed a hand to the window. The glass fogged under her touch, her voice rife with desperation. "Wait. Please."

"Not this time." Too much time was already wasted waiting. Reuben tapped on the driver's seat. "Drive."

~~~

Maggie remained in the late February chill long after Reuben stormed off, dumbstruck and numb. The bitter wind whipped around her legs, sending a shiver down her spine, and she barely felt it.

Her father was dead. Reuben's parents were dead. And she had no idea how it happened.

TWENTY

"Ticket, sir?"

The railway attendant's outstretched hand successfully derailed Reuben's mind from the task he'd just completed. He held his ticket out with a smile, received his tear, and wished the attendant a pleasant evening.

"Why thank you, sir! And you as well!" With a tip of his hat, the attendant continued down the line.

Reuben returned the ticket to his coat pocket, exchanging it for the penny magazine rolled within. As he flipped the pages to find his place, a thin cream envelope fell from its depths. He laid the magazine aside, and stooped for the letter. He fingered the edges, lingering on the pressed wax seal he himself had set only days before at the request of Laurence Archer.

Tena had delivered her father's summons the twenty-second afternoon of February. "Father asks to see you." No further explanations, but something in her voice told him he had no choice.

Reuben entered the other man's bedroom, shocked by how worn Laurence appeared in his feeble state. Unlike Harris Radford, Laurence's illness had developed slowly and lingered, a series of mountains and valleys, better and worse days, until it

135

drove him to his bed two weeks prior. It didn't seem fair that an otherwise mentally strong man in his mid-forties was about to die. But Reuben's mother had been the same age, his father five years older. Mira was only thirteen when she was viciously snatched from the world. It was the way of life.

All pretenses were forgotten in the instant Reuben closed the bedroom door. No hellos, no accusations, no petty small talk. Laurence wheezed, his labored breathing and pale face all too reminiscent of Reuben's father's own demise two months prior. Waking to his father's lifeless corpse had made for a most rotten Boxing Day. Reuben clutched the watch within his pocket. Laurence, like his father, had run out of time.

Reuben sat, calmly taking Laurence's hand when it was offered to him. The older man clutched it, as though he could tether himself to the world through Reuben's touch.

"Which day would you redo?" Laurence asked urgently. Maggie told him her father believed it was the most important question when he decided a person's worth—a question she herself had never answered correctly.

"There are so many," Reuben replied honestly. "How could I choose only one?"

Laurence squeezed his hand. "You must."

Reuben thought of all those who went before him, men and women who lost meaningful lives too soon. Tena, forced to care for her ailing father alone. And Maggie, unable to see past the tip of her own nose ... Reuben had to believe, in the end, she too would mourn his loss.

Reuben's parents were already gone. If he could spare those two women even an ounce of the same grief he'd experienced, surely he must.

"Whichever day would save you for your daughters. That is the day I would redo."

Laurence offered a nod, although he provided no response. Something in Reuben's heart knew that, as selfless as his response had been, it still wasn't the answer this man sought. Nevertheless, it must have been good enough to invoke the next words from his mouth.

"Take care of my daughters." Laurence's eyes held Reuben's as though they were the last thing he would ever see. They were the same color as Tena's; even in death, they blazed with determination.

"How can you expect me to do that?" Reuben asked. He had failed his own family; how could he be expected to protect Maggie and Tena?

"I know you," said Laurence. "You'll find a way."

"We've only spoken twice before today," Reuben argued. "You don't know me."

"I think—" Laurence coughed, clinging to the bedcovers and Reuben's hand. "Hmm ... mmm. I think I know who you want to be."

Reuben released Laurence's hand. "How can you? Even I don't know that. You were right to not give me your permission with Maggie."

Laurence fumbled for an envelope lying open on the side table. He pressed it urgently into Reuben's hands as their eyes met. "Sometimes, Reuben, even old men make mistakes."

Reuben flipped the envelope in his hands, only the paper was blank. "What do you want me to do with this?"

"Give it to my daughter," Laurence whispered. Reuben nodded, even assisting with the seal, but later that night, Tena knocked on his door with news of her father's passing. Sitting on his porch, she cried upon his shoulder until they both forgot their families were slowly disintegrating.

Her presence brought comfort to an otherwise lonely existence, and before long the first rays of dawn began to climb the horizon. Tena made to leave, pecking a quick kiss on his cheek. "Thanks for tonight," she said with a smile.

Reuben still regretted what he'd done next.

He pressed Tena's hand to his cheek, allowing the warmth to linger against his skin. Her eyes followed his, their color distant from the stormy eyes of the woman he missed so much. The only sound around them was the wind and the steady rhythm of their breath. No animal noises; there was only the cold and them. And the empty space where Maggie should have been. Tena's lips were slightly open, so supple, so inviting. He missed Maggie even more.

Tena hands flew to deflect Reuben's kiss. "Reuben, no. Charles."

Abject mortification wasn't harsh enough to describe Reuben's embarrassment. Tena belonged to his best friend! "Oh, Tena, what is wrong with me?" He sprang to his feet, pounded a fist against the door, and rounded back to Tena. "I'm sorry. Please forget this happened. Please, Tena. Don't tell Charles. I didn't mean it." He continued apologizing repeatedly and promising it would never happen again, sure she would hate him forever.

Offering only an uneven smile, she gently brushed the hair from his eyes. "I understand. I miss Maggie too."

Four days later, they buried Laurence Archer, and his letter remained in Reuben's coat pocket, all but forgotten.

Reuben's vision swam as he stared at the letter in his hands. A dying man's last wish and he had crushed it. He should take the letter to Maggie. He should go back and apologize. He should let her explain.

What explanation could there be for abandoning the father and sister you claimed to love?

Mira nodded thoughtfully from the opposite seat. "At least you made one good decision," she said. "Laurence Archer shouldn't have trusted you. His daughters are better off."

"For once I agree with you. They are. And I'm better off without you."

Mira's face darkened to a disgusting blackish red until it resembled the horrible destruction of the train accident. Reuben turned his attention to the passing landscape, but nothing could erase the images of that day. They were as painful as a branding iron applied directly to his brain. He could only hope someday they would lessen from open wounds to merely scars.

"Be careful, Reuben," Mira said coarsely. "Someday you might genuinely want to be rid of me and, well, that can only end one way." She pointed her fingers at her head and made a gesture like a gun firing.

Reuben crossed his arms. "I am not going to blow my own brains out."

"That's not how it looks from where I'm sitting. But do what you will." Mira picked absently at her fingernails as though she couldn't care less if her brother did himself in. "But, merely out of curiosity, can I ask what's keeping you here?"

Reuben opened his mouth and left it hanging. He could have caught a fly. With his visit to Maggie, he'd dissolved the last friendship he had in this world. He'd lost his parents to death and he'd lost Charles and Tena to each other. His last bit of purpose was attached to a psychotic episode in the guise of his sister. He would quite literally become exactly like his mother, until he withered away and died alone. No one would even know. Who would even bother to look?

"I hate you," he spat.

"I know you really mean that." Mira gave a twisted smile. "And I also know there's nothing you can do to change it."

TWENTY-ONE

MAGGIE CLUNG TO HER STEAMER TRUNK, fingers curled around the handle even as the railway attendants tried to carry it away, reluctantly releasing it only when the train whistle sounded. While trading her predictable downstairs life in London for an unforeseen future in her mother's house was a terrifying prospect, she had already rescheduled twice, and knew she couldn't delay any longer. Running away from her problems was what landed her in this situation to begin with. A further act of cowardice wouldn't improve her situation any more than the first.

How could she face home without her father there? Especially returning only days before the Easter holiday? Father defended her; confronting her mother without his support was unthinkable. And how could Reuben ambush her the way he did? He hated her for something she hadn't even known and didn't give her time to explain. She begged him to listen, but he walked on as though he didn't even hear her. What happened to the boy with the tender eyes and the affectionate smile? The Reuben she knew would never judge so harshly without having all the facts.

What else happened while she was away? How was Tena? What was the town saying? Had Lloyd followed through on his threats?

Not that it even mattered now. Her father was dead, and she hadn't been there. Either way she'd failed him.

Barely cognizant of how she arrived there, all too soon Fontaine whirled past the windows, and the train slid into the station with a whoosh of steam. About twenty or so people waited on the platform, anxious to reunite with their family and friends. Maggie skimmed the faces, her chest clenching.

Would Tena come for her? Would she be angry? Would she insist Maggie lodge elsewhere? Maggie sent a telegram last week, and Tena replied with only three words: *See you then.* It wasn't much to go off of. Then again telegrams weren't exactly cheap.

Someone shouted her name before she even exited the compartment. Peering out, she saw a recognizable face, only it wasn't Tena's. She jumped the last two steps onto the platform.

Maggie stared in disbelief. "Mr. Kisch?"

Charles pressed through the huddle and extended a hand for her luggage. "Where's Tena?" she asked, relinquishing her case.

He scrutinized the crowd. "She should be here. Maybe your mother found out."

"Found out?"

"That she planned to meet you. Your mother was not pleased when Tena informed her you were coming home." Charles looked around again as he muttered, "She was not the only one."

"What do you mean by that?" Maggie asked gruffly.

He continued to scan without reply.

"Mr. Kisch!" she exclaimed, and he finally looked at her. His hostile glare was more intimidating that she remembered.

"Do you understand the impact you have had on Tena?" he asked. "It is utterly shameful."

"Why are you even here?" She didn't need the third degree right now from an almost stranger. She wanted to go home, summon Olivia to fix her a snack, and take a seriously long uninterrupted nap.

"I shouldn't be. You are as bad as your mother."

Maggie had a strong desire to punch him. On May Day, he'd seemed so timid, so reserved, so ... so boring. Had he found some new burst of candor or was he suffering from low blood sugar? Either way, her pent up frustration wanted to cause bruises all over his perfectly formed face.

Luckily for Charles, she had enough sense to restrain herself.

For now at least. She'd make no promises if he pressed.

"No rebuttal?" Charles asked smugly. It was an unsightly change to his usually charming features.

"Listen here, Mr. Kisch, Reuben already told me what a rotten person I am, so save it, will you?"

"You expect me to believe Reuben went all the way to London just to tell you to sod off?"

"He's *your* friend—didn't he tell you? And I don't care if you believe me or not." She ripped her case from his hands. "I'll take it from here, thanks."

Maggie huffed away, leaving Charles no choice but to follow her. "You should wait for Tena."

"Why?" Maggie spat. "So she can yell at me too?"

Charles reached for her arm then, forcing her to a halt. "Tena would never do that. The second she arrives, she will forget everything. She will be so overjoyed to see you, it will no longer matter that you treated her like rubbish."

"I sent letters apologizing! Why didn't she write me back?"

Charles's face didn't soften. If anything his skepticism deepened. "If you wrote her letters, where are they?"

"Tena doesn't have them?

"No."

Another migraine crept up, the likes of which Maggie hadn't experienced since May Day. She'd sent Tena ten letters, one every month she'd been away. Each one the same as the last. She began by telling Tena all about life in London, asked how everyone was back home, then finished with her apologies: *I'm sorry. I miss you. I wish I could come home, but I can't, and I can't say why, but I hope you forgive me. Visit sometime and please write soon.*

As time passed without a response, eventually her letters

shortened to simply: *I'm sorry. I miss you. Please write.*

Maggie knew she made a dreadful mistake when she left without a word to Tena. Her sister was her closest friend and confidant. Besides their father, Tena was the one person who might have possibly understood. It was no wonder she felt slighted.

Even so, how could Tena leave her alone for months without contact? Why wouldn't she write to find out why Maggie *hadn't* written? It didn't make sense.

Charles gave her a long hard stare, and Maggie hoped he was actually considering the possibility that she was being truthful. Unfortunately, his only reply was in highly aggressive German.

"What does that mean?" Maggie huffed as Charles proceeded to spew another diatribe of foreign hostilities at her.

She clenched her traveling case, the urge to smack him resurfacing again. Even in another language, she knew when she was being insulted. "Stop! You're in England, speak English!"

Charles seamlessly transitioned as though he had been speaking English the entire time, and she was the one with the problem. "Frustrated, *fräulein*? Now you know how Tena felt living with an ill father and an insensitive mother, and all she wanted was you. I could not help her. My family could not help her. It tortured me to keep silent, to stand to the side at your father's funeral while she cried alone."

Maggie was incredulous. "You aren't still seeing my sister, are you? It's almost been a year!"

"Of course I am still seeing her. You know that!"

"How could I possibly know? I assumed that would all be over with by now."

"You were with us on May Day. You are neither blind nor brainless so, pending a severe bout of amnesia, how could you not know?"

"Tena gave a brilliant speech about living for the moment, but her defiance has always been short-lived. Mother abhors your kind, and Tena wouldn't displease our mother for long."

Charles's mouth hung open a few inches, his jaw working furiously to form words. He shook his head as though he'd forgotten he was in the midst of telling her off. "You really did not receive any letters, did you?"

"By George, I think he finally gets it," Maggie muttered.

Charles appeared strangely apologetic, more reminiscent of the reserved young man she remembered. He positioned his palms up in defense. "Everything has changed since you left."

"Is that so?"

Charles nodded. "I'm more than seeing your sister. I'm her fiancé."

TWENTY-TWO

MAGGIE DROPPED HER CASE. It clunked on the wooden planks and fell over with a dull thud. Charles bent to retrieve it, while Maggie struggled to decipher how she'd managed to suffer a stroke and still retain any brain function.

"You're engaged?" sputtered Maggie. "How? When?"

"About a month ago. And there is one more thing you need to know—"

"Oh heavens, Tena's expecting, isn't she?" No wonder Tena and Charles were hiding. Their mother would literally kill them both.

Charles appeared scandalized. "No! That's not why—"

"What else could there be?" Maggie's chest constricted. "I'm having a heart attack. First a stroke, now a heart attack. I hope it kills me."

Fortunately, before her body had a chance to expire, she was knocked backward by her sister's forceful embrace.

"I missed you so much!" Tena cried with tears in her eyes. Maggie held her sister at arm's length and refused to allow any of her own emotions to leak from her eye sockets.

The months had been kind to Tena. Now only one month shy of her nineteenth birthday, there was an assurance about her that wasn't visible before. With an almost regal stance, the crisp ebony of her mourning dress slimmed Tena's already trim figure to perfection. Delicate honey curls peeked from beneath her fitted cap. Thin brow creases were the only indication of recent turmoil.

Maggie focused on the amber broach at Tena's collar rather than her sister's watery eyes. "I should never have gone."

Tena responded exactly as Charles predicted. "All is forgiven. I'm so glad to have you home!" Charles's face said, *I told you so.*

She clasped Maggie's hand and began to talk animatedly as she ushered them all into a waiting taxi. "So much has happened since you left. Edith is married to Christopher Hartnell and Bianca's engaged to Colin Smith."

"He's so old," Maggie grimaced, taking the seat opposite her sister. Charles stowed Maggie's case and joined Tena on her side of the bench. With a rap of the reins, the carriage jerked down the road in the direction of number seven, Union Street.

"I know," agreed Tena. "It's completely revolting. But he's rich and you know Bianca ... Oh! Rumor has it Edith might even be showing hints of the family way, although she's admitted nothing yet. I keep trying to make her tell me, but she's so nasty; she simply refuses."

"Is that so?"

"Oh, you know them. Mr. Winchester pushed them to the front of the line for marriage as soon as they became of age. It's no surprise they'd have babies right off. Although Bianca isn't quite being square with me either. She's engaged to Colin, but I would wager she has a handful of fun on the side, if you understand my meaning."

"No surprise."

"And that isn't even the best news, is it, Charles?" Tena gave a very uncharacteristic squeal. "Oh Maggie, I'm certain you read all about it in my last letter—I hope it wasn't too dreadful to read. Look!" She retrieved a long chain hidden beneath the high collar of her dress. It contained two plain golden bands, one slightly thicker than the other. "They're lovely, aren't they? I agreed to the German tradition of a plain band in exchange for an English wedding ceremony. We can't wear them yet of course—I promised it would be soon!" Tena warded off Charles who had started to refute her and replaced the chain beneath her dress. "I want to tell Mother on Easter. Goodness, that's only three days from now. Oh, Maggie, I'm so relieved you made it home in time." Tena leaned across for another quick hug, the carriage's movement jostling her into the seat beside Maggie. "Maggie, you will be at the wedding of course? Oh please say you will?"

"Yes, of course." Maggie's mind was swimming. She had so many questions. Tena didn't let her ask any of them.

"Splendid! You must come over early to help me with everything. And see our new home! St. Louis must be such a beautiful city. The Kischs live in a German area, some place Emil calls brewery row."

"Because there are a number of breweries nearby," supplied Charles.

"Don't worry, though," Tena continued, "It isn't only Germans. Charles's mother wrote about a Czech family a few blocks down from them, and they met a Serbian couple at the market the week after they arrived. Not too far away is an Italian section. Can you imagine? It's all so exciting!" Tena paused breathlessly. "Also a touch overwhelming I must admit. Charles has been teaching me the language, although I'm afraid I'm not very adept."

"Nonsense," Charles amended. "You are doing very well with your lessons."

"That's sweet of you to say, but you needn't lie for Maggie's sake." Tena leaned into Maggie. "I'm rubbish at it."

Maggie didn't even know how to reply. What in the world was her sister talking about? She opened her mouth to ask.

"So Maggie," Tena continued, barely a breath taken. "Tell me about London! How was it as a lady's maid? Did they take you anywhere exciting? Did you see the king?" Tena squeezed Maggie's hand and giggled in a way Maggie hadn't heard since they were little girls. It meant her nervous laugh and bubbly enthusiasm was all for show. "Did you meet any handsome fellas? Did they take you dancing? Did you—"

"Tena!" Charles interjected. Tena threw him an annoyed stare that he returned in kind.

"Whatever is the matter?" she asked him. "I have eleven months of news to catch up on."

"You may be more interested that your sister has no knowledge of anything you told her."

"I wrote her letters." Tena turned back to Maggie and asked innocently, "You did read my letters, didn't you?"

Maggie counted the passing houses. Two more blocks to home. "I didn't receive any letters."

"Pfff, I wrote nearly every week. The post isn't *that* incompetent."

"I don't know what happened to them, but they didn't end up with me."

"Or you didn't read them."

Maggie met her sister's heated stare. "I would have if I had them to read!"

Charles stepped in before the situation got out of hand. "Tena, you should listen to her."

Tena's head swiveled between Maggie and Charles. "All those letters and you never saw them?" Her eyes glossed over. "So you really don't know? Our engagement? Leaving England?" A tiny gasp escaped her throat. "Father?"

"I know about Father, and Charles told me about your engagement. He wanted to send me to the wolves for not writing you back." Maggie held her sister by the shoulders. "Except I did write. I truly missed you."

Tena bit her lip, a tiny sob escaped her throat, and she burst into tears. "Oh Maggie, it was horrible without you here. I thought you didn't care!"

Maggie caressed her sister's hair as Tena's sobs dampened her front. The truth was she cared too much, and she hated herself for it. If she didn't care, she wouldn't feel guilt over missing her father's funeral or the pain she had caused to everyone around her.

What if she had stayed? What if she agreed to Lloyd's proposal? Despite his last threat, he still seemed a good man, or good enough anyway. She may not have loved him, but he would have made her life easy. Their marriage would have pleased her parents immensely. Marrying Lloyd wouldn't have saved her father's life, but at least she would have been with him at the end. He wouldn't have died wondering what happened to his little girl, assuming what everyone else did, asking why Maggie didn't even care.

TWENTY-THREE

THE HOUSE LAY DARK AND SILENT when they arrived. Cold drafts floated through the halls like ghosts. The door to their father's study, always open and inviting while he worked, was now closed, only blackness beneath the door. It was a harsh reminder of the last day Maggie was home, when she stood in that same room with her father and made a decision which seemed like a mistake now. A million regrets hung like lead weights, a million what-ifs that might have made a difference.

The study's familiar scent filled Maggie's nostrils before she opened the door. Unlike the rest of the house, it still retained Laurence Archer's essence—worn books, ink, sage. The familiarity wrapped her like a warm blanket on a cold day.

Maggie turned the wall switch, sparking the room with bright warmth. Even a month after his death, everything remained exactly as it had been. Ashes dusted the firebox. Ledgers lay open on the desk, papers tucked haphazardly beneath them. All of Laurence's beloved books lined the shelves. They were the ones her mother didn't deem acceptable for a place in the parlor, not sophisticated enough to be on display for their guests.

Maggie ran her hand absently along the spines, recalling smuggled moments reading them in the moonlight with Tena long after their mother thought they were in bed. Or the night their father caught them and, instead of punishing them, offered them candles for more light.

He'd given them each a kiss and a wink. "Don't forget to open the window so your mother doesn't smell the smoke." The girls stifled giggles behind their fingers, believing they were getting away with something worse than murder.

Maggie chucked the first available book across the room in frustration. It bounced off the back of the armchair, landing in the corner with a dissatisfying thud.

She swore. Apparently throwing things didn't help either.

"Did that story offend you?"

Maggie whipped around to face Charles. Stooping, he retrieved the book from behind the armchair and read the spine. "This one is Reuben's favorite. Is that why you threw it?" He held it up so she could see the cover. *The Time Machine.*

Of course it was.

"No, I didn't even see the title." She sank onto the couch and curled her legs underneath her skirt. "I'm frustrated. It was either the book or lighting the house on fire."

Charles chuckled. He tossed her the novel, and lowered himself into an armchair. "By all means, please proceed."

Maggie examined the book's worn binding. "Shouldn't you leave? What if my mother finds you here?"

"Your mother is out for the evening. Tena is checking with Olivia about dinner arrangements for the three of us."

"My mother's not here?" She hadn't expected her mother to be waiting at the door, of course. An abundance of affection would have drawn more suspicion than relief. Even so, after almost a year apart Maggie believed her mother would still toss her an obtuse acknowledgement when she arrived. Just as well, thought Maggie. She wouldn't have to stand on pretense anymore.

"So, you and Tena are leaving?"

Charles pulled at his collar. "*Ja,* I wanted to tell you at the station. We sail on Wednesday."

"Wednesday?" Maggie blanched. That was only six days away!

"My family is eager for us to join them. They traveled in January. I remained only to sell the house and put the rest of our affairs in order."

Maggie turned an eye at the fireplace's cold ashes.

"I wanted to leave sooner," continued Charles gently. "After your father passed, it seemed like the perfect time to go. Tena wished to wait for you."

"I'm back now so why don't you just leave then?" Maggie spat. She chucked the book and Charles caught it with both hands before it flew over his head, then handed it back, to what end she didn't know. Perhaps he enjoyed being assaulted with literature. She was about to hurl it into the fireplace when Charles spoke again.

"I want you to join us."

Maggie froze, her arm still poised in the air. She set the book down on the table. "*You* want *me* to move to America with *you*?" Maggie asked, releasing each word slowly to comprehend what he was offering her.

Charles held his hands out in offering. "Yes. Will you come with us?"

"Why? You don't even like me."

Charles folded his hands in his lap, considering her in the same way one might defuse explosives. "I hoped we might change that."

Maggie didn't answer. This was all too much to take in.

"Tena wants you there," Charles said thoughtfully. "She missed you every day you were gone. I know she will go wherever I ask her to, she said so herself, but I want her to be happy. I fear that without you she will always feel incomplete, and that is a part of her I could never replace." He removed an envelope from his breast pocket and placed it on the table between them. "There is a ticket here. You need only agree."

Maggie stared at the envelope open-mouthed, then peeked inside. Sure enough, a second class ticket was contained within.

"But at the station you said—"

"Forgive my behavior at the station. I was angry. Nevertheless, I would have asked you this even if my accusations were true."

Maggie held the envelope out to him. "If Tena wants me to go, she should ask me herself."

Charles smiled sympathetically. "There are certain people Tena will never ask you to leave behind."

Maggie bit her lip, eyes back on the envelope. Who did she have to stay here for?

She thought of her mother, she thought of Reuben, she thought of Lloyd, then she foolishly thought of Reuben again.

Then Maggie thought of Tena if she didn't go. She was as certain of her choice then as she was the day she chose London over everything else. And as equally certain that she truly had no choice at all.

Maggie forced a half-hearted smile. "You know as well as I do, Mr. Kisch. Tena's the only person we can't give up."

TWENTY-FOUR

FOR TWO DAYS, THE ARCHER SISTERS sorted through the remains of their father's life. Documents reviewed, final debts paid, personal items organized for sale or charity collection. Despite Father's gaping absence, life at number seven, Union Street was pleasant for once. Their mother called on friends from morning until night, only returning after supper. Those Beatrix-less hours freed the girls to rebuild lost time to the tune of shared memories and the crackling gramophone. Maggie slid between her covers Saturday night humming *Oh, You Beautiful Doll* and woke Easter morning with a smile on her lips.

Unfortunately, the holiday remained anything but cheery. By late morning the sky turned an ominous sheet of grey, ready to unleash at any moment. Collecting hats and umbrellas, the Archer women piled into the enclosed carriage for the church, riding in dreary silence while a steady rain beat upon the windows.

Concentration during the service was impossible. The pastor gave the same resounding sermon about forgiveness and new life after death that he preached nearly every year. Maggie heard none of it. Today was her last Sunday in Fontaine and her last Sunday in England. When her father was alive, Sundays were her favorite day of the week. Now she was adorned in black linen from crown to ankle, longing to complete this one last Sunday and never be

154

reminded of her home again.

The rain had recently ceased when they emerged from the church, although dark clouds still hung heavy over the cemetery. Leaves dripped water off their hat brims as the three women stepped around puddles on the muddy path.

The newest addition to the cemetery, their father's solitary grave stood near the rear fence shaded by yew trees. Mud splattered the bottom of the stone where a woodlark picked at the moist soil. Engraved upon the rounded stone, flanked by deep cut blossoms and simple hewn crosses, were the words:

Laurence K Archer
19 Oct 1868
22 Feb 1912
Husband, Father, Friend

Maggie slid her arm through Tena's to clasp her sister's hand. This was the first, and only, time she would stand at this gravesite. Once was enough. Cemeteries were ghastly places designed to remind one of horrible events that happened to good people. All those stories she'd manufactured before about the incredible lives these people led ... Their real stories were in reality no better than her father's. A normal man with a normal life who died full of disappointments. He died before either of his daughters had a chance to fulfill any of the dreams he had for them.

Maggie would never suffer the pain of such disappointment. No one would be left behind to mourn her loss, save maybe Tena. But no husband, and no children. Her father's death made real in a slab of granite resolved her decision now more than ever. She would die alone. Tena was unwise to choose anything else. What could Charles offer her? Nothing eternal. Nothing more than temporary happiness laced with difficulty and the same finality everyone must face.

The door into death was taken alone. Why not follow the road there in the same way?

Lost in her own thoughts, Maggie didn't even notice when her mother left. Beatrix vanished without a single word.

Tena's grip tightened on Maggie's arm. "Maggie?"

"Hmm?"

"Can I ask why?"

"Why what?"

Tena pressed her foot into the soil to repack the mud where the rain carved grooves through it. Not a single blade of grass had grown yet. "Why did you leave? Father said you didn't want to marry, so you'd taken a position as a lady's maid. He'd encouraged you to take it."

"So?"

"So, why didn't you tell me?"

"I thought you'd talk me out of it."

Tena's eyes shifted to Maggie's face. "Why would I talk you out of it when I made the same suggestion?"

"Oi, Archers!" The girls glanced over as Edith and Bianca pranced up on the arms of their respective men, Colin Hartnell and Christopher Smith.

"Maggie! We heard you were home!" Bianca cried, smothering Maggie with unbidden hugs and kisses to her cheeks. "We missed you so!"

"Yes, here I am." Maggie forced a smile. She hadn't given much thought to Edith and Bianca while she was gone, and couldn't say she was suddenly overjoyed at seeing them now. She still hadn't forgiven them over their little may queen stunt.

Edith seized her husband's arm. "Maggie, you remember Christopher from last year's Christmas party? We're married!" She extended her hand, flaunting her exquisite diamond ring.

Maggie gave a polite smile. "And did I hear you're also expecting?"

Edith shoved Tena playfully. "Oh, you heard that little rumor from your sister! She's so obnoxious, trying to pry information out of me, but I'm not telling! No, I'm not!"

"I'll tell!" Bianca cut in, shaking her shoulders saucily. "I'm not ashamed to admit Colin and I *are* expecting something a bit unexpected."

This piece of news was of no surprise. The surprise to Maggie was how Bianca had managed to turn eighteen before it happened.

"Aren't you going to congratulate us?" Bianca pressed, tossing her hair over her shoulder with a flourish.

Maggie gave a slow clap. "Bravo. Good show." Bianca frowned, wrapping her arms around her belly.

"You know," Bianca said icily, "We heard about your scandal with Mr. Radford last May. Made for some positively sinful gossip! Who would have guessed our Maggie could be such a little tart?"

Maggie opened her mouth in outrage, but Edith cut in eagerly. "What about when we saw Tena going around with him?" She nudged Tena and sniggered. "She still won't tell us the truth, will you, you naughty girl?"

Maggie gawked at her sister. *Later,* Tena's eyes pleaded.

"Lloyd Halverson was asking around about you again," Bianca continued, sidling up to Maggie. Maggie tried to shove her off, but she simply wrapped her arm through Maggie's and held on. Bianca lowered her voice conspiratorially. "I for one was most surprised he would still be interested. He was so upset after your betrayal. No need to worry though, one night and I convinced him he belonged with someone else."

"Bianca, your fiancé is standing right there!" Tena exclaimed.

Mr. Smith stared off in the other direction. For as old as he was, Maggie wondered if he'd even heard her. Bianca shrugged, barely giving her fiancé a glance. "That was months ago. Colin knows I'm completely devoted to him now. Don't you, sweetie?" Bianca leaned towards him for a kiss. Maggie and Tena rolled their eyes at each other. Would wonders never cease?

"So, will you take Lloyd back?" Edith asked.

"No," Maggie asserted. "My father made it very clear to Mr.

Halverson that there wouldn't be anything between us."

"Planning on more one night trysts with Mr. Radford then?" Bianca smirked. "Not that I'm judging of course."

Maggie gritted her teeth to stay calm. "No. There's nothing with him either."

Edith tsked loudly. "And after all the help we gave you, too. Here you are, still single." She turned to Tena instead. "And what of you, Tena?"

Tena blushed three shades darker. "Oh, no one special. Not yet."

Edith tsked again. "What must your poor mother think? Both of you are nearly at the end of your second decade and no prospects. It's utterly shameful if you ask me." She shook her head disparagingly and received Mr. Hartnell's arm. "Well, it's been lovely. Do call on us for tea, won't you?"

"Maggie, perhaps you can take a post as our nanny," Bianca remarked. "I hear you do love a bit of servitude."

Maggie started a well-placed colorfully-worded remark until Tena elbowed her in the ribs. Edith and Bianca giggled away down the path.

"They're horrible," Maggie muttered. "I don't like them one bit."

Tena chuckled. "Oh, Maggie, is there really anyone you do like?"

Maggie rolled her eyes. "You're hilarious. What I would *like* to know is how often you see Reuben."

Tena shrugged. "All the time."

"I thought you were with Charles."

"Oh, Maggie, it wasn't like that," Tena asserted. "We didn't see each other much at first, but then, well, Reuben needed a friend, and I needed one too and we both knew Charles so ..." Tena laid a hand on Maggie's arm reassuringly. "I promise it is only friendship."

Maggie tossed Tena off and turned back to Father's grave with folded arms. "Reuben hates me."

"I've never heard anyone talk about someone they hate the way he talks about you."

Maggie wished her heart hadn't started racing just then. "What did he say?"

"Nothing really. He's so guarded. But the way he sounds when he asks about you ... I doubt he asks only to fill the conversation."

Maggie didn't reply. She didn't even know what to think. Reuben might not completely despise her; she couldn't tell if she was relieved or disappointed. It troubled her when she thought he hated her, but it would have been easier to deal with than if he retained actual legitimate feelings for her.

"He needed you, Maggie," Tena said softly. "We both did, but I believe he needed you more. His mother was never right again. His father gave up completely after she died. I at least had Charles. Reuben was all alone."

"You make it sound like it's my fault!"

"No, I'm not. I simply want you to understand. Reuben doesn't hate you, Maggie. He never did. His heart hurts—"

"We lost our father too," Maggie argued. She pressed her palms against the gravestone's cool granite. "All of us are hurting."

"We are," Tena placed her hands on top of Maggie's. "But our pain doesn't make his insignificant."

Tena was so calm. How could she be this composed when they were standing before their father's grave? Maggie lashed her foot into the side of the stone. It was as bad of an idea as it sounded. "Confound it!" Maggie felt the blood in her toes pounding. She hopped in place clutching her foot. "That hurt!"

Tena's face broke into an amused smile. "I missed your silly tantrums. Life was no fun with only mother to argue with." Tena pulled Maggie into a tight hug, laughing at her sister's expense. "I'm so glad we don't have to say goodbye again."

Without warning, or perhaps because they hadn't paid enough attention, the sky opened up upon them.

Tena shrieked and made a grab for their umbrellas. She tossed one to Maggie and opened her own, swiping the rain from her coat and patting her hat self consciously. Maggie unfolded hers as the rain splashed across her shoulders. She shivered as a stream dribbled beneath her collar into her dress.

The girls huddled towards the cemetery entrance, as the rain tapped a steady rhythm against their umbrellas. Maggie was thankful to be free of this place of misery. A few more paces and she would be out on the road.

Hold tight to Tena's arm. Don't look back.

Tena inhaled sharply.

Maggie followed Tena's gaze and lost her own ability to breathe.

Reuben hunched low over his family's grave, violets in hand, head bowed against the downpour. If time had worn well with Tena, it had been the opposite for Reuben. Rain plastered strands of chin length hair against his cheeks and jawbone. Enough stubble lined his face to be noticeable even from afar.

Maggie dislodged her arm from Tena's grasp at the same instant Tena said, "We can go home. You don't have to—"

"I do. I'll never have another chance to set things right."

Tena held her sister at arm's length, nodded slowly, then reluctantly backed through the gate. Maggie waited until her figure was only a speck on the horizon.

Then she marched into the trenches.

TWENTY-FIVE

AT THE CONCLUSION OF EASTER SERVICE, Reuben dwelt in the church's shadows until the last of the congregation completed their holiday greetings, and the pastor dimmed the lamps. Vacating the empty pew, he retrieved the tied bouquet of violets from the outside stoop, gently shook the rain from their delicate petals, and navigated the sodden grounds to his family's gravesite.

Two new names lay stark against Mira's duller engraving, the markings not yet beaten down by weather, dust, and time. *28 April 1907, 19 October 1911, 26 December 1911*. Lives stolen in an instant.

"So tell me, Father," Reuben asked. "You promised me you'd fix our family. Only now you're with them, and I'm still here. Tell me, was it always part of your plan, leaving me behind?"

Harris and Florence Radford's names melted together with another fresh sea of emotion. Reuben pressed his thumbs into his eyelids. He promised himself this morning he wouldn't do this anymore. Today would be the last time he ever stepped foot in this cemetery.

Then again, he'd made that same pact every day since he returned from London.

Each morning he rose before the sun and walked the mile to the cemetery before work. Every evening he went another mile out of the way to visit their grave before heading home. And there he sat broken and alone, his mind a blank slate for his hallucinations' torment, until he woke up and did it all again.

Reuben missed his friends. Prior to Laurence Archer's funeral, not a week passed without Charles or Tena in it, and now over a month had come and gone. Just another unfortunate side effect of his life's ever expanding muck pile.

Dark clouds settled above the cemetery releasing a light drizzle rapidly shifting to a steady downpour. Fat drops splattered off the stones and soaked Reuben through in minutes. Stooping to arrange the violets before the gravestone, he touched two fingers to his lips before pressing them to the stems. *This is the last,* he promised. *The next time I'm here, I'll be under the dirt with you.*

Reuben sensed the shadows approach before the rain vanished above him. He raised his eyes to the empty air, knowing full well it was her face he would see. Reuben flicked the mud from his knees and stood up.

Maggie held an umbrella high over them both, her eyes the same torrid color as the sky, her lips creased in a tight line. "Hello."

"Hello." Reuben slicked his hair back, wringing the excess water to the ground. "You're home?"

"I am."

"Were you visiting your father?"

"Yes."

"Good."

A wren flew from the trees to preen itself on a headstone two rows over. Thunder rumbled overhead. Maggie didn't reply and Reuben didn't persist and so they remained in silence. If they didn't talk, then nothing had to change—good, bad, or otherwise. One of them could walk away right now and never have to see the other again.

That was just as well. Let it be him. "Goodbye, Maggie."

Maggie stepped in Reuben's path. "Wait."

"No, Maggie. We're done here."

Maggie gripped her umbrella tighter. "Two minutes. That's all I ask. Please."

Reuben checked the time on his pocket watch. "Fine. Two minutes."

"I didn't know about your parents," Maggie said slowly. "Or even my own father. The last eleven months are a void for me."

"How could you not know?" Reuben snapped. "Tena wrote you dozens of letters."

"If I had, you *know* I would have come."

All Reuben *knew* was that her clarification only embarrassed him for raging to London like he did. "Even if that's so, you still went away without so much as an explanation." He glanced at his watch. "One minute."

"That was wrong of me." Maggie reached for his hand. "I never wanted to go."

Reuben yanked his hand away. "Why did you?"

"I *had* to. I needed to be alone."

"We needed you here."

Maggie pointed to the watch still open on Reuben's palm. "How much time do I have left?"

Reuben stared at its tell-tale hands. "Time's up." He snapped the watch shut and returned it to his pocket. "Where will you go now? Back to London?"

Thunder crashed, but it was Reuben to whom Maggie gave a wary glance. "Charles didn't mention it? You do know they're leaving England?"

"Of course they told me." The truth was Reuben knew Tena and Charles's plans long before Maggie did.

The day of Laurence Archer's burial, Reuben was one of the last to leave. He stood shoulder to shoulder with Charles, the mound of earth separating them from Tena. The winter wind glued her veil to the unchecked tears rolling down her cheeks. In hindsight,

Reuben realized she probably felt as alone as he did.

Tena gave a small sob and fled towards the church. "Go," said Reuben. Charles didn't need further urging. He took off at a sprint.

Reuben slowly followed, pulling up short of the church steps where Charles knelt before Tena's hunched form. She'd tossed her hat and veil away and pulled half a dozen pins from her hair.

"I am afraid my words come at a most inopportune time," Charles said, "however, there is little time remaining to say them." He slipped a golden ring onto Tena's left hand, and she gasped, whispering words inaudible to Reuben's ears.

Charles held her petite hand in his much larger one, covering the ring to force her eyes back to his. "I would have much preferred to ask for your hand long ago, and from your father first, but propriety arrested my desires. You are a woman who required careful courting, and I knew you would not find favor if I rushed into a proposal. Untimely though this one is, I can only delay my departure overseas a month at most, and I find my time with you swiftly racing to an end. It would find me miserable to leave you behind, however I cannot force you to leave your family either."

Tena raised both his hands to her lips, gently kissing the tips of his fingers. "I would miss them," she said quietly, "but I think I would miss you more." She leaned in for a tender kiss, their hands still pressed between them. As she pulled away, her smile was genuine. "I love you, Charles. And I'll go wherever you ask of me."

Charles kissed her again softly. He pulled her close, running a hand over her disheveled locks. "I promise I will make everything better."

Tena's bright smile flickered then faded from her face. "I wish Maggie were here."

Reuben marched straight out of the cemetery and onto the next train to London, anger fueling him in a way he never thought possible. He wanted to rip Maggie to shreds for leaving Tena to shoulder her burdens alone.

Only standing before her now, Reuben didn't care anymore what happened next. Being rejected by her could never hurt as much as the blackened heart he inflicted upon himself through so much misunderstanding. He wanted her in his life; time had shown him how unbearable life without her could be.

Reuben snatched Maggie's umbrella from her fingers, flinging it to the side. She shrieked as the rain washed over her head to her dress, matting hair to her cheeks and rolling across her neck. She made a move for the umbrella, only Reuben was quicker. He wrapped an arm around her waist, swinging her back around to face him.

"Are you mad?" she exclaimed.

Reuben lifted his face to the sky, letting the water run down it as laugher spewed unbidden from his lips. "I am mad, Maggie! Crazy and stupid and nothing in my life makes sense. I have been so foolish not to trust you. That ends today."

Reuben's hands found Maggie's waist, gently pulling her body to where his lips at long last found hers.

Maggie broke the kiss, slipping on the muddy ground in her haste. "What are you doing?" she gasped.

Reuben smiled. "Kissing you. Now come here so I can do it again."

Maggie tapped her fingers against her flushed lips. "No—no—no. Reuben, you can't. I'm leaving on Wednesday."

"Wednesday?" Reuben shrugged. "Surely London won't mind if I borrow you a bit longer?"

Maggie's fingers froze mid-dance. "No, that's what I tried to tell you. I'm leaving with Tena. Didn't Charles tell you?"

Thunder exploded directly overhead. Reuben couldn't move. Surely he was imagining this.

"Stay," he said, as if there could be no question otherwise. He let her go once, and her absence had nearly defeated him. If he watched her walk away again, it would surely do him in.

Maggie's hands rose in an impenetrable barrier. "There's

nothing for me here."

Reuben edged forward until his chest touched her outstretched palms. "I'm here. Stay with *me*."

"I can't stay."

She was so close. Only inches separated them. Dark hair plastered Maggie's cheeks, slowly dripping against her shoulders. Rain clouds converged behind her lashes, as devastatingly beautiful as the day he'd met her. The fabric of her black dress conformed to each curve. A completely insane thought crossed Reuben's mind in that moment and, as is typical with insane people, he thought it a perfectly sensible idea.

"Then let's leave," he whispered. "Just the two of us. Let's leave this place and everything behind. No one will tell us what to do or what to think." He paused. "Or who to be with. Only us, Maggie."

Maggie's eyes grew as round as dinner plates. She was contemplating a million things at once, and expressing none of them. Reuben rushed ahead before she could.

"Remember when we were in Southampton and you wanted to stow away on that ship? I thought it was crazy at the time, but now, well why not? We can go to Iceland. I promised I would take you!"

"Reuben, we can't go to Iceland."

"It doesn't matter where we go." He wrestled her hands between his, kissing her palms. "As long as I'm with you."

Maggie wrenched her hands from his. She gestured between the two of them. "Are you asking me to marry you?"

"Uh ..." It was Reuben's turn to hesitate. He hadn't intended to ask that when he thought of his proposal. But he supposed that's what it had to be—a proposal. It had to be all or nothing.

Reuben didn't even know how to begin. He hadn't planned this. He didn't have a ring. Laurence asked Reuben to care for his daughters—would that count as permission? Reuben had refused though—that probably wouldn't gain approval. Should he ask her mother? The thought sent shivers down his spine. He'd have to wing it.

Reuben dropped down to one knee in the mud. "Maggie Archer—"

"Seriously? Stand up."

"Very well ..." Reuben stood and wiped the mud from his knee. "Maggie Archer," he began again.

"No."

"But—"

"*No, Reuben.* We are *not* getting married."

Reuben pressed his palms to his temples. He could feel Mira demanding attention, straining to escape. Maggie couldn't leave him alone. Not again. Not with *her.* "Please, Maggie," Reuben implored.

Maggie pressed her finger to his lips. "Stop. I do not want to be a wife, and yes, as flattering as your proposal is, you can't make me forget that. Once you have time to think this through—"

"She's right, you know," Mira hissed in his head.

"I don't need time!" Reuben retorted. "I've thought this through. Just now."

"I'm glad you've given our future together an entire five seconds of your time!" Maggie stooped to retrieve her umbrella and shook off the water from the puddle he'd thrown it in. It seemed she would leave without even a backward glance, until she turned to consider him with those expressive eyes only she could have. "I'm truly sorry, Reuben. I just can't. Especially not with *you.*"

Reuben felt a sudden rush of anger. "What does that mean—especially not with *me*?"

"Oh let me count the ways!" laughed Mira.

"You deserve better," said Maggie. As though that explained everything.

But it wasn't true. He'd determined last year on the Southampton pier that he deserved nothing better than the girl standing right in front of him. Now he doubted if he deserved even that much.

This was his fault. He'd known better.

"Before today you found me unbearable," Maggie continued. "Just pretend like we never spoke. And you'll see how easy it is to erase me from your mind."

He shook his head vigorously. Nothing in his mind was easy to erase. Oh, how he wished he could. "Maggie, how can you think a few months of misunderstanding will erase our *years* together?"

Maggie looked upon him then with nothing short of pity. He knew he had lost. He closed his eyes, and she proceeded to slice him open with her words. "We don't have *years* together, Reuben. We have *days*. And that's all I can give you, just days. You should wait for someone who will give you her entire *life*." Maggie lowered her voice to barely above a whisper, as though she didn't want to admit what she said next. "But know that, of all the things I must leave behind, you are the only one I will miss."

Reuben heard her footsteps squelch away through the mud. The sound grew fainter and fainter until it vanished. Then he counted to ten before he dared open his eyes. He was alone in the cemetery once more, rain-soaked to the bone, surrounded by stone. He wished he had never come.

Mira's laughter echoed in the storm. "Regretting yet another decision?"

Reuben stalked towards the gate, casting it aside with a metallic clang. Mira was right. It was time to ensure he never had another regret.

TWENTY-SIX

MAGGIE DRIFTED HOME IN A DAZE. She didn't bother shielding herself against the ongoing torrent. It couldn't hold a candle to the storm inside her head, thoughts flitting in sharp segments rather than coherent messages.

Reuben proposed to me?

No, he didn't. I slipped in the mud. I hit my head. I'm unconscious right now.

Wake up, Maggie. Confound it! Why won't you wake up? Pinch yourself.

Blast, that hurt.

Reuben asked you to run away with him.

You should have stayed in London.

Tena would never have forgiven you.

You shouldn't have talked to him at all.

You wouldn't have forgiven yourself.

Why does he even like me? I don't even like me.

I have three days. I can find him someone else!

Maggie, be frank, Reuben's a colossal emotional overload. Who else could deal with that?

Trying to contemplate all the wild emotions whirling around in that man's mind made Maggie want to take a three-day nap. Thank goodness she was leaving the country. It seemed only an ocean's distance would stop Reuben's lunacy.

What about your own lunacy? A little voice nagged. *Part of you actually thought about accepting, didn't it? Part of you wants to stay with him.*

Don't be absurd.

You missed him.

Shut up. I did not.

So engrossed in her own thoughts she was, that nothing else entered Maggie's mind until she was handing Olivia her umbrella.

"Caught in the storm, Miss?"

"Literally and figuratively I'm afraid." Maggie peeled off her sodden gloves and coat, handing both over. It didn't help much. She still retained the appearance of a drowned rat. "Please excuse me, Olivia. I need to freshen up before luncheon."

"Yes, miss. Your sister is already waiting for you in the dining room."

"Thank you, and my mother?"

"Upstairs. She will join you momentarily."

This afternoon was the first time the three Archer women would sit down for any stretch longer than a few minutes. They had attempted to complete tea the last two days, but both times more cups were rattled than drunk from. Surely for Easter though they could have one civilized conversation?

Any hope for that vanished thirty minutes later when, freshly dried and dressed, Maggie opened the dining room door. The scene before her was potentially more devastating than if she'd accepted Reuben's proposal.

Sitting at the table was a highly sophisticated, properly dressed, handsome and well-mannered young gentleman. Unfortunately, should this same man choose to remain in his seat when her mother walked in the room, they would all suffer a wrath like never before.

"Back again, Mr. Kisch?" Maggie sighed. "Will today's surprises never end?"

Tena startled, knocking over her still empty water glass. She stood, straightened her place setting, and gave a nervous twitter. "I invited him."

Charles also stood with a quick nod to Maggie. "We are telling your mother about us."

"Don't be absurd." Maggie strode over to Tena's chair. "What is he really doing here?"

"It's as he said. We're telling Mother." Tena rearranged the flowers on the table even though they were perfectly positioned. Her fingers fumbled with the delicate petals, knocking several to the table. She poked and prodded, pulled stems out and replaced them.

"You are not," Maggie reasoned. "We leave in three days, Tena. Suppress your inappropriate theatrics until then."

"Oh, in the same way you suppress yours? What happened with Reuben today?"

"You spoke with Reuben?" inquired Charles. "How is he?"

Maggie glared at him. "Are you seriously allowing this?"

"Why shouldn't he allow it?" asked Tena as she collected the fallen petals. She crossed the room to toss them from the window before slamming it shut. "I'm through with lying, Maggie. Every day for a year I've had to grit my teeth while Mother looks down on me. Edith and Bianca carry on and on about their perfect men, and I can't say a word. Charles is a finer catch than both their scabs combined!"

Maggie placed a hand on either hip. "You know this is a bad idea."

Tena's face flushed crimson. "So was leaving me because of a boy!"

"I—told—you—that wasn't the reason."

"Then why!"

Stillness descended with the creak of the dining room door. Beatrix smiled as she entered, as sweetly as a spider greets a fly. Her eyes slid over Charles's petrified form to her youngest daughter, now exhibiting a dull jade sheen. "Mr. Kisch? I do not believe we invited you."

Charles stood with a brief nod. "Apologies certainly, Mrs. Archer, however, I *was* invited." He looked to Tena for assistance, but she was rooted in place by the window. Maggie pinched the inside of Tena's elbow rather harder than she should have. Nonetheless, it did the trick.

Tena walked around the table to Charles's shoulder and raised her chin to meet her mother's. "I invited him, Mother."

"Why would you do that, dear?" Beatrix asked in the same falsely honeyed tone.

"Uh ... well ..." Tena stuttered. She, in turn, looked to Maggie for support. Maggie stared at her mother instead. She didn't agree with her sister's decision, and for once she wasn't in the lion's den. It seemed foolish to purposely jump in the pit. Tena could save herself from her own bad decisions.

"Mrs. Archer?" Charles spoke again. Fiery eyes turned in his direction.

Tena clutched at his arm. "Charles, no."

"Mrs. Archer?" Charles repeated. "Tena has allowed me to court her—"

"Oh, has she?" Beatrix asked calmly. "Well, please forgive me. I'm afraid I don't recall being asked if *I* would allow it." She floated to the table, resting her fingers on the back of the head chair and smacked her lips. "Tena, how long have you been lying to me?"

Tena avoided her mother's eyes. "I never *wanted* to lie to you."

"How long?"

"Fifteen months."

A knock at the door sent them back into resounding silence. Olivia entered, efficiently filling wine and water glasses while the rest of them watched without comment. Their cook and kitchen maid arrived soon after with the luncheon meal.

"Serve quickly and don't return until I send for you," Maggie whispered to Olivia. With a tight nod, she ushered the staff through service and scampered from the room.

Beatrix sat, placed her napkin on her lap, and nibbled at the corner of a potato. "Tena, this will be the end of your cohorts with this man. Take your seat. Maggie, you as well. Mr. Kisch, you are dismissed." She sipped her wine and continued eating.

No one else moved. "Mother," Tena ventured. "Charles's family is well-respected. Decently wealthy. He plans to take over their business with his brothers. He had top marks in school. He's kind and compassionate and, most importantly, he loves me."

Beatrix sliced through the ham on her plate. "He's German." As if that called for no further detail.

"But you originally picked him for Maggie!" Tena pouted, having used up the last of her calm reserves.

Beatrix waved her fork. "I was desperate. I wanted grandchildren. Anyone was better than Maggie ending up a spinster, even marrying one of them." She said the last word in disgust. "But *you*, Tena, are my respectful daughter. Dutiful to a fault. I trusted you would make better decisions." Her tone was so condescending and full of obvious disappointment that a great sympathy spurred in Maggie for her sister. Maggie had been on the receiving end of their mother's disdain most of her life; by now it was as ordinary as the rising of the sun. Until last year, Tena lived entirely the opposite—always trying to live the way she thought their parents wanted.

Charles placed a protective hand on Tena's shoulder. He met Beatrix's eyes without a hint of fear. "Mrs. Archer, Tena and I are engaged."

Maggie's hands flew over her mouth. Charles was either the bravest or the most idiotic man she had ever met.

Beatrix chuckled and continued eating.

Tena swallowed. "I'm sorry, Mother, but it's true. We're getting married."

Beatrix's chair slid into the wall with a crash. "Not to him, you're not!" she spat. And then their mother called Charles something so vile, so incomprehensible, that even Maggie was shocked speechless, and very few things about their mother surprised her anymore. Beatrix was always so pristine with her language, careful with her wording, but in that moment the words flying from their mother's mouth simply couldn't be believed.

Beatrix glared daggers between her daughters. "What sin did I commit that both of you turned out so horribly?" She pointed a long finger first at Maggie then back at Tena. "One of you throws your virtue away and the other one wants to ruin yourself with this foreigner."

Charles cleared his throat. "England has been my home for over ten years. I am no longer considered a foreigner." His hand moved from Tena's shoulder to seize the table edge. Maggie secretly wished he would give up his politeness, clout their mother, and be done with it.

Beatrix gave a derisive snort. "Mr. Kisch, when your family has lived here over four hundred years as ours has, I will gladly listen to your arguments. Thankfully I will be dead when that happens. Now get out of my house."

"No, Mother!" Tena cried. "He's not leaving!"

Beatrix marched to the door and screamed for Olivia. When there was no response, she stalked the length of the hall yelling the poor girl's name. Thankfully, after six years in the household, Olivia was smart enough to obey Maggie's orders and steer clear. Beatrix swept back into the dining room and pointed at Maggie. "Show Mr. Kisch the door."

Charles spoke before Maggie could. "Mrs. Archer, with utmost respect, I should have defended Tena long ago. You must listen."

Beatrix held the door open. "You, Mr. Kisch, have overstayed your welcome, for there was no welcome to begin with. Get out!"

"Please—" Charles was cut off by Tena's firm grip on his wrist.

"Maybe you should go," she stated in an attempt to lead him towards the door.

Charles gawked incredulously and refused to comply. "Tena, we agreed—"

"Please, Charles," Tena pled. "I'll call on you tomorrow."

Charles yanked his arm from her reach, and remained silent. Whatever fire he'd lit under himself had been extinguished by seven little words. He exited the room without a backward glance at his fiancé or her family.

Silence fell over the room. Beatrix righted her chair and continued eating. Tena dropped into her seat and stared at her full plate, hands in her lap and eyes brimming with tears. Maggie sat, reeling from the injustice of it all.

No matter her intentions in leaving, she had left Tena to fight her battles alone for the eleven months. If Maggie said nothing now, it was as bad as if she was still in London.

"Mother, if Tena found someone she loves, we should support her."

Beatrix slammed her fork down on the table. "Love has nothing to do with it, Maggie! I know that better than anyone."

"Father loved you," said Maggie quietly, "and we love you too." She didn't like that it was the truth, but there it was. Despite everything, Maggie loved her mother, even if Beatrix did not return her affection.

Beatrix returned to her meal as if Maggie hadn't spoken. "I have half a mind to disown you both."

"Then disown us."

Maggie stared across the table at Tena. No sensible woman would ask to be cut off from her family. "You don't mean that."

Tena peered over her plate. Something smoldered in her eyes like the flint as it meets the spark, the slow simmer before the boil. Palms flat to the table, she leaned in with conviction. "I do mean it. I *am* marrying Charles, Mother. In two days' time, we are leaving England. Maggie's going too. Come with us if you wish. Or stay here. Disown us. Or keep us as your daughters. Do whatever you like. I'm no longer asking permission as I no longer care."

Tena pushed back her chair, threw her napkin on the table, and stalked towards the door.

Maggie dropped her fork. It clattered against her plate. "Where are you going?" she cried.

"To apologize to my fiancé."

"Tena!" Beatrix shouted, but the front door slammed the conversation's conclusion.

The following silence was deafening. Maggie shoveled food in her mouth so she wouldn't have to speak.

"So, you planned to traipse off to another country and leave your poor widowed mother here alone?"

Maggie emptied her wine glass. "You are hardly a victim, Mother."

"Why did Tena bother to tell me now? It's clearly too late to change anything."

Maggie twirled her green beans on her fork. She had never seen eye to eye with her mother. Beatrix told her daughters flat out that sons would have been preferred. She had even now threatened to disown them. Yet Maggie felt compelled to try to make amends for Tena's sake. This was their mother after all; maybe they could still resurrect things.

A nagging voice in the back of her mind acknowledged what a dim-witted endeavor this was, but she ignored it. "It's *not* too late, Mother. You could come with us."

"No, Maggie, I cannot. More importantly, I do not *want* to go with you. You have always been an insolent selfish child. Why else do you think I kept those letters from you and Tena?"

Maggie sprayed green beans across the tablecloth. She should have figured her mother was behind it all. What other reason explained how over four dozen letters were mysteriously *lost in the post*?

Maggie couldn't even muster outrage at her mother's newest low. She wasn't even a bit surprised.

Beatrix laid down her utensils, patted her lips with the napkin, and gave a patronizing smile. "It was embarrassing to hear gossip of my daughter's indiscretions everywhere I went. Having to deny Mr. Halverson's proposal after I worked tirelessly to make him appealing to you. He was perfect, Maggie! I hoped if you thought no one cared where you had gone, you would decide to remain in London permanently. Perhaps later, after you found a suitable husband, we could consider your return."

Maggie stretched for Tena's wine glass. She'd need more than her wits to continue this conversation. "Did father know you did this?"

"Of course not. Your father would never have allowed it."

"How could you keep his death from me?" Maggie couldn't squelch the overwhelming resentment filling her chest. She wrapped her fingers in her skirt to calm the tremors coursing through them.

Beatrix walked across the room to pull the bell for Olivia. "Your father was a deplorable fool. He gave you girls too much. He was so forgiving, and far too lenient. He refused to believe the worst even when it stood right in front of him. Mr. Halverson was still willing to have you after that incident with the Radford boy last May! But your father condoned your disgraceful behavior right until the end." Beatrix moved her hand in front of her eyes and sighed. "Laurence even had the audacity to invite him here."

Maggie straightened. "Reuben was here?"

Beatrix nodded. "The day your father died. I found him leaving Laurence's room only hours before. Your father refused to provide a reason, but I knew why."

"Why?" asked Maggie.

"Oh, Maggie, don't be so thick! You were supposed to marry Mr. Halverson, not throw it all away for some girlish fling. In his final moments, the finality of your father's betrayal was apparent. He chose his daughters over his own wife."

Maggie wanted to scream, to release a torrent of emotions building for years. Unfortunately, railing at her mother wouldn't calm the revulsion she saw in Beatrix's eyes. It wouldn't bring back the months Maggie lost with Tena or magically raise their father from the dead. And it certainly wouldn't create a picture-perfect family.

This was the woman who helped give Maggie life, who held her as a child. She shared Maggie's dark hair and stormy blue-grey eyes. But this woman was also a stranger, a person who looked like Maggie, only didn't understand her at all. She hadn't understood anyone in their family. Even now, the only person Maggie's mother understood was herself. Perhaps not even that.

"I wish you knew how much you don't know," said Maggie. "Father never betrayed you. He simply saw all the things you couldn't."

Maggie thought about her last moment with her father, when he hugged her goodbye at the railway station. It was just the two of them with the promise that he would tell the others when he returned home. "I love you, little girl," he'd said, holding her with such veracity that, in hindsight, she wondered if he suspected it might be the last time they'd have together. "I'll miss you more than anything."

She laughed him off at the time. "Don't be silly, Father. I'll be home before you even have time to miss me."

Those were the last words she ever said to him.

Maggie stared down the expansive table at her mother. She wasn't a little girl anymore and this time she couldn't hide under it to avoid her parents' fighting. All that remained were two grown women and all the words left to be said.

"It doesn't matter anymore what I did or didn't do or should have done. That's over now. What matters is Tena deserves to be loved, and Charles gives her that." Maggie forced a lump down her throat. "My father loved you more than you will ever realize. You will never appreciate the sacrifices he made for you. He was a good man and I wish you knew that."

Maggie left the remainder of her meal untouched. She slowly made her way to the door and paused with her fingers on the knob. One final opportunity for her mother to call after her and offer to put the past behind them. To say it wasn't too late.

Only the minutes continued in silence. Maggie gradually turned the knob and cracked the door. She stared at the wood's smooth grooves, traced their path with her eyes. Still no response.

Olivia's silhouette appeared through the visible space. Maggie was out of time and out of chances.

"I forgive you. You don't deserve it, but I still forgive you." Maggie's words were barely audible, but she knew her mother heard them. "All I hope is someday we will both understand why."

TWENTY-SEVEN

FORGIVENESS. ACCORDING TO THE 1912 edition of the *New Websterian Dictionary*, forgive was defined as "to pardon; remit as a sin, offense, debt." Pardon's definition was simpler: "to absolve." *Absolve*—now that was the one term Reuben struggled with.

Absolve: "To release or set free, clear of crime or guilt."

Absolution required more than a mere apology. He couldn't achieve absolution for his mistakes through any amount of grieving or attempts to change his life for the better. He'd tried.

As Easter's afternoon gradually faded into evening, Reuben passed through his family's familiar rooms with the care of a father tucking his children in for the night. Each space held the memory of a lost life and a forgone future.

Reuben's bedroom was last on the list. He closed the door with the faintest click and observed the place he'd called his own for twenty years. The bed stood lovingly blanketed in his mother's handmade quilt. His father's boyhood stack of worn penny dreadfuls sat on the floor in the corner, now covered in a thin line of dust. Atop his dresser was one of the last photographs of his baby sister, stolen from his mother's belongings after her death. All there to remind him of what might have been.

As a child you're always told one day you'll wake up and

discover you've become your parents. You never believe it. And when you finally do believe it, you hope and pray you've only inherited their endearing qualities and none of their flaws. For some, such as Charles, that was true. But Reuben had never been quite so lucky.

He would leave this life in the same way his parents had: talking to disembodied voices like his mother, brooding in a dark house like his father. He'd been disregarded by his remaining friends and spurned by the woman he loved. "What is the point of it all, Reuben?" his father asked that final Christmas morning. Precisely, Father, precisely.

You live. You die. You're forgotten. His hallucinations told him so. He would end up another indentation on his family's gravestone. A name some youthful girl like Maggie would spin a story for. He hoped his narrative in death was better than the one he had in life.

Mira sat cross-legged on the bed, observing his movements. Reuben didn't want to be constantly haunted by his past, tortured by the mistakes he had made, the promises he couldn't keep, and the people he betrayed. And that's all he could guarantee his life would be. For an instant, a faint glimmer of a moment in the cemetery, he'd dared to believe he could achieve something more. But if it was not meant to be with Maggie, it could not be with anyone.

If Mira was to be his sole companion, then Reuben wanted the real one. He chose the sister who was full of life and love, not this apparition who whittled away at his emotions until he broke in two. He had always believed there was something after this. He believed in a heaven and he wasn't senseless enough to deny there must be a hell then too. Perhaps God would forgive him and he would see his sister again. Maybe He wouldn't and he'd burn for it. But at least his crazy delusions would burn with him.

Absolve: "To release or set free, clear of crime or guilt." Any direction he examined it from, there was only one method left to secure absolution. There was only one guaranteed path to freedom.

Reuben turned down the lamps and drew the curtains, the near darkness throwing stark contrast against his features in the dresser mirror. He wondered when his outward appearance began to reflect the hidden nature of the man within. He felt presentable at Easter service, but now his coat and tie were forgotten downstairs, his shoes thrown in a corner, and weariness washed over his features as plainly as the beard he wore. He was ready.

Reuben reached for the British Bull Dog in his top dresser drawer. Originally belonging to his grandfather, the revolver's legacy would now die with him. Reuben inserted one round into each chamber, five in all. There would be no chance for error.

Mira's face reflected in the mirror. "You're not serious."

"I want to be rid of you. This is the only way I know how."

"If you think I'm going to stop you, I'm not."

"Good. I don't want you to."

"It'll be painful. And messy."

"I hope so. When I woke up this morning, I thought, 'How can I inflict intense amounts of bodily harm on myself today while ensuring that the house gets much needed redecorating? Ah yes, that forty-four father left behind ought to be the ticket. This room will look brilliant in red.'"

Mira raised her eyes to the ceiling. "You're an idiot ..."

"No arguments here."

"... and a coward."

"It's the Radford way. Our family crest reads, 'A family of ordinary birth who turned tail and fled at the provocation of 1912. Look at those pansies run!'"

Reuben managed a faint laugh, until the revolver's weight in his hands dispelled all the humor of the situation. He wiped his palms on his shirt sleeves.

"You can't do this," Mira said furiously. Reuben swore her irises were now the deep tint of day old blood.

He ran his finger through the trigger. "Watch me."

Just count to three and it'll be over, he told himself.

Reuben closed his eyes and raised the revolver to his temple. His brow twinged against the sharp pressure of the icy metal, the weight of the instrument a vice upon his skull.

One. His hand shook violently at the thought of what he was about to do. He was insane. He knew this. But he had no choice.

"Hello? ... Reuben?"

He opened his eyes. Mira hadn't spoken. Was he hearing other voices now? Even more of a reason to end his madness.

Two. "God, please forgive me." If He was merciful, the real Mira would be waiting for Reuben on the other side. If not ...

"*Three*." Reuben's finger twitched above the trigger.

"Go on then," Mira offered. Her face was marred with twisted amusement. She didn't think he would do it, but he couldn't let her win. Not this time.

Reuben watched the person in the mirror. A petrified boy returned his stare, still holding a revolver to his head, eyes silently pleading in terror. Reuben aimed the gun straight at the boy's eyes then back between his own. "Just do it, you horse headed pansy!" Reuben choked. "What are you waiting for?"

"Please, Reuben," the boy whimpered back, as tears worked their way from his eyes. He used the back of his free hand to wipe his face then adjusted his sweaty fingers around the revolver and swallowed.

"Do it," Mira said again.

"Reuben? The door was unlocked..." In slow motion, Reuben turned towards the sound. *That* was no hallucination; he knew her voice.

A sob escaped his throat and he threw the revolver. It skidded across the room and disappeared under the bed. Reuben dropped to the rug, his forehead against his knees, his breath coming in shallow gasps.

Footsteps ascended the stairs, the floorboards creaking loudly in the otherwise silent house. He felt lightheaded. Oxygen wouldn't enter his lungs.

"Are you here? I'm looking for Charles. You will never believe what happened—or perhaps you would—you know how my mother is—" A stretch of light followed the door's standard creak and then, "Reuben?"

Quickened steps crossed the room and Tena fell to her knees beside him. "Are you all right?"

What a stupid question. Does it look like I'm all right? Reuben shrugged her away and kept his head to his knees. "Why are you here?" His voice was hoarse and rough and very much not his own.

Tena's sounded equally strained. "Searching for Charles. We told my mother. I'm afraid he's quite upset over how I handled it."

"Why do you think he's here?" came Reuben's muffled reply.

Tena shifted uneasily. "He's not at his house. I checked there first."

"Of course. Why bother coming here otherwise? Get out, Tena. I'm busy."

"With what?" Tena countered. "Necking the floor, are you? Those boards do look mighty lonely."

"Oh, you're a regular jester. Go away."

Tena smoothed a few long hairs away from Reuben's eyes. Her fingertips lingered lightly against his jaw. "Look at me. What's wrong?"

Reuben vehemently stared at a worn spot in the rug between his legs. The weight in his brow tripled as blood rushed to his head. "I don't need to be mollycoddled."

Tena wiped her hands and stood up. "Fine, Reuben. I've had a difficult enough day without you making it more so. If you want me to leave, I'll leave."

As her dainty shoes slipped out of his peripheral vision, a fresh wave of desolation slammed down. Reuben lunged away from the bed and the revolver's magnetic pull, clutching Tena's ankle. He was drowning and she was his only remaining life line.

Tena instinctively yanked her foot away in an effort to retain her balance. She fell forward anyway, landing hard on her palms. "Reuben, what are you—" Tena rolled onto her hip where her aggravated words ceased with the sight of his haggard form. They hadn't seen one another since Laurence's funeral and Reuben's appearance tonight was far reaching from the man she'd seen then. Lines creased her face in silent question. She probably wondered if she'd interrupted a crazy lunatic about to eat the furniture.

How could he begin to explain? Reuben ran both hands over his eyes as all his facial muscles scrunched in pain. He didn't want to look at her. He didn't want her to look at him.

He waved aimlessly at the door. "I'm sorry, Tena. I'm fine. You should be with Charles."

"I believe that was my line last time," Tena said gently, "and I was far from fine."

The last time she was here was the night her father died. He had comforted her then acted like a ruddy fool, and she forgave him as if it were inconsequential. She'd patiently listened while he explained all about his parents, the decline in his mother's health, and how much he missed them. With Tena there, he'd even managed to forget about his own inner sickness. For one night, his mind had been his and his alone.

"You have no idea what lurks inside me," Reuben began. "Not even Charles knows. If you knew what I live with every day ..." His voice sank so low he couldn't believe Tena had even heard him, but she must have because the next instant her smooth fingers cupped his cheeks to force his eyes to hers. The faintest smile played across her lips. "Then tell me," she breathed. Not a pitiful ask, not a command, only tender interest.

Reuben was seized now by a nearly overwhelming feeling identical to their encounter in Southampton. He wanted—no, needed—Tena to know about Mira. It was essential that *someone* understand. Reuben's eyes searched her face for assurance. Those golden phoenix eyes stared right back daring him—no, offering him—her trust.

"After my sister died, I sometimes see—"

You bloody idiot.

Reuben faltered. His eyes swept the room, searching for Mira, as her omniscient threats seeped into his brain. *Tell her and she'll declare you insane. Charles too. They'll have you committed. You will have spared your life for nothing.* Cackling filled Reuben's ears with the force of a roaring wind.

And in that second the good feeling was gone. It mattered little what he wanted; Tena was his best friend's fiancé and the sister of the woman who already rejected him. If he couldn't trust Charles or Maggie with the tortures of his mind first, he couldn't trust Tena either. Better for Tena to assume he was just a brilliant cur.

Reuben swatted Tena away and yelled in frustration. He struggled to his feet, hauling Tena up by the elbow and over to the open door. "Get out," Reuben growled.

Tena edged across the threshold. "I only wanted to help."

Reuben advanced, forcing Tena into the narrow hallway. There was one confession he felt compelled to make, which also proved a useful cover for his altered emotional state. "I went to London the day of your father's funeral."

Tena's face went slack. "Why?"

Reuben laughed. It was an ironic bitter sound that only added to the madman affect he was exuding. But if he didn't laugh he would break down and cry like a little baby. "Why do you think? Maggie wasn't there for your father. I wanted her to know that in my eyes that was the worst mistake she could ever make."

"It wasn't like that!" Tena said excitedly. "Didn't she explain? Oh, Reuben, I was angry with her too. I was near on to almost hating her for what she did until she explained everything! Didn't she tell you?" Tena's words fizzled out with the cold fire of Reuben's glare.

"He was your *father*, Tena. How can you forgive her for that?"

Tena maintained his gaze. "Maggie never received my letters. She had no idea Father was so bad off."

"Ha!" Reuben leaned against the wall. It tore him up to say his next words, although he found himself doing so effortlessly. "Tena, you're so naive. That's the same cock and bull story she fed me, but she's lying. She doesn't care about you. Maggie never cared about any of us. She found something better and she took it."

Tena glared at Reuben. "Why are you being so cruel? You, of all people, should understand. My father's gone! She's all the family I have!" Tena pointed her finger in Reuben's face and shouted, "I know you love her! Stop being a coward and admit how you feel."

Without waiting for a reply, Tena stormed from the house. Reuben followed as far as the entryway. The evening sun burned his eyes after the darkness upstairs.

"See?" said Mira. "You don't have any friends. Not really. Shall we go upstairs and finish our little game?"

Three seconds and it could all be over. For him at least. Not for the person who found what was left of him. Reuben understood the agony of seeing his little sister's mangled body in an end she would never have chosen. Thinking how he'd almost inflicted the same horror on Tena sent a furious pulse grinding against his skull. If he chose to do that to someone else, anyone else, his soul deserved to be tortured for all eternity.

"I knew you couldn't do it," said Mira with a cold calculating smirk. "You know you'll never be rid of me now."

Reuben watched Tena's retreating back. "I know."

BANG!

Reuben startled as a wind gust sent the coat rack crashing. His one lonely overcoat hadn't been heavy enough to keep it upright. From the coat's creases peeked a worn envelope twice now forgotten.

Reuben retrieved the letter as he righted the rack. The envelope was crinkled, but the seal was still intact. The letter beckoned him to Maggie like a siren calling him to his death on the crag.

He struck across the yard. Laurence had one last message for his daughter, and Reuben was going to make sure she received it.

"Stop!" Mira yelled after him. "Talk to Maggie, and you may as well take the revolver with you."

Reuben didn't turn around. His jaw set in determination. "That's why I'm not giving it to Maggie."

TWENTY-EIGHT

TWO MINUTES. THAT'S HOW LONG Reuben expected his visit to last. He could maybe shorten it to one minute if Olivia didn't ask any additional questions.

She would open the door. He would nod and hold out the letter. *Good evening, ma'am. Please give this to Miss Maggie Archer,* he'd say. Olivia, not recalling his face after a year's passing, would ask, *Who is the sender?* He'd reply, *It no longer matters.* Being an orderly servant, she would refrain from further prompting and wish him a good night.

Easy as pie.

Reuben rang the bell and made a last ditch effort to mollify his appearance. He buttoned, tucked, and snapped his shirt and suspenders into place. He wished he'd restrained himself long enough to fetch his shoes before streaking across town. His bare soles now screamed from the trek.

"Is that better or worse than your brains splattered across the wall?" asked Mira.

"Shove off," muttered Reuben. She blessedly complied as the door opened.

One very irritated Tena glowered back at him. "What do *you* want?"

Well that didn't go as planned.

He brandished the envelope. "This is from your father."

Tena's fingers settled across her hip. "That's a terrible joke. I think you should leave."

"I'm not trying to be funny. This really is from your father."

Tena's expression switched from aggravation to incredulity. "You're serious? How? Father's dead."

"It was the day you brought me here. Truth is I forgot I still had it."

Tena accepted the letter gingerly. Her fingers slid over the envelope with something akin to wistful nostalgia.

"Thank you, Reuben," she whispered. "Father's last words to us. This means so much."

Reuben shuffled his feet and focused on the second story windows. The second to last one was open. He wondered if it was Maggie's. "Um ... He, ah, only gave me the one letter. For Maggie."

"Oh. Just the one?"

"I'm sorry." And he was. So much so that he wanted to forge another letter himself.

Luckily, Tena was blazingly fast at recomposing herself. She slipped the envelope in her pocket and smoothed down the folds of her skirt. "Well, no matter. I'll see that Maggie receives it. Good night."

"Wait." Reuben's fingers caught hers and held on. "Earlier, I didn't mean to imply that your feelings don't matter. They mean a great deal to me. My life is just a mess right now and you happened to walk in at ... well, a time when I was less than impressive with my manners."

Tena cocked her head to the side. "That almost sounded like an apology."

"Was that your way of accepting my contrition?"

Tena's lip curled in a half smile. "Consider it as such. You know I can't stay mad at you for long."

"Good, because I hate it when you are." He released her hand. "Did you find Charles?"

Tena sighed. "No. He doesn't want to see me and I cannot blame him. Not after the bomb I dropped on Mother this afternoon."

"You reduced your mother to a pile of ashes? Look at you, you feisty she-devil." Reuben pretended to wipe a tear from his eye. "I've got to say, I'm proud."

Tena frowned. "I'm truly not in the mood. If you can't be serious, then leave."

Reuben had two choices: concede and run further risk of uncomfortable associations with his botched un-fiancé or go home to contemplate what was left of his sorry life. Some choice there.

He pulled the door shut, forcing Tena onto the porch with him. "I apologize ... again. Why don't we walk and you can take your mind off it?"

"But you're barefoot," Tena asserted. "Why exactly *are* you barefoot?"

"That's a terribly long story for another day. I don't mind though."

"Nonsense. Wait here." Tena disappeared into the house and quickly returned with a pair of men's socks balled inside patent leather oxfords. "Here."

"Thanks." Although a tad large, the shoes were an almost perfect fit.

Evening faded into night as they strolled down Union Street, over the ridge alongside the cemetery's border, and on farther still to the town square. As they walked, Tena shared the tale of that evening's confessions to her mother, sending Charles away, and including in no uncertain terms exactly how she felt about her mother's reaction to their engagement. Reuben listened without interruption, savoring the cool breeze against his face and his friend's hand in the crook of his arm. Warm light patterned the walk from homes merry with Easter celebration. Only the town's center lay dormant, shades drawn until business commenced the following day. Except for a stray passing carriage, they were alone.

The lamplighter emerged right on schedule. His nightly routine flickered the roads into life with dozens of glowing pools under the moon's waning form. The light rested upon the maypole erected in the center of the green to rehearse for the upcoming festival. Colorful ribbons wrapped the timber, secured at top and bottom with twine.

Tena slid her arm from Reuben's to run her fingers over the fabric. "It seems strange to not celebrate this year. Or buy a new dress. Or hope someone will notice me for once. To please my mother. So much of my life that was what I wanted. Now all I want is to be Mrs. Kisch." Her fingers fell slack. She turned her back to the maypole and offered Reuben a withered smile. "Then I insulted my fiancé *and* asked my mother to disown me. Am I so very foolish?"

"Foolish is not a word I would ever use for you. Charles will forgive you, and your mother ... well, sometimes our parents are who they are."

"At least Maggie seems to understand. I expected her to be least forgiving about my engagement. You know how she feels about that sort of thing."

"Do I ever."

Tena pressed two fingers to her lips and gave a little smirk. "And how exactly *would* you know?"

Blast, though Reuben. He'd walked straight into that. "It's Maggie. She may as well carry a sign that reads, 'I detest all men.'"

Tena's eyes narrowed. "Don't be cheeky. I put up with six months of your painfully obvious feelings disguised as unobtrusive questions. I found you in the midst of an emotional contusion after talking to her this morning. Plus you're dressed like a disgusting vagabond. Something went on between you today and I want to know what it is." She folded her arms, leaned against the maypole, and waited.

Reuben sighed. He'd had so many perplexing encounters with the Archer women in the last few months, at this point in the game, what was one more? He held up a finger. "Mistake number one, never trust Maggie with your emotions. She'll slap you with them harder than a baby's bottom on their birthday."

Tena's brow furrowed. "Excuse me?"

"It's simple, m'lady. *You* told me—many times I might add including tonight—to acknowledge my *undying attraction* as you put it."

Tena smirked. "You picked up on those subtle hints, did you?"

"Yeah. I did. And the not so subtle ones. And I believe I refuted your suspicions many times."

"But I was right, wasn't I?" Tena said smugly.

"Are you telling the story or am I?"

"Sorry."

"So I took your advice. I told her how I felt. She didn't feel the same. I was hurt. I overreacted. End of story."

"Oh."

"That's all you have to say? Oh?" It was a bit disappointing after all the work up. He'd expected a lengthier inquisition.

Tena pinched the bridge of her nose and exhaled. "What do you want me to say? I'm disappointed. I always thought you'd be the one to calm her down. Maybe even have you for a brother someday. But you tried and it obviously didn't work. I don't understand Maggie any more than you do. Just make me one promise."

"Anything."

"Stop being a loner locked away in that dismal house of yours. Find someone else to spend your life with. And please don't end up with Edith *or* Bianca."

"What about Edith *and* Bianca?" Reuben jabbed. "Is that on the table?"

Tena laughed. "Goodness, you are incorrigible."

"I try to be." It seemed so strange for Reuben to laugh only hours after he'd almost given up. He would miss this after Tena and Charles left ... Reuben pulled her to him; it didn't matter if a thousand rumors circulated now. "I'll miss you, Tena."

"Me too, Reuben."

"Write to me from the States, will you? Tell me when you set the wedding date. Do you think Charles will inherit some odd accent once you're there? Begin spouting random American phrases like he does English ones?"

Tena's cheek rested upon his shoulder, her warm breath fluttering against his Adam's apple. The pace of her heart quickened at Reuben's question. "Reuben?" she whispered. "Can I make a completely insane proposal?"

Oh bugger, what could this mean? Reuben thought. Tena didn't make insane proposals. Well, except for the time she'd stolen her father's money and led them on a crazy escapade in Southampton. And tonight when she'd openly defied her mother and admitted to "fraternizing" with Germans. What could be left for her to accomplish?

Not that he could talk. Today alone, he'd proposed to Maggie, contemplated suicide, thrown a fit in front of Tena, and had a lengthy conversation with his dead sister. Nope, that wasn't insane at all.

Reuben absently ran his fingers through Tena's hair. If a season could even have a scent, hers smelled of impending summer. Lilac, fresh baked pie, and the perfume after a rain shower. Reuben squeezed her tighter. "Don't worry," he whispered back. "We're all mad here. I'm mad. You're mad."

"How do you know I'm mad?" Tena quipped.

"You must be or you wouldn't have come here."

Tena grinned. *"Alice's Adventures in Wonderland."*

"I love that you know that."

"It's my favorite."

"One of mine too." Tena lifted her head from Reuben's shoulder. Her eyes glowed softly in the moonlight, never once leaving his gaze. It was a new feeling for him. Maggie was exactly the opposite; when she had something important to say, she refused to meet his eyes. Attempting to scry Maggie's true emotions was like beating on a door that never opened.

Maggie and Tena might have been sisters, but the closer Reuben became to them, the more he discovered how very different the girls truly were.

Tena released a quick exhale and rushed forward. "Charles is my fiancé, but you are his dearest friend. He doesn't have enough gumption to ask this of you—men never suggest such things—but I know it breaks his heart to think we may never see you again. Goodness, this is difficult to even ask ... but would you be willing..." Tena stepped away, shook her hands out, wiped her palms on her skirt, and began again. "Reuben, might you consider coming with us?"

A mere seven hours ago those words were all he dreamt of hearing from Maggie's lips. He'd done everything to convince her and she'd taken a cleaver to his scrawny neck.

Sometimes in life you were the chef and sometimes you were the chicken.

Reuben didn't want to be the chicken anymore.

Chickens were pathetic birds. They couldn't even fly properly. Plus they were one of God's more unattractive creatures. Reuben wanted to be something a little less depressing, like an eagle or a falcon. He'd even settle for a common sparrow.

His father's gun sat under his bed, inviting him to return. To bite the bullet if you will. Reuben's mental state was so fragile right now that, left to his own devices, he might be only a few lonely weeks away from changing his mind. Better to take some risks now and potentially change his life than sit by helplessly waiting for the slaughter.

"Tell me where to go and when to be there."

"Oh! *Wunderbar!*" Tena exclaimed and for once Reuben decided to bite his tongue. He spun Tena in a tight circle, throwing her off balance and nearly twisting her ankle. "Gah, what was that for?"

Reuben grinned. "Are you going to tell Charles you asked me to run away with you?"

Tena made a swipe at him. "Stop it," she scolded, although her upturned lips betrayed her. "I'll bring your passage by tomorrow evening. You may pay me back then."

"Nonsense. I'll go with you. A lady shouldn't bash about London by herself."

Tena placed a hand on each hip and gave Reuben a cold stare. "A *lady* shouldn't bash at all."

Reuben laughed. "Allow me to rephrase. A lady shouldn't gracefully stroll through the downtrodden streets of London alone."

She nodded. "Thank you, much better. And I wouldn't be alone. I'll tell Charles the news in the morning and ask him to escort me." Tena's gaze sank. "Unless tonight convinced him to call everything off."

"There's not a chance of that," Reuben assured her. "Leave Charles to me. I'll tell him the plan and charge a taxi to collect you at, say, nine? We'll have lunch together in London. Just like old times."

Tena looped her arm through Reuben's with a smile. "Good. I've missed old times."

PART TWO

~~~

Treacherous Waters

TWENTY-NINE

"Stop scolding, Tena. We will not be late."

Maggie hefted her case onto the hotel room bed, removed the entirety of its contents, and began the task of collecting yesterday's garments strewn across the carpet. Rather than fight the rush of passengers on the morning transit to Southampton, Charles booked two rooms for the prior night. Unfortunately, because it was closest in proximity to Berth 44, he chose the Goshawk Inn and Tavern, the same hotel she and Reuben occupied last May Day.

Tena bounced down beside her, folding clothing as Maggie tossed them upon the duvet. "You should have packed before breakfast like I did," Tena stated. "Also, speaking of breakfast, Bianca told me once how all White Star Line meals are positively sinful. 'You'll feel as though you've lost your innocence to those little floozies,' she told me. 'Wrapped up in decadence, each bite is like an exquisite little tart!'" Tena's pitch raised an octave on the last phrase, giving a prime rendition of Maggie's least favorite Winchester sister.

Glancing up from repacking, Maggie cast a dark look through her lashes. "Sound like Bianca again and I *will* toss you into the harbor."

"You would not." Tena picked up Maggie's stockings, folded one across the other and deposited them into the case. "I left a letter for Edith and Bianca with the front desk this morning. Think how jealous they'll be when they hear we're on *Titanic*."

Ducking below the bed for yesterday's shoes, Maggie managed to conceal an eye roll. It was precisely like the Winchesters to faint in distress over missing the social highlight of the month, while Maggie, for one, couldn't fathom why any ship should be considered newsworthy.

Olivia had nearly lost her mind when Maggie tried to express the depths of her indifference. She danced across Maggie's room, organizing the war zone of strewn belongings into their assigned trunks.

"*Titanic!*" she exclaimed. "My cousin, Maude, accompanied the Adelaires on *Olympic* and says it was the grandest around! Important people, exquisite food, beautiful decor ... pomp and circumstance, snooty rich folks overreacting." Maggie's brain turned off somewhere around "exquisite food", so she could really only guess at the actual remainder of Olivia's approbation.

Regardless of society's opinions on the matter, to Maggie the ship was nothing more than an oversized boat constructed of steel and wood, the same as any built before her. In fact, give or take a few details, the aforementioned *Olympic* had been built to nearly *Titanic*'s exact specifications. Maggie's fellow staff members followed the *London Times*' coverage of the *Olympic*'s maiden voyage last June with the same fervor they probably sought now for *Titanic*. Why, Maggie hadn't the faintest.

Did everyone get all excited when someone purchased a new carriage or motorcar? Did they fall to pieces over a new locomotive on the rail lines? No. Nor would she.

"I would think," Maggie told Tena as she bent to retrieve her chemise from the floor, "That the Winchesters would be more upset you deprived them of a year's worth of gossip over your illicit romance. You did remember to tell them that little bit about Charles, didn't you?"

"Of course I did." Tena gave a shy smile. "Every toe-curling detail."

Maggie's jaw hung slack as she took that in. Then she tossed a pair of silky cream bloomers at Tena with a saucy grin. "Tena Elizabeth Archer! Edith was right—you are a naughty girl!"

A bold blush brightened Tena's cheeks. "Not at all. But they don't need to know that." She shook her head, depositing the bloomers into Maggie's case. "In truth, I'm thankful Charles is too honorable to even propose such a thing. Our first night together has me in knots, and it's still a year away. It seems unbelievably strange to allow him to see me in that way." Tena removed the embroidered mourning shawl from atop her own case, the silken black fringe flowing through her fingers. She folded, unfolded, and refolded the shawl, rubbing the fibers between her thumbs. "I shouldn't say these things. You'll think I'm afraid of being a bride."

Maggie stole the shawl from Tena's hands, swinging it around her sister to knot above Tena's breastbone. "Not at all. I suspect we're all afraid the first time ... at least a little. If you can't tell your sister then really, whoever would you expect to listen? But one word of advice? Given the right conditions—such as relief from parental disapproval—propriety is a quickly fleeting thing. Don't be surprised if Charles's honor only survives as far as the ship's gangplank."

Tena turned scarlet from her ears straight beneath her black crepe trimmed collar, but Maggie could tell embarrassment was only half the reason for her crimson features. With a hasty tug, She untied the shawl, wadding it in a tangled mess before smashing it into her traveling case. Securing the latches, she narrowed her eyes at the silver timepiece pinned to her dress, and pressed her lips into a tight line. "Do hurry, won't you? We're to leave for the pier at eleven. It's nearly half past ten now."

Maggie scooped up the rest of her belongings, tossed them into the case without care, and dashed after Tena, finally catching up to her in the tiny parlor. The girls claimed the table beside one of two windows on the front wall, the other two green and gold papered walls hidden behind a blazing modestly-paneled fireplace flanked by floor to ceiling bookshelves. Besides their table, a young couple barely older than themselves sat in the opposite corner. Another couple with two school-aged children occupied the third sitting area comprised of a navy flowered sofa and two crimson armchairs. Charles hadn't arrived yet.

Outside the window beyond the few remaining fishing boats, a sea-weathered tugboat labeled *Neptune* churned across the waves and out of sight, traveling in the same direction as the carriages and motorcars pressing their path through traffic to Berth 44. Stacks of luggage were the only indication of which carried ship's passengers versus launch observers hoping to claim the day's passing fancy. Whether passenger or observer, they knew their destination—their plan. Was it of their own devising? Was Maggie's? She felt so free when she slammed the door to her old life yesterday afternoon; why now did the old questions keep crawling back?

"I'm sorry for what I said about Charles," Maggie said, turning away from the window. "Buried deep, I wonder if I'm not jealous of you. You have everything worked out. And I hardly know where I'll be tomorrow."

Tena maintained her gaze on the harbor. "London has made you extremely ill-mannered. If you *are* jealous of me—which I very much doubt—you may wish to refrain from flapping your opinions and causing general disgrace to what's left of our family."

Maggie held up a hand in protest. "That is simply uncalled for."

Tena waited a breath and turned to face her sister. "Regardless, I would hardly consider being disowned by my own mother 'having everything worked out.' However, it does mean something that *you* think so." The wisp of a smile pulled at Tena's lips, the mid-day sun spilling across her face through the window.

"Do you think I'm an idiot for leaving Lloyd behind?" blurted Maggie. She hadn't intended to ask, hadn't even thought about her decision in nearly a week. Not since the day she returned home and wondered if becoming Mrs. Lloyd Halverson would have made a difference in anything. Now, sitting here, only an ocean's distance away from Tena becoming less sister and mostly wife, Maggie couldn't help but consider what she would do without her.

Tena examined Maggie's features. "Are you sorry you did?"

Maggie paused, watching the young couple at the corner table. The man tilted his head forward, sliding his finger over the girl's wedding band as he spoke. His wife's lips parted slightly, eyes twinkling with her response. "No," Maggie said firmly, returning her focus to her own conversation. "But he *would* have made a fine partner. Wealthy, charismatic, well-traveled. I would have had everything and gone anywhere I wanted. Mother and Father approved. And it seemed you even liked him.

"I did ..." Tena gave a slight shake of her head. "Except you don't love him."

"No, that's true, only that's the best kind of marriage. Isn't it? Look what happened to Father. It's easier when you're not attached."

"Nothing has been simple since I met Charles. What is easy doesn't matter to him over what is right." A soft smile flitted over Tena's lips. "It's why I love him."

Maggie frowned. "Do you really believe honor will always prevail in the face of disaster?"

Tena chuckled. "That's my sister, always the cynic. I do wish you would at least *try* not to take after Mother so much."

While Maggie knew her sister to be joking, the words still ran a barb. It was indeed a worry she'd played over before in her mind— if she shared her Mother's outward appearance, was there a part of her destined to mirror the inside as well? True to fashion, their mother didn't leave them with so much as a "Good luck" or even a "Goodbye" when her daughters departed their childhood home.

Even a "Good riddance" would have evoked some emotion regarding their exodus. Beatrix behaved as Maggie had when she went to London, disappearing before her daughters woke with no explanation and no farewell.

Tena cried as they closed the door to number seven, Union Street with a depressing finality. "Perhaps it is too difficult to see her babies leave her."

Maggie watched as each familiar house passed by the taxi window, wishing she didn't feel the tug at her heartstrings seeing them go. Fontaine was her home for nearly twenty years. This place buried her father, and she would miss *him* every day. But she would not miss her mother. Could not miss her. It was impossible to miss someone who was never really there to begin with. "To have babies you must be a mother," she told Tena as the taxi turned off Union Street for the final time. "A mother loves her children. Beatrix Archer was many things, but I doubt she was ever our mother."

"Do you think we'll ever see her again?" Tena asked, picking at the Goshawk's frayed lace tablecloth.

Maggie watched Tena's nails unravel the threads of a flower. "Oh, Tena, I know how difficult this must be. You always valued Mother's opinion, which is something I never cared about, yet even still—I tried. Believe me, I tried to make her understand for your sake."

She reached across the table to press a reassuring squeeze onto the hand now containing Tena's engagement band, and invited Tena's eyes to meet her own. "We may not have Mother," Maggie said gently, "but we do have each other. And you never have to hide what you want from me. Promise, no more secrets?"

Tena's eyes went wide. She slid her hand from Maggie's grasp and began fervently twisting her new ring against her knuckle. "Perhaps one more secret to tell?" she said.

The fire did nothing to keep the chill of Tena's tone from sweeping across Maggie's skin. "What did you do?"

"Please don't hate me."

"Why would I— " Maggie's heart faltered. Tena used that same phrase once before; the inflection in her tone matching beat for beat. Last May Day, seconds before Maggie opened the dining room door to find Charles and next to him ...

Twisting in her seat, Maggie scanned the entirety of the parlor until her sight fell on the open doorway, across the foyer, and into the tavern on the other side. There, seated in jovial discussion with Charles, was the very person she had planned to never see again. Lines crinkled the corners of Reuben's eyes in a way she hadn't seen before, or perhaps only never noticed. The desperate man who proposed to her seemed to have vanished. Gone too was the lonely boy she'd first met in the cemetery. Before her now remained a man fashioned of a very handsome nature: charcoal suit, watch chain dangling against his trousers, and a sturdy leather satchel at his side. Unkempt hair and neglect were now exchanged for a sleek trim and smooth face. His repose juxtaposed to the tension seizing her neck and shoulders.

For a second, barely longer than a breath, those chocolate eyes met hers followed by a nearly imperceptible nod of acknowledgement without a hint of animosity. The left corner of his mouth crept into a shy half smile, asking her to remember his proposal only days before.

Stay with me, Maggie.

Her heart shocked back into motion, swinging herself back around to meet Tena's anxious expression. A nervous laugh escaped, half twittering wren, half caw of the raven. She cleared her throat and waved a hand behind her. "Your worry will age you before your time. Why would I hate you because Reuben came to see us off?"

Tena reached for Maggie's hand, however instead of the same reassuring squeeze she expected, Tena flattened Maggie's palm to the table underneath her own.

"What is the matter with you?" Maggie yanked her hand away and failed. Clearly she had underestimated her timid sister's physical strength as well as everything else lately. "Will you please let go?"

"No. You're hot-headed when it comes to Reuben. You don't think clearly. And I do not want you to ruin this entire voyage for me."

Maggie rolled her eyes. "Well, that's a bit melodramatic, and hurtful, I might add. I am perfectly capable of controlling my emotions for the next ten minutes he's here. I'm not five, Tena."

Tena drew in a breath and slowly shook her head, the same as one might react to a petulant child who'd already been told twice to listen and refused to comply. She released Maggie's hand and folded her own in her lap. "Reuben's not here to see us off," Tena stated flatly. "He's here because he's coming with us, and I need your word you will be civil."

Tena should be thankful they weren't still holding hands. Maggie might have dug her nails in until Tena's palm bled. *Eyes open, Maggie,* she told herself. *Eyes ahead.* But all she saw was a red haze sweeping over and ruining everything. There was only one reason why Reuben would uproot his life for an unknown country in the course of two days' time. If he was chasing her in hopes of a second chance he was out of his bleedin' mind.

She could promise civility. Of course she could. But with Reuben civility only went so far.

THIRTY

"HOW WOULD YOU SUPPOSE MAGGIE is taking the news?" asked Charles. He swallowed the last swig of his ale and slid the empty glass to the table's center.

Reuben didn't know what to make of Maggie's wild hand gestures. When she'd seen him watching her, her reaction could only be described as a hint of delight mixed with a heaping spoonful of acrid astonishment. The fact that he, even now, found that look alluring confirmed he needed to invest in a psychiatrist post haste. The fact that it was Maggie pushing him to consider a shrink and not the crazy wonderland in his head confirmed his priorities were seriously off balance.

"Judging from your fiancé's expression," Reuben said, "I'd say Maggie's taking it the same way she takes everything else—by being difficult." Although Maggie had turned her back to him, Reuben still retained a clear view of Tena. He recognized the nearly indistinguishable crinkle in her brow and tightly upturned lips as an indication of her exasperation. It was the way she said, "I know you're wrong, but arguing is a hopeless endeavor." Whenever he saw that look at the conclusion of a conversation with Charles, there was guaranteed to be a follow-up exchange with Reuben about her true feelings. He should pencil it in now: *Listen to Tena rant about Maggie's obstinacy. 3 p.m. Aft Boat*

Deck.

Charles eyed his fiancé with barely an acknowledgement. "She does not appear too upset. Besides Tena assured us Maggie would be pleased."

Reuben downed the remainder of his own beer, leaving his fingers curled around the empty glass. "No, she assured us Maggie would be cordial. That isn't the same thing. It would translate closer to begrudging politeness."

"Ignore her complaints, Radford. I, for one, am certainly glad you are with me." Charles arched one brow. "Does my opinion count for so little?"

The morning following Easter, true to his word, Reuben spoke with Charles. He explained everything, including his conversation with Tena at the maypole and dim-witted proposal to Maggie, and minus his conversation with Mira and near decision to paint the walls red. Charles, as expected, was quick to forgive his fiancé and exuberant to have Reuben along for the ride. Reuben had to hand it to his friend; Charles listened to his sad sob story from dismal beginning to promising end with more attention than it deserved. Reuben had been a sorry excuse for a friend these last long years, and it wasn't any wonder Charles sought refuge with Tena.

Not anymore. Never again would their friendship suffer at Reuben's hands. His morning dawned to sunlight streaming through his hotel window and Mira hadn't visited in three days. Coupled with the spring in his step, Tena's impromptu invitation couldn't have offered him more opportunity for future happiness. And he wasn't about to allow Maggie's sour mood to cloud his own.

Reuben stood, bending to lift his satchel strap over his head so it lay flat across his sternum. "Not at all." He grinned. "Mates for life, right? I'll always need you to talk my sorry self away from the next fool headed thing I decide to do."

"As if you would listen." Charles tossed their drink expense on the table and pushed his own chair back. "You were not so brash a few years ago."

"That's the funny thing about time, Charles. Fight it if you like, but it always changes things." Reuben rolled one shoulder then the other, swinging his arms in front of him. "Now then ... Race you to the girls?"

Not waiting for a response, Reuben sprinted across the room. Charles let out a yell and gave chase, narrowly avoiding a middle-aged couple to snatch the tail of Reuben's jacket and bowl them both against the girls' table. Tena threw her hands out to cease its descent into the wall, eliciting laughter from the school children on the couch in the corner and a sharp cluck of disapproval from their mother.

"Our sincerest apologies," Charles nodded to the family, then took residence beside Tena's chair, gently bending to kiss her crown. "I have missed you, darling."

Tena smiled, tilting her chin upwards. "It's only been an hour since breakfast. We spent longer apart while we slept."

Charles returned her smile as he brushed a stray hair from her cheek. "I want to make up for every minute we lost."

"You are both positively nauseating," Maggie noted. She retrieved a pair of black gloves from her handbag, wriggling into the close fitted fingers before turning her own sights on Reuben standing over her. Nothing in her eyes indicated discomfort or pleasure either way. "'Morning, Reuben."

Reuben plastered on what he hoped passed for a completely-platonic-let's-forget-what-happened-before smile. "Good morning, Maggie. It's nice to see you."

Maggie couldn't hide her surprise. "Is it? Why didn't you tell me your travel plans when last we spoke?"

Reuben shifted, all too well aware of Tena and Charles's close proximity. "It was a spur-of-the-moment decision."

"Interesting. You seem to be making quite a few of those lately."

"Yes, well, spontaneous decisions are like shots of whiskey. The first one might burn like fire, but each subsequent glass hurts a little less so why not drink another?" Reuben moved his attention to Charles then, interrupting a silent exchange between him and Tena. Reuben didn't need to be an expert at lip-reading to catch Charles's last words as, *Can we take our own ship?*

"So, Kisch," Reuben said. "Should we head to the ship? I'd like to roam about before lunch and then maybe we can take to the smoking room for cards? Let the ladies do whatever it is ladies do in their parlor."

Charles exchanged another look with Tena, this time somewhere between sympathetic and merely finding Reuben pathetic which he found condescending. He was not moping, nor had he given any indication of the sort to Charles or Tena since their initial conversations. And he had no intention of becoming a sniveling mess now.

Maggie threw her hands in the air. "If there's something on your minds, for heaven's sake just say it. Don't keep us guessing."

Charles ignored her. "Reuben, did you know Ireland was named after a goddess?"

Reuben ran his fingers through his hair, startled to come up short from his recent trim. "I did, yes, but blimey, what is your point?"

Charles entwined his left fingers with Tena's right, brushing a delicate kiss on her brow. "This woman is a rare commodity to be treasured far above any goddess. Reuben, you captured my attentions last evening, and this morning, and at some point, it is my intention to level you in shuffleboard. When we sail from port in Ireland tomorrow, come find me. Until then I belong to Tena alone."

"I suppose I'm nothing more than an unnecessary wheel then?" Maggie admonished.

"Of course not!" Tena exclaimed, snatching Maggie's arm with her free hand. She nodded at Reuben. "Reuben, you've been appointed."

"For what?"

"Maggie needs a ship escort," began Tena, eliciting a resounding, "No. I certainly do not," from her sister. She cast Maggie a pointed look. "This will give you both a chance to work out your unresolved issues."

"Fine with me. I have no unresolved issues," stated Reuben at the same time Maggie spat, "Not a chance. I'd rather leave them unresolved."

"Maggie ... please," Tena said. "You promised me you'd try."

Maggie rose abruptly from her chair, leaning over her sister and elbowing Reuben in the process. Her nails dug into the table edge. "I promised you I'd be civil. I never promised to spend the voyage under false pretenses. You are not Mother so don't you dare assign me an escort. Especially not *him*."

Failing to keep his annoyance in check, Reuben caught the opposite edge of the table in his own grip and found his face barely a foot from Maggie's. This was not where he'd intended to end this conversation, but so be it. "There's that phrase again: *especially not me*. What is it about *me* in particular that you find so revolting? You could at least be a bit more polite after you—"

"After I what?" Maggie demanded. "After I rejected you because you made a ridiculous request?"

"It wasn't so ridiculous. Of course, I forgot people call you the 'perpetual spinster'. Definition should have spoken for itself."

Maggie smirked. "Maybe you just don't have what it takes for a girl to say yes."

Reuben returned her smug look. "Bianca? Edith? They were more than happy in my company a year ago. Tena was even considering me before Charles came along."

"Preposterous," Maggie scoffed. "As though Tena would ever be seriously interested in you."

Tena laughed at Charles's raised eyebrow. "I wasn't. I only promised him a dance at Christmas."

"A dance and a night alone on his porch," muttered Maggie.

Reuben's jaw dropped. He couldn't have concealed the shock

on his face if he'd tried. Utter and complete silence filled the room from every corner as he became painfully aware of six complete strangers watching their conversation like the latest theatrical production. Only then was he able to step away and pray Maggie wouldn't say any more about that night. Hopefully, she didn't know ...

Tena leapt to her feet, a deep flush brightening her skin from collar to hairline. "I told you that in confidence, Maggie." Another agonizing moment passed before Tena finally spoke again. To her credit, she met Charles's eyes with unwavering confidence. "I went to Reuben's the night Father died. We talked, nothing more. I promise."

Nothing more than my attempt to kiss your fiancé, thought Reuben, but he would rather cut out his own tongue before admitting to that obscene blunder. If he admitted it, Charles would probably remove Reuben's tongue for him.

Instead of acknowledging Tena's statement or knocking Reuben out, however, Charles turned his anger on Maggie. "I cannot understand why you would say that. Are you wanting to ruin this for us?"

Maggie shrugged. "I cannot understand why you didn't already know."

Charles possessively placed Tena's arm through his own. "I believe my fiancé. I trust her. I do not, however, trust you yet. I invited you to come with us as a measure of good faith because I believe you have Tena's best interests at heart. Do *not* prove me wrong." He flicked his gaze in the direction of the mantel clock. "It is nearly eleven. If we are finished bickering, we should make our way to the ship."

Hefting his satchel, Reuben dug a hand into the bag, rearranging his few belongings as much to ensure his passage and money were in close reach as to give Tena and Charles some privacy. Not fully trusting the entirety of his valuables on board in the cargo hold or with the purser, Reuben had stashed inside his satchel a large sum of cash along with his few family heirlooms, a selection of his father's penny dreadfuls, and his worn out copy of *The Time Machine*. He sold his father's British Bull Dog to the estate agent when he signed over the papers on the Radford home. There was no guarantee how quickly a buyer would be located, but the agent promised to see to maintenance and forward payment when one was found.

"Are you planning to join us?" Reuben asked Maggie, who remained firmly planted beside the window. Behind them, the clock chimed out the eleventh hour, and the remainder of the room cleared, assumedly for Berth 44.

The young married gentleman offered Reuben a sympathetic glance as he passed by, tucking his wife's arm tighter within his own. "Good luck, mate," he whispered. If this was how the remainder of the week would go or, heaven forbid, this absurdity continued on the mainland, he would need much more than luck to survive it.

Maggie pulled her attentions away from the harbor. "Give me an honest answer, Reuben—when we make it to America, do you plan to live in St. Louis?"

"Of course. Didn't Tena tell you?"

"She did, although I would have preferred to hear it from you," Maggie crossed her arms in defiance. "Now that you've confirmed it, unless you also plan to give up seeing Tena and Charles, we're stuck with each other. And I can't accept that."

"We can't even live in the same town?" Reuben sputtered. "That's absurd! I thought you were willing to be normal about this." He gripped his satchel strap, flexing his fingers in irritation. He was more than apt to be civil, and had every intention of accommodating Maggie's erratic emotions, but only if she occasionally gave him something remotely reasonable to work with. Her mood had already taken a couple left turns this morning, and it was all he could do not to shoot back expletives until his throat was raw.

"Maggie, you're being ridiculous," Tena interjected.

"Tena is correct," Charles agreed. "We will be in close quarters on this ship, but St. Louis is far more extensive than Fontaine. It will be easy enough to avoid one another."

"They shouldn't need to avoid each other," Tena argued. "She's being childish."

"See, Maggie," said Reuben. "We have a week on the ship, and then you never have to see my ugly mug again."

"It won't be only one week," countered Maggie. "I assume you're not going off into the wilderness once we arrive?"

"You know I'm not."

"Then we'll have to see each other. Your best mate is marrying my sister; there'll be no avoiding it." A thin veil of victory slid over Maggie's lips as she slowly rose from her seat to level her eyes at Reuben, and he retreated a step before he could stop himself. "Here's my proposal," said Maggie. "You, me, and our old friend, the tavern. The game is Snap. Standard rules, whoever claims the cards, the other has to drink. First one to find themselves completely obliterated has to retrieve their belongings and return to Fontaine. Winner takes all the spoils."

Tena seized her sister by the shoulders with a profound shake. "Maggie, wake up. Even with as irritated as I am right now, you are still not going back to Fontaine."

"Did you learn nothing from the last time we were here?" Charles exclaimed. "You and alcohol do not mix!"

"How certain are you I will lose?" Maggie kept her eyes on Reuben, her challenge clear.

"You're not sending Reuben back either," Tena stammered. Her voice rose against fighting emotion. "I won't leave either of you behind."

Charles wrapped his fingers at Tena's elbow, and eyed Reuben carefully. "Be still, darling. Reuben is not going to agree to this lunacy. And if he does, I will drag them both on board and lock them in the hold."

Reuben knit his brows together, considering if Maggie was calling his bluff. She would be in serious trouble with her sister if she lost this ... of course, she didn't need to win in order to win. She only needed to keep him distracted long enough to excuse herself to the toilet and never return. Playing the game Maggie-style as was her forte. Tena would simply have to forgive Reuben for returning Maggie's serve.

He raised one finger. "I accept, with one modification. No one goes home. Instead, meals notwithstanding, the loser remains in his or her cabin throughout the duration of the voyage. No other gauntlets thrown on international waters. Fisticuffs resume May first. You give me until May Day, and I'll offer you an acceptable solution to our debacle. Sound reasonable?"

Maggie gave a satisfied nod. "Agreed."

Charles's jaw visibly tightened. "Reuben, remember when you asked me to stop you from being a fool? The moment has arrived." He captured Tena's arm once more. "But you only learn from your own mistakes. We will see you on board." With one final crestfallen glance, they collected their traveling cases and departed to the tinkling of door bells.

"This is stupid," Reuben said. "I weigh twice as much as you. Don't for a second think you can win this."

With a haughty grin, Maggie spun on her heel, motioning for him to follow. "We shall see, Reuben. We shall see."

Mira rubbed her hands together with glee. "Ooh, this should be entertaining."

Reuben's chin fell to his chest with a sigh. "I suspect it will be."

THIRTY-ONE

FOR THE REST OF HER LIFE, Maggie would endure stories about the glory of the ship, how majestic she had been, and how refined. All that may have been true to those who actually sailed on her. But in the space of three whistle blows, *Titanic* became a horrid piece of ugly steel sailing away with the remnants of her future. She jostled against a sea of the ship's adoring fans, issuing farewells for loved ones. There were women waving lace handkerchiefs and small children hoisted on their fathers' shoulders. Maggie shoved aside one then the next in her scramble to reach the pier. She surely appeared a madwoman in her haste.

"Let me pass!" she screamed. "I have a ticket! Please, sir, I have a ticket!" She pulled her passage from her handbag, waving it in the face of the nearest docker. "You must have the ship turned around."

The older man narrowed his eyes. "Sod off. No one's calling for fifty-two thousand tons of steel to turn about for some brainless woman. Can't ya tell time?"

"You are rude indeed, sir! Do you know who I am?" Maggie admonished, stomping her foot at his egregious behavior. She prayed he wouldn't dispute her on her challenge.

Of course he did. "You're nothin' little miss. You ain't nobody neither. Now get off my dock."

Maggie pushed her way against the crowd until she came to a second docker. This man was far younger and significantly more attractive, in all probability no more than five years her senior. She sidled up to him with her most withering smile, praying her feminine wiles would do the trick. She was pleased to see him give a coy smile back. "Please, officer—"

The man puffed out his chest. "Thank you, miss, except I'm not an officer."

Maggie fluttered her lashes at him. Time was wasting. "Oh heavens, forgive me, you seem so authoritative. I hate to ask, only I need a teensy favor."

His eyes widened in interest. Gaining confidence, she risked another step closer, her arm lighting against his. "I'm afraid I've missed my time to board. How careless of me! I had so hoped a superior sailor such as yourself could find me a way to the ship."

"Maggie, what are you doing?"

Reuben shouldered his way out of the crowd, now gripping his satchel strap in a way suggesting he'd be pleased to throttle Maggie instead. "Excuse us, sir. She is only now realizing she's mistaken."

Reuben clasped her arm, roughly removing her back into the center of the crowd. Maggie twisted in his grasp, only managing to strain her muscles and tighten his grip. "Let go!" she yelled. "I had him! He would have taken me to the ship!"

"Oh, Maggie, Maggie, naiveté is not a look you hold well. Even flirtation doesn't have the power to turn ships around." He peered down at her as though she were an ignorant child, burning Maggie with fury.

"I know that! He would have sent for a tender."

Reuben snorted. "Hardly. We're stuck here, you and I." Maggie stopped dead in her tracks, bringing herself full face with Reuben. He was breathing heavy, his eyes bright with anger as the crowds jostled against them.

She'd been an idiot, played at her own tricks. The game went exactly as she'd planned and then turned disastrous somewhere along the way. Had she finished four drinks or five? Reuben chose the first two and they'd been stronger than their previous tavern visit, that was for certain. Every time she came close to winning, Reuben inexplicably managed to turn it all around. His skill was uncanny. Cheating was the only explanation.

Just when Maggie's luck finally found a strong upturn, the door to the tavern flew open. "Ahoy!" came a shout, "She's cast off!" Three whistle blasts sounded loud and long, seeping into their ears deep enough to rattle their attention away from the game. Reuben and Maggie locked eyes in one brief second of acknowledgement that their match was a draw in the worst way possible.

Maggie now itched to shove Reuben into the harbor.

"I would have won!" Maggie spat furiously. "You wanted to keep playing. You wanted this, didn't you?"

"You think this is what I *wanted*?" Reuben gasped.

"You couldn't let it rest," Maggie retorted. "Trapping me here won't change my mind. How many times do I have to say no before you'll listen?"

She flinched as Reuben grabbed her shoulders and spun her into the crowd. "Find your new beau. He'll be pleased to have you."

Maggie refused to satisfy him with another sarcastic retort. She would find a sailor and make him see reason. She would be on that ship, and she would do it alone.

THIRTY-TWO

REUBEN THRUST MAGGIE INTO THE throngs of bystanders and didn't bother to follow her. Instead, he sank onto the nearest bench until the crowd dispersed. A number of smaller vessels stood out against the bright afternoon sky, and a second tugboat trudged through the waters to the pier. In the distance, he could make out the dark outline of *Titanic*'s departing form, descending slowly until she vanished into the horizon.

He puzzled over where Maggie ended up. Had she taken up with the sailor as he'd suggested? The louse had been a hair's breadth away from fully undressing her with his eyes. Maggie was a stunning woman; how any man could say no to her would be a wonder. Reuben certainly hadn't been able to resist. As a result, she was possibly being felt-up by some grabby sailor while he was stranded here alone.

"Oh you're never alone," Mira said, appearing beside him.

Reuben refused to look at her.

"Why the long face, brother? You know you secretly wanted this—more time with Maggie. Isn't that why you left Fontaine?"

Mira as usual, being in his mind, was accurate in her evaluation of things. Reuben's heart still twinged with the chance that Maggie might accept him in time. But she would never do so if they were an ocean apart.

"You can change her mind," said Mira. "Force her to."

"I'm not going to *force* her to do anything. I'm not like that."

Reuben marched to the water's edge, resting his elbows on the railing, and thankfully Mira didn't follow him. His thoughts were overtaken with foul memories of years past, struggles he suppressed whenever they swam to the surface. How he longed to drown them forever!

The nearest clock tower chimed the two o'clock hour before Maggie joined him, breathless from hefting her traveling case for blocks in the afternoon sun. She cast her gaze across the water in the direction Reuben stared. "Your seafarer didn't meet your needs, Miss Archer?"

"No. It would appear Southampton men are not as accommodating as London men. Also," she huffed. "Miss Archer? Really, *Mr. Radford*? After everything else, why would you stand on propriety now?"

"Because *Miss Archer*," Reuben repeated. "The timeframe for such informality has passed. As you outlined quite clearly, we are not lovers nor does it seem are we friends. As such, there is no other situation that would warrant such familiarity between us."

Maggie opened her mouth once then shut it and said, "That's fair." A seagull flew by, skimming its wingtips upon the water until it snatched up its dinner from the waves.

For the next hour, Reuben observed that bird—whom he decided to name Ben—sail across the water, perch upon the nearest fishing vessel, and then take flight again only to find a new place to land. Always moving, never quite satisfied with where he was, continually wondering why he sang solo while other birds chirped in harmony.

Behind them, vendors pushed carts along the pier. Fishermen whooped as they pulled their latest catch out of the water. Even a police officer regarded them but passed on by. The world was revolving without a second glance to their plight. Maggie gave an exasperated sigh ... twice. And still, Reuben said nothing.

"So what do we do now?" Maggie finally demanded.

"Step one, find a place to stay for tonight. Step two, find passage to New York."

"Hotels are expensive."

"If you have another idea, please tell me."

Maggie considered the line of boats at the other end of the harbor. She had a crazed look in her eyes. "We could steal a boat."

Reuben snapped his fingers in front of her face, jerking her back to reality. "We could not. Neither of us know how to sail, nor do my travel plans involve being arrested."

Maggie scowled at him. "Mine didn't involve being stuck here with you."

"Then it's mutual," Reuben said, starting another twenty minutes of long-suffering silence. He paced in angst over whether he was willing to start another argument before eventually returning to his place at the railing. "What if we shared a room?"

Maggie snorted. "Yes, because that idea worked out marvelously last time."

"I have enough money for two rooms—actually, wait on that." He extracted his billfold from the satchel and shuffled through the money, counting silently. Their tickets would transfer to another White Star Line ship, but there was still the fact that, minus their two cases and his satchel, all their belongings were on *Titanic*. They needed to purchase personal items and meals in addition to their hotel room rate and train fare from New York to St. Louis. Financially, he was more prepared than Maggie, but what he had wasn't nearly enough for both of them without running him dry. "Actually," he said, "We don't know how many days we'll be here. I shudder to even ask, but would you be willing to wire your mother—"

Maggie turned colder than the North Atlantic. "Choose your words carefully, Mr. Radford, because if they involve asking my mother for assistance, I will swim to America. If you like my mother so much, you should return to Fontaine and ask her yourself."

"She's *your* mother; why do *I* have to go?" Reuben demanded.

"She disowned me, remember? Besides, I still have my sister, and she expects me to meet her. You don't—" Maggie instantly stopped talking as she realized her mouth spoke before her brain could process the words.

Reuben finished her sentence for her. "Don't have anyone," he said calmly. "You have someone and I don't. I'm expendable."

Maggie pursed her lips, and remained silent.

"Here's a marvelous idea." Reuben returned to the bench and ran his hand over the wooden slats. "I'll take the room and you can sleep on this bench. It should be perfect for someone as cold as stone."

Reuben glared up at her glaring down at him, and wished she would sit down. Hovering over him with that angry, exasperated look on her face was too intimidating ... and yet, he also found the intimidation factor strangely enthralling.

What he found enthralling was irrelevant. She'd just insulted him—how was that alluring anyway? Seriously, what was wrong with him?

Mira popped up behind Maggie's left shoulder. "Oh, loads. How much time do you have?" Reuben blinked and she disappeared again.

"One room then," Maggie said as though they hadn't just exchanged verbal slaps. "Let's hope we don't see anyone we know this time."

"Why do you care?" Reuben asked. "What does it matter if people think you're a Greek goddess or the town harlot? *I* know who you are." *Beautiful, but able to strike men dead with a single word,* he thought. *Yep, Greek goddess in a nutshell.*

Maggie crossed her arms, her scowl deepening. "Why *don't* you care? You used to. When we first met, you wouldn't even ring a stupid bell."

"As you so graciously just reminded me, my entire family died.

And I realized the only person whose opinion of me really mattered was my own." Although his own opinion was pretty shallow too.

Maggie settled beside him on the bench, obnoxiously close. Reuben sighed. She was about to play one of her games again and she probably didn't even know she was doing it.

"Then why do you still want to be with me?" she asked, lashes fluttering like a moth's silken wings.

He could have given an honest answer, but instead scoffed at the very notion, "I don't. That ship has sailed."

Maggie shifted uneasily on the bench. "Really? Why are you suddenly giving up on love?"

"I'm not giving up. Give me one day in America. I'll find someone much nicer than you."

It was Maggie's turn to scoff. "Oh, you think you could? And in only one day?"

Reuben leaned back casually on the bench. "Easily. There are plenty of other fish in the sea." Maggie rolled her eyes at his nautical reference. That's when he thought of another. "America surely has a boatload of beautiful ladies to choose from."

Maggie groaned. "Please stop." Reuben laughed. This was fun. Now he knew what it felt like to be Emil. What a fine life that boy must have.

"Aw, Maggie, don't take the wind out of my sails."

Maggie frowned. "And that was one too many."

Reuben grinned, glad some of the tension had finally been relieved. "You know you missed me in London."

"So what's your plan for our escape from the English?"

Reuben shrugged. "My plan is currently no plan. We figure out tonight and tomorrow will take care of itself."

"Oh, wonderful plan. We'll never get there."

Reuben was surprised at how suddenly Maggie was using words like "we" and "our." It probably meant nothing and he should assume as much, nevertheless that little glimmer of optimism laced with stupidity reared its ugly head again. "We?" Reuben asked. "Does that mean you're good with my living nearby?"

The corners of Maggie's eyes turned down faster than Reuben could blink. "You never exactly said why you decided to leave Fontaine. Why now? Why Saint Louis? No one mentioned this to me until this morning. Surely Tena would have told me the reason unless the reason was me."

"Don't flatter yourself. I told you, I'm over it." Reuben stood and walked a circle around the bench. "If you must know, I heard Charles propose to Tena at your father's funeral. They didn't know I overheard." Reuben buried his hands in his pockets, caught short at the memory of Tena's tear streaked face and Charles's battered emotions. "It was such an important moment for them. You said I don't have any family, but I do. Charles is my brother, and I hated the thought of missing out on his life. His wedding, his children—important moments should be shared, right?"

"I missed everything, didn't I?" she said softly, her gaze drifting across the sea in the direction *Titanic* disappeared. Maggie inhaled sharply. "And I'm missing it all again."

"We'll see them soon." Reuben offered a half shrug. "I know it's not much consolation, but ... well, I'm still here."

"Why *are* you here?" Maggie asked. "Why don't you leave me to fend for myself?"

He didn't think now was the time to bring up her father's request or Reuben's unresolved feelings. Both topics were sure to only invoke hostility. He chuckled nervously. "Same reason you are. You're the only person I know here."

Reuben pulled her to her feet. "Let's return to the inn. We'll figure everything out tomorrow."

THIRTY-THREE

Two DAYS. THAT WAS HOW LONG Maggie and Reuben managed to avoid anything resembling a serious conversation. Literature, musical composition, conjecture on the true nature of Americans? Sure. The overdone fashion sense of the overweight lady in room four? Of course. Speculating whether the peculiar man in room six would slaughter them in their sleep? Hesitantly, but still yes. How to escape their current predicament or anything occurring prior to the eleventh of April? Unacceptable.

Despite their polite conversations, sometimes even eliciting a light chuckle, there was frustration at the edge of every smile. Reuben was missing when Maggie woke and remained away until dinner both evenings. Not that she was waiting around the inn for him to return. The concierge was more than accommodating to any of her requests for information, directing her to the White Star Line office on the first morning. After waiting twenty minutes to speak with someone, she was finally seated before a lanky man with a bottlebrush mustache.

"I wish to request transfer of my passage," Maggie explained, retrieving her *Titanic* ticket from her handbag. "Any ship will do."

He took her ticket, examining it from every angle, then held it up to the light and sniffed it. Apparently content with its legitimacy, he said, "Missed your passage on the great *Titanic*?

What a shame. What–a–shame."

"Yes, yes, I'm quite broken up about it. Now tell me how soon I may leave this city."

"Two weeks."

"*Two weeks?*" Maggie sputtered. It couldn't be. They couldn't stay here for two weeks. She'd used over half of her own funds so far, and Reuben's money was sure to run out before long. A slow pain took up residence somewhere in the area of her temple. She slid her hand across the desk in a silent plea. "Please, sir, there must be something sooner."

"White Star transferred the coal from many of our ships to *Titanic* due to the strike. It will take time to have them up and running again. As I said, the next passenger ship in this port departs in two weeks." His lips drew into a pitiful smile. "Of course, there are always other lines to choose from. I believe there's a ship arriving from Bremen in a few days time."

Other lines! She hadn't thought of that. Breathing a sigh of relief, Maggie said, "That will be perfect."

"Oh. No, miss." The man smoothed his desk papers repeatedly. "Your ticket will not transfer to another line, although I can provide you the address of their office." He scribbled an address on a piece of paper, slid it across the table and stood. With a final "Good day, miss," he strode across the room and through a door, leaving Maggie with nothing except useless passage and an unfamiliar address.

How could she ever hope to find the funds by tomorrow?

A horrible vision sprang to her mind of trollops on the street, selling their bodies to the highest bidder. It would certainly earn her enough money. If she felt generous, she could maybe earn enough for Reuben's passage too. Although it wasn't a matter of her generosity, but the generosity of the men who purchased her.

Maggie dug her nails into her palms just short of drawing blood. *Maggie, what is the matter with you? You've done some unseemly things in the last year, things Father might climb from his grave if he knew, but prostitution was not one of them. Pull yourself together. You have other options.*

Sure, she countered. *Stay here for two more weeks living on the streets because I can't afford a room? How is that much different?*

You'd have Reuben with you.

Ugh, no thank you. That man confuses me.

There's another way. Ask for help.

Ask for help? From whom? Oh ... of course.

There was another way. She would simply ask for the money. And she suspected it would be only too easy to get it.

Maggie strode to the nearest desk, her head held high and shoulders back. "The address for the wireless office, please. I have an urgent message to send."

THIRTY-FOUR

UNFORTUNATELY, BY THE FOLLOWING evening Maggie's nerves were nearly shot waiting for a response to her message. Anticipation clenched her chest and rolled the dinner settling in her stomach. Originally expecting an answer within hours of sending her desperate plea, she understood now the unrealistic nature of her request. Having made more stolid acquaintances than actual friends over the years, and repeatedly disappointing those friends she did have, there was little chance of anyone taking pity on her. If she didn't hear a response by tomorrow morning, she would wire her mistress in London requesting a staff position until she earned enough for another ticket. By her math, that should place her in St. Louis by her twenty-fifth birthday. Long enough to miss her sister's wedding, two or three babies, and secure herself on Tena's black list for all eternity.

If Reuben caught on to her unusual behavior, he wasn't acknowledging it. Using no more than five word sentences didn't deter him from initiating a conversation about the existential ramifications of *Moby Dick*.

Was the whale a symbol of man's need to mask the true nature of his soul? *Who cared?* She now regretted ever mentioning that her father owned a copy, and no, she never planned to read it ever. After listening to drivel about marine animals for over an hour, desperation led her to suggest one of her other least favorite activities: chess.

Maggie detested chess. She was no good at it, never had been. It didn't matter who she played against—her father, her sister, or a five year old—everyone was capable of besting her in a minimal number of moves. That night, more than ever, her clustered brain brought her lousy skills out in spades. But eight o'clock was too early for bed, and the game stilled her angst over a wire that would never come.

"Captured your queen!" Reuben cried victoriously, only twelve moves into their second game. He wagged the black piece in front of her face before adding it to the other defeated men on the table. "Shame your pawns won't live long enough to save her."

Maggie gritted her teeth and scanned the board for other possibilities. "I'm biding my time. Wait five minutes, and I'll unleash all my secrets."

Reuben studied her across the board. "Is that a promise? Care to make a little wager?"

"Certainly," said Maggie choosing first the rook then replacing it to move her knight instead. "If you win, you may ask me any one question ..."

Reuben sat up with hungry eyes and promptly knocked her knight into oblivion.

"But-" Maggie continued, lacing her fingers upon the table ledge. "If I win, I claim the same of you. Agreed?"

"Fair enough." Reuben rubbed his hands together and narrowed his eyes at the board. "If you're going to tell me anything, I better make my question good."

Now, Maggie wasn't a complete fool. Such a high wager would have him carefully calculating every move and she would need to do the same. And by *do the same*, she meant *cheat*.

Maggie plucked a previously won pawn from the table and rolled it between her fingers. As Reuben bent to choose his piece, she bounced the piece off his shoulder, sending it skittering across the floor into the lobby.

In response, Reuben knocked her bishop off the board with his rook. She opened her mouth to protest until he shook a finger at her. "Sorry, Miss Archer, but you'll need more than a renegade pawn to distract me." She frowned, sliding her other knight into battle position. She could capture his queen on her next move.

That is until Reuben captured her knight with his bishop. "And that is how that is done."

"Just you wait," Maggie challenged. "I'm planning my attack." She moved her pawn, which was swiftly captured by Reuben's.

He folded his hands on the table. "Are you even paying attention to where you move? Your game play is disgraceful."

Maggie decided to switch tactics. She gestured out the open doorway where two pretty teenage girls were waiting with their parents. The daughters were undeniably attractive—all smooth skin, freckles, and shiny scarlet hair—details no man's eyes would miss.

"Do you think the right girl is waiting in Missouri?" she asked and quietly slid her queen four spaces closer to Reuben's king.

"Hmm?" Reuben murmured, still watching the girls. Maggie coughed loudly, redirecting his attention. "Sorry. What was the question?"

Maggie pointed at the girls. "Do you think the girls in St. Louis are as pretty?"

"I'm sure they are." He moved his rook towards her king. "Check."

She positioned her bishop in front of her king. "So then, hypothetically speaking, what would your three questions be?

"What questions?"

"Remember? My father always said to ask three questions. To see if someone's worth knowing."

Reuben glared at the board and slid his queen over as reinforcement. "I would start by asking her name."

"Obviously," Maggie affirmed. "That doesn't count for a

question." She positioned her rook at the opposite end of the board, and he quickly swiped it with his own.

Reuben glanced up from the board. "Then I would ask her what she's so afraid of."

Odd question, Maggie thought, but didn't comment. She moved her pawn. He moved his bishop.

"I would ask my third question at the end of our meeting, after I asked for a second date and she told me no."

"How do you know she would say no?" Maggie asked.

Reuben leaned his elbows on the table, his fingers automatically tenting against his lips, and stared her down like she'd failed to answer the world's most mundane math equation. "Because *you* did."

Maggie scowled and moved her rook, knowing it was a mistake when her fingers left the piece. "Every girl is not the same."

"Why did you really say no, Maggie?"

"No, sir. No questions for me until you win."

He struck her rook off the table with his bishop, sending it flying against the nearest bookcase. An elderly couple tsked at them from the corner of the room. Reuben lowered his voice. "Shall I phrase it another way? Explain."

Maggie captured his knight, left unattended when he blew her rook off the board. Reuben cursed under his breath and moved a pawn. "You made the wrong choice," she said.

"That was a perfectly legal move!"

Maggie shook her head. "No. I mean, I told you no because I didn't think you made the right choice."

Reuben glared at her. "That isn't for you to decide! You had your pick of men and you didn't choose at all."

She glanced around the room. People were openly staring at their conversation.

Maggie reduced her tone back within the confines of their table. "Reuben, think about it. My choice would have been the wrong choice, just as wrong as yours, so I chose not to choose."

Reuben's mouth hung open. "What does that even mean?"

Maggie gasped as she saw her perfect opening in the game. She placed her rook on Reuben's end of the board and giggled. "Check!"

"Miss Archer?"

A hotel steward approached the table, holding two sheets of folded parchment on a small silver tray. "A wire arrived this afternoon. My apologies for not seeing it to you sooner."

"Thank you." Maggie handed him change from her coin purse. One shilling. It was all she had. He raised an eyebrow at his still outstretched hand until he realized no more was to come and returned with a frown to his post in the adjoining room. Well, what did he expect? The message *was* late.

Reuben raised an eyebrow. "Tena?"

"No—I mean, yes," Maggie stumbled. "That is, I wired her a message this morning, but she hasn't replied. I hope she received it."

"Then who is it from?"

The papers in her hands—a telegram and a wire transfer—were the very thing she'd been hoping for. Her breath caught when she read the sum on the transfer. That was a mess of money in her hand. More than enough for a second class ticket. She glanced at Reuben—plenty of money for two tickets even.

"Who sent it?" Reuben pressed.

Maggie didn't want to say. Unbidden queasiness bubbled up her throat knowing how furious Reuben would be; however, her pride took over as it always did. If he was angry, it was by his own deception and would be his undoing, not hers.

"I asked Lloyd to send money for our passage."

Silence. Dead silence. Reuben's hand held his rook frozen above the board, too dumbstruck to finish his move. "You did *what*?"

"I asked Lloyd—"

"I heard you." Reuben snatched the telegram out of her hands, his eyes growing wider by the minute. "Blimey," he breathed.

"That is a lot of money."

Maggie exhaled. "It's enough for both our tickets."

"I will *not* be indebted to him," Reuben hissed through gritted teeth. His hands clenched the bank note as though he intended to tear it to shreds.

"You won't be," Maggie assured him. "I didn't mention you in my request. I'll take responsibility for the repayment." She wasn't sure how—it would take her years to earn back the money—but she couldn't ponder over that now.

Reuben considered her with—what was that look—betrayal? "You should have let me take care of it. I would have found a way."

"That's not your obligation."

"Oh, so it's *his*?"

"No!" Maggie tried to sit taller, impossible being half a foot shorter than him. "It's no one's responsibility but my own. We need a solution and I found one. Simple as that."

"So, that's it then?" Reuben huffed. "I don't have a say in this at all?"

"Not unless you care to get over your childish grudge against him."

Reuben considered the chess board only a second before he knocked over his king and slouched backward in his chair. "Checkmate. You win."

Maggie didn't even bother arguing that he moved twice in a row ... or his second move wasn't even a legal move ... or that he took out his own piece. The time for making light had passed. She wished she could go back to discussing whaling ships and harpoons again.

Maggie cleared her throat. "The next ship sails the morning of the 14th. The day after tomorrow. I'll purchase our passage in the morning."

Reuben nodded. "I didn't tell you my third question." His eyes met hers across the board and she forced herself not to look away, even though her heart skipped a beat with his stare. "Was there ever a world where you would have said yes?"

Was there?

In another world perhaps things could be different for them. In a world where little girls didn't die and mothers didn't go insane. In a life where Maggie's mother loved her father as much as he had loved her. In a place without duplicity. In *that* world, the right man wouldn't be just a visitor. In that world, he could *stay*.

But such a world didn't exist. It wasn't even a possibility. And anyone who convinced themselves otherwise was a fool.

Maggie said nothing. She stared directly at Reuben and didn't say a word.

Reuben's intensity faded to void sentiment. He slid the bank note across the chess board and stood. "You've placed your trust in the wrong man."

~~~

The hotel room was dark when Maggie quietly entered hours later. She lost track of how long she had remained in the parlor—long enough for the other guests to retire upstairs and the hotel's night steward to cast her inquisitive glances.

A sliver of moonlight now shone across the bed through the open draperies. Reuben lay stretched out atop the covers, his hands beneath his head and eyes closed.

One hand lingering on the knob, Maggie remained in the doorway until she was confident he was actually asleep and not merely feinting. Seeing him in dreams, she was reminded of the boy she met on that first May Day. It was similar to how she'd been told a parent feels for their child—the angelic nature of their sleeping makes you forget all the aggravation they caused when they were awake. While she may not have chosen to spend the last few days as she had, she *was* glad he was the one she spent them with. She ought to apologize for the telegram.

Maggie shook her head, dismayed with herself.

But what do I have to apologize for? she scolded. *I did nothing wrong.* Her head pounded with the mess of thoughts floating through it.

It was decided; she would speak to Reuben in the morning. Yes, that was best. A night's rest apart would help her decide what to say. She snatched the spare blanket from the chair in the corner and hurried back down to the parlor.

~ ~ ~

Reuben opened his eyes with the click of the door. He turned to face the window, gooseflesh rising on his bare forearms. Maggie didn't understand. She didn't know. It was no wonder she didn't trust him and never would. He didn't trust her either. There was no one he could trust.

Reuben rolled over again and closed his eyes, finally allowing exhaustion to overtake him. He imagined her gentle fingers stroking through his hair, calming his scalp as he faded off to sleep. Her soft voice soothing away his doubts. If only she could.

If only Lloyd had never existed.

If only Reuben could tell Maggie the truth.

"If only, if only, if only," Mira crooned in the space between what was real and what was a dream. "If only."

THIRTY-FIVE

IT TOOK NO LESS THAN EIGHTEEN hours for Reuben to assess that his argument with Maggie wouldn't be returning for another round. Or not while they were still on dry land at any rate. Even with his seven o'clock arrival for breakfast, she wasn't to be found and still hadn't made an appearance by luncheon. That was just fine by him. Between Mira's whispering and his ever wandering mind, what little sleep he had achieved was restless, and his mood was not fit for arguments or rebuttals.

Rest was what he needed most right now. He would return upstairs for a short respite before continuing to search for temporary employment. There were eight or nine hours left to turn this around ...

He took the stairs two at a time, and quickly packed his satchel, checking if everything was still in order. It was then he noticed his worn copy of *The Time Machine* sitting out, a thick packet of letters wedged between its pages. Only, upon investigation, he discovered they weren't letters at all. Instead, he held a sizable stack of twenty notes wrapped securely between a second class steamship's passage and a short message in Maggie's hand: *{Here is your passage for tomorrow. Sails at one. You may have this room. I reserved my own for tonight.}*

His own room. At least they wouldn't need to skirt around the hot tension bumping into them at every turn. On the ship they wouldn't even see one another save perhaps at dinner, and, even then, he could turn his attention to other passengers.

Reuben's gaze went to the window; the harbor water was as calm as his thoughts were choppy. Why did she have to take the money? Why did she have to ask *him* for help? Was she so proud she couldn't go to her mother instead?

Just as proud as you are to refuse help from Lloyd, he thought. But Lloyd was different. His history with that man was complicated and dirty. He brought out the worst in Reuben, dark intentions he found difficult to control. If Maggie threw her lot in with a man like Lloyd, in the end Reuben would be forced to interfere. He couldn't leave her to her own devices; she didn't know what Lloyd was capable of and too naive to believe it if she knew.

Reuben's fingers squeezed the passage still in his hands, finally reading its contents: *{Received payment for second class passage of one adult, Reuben Radford, from Southampton to New York on the Steamship Höllenfeuer to sail 14th April 1912 at one o'clock p.m. from Bremen Rhein piers, Southampton unless prevented by unforeseen circumstance.}*

Any delight Reuben may have felt over sailing on a German ship quickly extinguished as he reread the ship's name.

Höllenfeuer. Hellfire.

He closed his eyes and breathed in then out. In then out. Each breath steady and sure.

The name was a coincidence. Unlike Reuben, Maggie couldn't understand German; she'd chosen that ship for convenience and a quick escape.

Still ... *Höllenfeuer* ... the word didn't sit right. One week prior he'd held a revolver to his head, prayed for death, and wondered if God would send him to hell. Seven days ago he would have welcomed it. Now he was about to step onto a ship that literally meant it. But, truly, what choice did he have?

Reuben wrapped Maggie's message back around the money and passage and hid the bundle at the bottom of his satchel. He slung the pack across his chest on his way to the door, sleep no longer a safe option. Now was not the time to be trapped alone with his subconscious.

THIRTY-SIX

BEING FAR TOO PROUD TO ADMIT her fault in the matter and far too obstinate to approach Reuben with a compromise, Maggie departed the inn alone in the early morning hours of April fourteenth with her single case in hand and her eyes on the horizon. She'd intended to speak with Reuben last night, except every time she thought of the ensuing argument, her stomach curdled and sent her running. One day soon she would deal with Reuben's fragile emotions, but it was not this day. If she was lucky, it would not be the next day either or the day after. If she was truly fortunate, it would be in St. Louis with Tena and Charles to distract Reuben from harboring undue resentment. There was, after all, a wedding to plan.

A wedding neither of her parents would attend. She missed her father. It seemed like years since she'd visited his grave and virtually decades since she'd kissed him goodbye on the railway platform. She would give anything to be a little girl again curled by the fire in his study while her father's soothing voice read her off to sleep.

A sharply attired steward directed Maggie to her cabin, situated in *Höllenfeuer*'s far aft upper deck corridor. The hallways here were narrower than *Titanic*'s, although not overly so. The decor was simpler yet still grander than anything she had expected to find in a steamship. More now than ever did she question the hype surrounding *Titanic*'s departure. Perhaps in first class there was reason for such uproar; however, *Höllenfeuer*'s second class accommodations were quite acceptable for her needs.

Two stacked beds, small sofa, sink, and general cramped living space? All accounted for. Random stranger of a cabinmate? Maggie returned the smile of the vivacious girl standing across the room from her. Although the girl's height was mostly legs, she still barely reached Maggie's chin; she couldn't be much older than fifteen or sixteen. Her ash brown plait swung over her shoulder as she bounced forward with hand outstretched.

She grasped Maggie's hand and gushed, "*Hallo! Mein Name ist Amara Müller! Es ist schön, Sie kennen zu lernen!*"

Maggie stared at Amara. It was hard not to. Since Maggie's second night home from London, Tena had gushed in earnest over how sensual the German language was. She thought Tena's absurdity was from the rose colored glasses of love as every foreign word uttered by Charles sounded like an insult. However, on this petite beauty, Amara Müller, the language took on new life. What a shame Maggie couldn't understand her.

"Sorry, I don't speak German."

"*Darf es sonst noch etwas sein?*" asked the steward, his eyes narrowed as though he wished to say, "Stupid English woman."

Amara stepped forward, counting out a few coins from her pocket. "*Nein, danke.* We have need of nothing else." She didn't bother waiting for the door to close before spinning back to Maggie. "Sorry. I assumed I would be paired with another woman from my country." She tapped her finger to her cheek. "Although, I should have assumed there were not many Germans lying in wait at an English port."

She flitted around Maggie to the sofa, patting a spot beside her. "You are from here then? You do not look it. Although I wouldn't know. All I have seen is the coastline! Can you still see it?" She dashed to the tiny porthole, standing on toe to peer out. "Yes! Still there! It is gorgeous. I hope someday Siegfried may bring me back." She craned her neck round to Maggie. "Did I receive your name?"

With a low whistle, Maggie dropped onto the couch. There wasn't enough energy to sustain herself with such vivaciousness in the room. Where were this child's parents? And who was Siegfried? A brother, perhaps? Most parents were not so unassuming as to allow their daughter to travel unaccompanied. "Maggie Archer. Are you traveling alone?"

"Not anymore!" Amara spun away from the window, landing beside Maggie on the couch. "Mama insisted I could handle myself, but Papa forced my promise I would remain in my cabin always. Now that you are here, you can be my companion! It will be so nice to have a friend."

"Why didn't your family travel with you?"

Amara grew quiet as her fingers slipped along her dark plait. "I left my parents and sisters back home. My brother moved to America five years since, and our cousin, Siegfried, has now requested me to join him as his wife."

"Siegfried's your fiancé?" Maggie exclaimed. "You're too young! How could your parents force you into this?"

"I'm sixteen, which is not so young. Regardless, this was my choice, not theirs." Amara held her gold banded left hand for Maggie to admire. "This was my grandmother's. She was fond of Siegfried before she died. She would have approved."

Few times did Maggie truly not know how to respond. Choosing to marry at an age four years younger than her own, a year younger than she was even presented? And to a cousin no less? Maggie understood that, especially in esteemed circles, it was still quite commonplace in England ... but without the societal pressures? Why then?

"I cannot fathom your decisions," she told Amara. "My mother would sell her soul for a daughter like you. In fact, she probably did."

"Your mother does not agree with your chosen path?"

Only the knock at the cabin door stifled Maggie's need to express where her mother could stick her opinions. Amara leapt up before Maggie could move, exchanged several highly pitched words with the stewardess in German, and shut the door with a triumphant grin. She tossed a folded note in Maggie's lap and squealed. *"Meine Güte! Er ist auf diesem Schiff!"*

"English, remember?" Maggie snatched up the note, her eyes flying over the few written lines: {*Miss Archer, meet me this evening on the lower promenade, aft rail. 7 p.m.*}

"He is on this ship!" Amara repeated in English. She quickly returned to her perch at Maggie's side. "Well?" she pressed. "Tell me about him. This beloved of yours."

Maggie took in the girl's flushed cheeks glowing with excitement and allowed a smile to fall upon her lips. This child was so ignorant to the workings of the world. The only exposure to love and romance she had was most certainly from her parents. If they'd maintained the illusion of happiness, Amara couldn't be expected to understand that not every relationship involved the anticipation of a proposal from half a world away. Maggie didn't need to hurry Amara's childhood away. Reality would be an unpleasant enough teacher when she arrived in Siegfried's arms.

"He's not my beloved," Maggie corrected. "Just a boy I know. I would rather hear about Siegfried."

Amara grinned, fingers flying over her braid again. "Would you take me on deck? I haven't been out for anything other than meals and the toilet."

Maggie nodded. A brisk walk in the crisp air would allow her to sort out what she could say to Reuben.

Amara bounded off the bed like an excited puppy. She drew on her coat, nimble fingers fastening the buttons before pinning her crimson hat on completely askew. Even if she added another dozen pins, it would fly away into the waves not more than five feet outside of the exterior door. Maggie shook her head, gently removed the pins, and refashioned the hat atop Amara's scalp. She licked her fingers to smooth down a few flyaway strands behind the girl's ears. "There. Tomorrow I will show you a few simple hairstyles. You will arrive the perfect picture of an American wife."

Amara examined her reflection in the looking glass over the sink. She turned either direction and extended her arms with satisfied flair. "*Danke*, Maggie! My first English friend! Wait, I should say my first *American* friend!"

Maggie laughed. "I'm sorry to say you are not my first German friend. My sister is engaged to one."

"What does your sister think of your strange suitor? Or is it a hidden romance? I do love a good intrigue!" Amara bounced on her toes, causing Maggie again to question how anyone could expect marriage of a mere child.

She ushered Amara into the hallway. "You're as nonsensical as my sister. Wait 'till we're outside. I'll tell you all about him."

THIRTY-SEVEN

FOUR HOURS INTO THE VOYAGE, Reuben was bored stiff. After depositing his lone traveling case in his cabin and cursing again that his trunk full base to lid with novels was sitting in *Titanic's* hold, he traversed the entirety of the deck, staked out the smoking room and even the toilet. Shortly after the five o'clock bell sounded, he made his way below, curious as to whether his cabinmate had turned up. The only indications the man existed were his crude personal belongings scattered about the space when Reuben arrived earlier that afternoon. While company would be welcome to Reuben after these last months living alone, he hoped the other man also appreciated the shared space.

In other news, Maggie still hadn't sought him out since leaving the ticket in his book. Not that he expected her to. He didn't know which cabin she'd been assigned, and figured he probably shouldn't ask a steward. They were liable to only think him lewd. He would simply wait to see her at dinner with everyone else.

Reuben opened his cabin door and stopped in his tracks. A sandy-haired man leaned upon the wash basin, suspender straps hanging from his waist and hands roaming every breathless inch of the disheveled stewardess pressed against him. She gave a faint gasp at his entrance and ducked the man's arm to fall from his reach. Her fingers fumbled with her apron as she tumbled past, gasping apologies all the way down the corridor.

Instead of chasing after her, the man advanced on Reuben, muscles flexed and dark eyes flashing. "*Wer bist du?*"

Reuben backed up. "Reuben Radford. And you are?"

"*Geh raus!*" The man shoved him through the doorway.

"Wait!" Reuben yelled, throwing his foot in the way of the closing door. "This is my cabin!"

"*Dumme Amerikaner!*"

"I'm not an American. And I speak German! *Ich spreche Deutsch.*"

The pressure against the door released slightly. "*Du sprichst Deutsch?*"

"*Ja.*"

The man retreated into the room with a grunt. Reuben eased into the room, but left the door slightly ajar. "So, we share a cabin then?" he ventured in German. The man shrugged noncommittally as he buttoned his shirt, adjusted his suspenders, and thankfully didn't attempt to toss Reuben from the room again.

Reuben gestured towards the door. "Who was the lady?"

The man shrugged again. "Met her in the corridor."

"I see." They obviously wouldn't be spending much time chatting about moral values. Reuben had kissed exactly one woman in his life. This man ... well that stewardess was clearly not his first ... nor meant for only a kiss. "Where are you from? And where are you headed?"

Reuben was met with the man's back as he rifled through his luggage. "Dresden. New York."

Also not a man of many words, thought Reuben. The next week would be tedious travels if they were unable to quickly find some sort of common ground.

Taking a chance, Reuben said, "We have round about an hour until we must dress for dinner. Care to join me on deck?"

No response.

Think, Reuben. What would Charles suggest? Probably to

fixate on Tena for nine hours and make no decision at all.

No, this man and Charles would be like oil and water. He needed to think like someone who didn't give two hoots. Reuben grinned. The answer was obvious. *What would Maggie do?*

"Drinks and cards in the smoking room?"

Another shrug. "Do you have money to lose?"

Reuben's smile broadened. Lloyd's money burned in his pocket. "Sure do. Let's call it blood money."

That caught the man's attention. He turned around as he pulled his coat on with slow movements. "Geez, man, you kill someone?"

"Almost, but no."

"Ba, horse shoes and hand grenades. Doesn't count." He clapped Reuben's shoulder, and his deep laugh revealed a ring of smoke-stained teeth. "Ulrich Klassen, and I bet the louse had it coming. They always do."

Ulrich checked his money while Reuben rifled through his satchel for the cigars he'd purchased yesterday wandering Southampton's streets. If they tasted as good as their sweet aroma indicated, he would save the last one for Charles.

"Cigars?" Ulrich scoffed. He flipped open a tarnished case packed with equally questionable cigarettes. "Nah, I ain't sophisticated enough for that stuff."

It was Reuben's turn to shrug. He returned the cigar to his pocket and tossed the satchel onto the bed behind him. "A smoke's a smoke, mate."

Ulrich snapped the case shut with a loud guffaw. "Hey boys, tell the warden! Turns out I'm a gentleman after all!"

THIRTY-EIGHT

"WHAT DO YOU IMAGINE AMERICA WILL BE LIKE?" Amara asked. She skipped ahead of Maggie down the corridor. "We lived in the mountains back home. Everything was beautiful."

"They have mountains in America too," said Maggie. "Charles told me they added a forty-eighth state not two months ago. You can see cities and fields, deserts, oceans, and rivers and never even cross a foreign border."

Amara giggled, pressing a hand to either hip. "Who is Charles? Is *he* your beloved?"

And they were back to that again. Maggie sighed as she opened the exterior door on deck. The English coastline forgotten, the sky now spanned before them in a seamless stream of brilliant blue hanging low upon the navy waters.

"No," Maggie said. "Charles is my sister's fiancé. Remember, the German friend I spoke of?"

"How wonderful for your sister!" Amara clapped. "Siegfried is truly the most—I do not remember how to say the word in English—*perfekt* is what we say. Oh, no, my hat!" Amara seized the brim before the wind could free it completely from her hair. It now lay askew, thick strips of fallen hair blowing wildly about her face.

Maggie slid the pins from Amara's hair, wrapped the loose

strands back into her plait as best she could, and settled the hat upon her head. She worked the hatpins in at the sharpest possible angle she could without attaching them directly to the girl's scalp. "There you are. And the word is *perfect* in English too."

Amara surprised her by throwing her arms around Maggie. "Siegfried was correct!" She grinned against Maggie's cheek. "We are not so different from you after all!"

"If only my mother understood that."

Slight creases edged across Amara's brow when she pulled away. "What do you mean?"

Maggie ran her thumb over Amara's pursed forehead. "Relax. Your face will be riddled with wrinkles before you're twenty." She nudged Amara's shoulder with the flat of her palm until the other girl finally relented. "Now then, I believe you promised me every story about your future husband."

Amara's eager ramblings proved her a girl full of surprises. She might exude naivety, but she was by no means ignorant of her situation. Maggie begrudgingly admitted Amara had been truthful when she stated marriage was her decision. In between her vivacious bouncing exterior indeed lay a carefully orchestrated life. Siegfried was four years her senior, best mates with her brother, and had purchased them a quaint home just last month. For three years, they exchanged monthly letters until finally, last September, he requested she join him. They would be wed the Friday after her arrival. In Amara's eyes, Siegfried loved her and she him and there was little else to consider. Her gleam was so similar to Tena's, it struck Maggie with unexpected pangs of homesickness. If only there weren't so many miles separating her and Tena and she wasn't again the cause.

Maggie turned her attention to the rapidly emptying deck. A smattering of men disappeared into the second class smoking room, although most passengers moved towards the interior stairwell, likely descending to their cabins for evening attire before the dinner bell. Seeing as her wardrobe now consisted of a mere handful of items, there was little reason to impress people she wouldn't see again in a week. She may as well enjoy the fresh air until they were cooped in their cabin for the night. No doubt Amara's enthusiasm would continue well past when Maggie usually retired.

Amara cast a glance at the sun's position, then at Maggie. "Do you see him?" She asked in earnest. "You still have not given me his name."

As if on cue, Reuben emerged from the smoking room with another stocky fellow at his side, both men buttoning their jackets against the evening chill. He clapped a hand to the other man's bicep and laughed in boisterous German—*Wait, when did Reuben learn to speak German?* Maggie wondered. However, her speculation moved to other interests when the men headed in the opposite direction. Reuben's companion lit up a cigarette and made a snarky comment causing Reuben to offer a dubious shake of his head and respond in kind. They then descended into the stairwell without so much as a glance her way.

Maggie stood flabbergasted. *Well, well, Reuben,* she thought. *You send me a note and then stand me up? I suppose I deserve it, and I suppose I should be glad it's not another woman ... but regardless ... you have no manners.*

"Maggie, is he him?" Amara asked. While Maggie glared at Reuben's retreating figure through the exterior porthole, Amara openly gestured towards a second man at the aft rail. She couldn't make out a face beneath his top hat.

"No," Maggie said in irritation. "Let's head to dinner. I'm famished."

The echo of their clicking heels reverberated across the now deserted deck, instantly drawing the unknown man's attention. The profiled line of his jaw was all she noticed before she dragged Amara around the edge of the smoking room wall. She prayed she was mistaken, however a quick second glance only confirmed her suspicion. Her ribs strained against her corset stays and a pulse now beating at what was, most assuredly, not a healthy rate.

Maggie flattened Amara against the wall and gulped air that, to her lungs, felt like breathing pure soot. How amusing that even surrounded by fresh ocean air, there simply wasn't enough oxygen.

Ten meters from her stood the only other man, besides Reuben, she left England never expecting to encounter again, and the only one whom it would have made logical sense to stay with. Lloyd Halverson waited at the railing, all calm and collected like ice tea on a summer's day, and she was on the verge of a panic attack. She took a few deep breaths and willed her heart to stay in her chest.

Maggie tapped her head repeatedly against the wall. What was he even doing here? It's only business, she reasoned. Halverson Shipping thrived on international business including with the United States. They had offices in four separate countries: England, America, France, and Ireland. It made sense, as his father's second in command, Lloyd would be sent out for status from each location. Confound her bad luck it happened to be at the same time they were there.

Oh, grow up, Maggie, she chided herself. *Reuben said naiveté doesn't suit you. You basically summoned Lloyd with your telegram. Why else would he be on a ship owned by a country he doesn't even do business with?*

"Are you ill?" Amara asked. "Should I summon the doctor?"

"No, no. I'm fine."

Wrinkles peppered the girl's brow again and Maggie forced a chuckle. She poked Amara's forehead. "I told you not to do that. Can you manage to change for dinner on your own? I'll meet you in the dining saloon?"

The tension in Amara's face eased only slightly. "I may go alone?"

"Why not? You managed to find your way the last two days, didn't you? What harm will another do?"

Amara's smile spread to the tips of her fingers. She bounced on her toes to kiss Maggie's cheek. "Oh thank you! Of course, I will see you there." She skipped across the deck and with an energetic wave disappeared into the stairwell.

Even before the door fully closed, Maggie recognized the approach of steady footfalls. When Lloyd rounded the corner, there was no surprise in his dark eyes at her presence.

"Why, Miss Archer," Lloyd beamed, and bent to kiss her cheek. "Good evening, my dear."

Maggie frowned. The cold surface of the wall seeped through the warm fibers of her coat, an appropriate juxtaposition to the two of them. "I presume it was you who sent the note?" she asked.

"Logically." Lloyd flipped open his pocket watch, checked the time, and returned it to his coat. "You're late."

"Forgive me for not meeting your vague request in a timely fashion."

His hand found the wall above her shoulder, close enough that she could feel his breath on her face. "*Au contraire*, as of late you are the one making requests of me."

Maggie ducked under his arm. "I had no one else to ask."

Lloyd pushed off the wall to face her. "Who was the girl?"

"My cabinmate."

"So you're traveling alone then?" he asked softly. Consideration stared back at her, set into cold grey eyes the opposite color of Reuben's. How she could even recall Reuben's eye color was a wonder when she avoided his gaze at all costs. Eyes stole too many emotions such as Lloyd was doing now.

She averted her own over his shoulder. "Tell me what happened between you and Mr. Radford."

Lloyd's face hardened in her peripheral vision. "Are you with him now?"

"No."

Lloyd visibly relaxed. He smoothed his fingers over his temple. "Then there's nothing you need to know."

Maggie's hands sank to her hips. "An honest answer, please, Mr. Halverson."

"If we are being honest, Miss Archer, then I never stopped thinking about you. We were so good together, Maggie."

Maggie sighed. "Those were enjoyable functions we attended, Mr. Halverson, but we were never together. We were a socialite couple; a fact I believe my father's notice made quite clear."

He inched closer, one brow flirting against his hairline. "How am I to believe you when it was I you wired for assistance?"

Maggie stepped out of his reach. "If you cared so much for me, why didn't you write when my father was ill? Why were you not at the funeral?" Her mother might have monitored all communications in and out of number seven, Union Street, but even Beatrix Archer couldn't control the entirety of the British post.

"Maggie, drop this charade and return home with me." An edge laced his voice Maggie had never particularly cared for. She heard it the last time they spoke in person, when he made threats against her father in Southampton. Fractures formed in his carefully crafted facade that day, cracks she had forgotten within her father's death. Only now they were widening.

"Why are you here?" she asked. "Are you following me?"

Lloyd smoothed his lapels and refocused his tone. "Yes ... and no. I have business for my father in New York which requires completion by month's end. Your telegram inspired me to embark on an earlier passage."

"I will repay you every pound."

"Every dollar as the Americans say," Lloyd corrected. "Assuming you truly wish to reject your home. My offer still stands. Don't make me ask on bended knee."

"Mr. Halverson," Maggie stated firmly. "I would prefer we depart ways as generous donor and grateful borrower."

He smiled. "Neither a borrower nor a lender be."

"Meaning?"

"I will relieve you of your debt if you relieve me of your insistence of this matter with Mr. Radford." Although his lips smiled and his tone remained light, the center of his eyes smoldered. "I will not stoke cold fires."

She wanted to scream. Between the two of them, Lloyd and Reuben caused more unnecessary drama than Edith and Bianca. Ugh. Confound the both of them. What Lloyd offered was a necessary break to her last tie with him and entry into America uninhibited. Tena would agree if she was here. "Just let it go, Maggie. Some secrets are better left buried." She would steer clear of the puddle before she rode through it.

Maggie extended her hand with a polite smile. "Thank you, Mr. Halverson. I accept."

Lloyd turned her hand over and raised her wrist to his lips. "Shall I escort you to dinner?"

"No, thank you. I would assume first class serves a more delectable meal than you could find down here."

Lloyd smiled. "In that regard, perhaps you care to join *me*?"

Maggie snatched her hand from his grasp. "I was not requesting an invitation. Thank you again for your assistance. Our business is concluded."

"As you wish, Miss Archer. However—" He opened the inner door, allowing her to pass by. "Intercontinental travel can be a tricky business. If you find yourself in need of assistance, I am located in cabin two-twenty-three."

~ ~ ~

The second class dining saloon was a veritable cornucopia of unfamiliar voices all blended into a low drone. German mostly, then a few words in Irish, followed by another language Maggie couldn't place. Two large rooms made up the dining area, decorated chiefly in dark wooden paneling and deep green and white wallpaper. Long wooden tables ran the length of either room with swivel chairs bolted to the floor eight to a table. Dining stewards held trays aloft as they passed between two sets of open double connecting doors.

Amara sat towards the rear of the second room with Reuben

and the mystery man from the smoking room. Two other unknown couples occupied the remaining spots at the table. Oblivious to her observation, they laughed through their first meal on board, making plans for the week to come. Once she took her seat, they would bombard her for every detail: where she came from, where she was headed, and why. Once they learned she and Reuben were from the same town—or as soon as Amara squealed out about Maggie's mysterious *beloved*—it would all be over. It wouldn't matter that the only German she knew was *ja, nein, and perfekt*. Amara would translate, and Maggie would have to choke on her food to avoid the conversation. She'd rather go to bed without eating.

Her cabin felt like an empty tomb when she returned. She changed into her nightgown, splashed water on her face from the little sink, and drew back the bedcovers. The thin material left the sheet too cool against her skin, and she longed for the extra hand embroidered blanket folded in her trunk on *Titanic*. She lay in the dark, staring at the metal frame of Amara's bunk above her. Was Tena as lonely and confused as she was? All those months alone in London were nothing compared to this.

THIRTY-NINE

REUBEN QUITE LITERALLY SPENT THE entire next day in his cabin for no other reason than he could.

For the first time perhaps in his life, he had nothing he was required to do. The days at sea stretched out before him like blank pages waiting to be filled by a writer's hand, which was pretty much how he felt about his life right now.

After immigration declared he wasn't going to poison the general population of America with some infectious disease, he was free to go wherever he pleased. He could travel to any state, do anything. He was no longer confined by the expectations of his father. Of course, he could carry on with journalistic endeavors if he desired, but it was no longer expected of him. He could become a ballet dancer or muck out stables. There was no one to tell him not to.

Very well, he admittedly would draw the line at dancing, but the point was still applicable. He was a free man.

"Free are you?" Mira asked.

And then there was her. His almost-suicide had most certainly cemented himself with a daily dose of crazy from now on. When the thought became overwhelming, he instead focused on his continued ability to still differentiate when he was having a hallucination—his mother's illness wouldn't overtake him completely.

He forced Mira away, partly because he was comfortably relaxing in bed, mostly because his cabinmate was currently in the room. Poor Ulrich didn't need to sleep with one eye open because he thought Reuben was off his trolley.

A sharp knock drew both their attention to the door. The cabin steward always knocked three times in quick succession and announced himself. Only no introduction accompanied this interruption. Unfortunately between the door's width, Ulrich's shoulders, and the already cramped space of the room, Reuben couldn't decipher who was on the other side.

"*Was ist das Problem, Frau?*" Ulrich demanded. *What is the problem, woman?*

Ulrich was sensitive like that. In the day since Reuben met him, Ulrich held nothing back. He was a single man pleased to live out his days however he pleased. His only cares included rugby, ale, and attractive women he didn't need to bring home to mother. And that was how he liked it.

Their guest returned an inaudible reply, and Ulrich tossed Reuben a smirk. "*Viel Glück, mein Freund.*" *Good luck, my friend.* He then mentioned his dislike for emotional women, his preference for prostitutes, and something about a potato which made Reuben doubt his translation skills. He snatched up his hat and coat before disappearing into the corridor, still chuckling random mutterings.

A beat after, Maggie stepped into the room, and Reuben knew things were about to become significantly more complicated.

He bolted upright, his head colliding with the underside of the top bunk. He rubbed the spot and mumbled, "What are you doing here?" When she wasn't at dinner the previous night, he figured she planned on avoiding him the entire voyage, which was preferable. He had enjoyed every minute with his dinner companions. Amara was a sweet girl and the other two couples at their table equally pleasant.

Maggie rested a hand on her hip. "You weren't at dinner

tonight. What were you doing?" She said it like an accusation of more sinister misdeeds.

"I took dinner in my cabin."

"You should have been at dinner."

Reuben wasn't sure what Maggie was on about. What did it matter where he decided to eat? "You weren't at dinner last night. What were *you* doing?"

Her next words hit harder than a ton of bricks dropped on him from an enormous height. "*Titanic* hit an iceberg." Her smoldering glare implied he was somehow at fault.

Reuben's chest hurt more than his sore head. *I will not overreact,* he repeated. *I will not overreact.* "Charles?" he asked, barely managing to retain a steady voice. "Tena? Are they safe?"

Maggie placed her other hand on the opposite hip. "I'm not sure. There are conflicting stories. Some say the ship was towed ... I can't remember where. Others say it sank. Amara heard nearly everyone was rescued."

He rubbed the center of his sternum as the panic subsided. "Thank God for that."

Maggie's nails tapped nervously against her side. "Nearly everyone doesn't mean all. *Oceana* wrecked last month, and the only deaths were those in a lifeboat. What if the same thing happened to Tena?"

Not a chance, thought Reuben. If he even considered the possibility, he knew he'd be lost. Mira would latch on to any shred of doubt and strangle him with it. "Maggie, look at this logically. If the papers say most were saved then the odds are on Tena's side. We'll see her next week, and our biggest problem will be recouping all our belongings." He groaned. "Guess I should have purchased the insurance."

Maggie nodded. "I did." She backed towards the door. "That was all I needed to tell you. I should leave before your cabinmate returns. Will I see you at breakfast?"

It was difficult to gauge her true emotional state when, as usual, she refused to look at him. He could assume the waters weren't calm, although he couldn't judge if they were a typhoon either. Deciding she probably lingered somewhere closer to the latter end of the scale, he decided to play the gentleman. Maybe they could at least bring their friendship back to neutral status.

"Ulrich's in the smoking room for the next three hours easy," Reuben said. "Then he'll attempt to chase down some ill-placed stewardess and return around midnight hooting about what a rush it was." He gestured to the couch. "You may as well stay."

FORTY

MAGGIE'S THUMB RESTED ON THE doorknob as she weighed her options. Go back to her cabin to watch Amara flit about like a restless butterfly, take to the deck alone to hyper focus on Tena's unknown life status, or stay here and have the argument they'd been avoiding for three days? It was a reflection on the sorry state of her options when she shut the door and cautiously sat on the edge of the couch, as lost as a raft floating amidst the waves.

Reuben asked a question, startling Maggie from her thoughts. "Pardon?"

"I asked if you found your cabin comfortable."

"I suppose. It's similar to this one."

"And your cabinmate? Have you gotten on?"

"Amara?" She managed a wry smile. "Oh, she's very agreeable. Perhaps too much so. She's meeting her fiancé when we dock and appears dead set I procure one of my own."

Reuben snorted. "Not bloody likely."

Maggie raised an eyebrow at him. "Excuse me?"

"Nothing." He ran both hands through his hair then extended them towards her. "What have you been doing since yesterday?"

What a complicated question. If she were honest? *Oh, not much. I played backgammon, strolled the deck, met with your most-hated enemy. Standard steamship fare.*

"I played backgammon with Amara. She won, of course."

Reuben smirked. "As lousy at that game as you are at chess?"

"Even more so." Maggie returned the smile, but when Reuben tried to hold her gaze a second too long, she wished she'd frowned instead. "What did you do today?"

He gestured around the cabin. "You're looking at it. Read, took a kip, now engaging in awkward conversation with you." She didn't refute his observation. The imminent discussion neither of them wanted stood in the tiny room like a morbidly obese man forcing his way onto a crowded lift.

Reuben absently picked lint off of his pants. "I heard rumor there was another gent who piqued your interest as of late."

Maggie gaped at him. "What *gent*?"

"Some English chap. Miss Müller mentioned him at dinner last night."

"Who—" Maggie began and immediately fell silent. It was Lloyd he referred to. Thankfully Amara didn't know his name.

She shifted uncomfortably, smoothing the folds in her skirt. "Ah, yes, there is a man I spoke with. He's traveling in first class, however, and I am well out of his league."

"I see. What a shame," Reuben said. His expression shifted to dark amusement. "At least Lloyd isn't an option anymore." The word *option* sounded far closer to *threat* than Maggie would have liked.

She needed to clear the air before it started to sting her eyes.

"I'm sorry I asked him for the money," Maggie said. Reuben remained so silent she wondered if she had only apologized in her head. "Lloyd's money," she clarified.

Reuben looked up at her. "I don't mind that you asked him for the money, not much anyway."

Maggie couldn't restrain her jaw from hanging loose. He was notorious for constant reminders of how terrible it was to associate with Lloyd. Now he didn't care? She found so violent a swing highly suspect. "I don't understand. Why the change?"

Reuben shrugged, that dark gleam hinting at the edges of his gaze. "You didn't know any better."

Maggie stood, needing to obtain the higher ground. "Then please, Reuben, explain it to me."

Reuben rose, gave her a long stare, and paced to the window. A full minute passed before he spoke again. "Maggie, why did you really go to London?"

Maggie folded her arms squarely over her chest. "I didn't want to be married."

"That's what your father said too."

"He talked about me the night he died? What else did he say?"

"No, not that night. He told me this before." Reuben retained his gaze on the porthole. "When he shot down my request to court you."

"Your *WHAT*?" Maggie felt her hands shaking with emotions that should belong to someone else. She wanted to lunge across the room and throttle him. How dare he bring her father into this lunacy! How could he even ask? "Father said no and instead of respecting a dead man's wishes, you still proposed to me? Are you insane?"

Reuben whirled around. He strode across the room quicker than Maggie thought humanly possible and seized her shoulders. She wrenched out of his grasp and brought her palm across his face with an instinct she was unaware she possessed. Without a word, he dropped onto the farthest corner of the couch, his hand caressing the stung flesh.

Maggie dropped to her knees beside him. She realized her mistake the instant her fingers touched his cheek. Horrible flashbacks of Florence Radford in the Winchesters' garden invaded. She'd called Reuben insane; he probably feared becoming like his mother as much as she worried about becoming hers. "I'm sorry, Reuben," she said softly. "This is exactly why I left for London. Can't you understand what a mistake it is for us to even be friends, let alone more?"

Reuben lowered his fingers. "Nothing about us is a mistake," he said firmly. "Can't *you* understand that?" It was impossible to decipher his expression. He was incredulity and sympathy both, frozen between emotions.

"How can you believe that?" Maggie demanded. "We're horrible together. We fight all the time ..." She counted on her fingers. "Christmas, Southampton, Easter, and let's not even mention every minute of this entire fiasco. Confound it—I just struck you! What in all of this makes you think our friendship isn't one huge misstep?"

Reuben scooted closer, one leg crossed on the couch, the other on the floor, facing her. He tucked a stray hair away from her face, his eyes taking her in. "Because it's not. And you know it's not. I don't have to convince you of what you already know."

His fingers brushed across hers, and Maggie instinctively edged away from his touch. He was intelligent enough not to try again. "What are you afraid of?" he asked.

That was a seriously loaded question—as in a loaded revolver ready to blow her life away. This was no game of Russian Roulette. All the chambers of this gun were equally deadly. If Maggie pulled the trigger, there was no going back.

"We can still go our separate ways," Reuben said, sensing her hesitancy, "If it's what you want. I won't try to stop you anymore. But I deserve to know why."

Confound him and his logic.

Maggie closed her eyes and exhaled slowly. She was going to regret this so much.

"I am completely terrified of a future with anyone. It scares me to death that, if I give in to someone, life will be terrible to us, or I'll be terrible to him. Someday one of us will have to watch the other die ... or worse watch our children die. I saw what it did to your mother. That's why I said no then, why I'm still saying no now, why I'll say no forever. I refuse for that to happen to me." Maggie opened her eyes.

Reuben didn't say anything. His gaze held her face as though he was seeing her for the first time and wasn't quite sure if he understood what he saw.

When he finally spoke, his voice was calm, and his gaze unrelenting. "Everyone I ever loved has been tragically ripped from my life. *No one* will ever understand your fears like I do."

Maggie's stomach flipped like a Chinese acrobat. After all these months hiding from what she felt, convincing herself there was no way he could possibly understand, and the answer had been so simple. Of course he understood—he loved her.

Reality crashed down. She'd run from it for so long, and it always followed right around the corner. Now here it sat staring her in the face. Reuben lost his family and she may have already lost the remainder of hers. The terror of living without Tena was overwhelming. For this moment, Reuben was still here, until the instant they stepped foot on shore. Then he would be gone too ... unless she asked him not to go.

Every chamber of the revolver unloaded at once, shattering everything. Right now the thought of being with him frightened her far less than the possibility of being utterly alone.

The only defense Maggie could see was to take Reuben in her arms until everything else disappeared.

So she did.

~ ~ ~

Reuben woke completely renewed. He stretched on his bunk, fingers to toes uncurling every ounce of tension. A deep blue sky filled the porthole, promising a more exquisite day than he'd experienced in years.

He slid his hands beneath the nape of his neck and exhaled. Last night he'd finally broken Maggie's walls—and overstepped every rule of propriety along with it. They were together in every way two people could be, and he didn't regret a second of it. How could he when she finally agreed to go to America with him as a couple? They would meet up with Tena and Charles in St. Louis, and more than a few parts of him were thrilled at the prospect. Not only would he have a beautiful woman on his arm, he would also have his best mates living nearby. Not a bad deal.

And the best part?

Mira didn't show her face since the moment Maggie knocked on his door last night. If she wasn't going to interfere in his new relationship, he must be doing something right. Mira was a difficult hallucination to please.

A full-fledged genuine smile raised his lips with muscles protesting from infrequent use. His grin only widened. *He had Maggie.*

He had won.

FORTY-ONE

As it turned out, optimism was quickly extinguished when your lover of eight hours ends up missing.

Maggie was nowhere to be found. She wasn't at breakfast nor lunch, not on deck, and by quarter after six, Reuben was past the point of worry. He checked the hospital, the ladies parlor, even the gentlemen's smoking room.

The more he asked, the more he learned, and the graver he felt.

It turned out the reports were incorrect when they announced most of *Titanic's* passengers as survivors. The truth was the opposite. Fifteen hundred to the opposite as it were. Only thirteen of the second class survivors were men.

Thirteen.

Reuben's stomach threatened to expel itself. He raced down the corridor, barely reaching the toilet before losing his lunch in a cold sweat.

Höllenfeuer's cheerful mood evaporated in a single afternoon. Gloom hung upon the ship, heavier than the whitest fog back in Fontaine. At dinner, whispers circulated throughout the dining saloon as fear took hold that they would be next to sink. Word quickly spread to the bridge and the captain himself arrived mid-meal.

Breathless silence fell as the stout captain faced them with a tight-lipped frown. "The loss of *Titanic* is tragic to be sure," he stated in a dialect so unfamiliar Reuben strained to decipher it. "However, we have no intent on meeting her same fate. Extra lookouts are posted in the crow's nest and on deck. Speed will slow during the evening hours, and if ice fields grow too treacherous, we will wait for daylight to resume course. All further inquiries should be directed to your cabin stewards. Good evening."

"What about lifeboats?" someone asked, but the captain had already rushed from the room, a din of voices erupting in his wake.

"Stopping for ice?" Amara asked Reuben. "Then it *is* serious? Do you think we could wreck?"

Despite the extra precautions taken by the captain and crew, Reuben wouldn't have batted an eye if their ship was sucked into the pits of the Earth for which she was named. Labeling a ship after the devil's lair was tempting fate. But right now he was focused on only one thing.

"*Kapitän!*" Reuben leapt up, sending his chair spinning, and ran after the captain. He caught up to him at the top of the stairs. "Sir, I wonder if you've received a survivor list for *Titanic*. I have friends on board."

The captain's face flooded with instant apology. "We have not. The lines are brimming over with ice warnings, and my men are struggling to catch up. If we hear anything, we will report it."

Reuben nodded, watching as the captain walked away, and Amara took his place. "Did you find out anything?" she asked.

Reuben shook his head. "Do you know where Miss Archer is?"

"Of course! She is awfully upset." Amara raised her hand to her mouth and whispered, "About your quarrel."

"Our quarrel?"

Amara's face blushed. "I am sorry. She asked me not to speak of it. I cornered her in our cabin before dinner and said, 'Maggie, you will tell me what's bothering you this instant. I will not lie for you anymore.' And she did tell me!" Amara threw up her hands with a flourish.

Reuben frowned, profoundly troubled. He didn't remember having a row with Maggie. He remembered doing many things with her last night, and another fight certainly wasn't one of them. She'd left his room with a smile.

No, she must be in straits over Charles and Tena. Who wouldn't be after the news they received today? He certainly couldn't stop thinking about it.

Sure enough, Amara knew exactly where Maggie was, hidden away in the ladies' parlor. Reuben idled in the corridor until they emerged, Amara dancing on her toes. "Here she is! As promised!" Amara gave Maggie a little push into the corridor and wagged a mothering finger between them. "Now apologize, the both of you." Maggie remained feet away, oddly subdued.

"Maggie," Reuben breathed. "I was so worried. Where have you been?" He attempted to take her arm, but she shrugged out of his grasp with no reply. He then tugged at her shoulders in an effort to make her face him, and she wrenched away as if his touch was painful.

"Please don't," Maggie hissed, stalking away towards the deck stairs. Reuben fought down the automatic rejection that swelled inside him. He had to be logical. There was no way he was only a one-night affair.

Reuben took the stairs two at a time to reach the exterior door. The wind lashed through his dinner jacket. Amara breathed her own blustery sentiments as she followed him onto the deck.

Maybe this was his fault, Reuben wondered as he reworked last night's events. It was all a bit of a blur and over far too quickly. Later, after Maggie left and Ulrich stumbled into the cabin half drunk, he'd kicked Reuben's bunk and offered a knowing laugh. "So how was she, my friend?" Half-awake, Reuben muttered, "Good, my man. She was bloody good."

But in the biting chill of the wind, "bloody good" wasn't exactly how Reuben would describe it. In truth, it had been a bit unpolished. He didn't know what he'd been expecting for his first time with a woman, only that after so long envisioning it he'd expected ... well, more.

Did I do it wrong? he wondered. *Was there even a right way to do it?* Reuben had assumed it was the first time for Maggie also, but what if it wasn't? He hadn't thought to ask at the time. Even though she claimed to ward off men, she'd also been in London for eleven months. She could have been with any host of men more attractive and experienced than Reuben. He probably should have asked.

Would it have mattered though?

No, not at all. Maggie could have made love to the entire British Parliament and the second she kissed him, he wouldn't have cared. He had already tried everything else to convince her to be with him.

Maybe *that* was the problem.

A throbbing pain spread behind his eyes as he recalled the final words he'd said to Maggie before she'd kissed him.

No one will ever understand your fears like I do.

He rubbed the back of his neck, stretching the tight muscles. That sounded like a line Ulrich would use to get under a young lady's skirts.

Now in the light of a new day, Maggie must have come to the same conclusion. He could bloody well quote it straight from *The Time Machine*.

"*It sounds plausible enough tonight,*'" he whispered into the evening wind. "*But wait until tomorrow. Wait for the common sense of the morning.*" He'd read that infernal book more times than he could count; how did he not think to take its warning *before* doing something stupid? How could he be such an idiot?

"And not one word from you!" he scolded Mira. She was nearby, tucked in some corner of his brain waiting for the perfect chance to strike. He hated that about her.

Maggie stared straight ahead when he approached. Her eyes focused on the night sky, lips pursed against whatever strained to break free. Gooseflesh stood out on her bare arms, and she didn't bother rubbing them for warmth. Always colder than ice, more unbreakable than stone when she wanted to be. Last night he'd seen her break, offering him a glimpse of who she could be. It had been so beautiful, and he feared she had already mortared herself back in.

Reuben lowered his voice as if it mattered. Amara wasn't even pretending not to listen. "Maggie, is this about last night?" he asked. "I promise I meant every word. I love you."

Maggie bent over the railing to watch the waves churn against the hull of the ship. "You shouldn't."

"Well I know I *shouldn't*. You're stubborn and impatient and rude, but I still do." He smiled and received nothing in return. *Note to self*, he thought. *Insulting a woman in jest is apparently still taken as an insult.*

"It's all my fault," she said, matter of fact. "I was stupid and now they're dead."

Reuben flinched. "Wait a minute. You blame yourself for what happened to *Titanic*?"

"No, I blame myself for what happened to Tena." She tightened her grip on the railing and righted herself to face him. Her eyes lay steely grey and bitterly cold, and he shivered in their wake. "Tena was drowning while I was seducing you. She died so I could act like a two-bit hussy."

"Maggie, you're being unreasonable," Amara cut in.

Maggie's head swung in Amara's direction, her cheeks flushing as though just now seeing her. She threw her hands up. "Oh perfect! Now you know too!"

Reuben captured her wild hands between his. "Maggie, listen to yourself. *If* Tena died—and I refuse to believe she did—she was already dead long before anything happened between us. Trust me."

Her eyes narrowed to mere slits. "You say I should trust you, but how can I when you continue to lie to me?"

Reuben's grip lost hers. "Last night wasn't a lie."

"Not that. Lloyd."

"Come on, Maggie, not this again. Can't we just have us and forget everything else?"

"I wish we could."

"I think you should," Mira cheered. She leaned casually against the railing between himself and Amara, tossing breadcrumbs to nonexistent birds. "She's going to find out eventually."

"How? Who would tell her?" argued Reuben. Charles wouldn't say; Tena didn't know; Mira and his parents were dead; and Lloyd was back in England, never to be seen again.

"Excuse me?" said Maggie quickly followed by Amara's, "Are you ill, Mr. Radford?" Both women wore identical masks of bewilderment.

Reuben shot angry daggers at Mira. His mind was becoming worse if he was speaking to her out loud in front of others. He stepped around Mira to face Maggie eye to eye, cupping her chin up to force her gaze, and pouring as much reassurance into his words as his heart held. "I haven't lied to you. I'm simply choosing not to rehash the past. It was a long time ago. It doesn't matter now. And it doesn't change how I feel about you."

In silence, she peered at him as she considered his answer. After a long moment, her face contorted inexplicably. "There's something I need to do, and I wish I didn't," she choked. "I'll beg your forgiveness later. Please don't follow me." Then she wriggled out of his grasp, her heels tripping on the wooden planks as she sprinted down the deck.

He jolted to follow at the same time Amara blocked his path, one hand raised to stop him. "Do not be the man who chases his woman, Mr. Radford. Think. If she cares for you, all will be well."

Reuben watched the love of his life run away from him. She was always running from him in one fashion or another. "*If* she cares for me ..."

Amara followed his line of vision as Maggie ascended the stairs to the adjoining deck. Not once did she turn back. "My Siegfried would never doubt my honor. Do not doubt hers. Maggie will tell her suitor she chose another and return to you."

Reuben couldn't contain his jealousy. "Who is this guy?" he snapped in Amara's face. "Maggie's with me now. Why does she owe *him* an explanation?"

"Patience, Mr. Radford. Maggie needs you, however she also needs time." Amara's voice was soothing, but not soothing enough.

"She's had two years. Isn't that long enough?" Not waiting for an answer, Reuben stormed off in the opposite direction, praying he didn't encounter anyone in his wake.

FORTY-TWO

MAGGIE WAS BEING ILLOGICAL. Reuben knew it, Amara knew it, and she knew it. Reasoning fate had struck Tena down because she shared a moment of intimacy with someone was as nonsensical as believing in fate itself. Especially when that moment of intimacy happened after the fact. But she didn't know how else to deal with the complicated emotions threatening to drown her.

Last night afterwards, she and Reuben ticked off the list of important topics: traveling to America, living in St. Louis, standing witness to Charles and Tena's marriage ... everything involved in planning a real future together. When she left a few hours later to return to her cabin, she kissed him and said, "You know, Mr. Radford, I do believe this is the first time we've parted ways amicably."

Reuben kissed her back softly and said, "Then you know what the solution is, Miss Archer? You never leave me again."

She left his statement hanging in the air. She could feel his heart beat against her chest, slow and steady unlike her own which pounded erratically. He wanted everything to be so all or nothing when it wasn't that easy. She could entertain the idea of being with him for now, but forever? For him, everything was black and white while her world spun in blurry shades of grey.

Yet inside her soul, she wanted it to be that simple, whether it was or not.

So she smiled up at Reuben, hoping her voice carried only sincerity with none of her doubt. "Never," she lied, praying when they arrived in America all her misgivings would miraculously vanish.

Now in the light of day with the specter of her sister's demise hanging over her like rain clouds, Maggie felt the significance of her doubt fall on her shoulders like hailstones.

There was so much she didn't know. For example, Reuben's troubled past or why his eyes threw daggers every time the subject of Lloyd was mentioned. It was this huge animal in the room with them, and it would follow them everywhere until it devoured them. Maybe the truth would be all it took to dispel her fears once and for all.

Reuben told her to trust him. His word should have been enough. But it wasn't.

Steeling the last of her reserves, Maggie knocked on the door to cabin 223.

Lloyd greeted her with the same devilish smirk he'd surprised her with on deck, his full dinner attire and slicked hair suggesting he had only just returned to his cabin. "Well, well, my dear. This is highly unexpected. Although not unwelcome I assure you."

"Good evening, Mr. Halverson." Maggie nodded. "May I enter?"

"Of course." Lloyd stood to the side so Maggie could walk by. The room, although larger than second class, was still too cramped for Maggie's liking. Dark paneling surrounded all four walls with a single present porthole, the night in contrast to the cabin's warm table lamp and sconces. A walnut bed with deep green coverings filled one side of the room while a sink and Lloyd's steamer trunk stood in the corner, papers scattered across the lid.

Lloyd lounged into the only armchair, crossed his right leg over the left, and gestured for Maggie to take the sofa opposite him. She shook her head and lingered closer to the door. "No thank you, Mr. Halverson. I shan't stay long."

"So tell me then, Miss Archer, what brings you to my cabin? Am I safe to assume your mind hasn't altered since yesterday?"

"Yours is a correct assumption."

Lloyd looked towards the window, sorrow heavy in his tone. "I heard the news of *Titanic*. Most unfortunate. My deepest sympathies about your sister."

"Tena is *not* dead," Maggie spat, even though she herself wasn't certain of it. They still hadn't posted survivors. She would demand a list from the captain after she completed the task at hand.

Lloyd stood. "If you do not need comforting, then I can think of no other reason for your visit. You may go." He made for the door, but Maggie reached for his arm. He turned into her touch, intrigue lighting across his lips.

Maggie released him. "I can't leave yet."

Lloyd gave a wry smile and returned to his seat, gesturing over his shoulder. "Then stay. Perhaps I can help you remember the real reason why you came."

"I would like to renegotiate our agreement."

"The terms were more than fair, Miss Archer. Your debt paid in exchange for silence." Lloyd gestured once more to the sofa, and again she disregarded his invitation.

She raised her chin and edged another meter into the room. "The situation has altered."

"In what way?"

"Let's suffice it to say I've obtained new enlightenment."

Although he didn't ask her to expand, Lloyd's expression was awash with curiosity. He raised a hand in her direction. "Shall we continue to treat this as a business transaction, Miss Archer?"

"I believe that would be sensible. Don't you agree, Mr. Halverson?"

"I do." Lloyd rose once more, thumbs looped in his pants pockets. A low smile slid up his lips, an expression one might take for timidity if they didn't know him as she did. "You want something from me, and I want something from you. I don't see why we can't both get exactly what we want."

Maggie flinched as Lloyd slid her coat off her shoulders, letting it drop to the floor. He ran his hands leisurely up and down her bare arms until the tiny hairs raised on end. She'd planned for this possibility and would coax him just far enough to find out what she needed without allowing her moral compass to swing too far south.

It wasn't as though she'd never been with a man before Reuben. If he had asked, which thankfully he hadn't, she could have admitted she'd been with three other men while in London. Second was Eddie, the dressmaker's son and a short lived flirtation. Third was Oskar, the three-week Norwegian sailor. First, last, and in between was Derby, the second footman in the house where she served. Pretty from his face down every inch to his toes, Maggie was not the only staff member who regularly found her way into his bed. It was Derby she sought out the night Reuben announced her father's death, and he happily obliged her requests.

"Are we agreed?" Lloyd asked, meeting her eyes. Tonight they were a fierce grey, reflecting the same stormy hue of her own. She nodded.

When he kissed her, she reluctantly returned the favor, and quickly found herself in a precarious situation. Despite how he irritated her, she was surprised by the smoothness of his lips, his hands; even his cheeks were shaved clean. So very different from what she'd expected and not altogether in a bad way.

Maggie tilted her chin upwards. "Tell me," she said, far more breathily than she'd intended.

Lloyd smirked at her reaction and extended a slow nod. "Reuben and I were mates in school," he said with a sad smile. "Unfortunately, as things sometimes go, he went quite deranged. I had to sever ties with him."

It was true then? Madness could be inherited? "In what way?"

Lloyd waved off her question. "He made some wild accusations against me."

"What accusations?"

Lloyd tapped his nose knowingly. "That's cheating, my dear. You've received all the information that first token will buy you." He extended his hand and she took it, allowing him to turn her around the room in a simple two step. Those charcoal eyes not once left hers. "Stay with me tonight," he crooned. "I can make you forget Reuben Radford ever existed. I won't need to beg you to return to England with me – you'll *want* to go."

Maggie stared up at him through her lashes. "If I agree, will you tell me what I wish to know?"

"Of course, my dear." He drew Maggie's body flush to his as they continued their promenade about the cabin. His lips whispered against her ear. "I'll gladly grant whatever you request."

"And my debt?" Maggie breathed.

"Your debt will remain paid."

Maggie calmly inhaled, held on for a five-count, and gave a slow exhale. "Well, then, Mr. Halverson, I believe our contract has been amended."

FORTY-THREE

THE BOAT DECK LAY DESERTED WHEN Reuben sank exhausted onto a bench after two hours wandering in argument with Mira. Solid black smoke spewed from the broad funnels above him, blowing soot straight from the coal boilers in the belly of the ship. The cloud trailed away through the sky and blocked the stars from shining through the grime.

Straight ahead hung the tautly covered wooden lifeboats, secured to the curved davits at the edge of the deck, their mass blocking his view of the ocean below. If he closed his eyes, though, he could pretend the air stinging his face blew off the lake in Fontaine. The whistle of the wind became the voices of those he missed.

Reuben removed the cigar from his breast pocket and rolled it between his thumbs. It wasn't anything special, not even one of the better made lot. Just a plain old English cigar given to him by his very German friend.

The night of his twentieth birthday—the same day Charles announced their move to America—was one of the best Reuben could remember. Long after Tena departed and Karl, Elsa, and Winnie said their goodnights, Charles, Emil, and Fred remained awake in the living room with Reuben. In Reuben's busy schedule of hallucinations, unrequited romance, and general misery, he oft forgot to include time with his mates, and greatly missed it. Hours passed playing cards, smoking cigars, and joking until their sides hurt. Ten minutes to midnight, Emil climbed on the table to present Reuben with a final celebratory birthday jig and even Fred forgot to reprimand him, he was laughing so hard.

As most people with siblings can testify, an annoying little sibling is often the ruin of everyone's fun, and this was certainly the case that night. Emil had proceeded to a second round of boisterous singing when Winnie stalked into the room, her night gown flapping around her ankles and hair flying. "Emil! I'm telling Mama!"

"Oi!" Emil tumbled off the table into Reuben's lap with a cheeky grin. He rested his head on Reuben's shoulder and sighed. "Oh, Reuben, after all this time? I knew we were meant to be."

Reuben stood, tossing Emil onto the carpet. "If you fancy me, then I'm a toaster."

"But a very pretty toaster."

Winnie kicked Emil in the thigh. "Go to bed! You're so loud, I can't sleep!" She padded over to Charles and climbed up into his lap, resting her head against his chest. "You wouldn't want me to have low marks at school tomorrow because I didn't have enough sleep? Would you?"

"*Nein*, Winnie. I am sorry we woke you."

"Will Tena visit again tomorrow?"

"Of course," Charles replied, a mischievous twinkle in his eye. "She promised me not to tell, but she crafted something special for you to do together."

Delight shone on Winnie's face. She wrapped her arms around Charles. "Thank you. She's the perfect sister."

Charles smoothed his sister's hair, gently kissing the top of her head. "I am rather fond of her myself. Now to bed," instructed Charles. He set her on her feet. "I will turn down the lamps and join you shortly." Clutching her night gown seams, Winnie bounced up the stairs.

Emil begrudgingly helped Reuben snuff their cigars and clear the table, stowing all signs of their late night revelries. "Good night, Reuben," Fred called with a yawn as he ascended the stairs.

Emil clapped Reuben on the back with a knowing grin. "Yes, good night, my friend. May your next year be as lovely and agreeable as the lady friend for which you pine."

Reuben slapped Emil in the back of the head. "And may yours actually find you a lady to pine over."

"Ha! Funny, Reuben," Emil mocked. "For your information, Beth Warren smiled at me yesterday."

Reuben nudged Emil between the ribs. "She *smiled* at you? Sounds like she's one day away from having your babies."

"Oh shove off. We talked too."

"What did she say?"

Emil reddened. "Hello."

"*Hello*?" Reuben failed to contain his amusement. "You better steer clear of her. Girls like that are trouble. Charles, would Tena think to speak to you in such a manner? *Hello Charles*? Think of the town's outrage. The scandal!"

"Would she, Charles?" Emil winked. "She's a feisty gal. I'd bet she's loads of scandalous."

Charles pushed Emil towards the stairs. "Go to bed, Emil."

He backed out of the room with a grin. "I don't fancy a sleep alone. Care to lend me your fiery girlfriend?"

"Emil!" Charles admonished while Reuben doubled over against the wall, tears leaking from his eyes. Emil bounded up the stairs, cackling the entire way.

Charles shook his head, muttering in German around the living room. He plucked two cigars from the humidor, cut and lit one, and took two puffs to calm himself. Reuben watched him, still wiping tears from his eyes. "You know Emil's only jesting, don't you? That's just him."

Charles remained serious. "I thought about what you said

earlier today. How I should marry Tena and take her with us. Otherwise you would steal her from me."

Reuben raised both hands in defense. "I wasn't serious. I would never—"

"I know you would not. You wanted me to think. And I did." Charles stared at his cigar, the smoke curling around his fingers and drifting upwards between them. "I do not think I will be so fortunate as to find someone like her twice."

"You'll marry her then?"

"Not before we sail. She needs to be certain. What if she is unhappy there? Then she hates me for trapping her in a marriage? If she changes her mind, she should be free to leave."

Reuben stole the cigar from Charles's hand. "This is making you stupid." He placed it between his own lips with a clumsy grin. "I on the other hand have no woman to impress with my intelligence."

Charles paused, analyzing Reuben carefully before he finally held up the second unlit cigar. "Take this one too. For next time."

Reuben exhaled, waving the smoke towards the ceiling. "Next time?"

Charles tucked the cigar in Reuben's breast pocket. "Today you helped me find the other half of my heart. Next time I will find you yours."

Reuben now rolled the cigar between his fingers, wondering if it was the best time to smoke it.

If Charles were here, he would have the annoying and yet completely solid guidance Reuben so desperately craved. "So what would you have for me tonight?" Reuben asked. "What would you do if you doubted Tena?"

I would never doubt Tena, Charles would say. *Have faith.*

He, of course, would be correct. Reuben would never doubt Tena either.

"Then tell me, Tena, what am I to do?" As if in answer, blustery wind swept around him, the bitterness embedding in his bones.

The lifeboats mocked him with their guarantee of safety. No one could make such a promise. Visions of his friends flew in, blue and frozen, then contorted and bleeding like his sister had been. Charles's limbs swollen with ocean water. Tena's golden irises holding onto Reuben's and yet unseeing.

Reuben bit his fist to stifle his rising sobs, tears blurring the lifeboats as though they too had gone down with the ship. He wasn't worried anymore. He was completely terrified. There was no denying the truth even when he wanted to convince Maggie otherwise. So few were rescued. He could continue to believe two of them were Charles and Tena, but it was like holding water in his hands. Why have hope when the odds were so sorely stacked against them?

He squeezed his eyes shut so tightly a prism of colors danced at the edges. Why did this keep happening to him? Was it his destiny to love again and again only to lose everything he held dear? Out of all of them, could it be Maggie who actually understood life the most? Was it better to *choose* solitude rather than be forced into it?

His friends would tell him that was no way to live. It wasn't even living.

"But what if you're dead?" he whispered.

What if we are? returned Tena's voice. *Would you wish you'd never known us?*

Tears trickled down his cheeks. To have never heard her laugh, never looked in those eyes or seen her smile? To have endured the last five years without Charles by his side? He would never wish for it.

Then be thankful. At least you still had the adventure.

Reuben returned the cigar to his jacket and wiped the tears from his eyes. He inhaled the salty air and shuddered as it froze through his lungs. He drew in a second breath, then a third, concentrating on Tena's words even as debilitating fear coursed through his veins.

An adventure? Is that what this was? Or a long walk off a short pier? Either way, he was drowning, and he doubted there was a lifeboat near enough to save him.

FORTY-FOUR

With unsteady fingers, Maggie slid the silver combs from her hair. In between the upheaval of Lloyd's confessions, the final state of her appearance had all been forgotten. She couldn't return to her cabin in such a state. Amara's innocence might shatter at the news of such illicit deeds, and Siegfried should hold such honor on their wedding night.

She tore at her hair, her mind more tangled than the strands beneath her fingers. She replayed the last hours like a scratched record.

She slept with Lloyd ... and enjoyed it. He'd been a far better lover than Reuben, and Maggie didn't even love him. She didn't love either of them, just as she hadn't loved Eddie or Oskar or even Derby. Marriage was still as far removed from the equation as it had ever been. Yet she'd made love to all of them without much hesitation. They'd been her means to an end, a cure for what would be an otherwise painful or lonely existence. They were her playthings and she was becoming all too proficient at mastering the game.

Not like Reuben. Reuben understood her. She wasn't a time out from his life; she was part of his life. Making love wasn't part of some scheme to him, but that's what she had used it for. She was still only inches closer to having the assurance she needed. And what answers she had found only left her with more questions.

Not even an hour after sealing their agreement, Maggie analyzed her reflection in the looking glass of Lloyd's cabin as she closed the buttons on her dress sleeves. His eyes watched her movements from the bed, finally meeting her gaze in the glass. "You owe me information, Mr. Halverson."

"It is half past ten already. Would you not rather wait until morning?" Lloyd propped himself on his elbow, allowing the sheet to fall from his bare chest. Maggie turned her attention to the buttons at her neckline instead of satisfying his request for her attention. She had already given him quite enough of that.

"My cabinmate will send for the guard if I don't return." She patted the trim at her collar, satisfied no one could tell what she had been up to.

"You forgot these." Lloyd held up the earrings she'd dropped on the side table near his pocket watch.

She moved to him, her open palm raised. Lloyd handed her the earrings, curling her fingers around them, only not letting go of her hand. His voice was oddly calm. "There is something you must understand about Reuben, Miss Archer. He cannot be trusted."

Her eyebrows shot up. "And you can?"

"You have nothing to fear from me. If you want to know what happened, I will tell you." Lloyd gave a gentle tug on her hand, beckoning her to sit beside him. Maggie perched on the bed's edge, feeling the air hover in her lungs while she waited for the words to explain everything. This was what she came for. This was why she threw the last of her moral fiber out the porthole.

Lloyd tapped Maggie's knuckles each in turn down one direction then back in the other. The movement reminded her of a metronome keeping time to his thoughts instead of a musician's melody. "I told you Reuben went deranged. We were fourteen, and finished school two months before. One day he snapped. He beat me within an inch of my life. Kicked my rib in." Lloyd's fingers stilled against Maggie's skin. He raised his piercing eyes. "My *friend* tried to kill me."

Maggie bit her lip, mystified at this new piece of information. Could the loving man she knew also have a callous side?

Yes, of course he could. She had seen it in his eyes. All he needed was a reason to unleash it.

Reuben asked her to trust him. If Lloyd's story was true, Reuben must have a reason.

But what if he didn't? What if it was exactly as Lloyd said? If Reuben had the same sickness inside him as his mother, eventually there might be no escaping it.

"I'm sorry I was the one to tell you," Lloyd said, and his eyes genuinely seemed to express his remorse. He held her hand between his and lightly kissed each of her fingers in turn. "I care about you, Maggie. You deserve to know the truth."

"Reuben would never hurt me," Maggie said even as doubt crept into the edges of her voice and knew Lloyd could recognize it.

He frowned. "You can't trust him. He tried to *murder* me when he was only fourteen. What kind of man does such a boy become?"

"I do trust him," Maggie replied through clenched teeth, momentarily forgetting the rouse she came to play.

"Oh, I don't think so. You wouldn't be here if you did. Now that you know the truth, will you consider returning home with me?" Lloyd's tone may have been sincere, but his eyes betrayed him. There was a glint of victory there, hidden just below the surface. The slightest touch of a smirk pulled at the corners of his down turned lips. It was barely enough to notice, but she did.

Maggie wrenched her hand from his grasp, clasped her fists to her chest, and gave a disgusted chortle. "I will not. My sister needs me."

"What if your sister is dead?"

She stood, at the same time pushing the earring loops through her lobes. "If she is dead, then I will be mourning her loss for some time. A wedding would be unthinkable." Maggie retrieved her coat from the carpet on her way to the door. Her words flung through the air behind her. "Good night, Mr. Halverson. Thank you for a most illuminative evening."

Throwing a stomp to the deck, Maggie wound her hair into a tangled chignon and thrust the combs back into place. One of the teeth painfully scraped her scalp. "Confound you, Reuben," she cursed to the night. "Why couldn't you just tell me the truth?" She would ask him right now and lay this affair to rest. He could corroborate or deny Lloyd's story, but one way or another he would finally talk.

Deep voices startled Maggie's attention. Ulrich and two unfamiliar men were crossing from the upper deck. The two men chuckled and gave a polite nod as they passed. Ulrich, however, took a long drag on his cigarette and exhaled slowly, holding her gaze as he passed by. He was trying to read her mind. Let him try. It was impossible for him to guess.

Even Maggie wasn't sure what she thought anymore.

FORTY-FIVE

MAGGIE KNEW REUBEN WOULD FIND HER.

The ship's engines lay silent now, leaving the wooden boards beneath her feet as still as the water below them. As a safety precaution, the captain had ordered full stop for the night. It would cost them sailing time, but she was grateful for his foresight; it wouldn't benefit anyone if *Höllenfeuer* also foundered.

Reuben's thigh pressed against hers when he slid onto the bench beside her. He tipped her chin up for a kiss and his lips lingered another moment when she reciprocated without argument. A row was inevitable with the hidden agenda she carried. She could allow him this one.

"Cold?" He slid his arm around her shoulders until her body settled into the curve of his side. His warmth melted through her coat until the cold remained in only her fingers and toes. She wiggled them to regain circulation.

"Where were you?" he asked. "What did you have to do?" She stiffened under his watchful gaze. They needed this confrontation. The last cards must be played. Still, she hesitated to admit the carnal atrocities she'd performed that night.

After all, he was her boyfriend now. And she, the philanderer. In biblical times, he could have stoned her without batting an eye.

"Miss Müller thought you went to reject that bloke in first

class," he continued. He slowly rubbed his palm back and forth against her upper arm.

"I did."

"But if you planned to reject him, why couldn't you tell me? Why did you say you would need my forgiveness? What did you do?"

"I don't want to say." Maggie rose from the bench, turning to the rail and the ocean beyond.

His gaze followed her. "Force yourself."

"You don't want to know."

Reuben joined her at the rail, his thumbs circling his temples. "No, I probably don't."

"Before you become angry, you have to listen to me. There are some things I need to know and you're the only one who can tell me. Promise you won't overreact."

"Fine. You can trust me."

But can you? something whispered in her head. *Did he really almost kill someone and hide it from you? What kind of man does that make him?*

Another part of her argued back, *Why are you listening to Lloyd? He only told you so he could have you. What kind of man does that make* him?

Yes, but what if he told you the truth?

Besides, you're one to talk. You're manipulating both of them.

Reuben faced her, his expression impossible to read. He was holding back, as she had always done. The usual deep brown of his irises reflected the warm amber of the deck lights. Were those really the eyes of a violent boy? They could be. After all, they had really only known each other such a short time. Anyone could hide who they were for a few days each year. She certainly had been.

"Lloyd's on the ship," she admitted. "He's the man I've been meeting."

Maggie waited for the explosion, but when it came it didn't take the form she expected.

She was in his arms in a flash, her thoughts silenced with a kiss so feverish it made her head spin and left her breathless. *Where was that raw passion last night?* she wondered. Maggie leaned into him, every worry temporarily forgotten.

Unfortunately, the moment was short lived. Seconds later, the exterior door opened, breaking their lips apart.

A middle-aged couple emerged on deck, arm in arm against the cold. They extended an apologetic nod, realizing they were intruding on a private moment. "*Guten Abend, Herr, Frau,*" the man regarded them politely.

Reuben responded in kind, exchanging a few more pleasantries with the couple in German. He smiled sheepishly as though he and Maggie were like any other happy couple. As the pair turned to walk away, the woman provided Maggie with a knowing grin. "We all must find a way to keep warm, must we not?" she noted in English before being led away by her husband.

Reuben ushered her into the opposite corner with their backs to the couple. Even though she was certain they couldn't hear, Reuben lowered his voice to barely more than a whisper. "When you said you were meeting Lloyd, in what manner did you mean?"

"We spoke on deck the first day. Polite conversation. It was innocent."

"And tonight?"

Maggie cast her eyes at the deck, refusing to look up even when he repeated the question. Tonight she had reached a new low, even for her. "I went to his cabin to insist he tell me what happened between the two of you. I had to know."

Reuben looked skeptical. "Did he tell you?"

"Yes."

Reuben scowled. "You're lying. He would never tell you what really happened. He has a reputation to maintain." He stepped closer and slid the combs from her hair, the locks falling against her back. Her spine stiffened when his fingers caught in the tangles she had missed.

Reuben narrowed his eyes on the ocean rather than her. Icebergs spiked ominously against the dark horizon. "Did you sleep with him?"

Maggie skirted out of his reach, her hair falling from his hands across her shoulder. She set all her features to scandalized, although positive she could only appear impossibly guilty. "Why would you assume such a thing?"

"Your hair ..." Reuben trailed off; his expression flickered between outrage and disbelief.

Maggie held her hand out for her comb. "Do you not trust me?"

"More than you trust me it would seem." Reuben laid the comb in her open palm, closing her fingers around it in a motion eerily similar to Lloyd's return of her earrings. The cold teeth of the comb pricked against her skin.

"And so we return to the age-old impasse of ours," she said.

Surprisingly, Reuben's eyes softened slightly. "Forgive me. I've unfairly accused you of things in the past, and I won't do it again. Tell me I'm wrong and I'll believe you."

He would accept whatever she told him even when the evidence screamed otherwise. He was too clever to be lied to, but how could he face the honest truth?

Enough of this duplicity, Maggie scolded herself. *You wanted answers and you will have them. You had a moment of weakness last night with Reuben—and tonight with Lloyd—but they were simply that ... moments. Own your sins, however sordid they may be. And regret nothing when he leaves you.*

She leaned against the railing, and spoke as casually as one might lay across the sand on a summer's day. "You're not wrong."

Maggie thought she'd already heard all the expletives in existence until he managed to dreg up a new one.

"Are you serious?" Reuben flung his arm out towards the upper decks. "With *him*? God, Maggie, you should have lied!"

She eyed the German couple. They had wandered farther down the deck with no obvious indication of hearing Reuben's outburst.

"So what if I did?" she shot back, gesticulating just as wildly towards first class. "I needed answers and *you* wouldn't give them to me. What if I'd made a mistake?"

Reuben blinked twice. He looked like he was trying to swallow a brick. "By being with me? That's what you mean, isn't it? You wondered if you'd given yourself to some lunatic? So you were going to be with *him* in order to find out?"

Maggie narrowed her eyes at him. "No, that wasn't my intent. It had nothing to do with you."

"Are you mad? It had everything to do with me!" He paced the deck like a caged animal. "Did you plan to compare notes afterwards?"

Unbidden panic rose in Maggie's chest. She rubbed her sternum to force the disgusting taste back down her throat. She'd witnessed him angry before. She'd seen him full of loathing when she missed her father's funeral. But never had she witnessed the pure unadulterated hatred which burned in him tonight. He no longer resembled the man who loved her last night.

She remembered the touch of Reuben's hands against her skin, slowly sliding across her body, attempting to drink in every inch of her through his fingertips. Telling her how much he loved her. How she was all he wanted.

No matter what she had done, no matter what she wanted, she still understood the ache of loneliness, and the insensible desire to be wanted. To be the last person in your family, clinging to the wreckage. Holding on by your fingertips to the only person who reached out. She couldn't take that from him. Not yet. Not now.

A bitter gust blew through the space. Maggie yanked her coat tighter, and the temperature only dropped further. She drew a ragged breath. "It didn't happen how you think."

Reuben turned from her and focused again on the sea. "How did it happen then, Maggie? Because how I think it happened was that my—" Reuben cursed, banging his palm on the top rail. "The person I love sold herself to the only person whom I truly hate!

How could you?"

"I didn't want to!" Maggie's voice caught in her throat like a mis-swallowed biscuit. Heat flooded her face and, with deep breaths, somehow managed to calm her racing heart. "In the end, he didn't give me any choice."

It wasn't a complete lie, but nowhere near the truth either.

She moved beside Reuben, carefully trying to decipher his expression. He was a slate of ashen emotion, increasing tension in his shoulder muscles visible even through his coat. Maggie folded her arms around her middle, and she swore the temperature dropped another twenty degrees.

"I know this is my fault. Even so, you agreed not to overreact."

Reuben captured her forearms and peered into her face with urgency. His eyes flickered over her body. "He forced himself on you? In what manner would that ever be your fault?"

"I basically asked him to seduce me. It's no wonder he didn't believe me when I later refused him."

"No." Reuben drew her within his arms. His hand eased her cheek against his chest, fingertips lighting over her hair. All the hostility of his previous statements evaporated in one word. Maggie closed her eyes, relishing the feel of his fingers through her hair. It was strange that here, in the midst of a terrible deceit, a piece of her wished this was real.

"No," he repeated. "That's what people like him tell people like you so you think you deserved it. You made a mistake by going, but it doesn't give him the right to take advantage."

He pressed his lips to her scalp and sighed. It wasn't a sound of contentment, quite the opposite. It was the resolve of one committing to the conclusion of long overdue conflict. "Find out how much money you have left. I might need you to bail me out of the master at arms."

Maggie's stomach clenched. "Why would I need to do that?"

"People like him never stop. Unless someone makes them stop." His voice remained eerily composed, so much that Maggie wished he would scream at her again.

In a flash, she remembered the story Lloyd told her.

She pried his arms off her body. "So you plan to finish what you started? Lloyd told me you attacked him."

At first, a steady stare seemed the only response she would receive. Until she considered that by not denying it, he was likewise admitting guilt. Her heart sank like a stone. "It's true?" she choked. "Why?"

"*Why*?" Reuben paled. "Because you're not the first person he's used force on." All repose shattered as his fist collided with the metal railing, then shook the pain away before he punched it a second time. Maggie's curiosity wanted to find out how he knew this, but was horrified to learn the answer.

"Mira."

The word echoed in her brain, and she knew she would never forget the haunted sound of Reuben's voice when he said it. Never before had one word conveyed more heartache.

"Mira was terrified I wouldn't believe her—in the end no one else did—but why *wouldn't* I? What child would tell such a lie? Mira was only twelve, Maggie! What kind of bloody lout does something like that?" He pressed his sore knuckles to his lips. "I was Mira's brother and she trusted me to protect her. Lloyd was *my* friend. *I* invited him into our home. What happened wasn't Mira's fault. It was *mine*."

Maggie hadn't a clue how to respond. The truth was worse than anything she had imagined. Her mind fought between disgust with Lloyd and relief that Reuben's behavior, while not to be commended, had a justifiable reason. "I'm so sorry," she whispered and immediately felt stupid for saying it. Her words were insignificant compared to the reality and the remorse she should be feeling, but wasn't.

Reuben's fingers made odd movements on the rail, flexing and tapping alternately. She hesitantly placed her hand over his, and it only resulted in his fingers clenching into a fist.

He spoke through gritted teeth, "I won't lie to you—I wanted to kill him. At the time, all I could think of was making him pay. It was Mira who stopped me."

He stared out at the dark waves as if witnessing the event for the first time. "Mira wasn't exactly the same afterwards. What Lloyd did changed her. And now every day I listen to that voice—" Reuben gave a sharp intake, and solemnly shook his head. "The *point* is I gave him far less than what he deserved."

His eyes shifted first to her, then to their clasped hands, then back to her face. Heaven only knew what he must have seen there. She only just managed to throw herself between him and the exterior door as his hand gripped the knob.

"Move." Reuben's face flushed with such ferocity Maggie visibly flinched.

She pressed her back to the door. "You wouldn't really hurt him, would you?" She swallowed, her palms slick against the metal door. "You wouldn't kill him? Would you?"

"How can you still care about him?" Reuben demanded. "This is exactly why I never told you." He swiped his hand across the air between them. "Why I never tell *anyone*. No one believed us then. They looked at me exactly how you are now—like I'm some kind of monster. But *he* was the monster! And he still is. I might have failed to protect my sister from him, and that's something I'll deal with for the rest of my life, but I won't regret making him pay for it. I did it for Mira and I'll do it for you."

An unfamiliar type of despair enveloped her, some emotion that very nearly resembled defeat. She knew he wasn't lying. And if he did this, he would never be the same. "You can't."

Reuben narrowed his eyes. "Give me one good reason."

His brow creased while he waited for her response. Her senses notched up every element around her as her brain racked for a solution. Calm waves rolled against the ship with barely any wind, yet its salt stung her nostrils. The once faint padding of waves on the ship's hull now thundered in her ears. She glanced down the deck. It must be close to midnight now, everyone turned in for the night. Even the German couple had gone below. Except for the fog of their breath and the beating of her heart, the night lay perfectly still.

Her mind drifted to the day Reuben hastily asked her to run away with him on an impulse. With him there were no financial arrangements with her parents, no disparaging looks at her deplorable behavior, no threats against her family. Here was a man who would follow her to the ends of the earth, who would defend her with everything he had, even when she betrayed his trust that very night. A man who loved her.

It will be just the two of us, he had said on Easter. *Let's leave this place and everything behind.* What if she had taken his hand and run? They wouldn't even be standing here if she had.

The interior lights shone through the door's tiny window behind her, illuminating Reuben's face through the darkness. His life held possibilities—a future so spontaneously conducted yet more incredible than any she could have planned for. She wanted to want him in the same reckless way he wanted to be with her, one day at a time, no questions asked.

Maggie wanted to feel that way ... only she didn't and probably never would.

But if she didn't find a way to stop him, she had no doubts Reuben would go straight to Lloyd's room and strangle him with his bare hands. She didn't want blood on Reuben's conscience— especially not on her account. Especially not because of a lie.

She wondered what Tena would do. Maggie wasn't like her sister—built to love unconditionally and trust blindly. Maybe it was the reason Tena was happily engaged. She was confident enough to do what Maggie couldn't.

A light flickered on in her brain, her nerves short-circuiting momentarily. An idea emerged so crazy it seemed to come from someone else.

She stared Reuben square in the face. "I want you to marry

me."

The resulting silence lay so profound, Maggie longed for the wind to return and indicate time hadn't stopped.

Reuben's expression shifted from anger to confusion to shock. He looked as stunned as if the skies opened and foreign invaders descended onto the deck. That would have been about as probable as the words he'd just heard.

Very slowly poignant hope emerged in his eyes. "Are you *sure* that's what you want?"

FORTY-SIX

REUBEN WAS THE TIME TRAVELER whom H.G. Wells wrote about. Only he didn't require a machine to stop time, reverse it, or see the future. True time travel was, is, and would always be impossible. Just as impossible as the words he'd just heard. Words he'd been denied when he requested them. Impossible. And yet, Maggie still said them.

"I want you to marry me."

Her eyes locked onto his, the dark swirls of the sky reflected back. Those eyes which never sought his out and never wanted his gaze. No matter what she had done, he could forgive her. Those eyes were the doorways to his doom.

He could go to the past and erase every mistake. He could create a perfect future with Maggie by his side. Time always changed things, and he would be the one to change them.

"Are you sure that's what you want?" he asked, daring to hope it was.

Maggie's answer never came. In the blink of an eye, the exterior door crashed open, sprawling her upon the deck. Light spilled over Reuben, a familiar silhouette filling the doorframe.

Reuben lunged at the same time Lloyd did. He grabbed hold of Lloyd's collar, swinging him in a broad arc as the other man jabbed a fist to Reuben's stomach. The blow loosed his grip and

Lloyd stumbled backward.

"You don't want to fight me!" Reuben gasped.

Lloyd grinned wickedly. "Oh, yes, I really do." Surging forward, he seized Reuben's arms as his taller frame pressed Reuben's chest against the stiff railing. The metal bars crashed into Reuben's ribs, pain shooting down his side. With a guttural yell, he jutted his heel into Lloyd's shin, unable to so much as loosen Lloyd's grip.

"This has been a long time coming, Radford," Lloyd sneered as he twisted Reuben's wrist. "Shame I have to embarrass you in front of your new *fiancé*." He said the last word as if it tasted of bitter grapes.

Of course, Reuben swore, Lloyd must have followed her. He'd heard every word they said.

He flexed his arms, straining in vain and cursing the day Lloyd decided to bulk up his otherwise scrawny teenage frame. After years wasted in a cemetery, Reuben had lost the physical advantage.

"Curse you, Lloyd! I should kill you right now."

Lloyd laughed. "You could try, but I've always had the upper hand against you. No one believed you then and they won't now. I don't know how you won Maggie over, but in time she'll see my side. As she discovered earlier, I can be *very* persuasive."

Maggie stumbled to her feet and threw herself on top of them, repeatedly clawing at Lloyd arms. He shoved Reuben away to fend off her ravaging fingernails, capturing her wrists only to drop them when his nose encountered the force of Reuben's fist.

Reuben may as well have punched a brick wall for the way his fingers buckled. The skin above the middle knuckle, already tender from taking his aggressions out on the railing earlier, began to darken with an angry red welt and shooting pain sliced down his wrist when he bent his pinky.

Taking advantage of Reuben's injury, Lloyd rounded on him with both fists flying, even as blood dripped from his left nostril. Reuben leapt back, forearms raised, foolishly leaving the rest of him unguarded. Reuben doubled over as Lloyd's fist hit his midsection, his breath haggard and heart pounding in both pain and wild despair. He was going to lose.

"Stop!" Maggie yelled. She reached again for Lloyd's arm, but he threw her hard to the deck, the wind forced from her lungs in a dry gasp. She rolled onto her back, hands pressed for breath against her rigid corset stays. Reuben's revulsion rose stronger than anything else on the deck—more volatile than the pain in his fists, more penetrating than the chill of the artic sea. He would not—could not—fail Maggie. Lloyd would have to kill him first.

Hands outstretched, he tackled Lloyd, sending them both to the deck in a heap. Before Lloyd could retaliate, Reuben heaved him onto his back, straddling his midsection. "What are you doing, you perverted—" Whatever Lloyd was about to declare Reuben was lost in the sound of Reuben's fist meeting Lloyd's right eye. Reuben only vaguely noticed the sting in his knuckles or the ooze of blood as one cracked open before he thrust another blow up Lloyd's nose. Maggie winced at the sound of bone meeting bone, but this time Reuben relished it.

His fingers wrapped themselves around Lloyd's throat. The thumbs ground against Lloyd's larynx, ever so slightly, enough to make the other man draw a nervous breath. "Time to end this," Reuben spat. "Last words?" He wanted to witness Lloyd in tears, begging for mercy. To grovel in his final moments and know he deserved his fate.

Unfortunately, Lloyd wouldn't give Reuben the satisfaction. He seized Reuben's wrists, his sneer mirroring all the arrogance he'd always possessed. "You wouldn't. You don't have it in you."

"Oh, no?" Reuben tightened his grip, and pressed his thumbs in a touch farther. "I have no reason not to."

Mira bent low over Lloyd's face, studying his expression. Her black eyes met Reuben's through her dark lashes, the irises vanished inside her distended pupils. "Do it," she whispered.

Like a man possessed, his fingers curled of their own accord.

Mira doubled over with cawing laughter, hands clutching a stitch in her side until she fell, rolling and cackling, to the deck. Reuben's fingers curled tighter. Far off he heard Maggie scream as though she were trapped in a glass jar, no air holes tapped into the tin lid, bouncing off the walls in an effort to escape.

"Stop! Please!" she screamed over and over. "Reuben!" His arm muscles only tensed. Lloyd's clawing fingers became inconsequential pinpricks against Reuben's bloody knuckles.

A trail of scarlet trickled down his wrist then frantically smeared by Lloyd's twitching hands. A second set of hands were on top of his now, pulling, heaving to save his victim.

Didn't she know he couldn't stop? He would toss Lloyd's body overboard and never think of his worthless form again. Reuben was beyond caring if he was damned for it. It was enough that Lloyd be damned too. They could grapple for all eternity if they had to. At least the living world would be free of Lloyd's crimes.

It was Mira who saved Lloyd all those years ago. The voice of the cackling delusion who goaded him to commit murder now also held the face of the girl who then pled for Reuben to let Lloyd live.

Charles had been the first to discover what happened. He walked in to find Lloyd unconscious on the Radfords' drawing room floor and Mira sobbing in a chair. Reuben stood over Lloyd's body, his destroyed knuckles dripping blood on the oak hardwood as he viewed the aftermath of his anger. Numb at the time, he hadn't been able to speak when Charles asked what happened. He could only look from Lloyd's smashed face to his own battered hands and wonder in horror if he'd actually killed him.

Through every police questioning, every argument with Reuben's father, every demand by Lloyd's parents to have Reuben locked away in the sanatorium, Charles was there. So many nights Reuben appeared on Charles's doorstep, preferring to stay there instead of in his own house. Emil would join them for stolen cigars on the back patio at midnight, Fred would lecture them about the evils of allowing a ten year old boy to smoke, and all three of them would laugh and blow smoke in Fred's face. Those nights, it was almost as though Reuben was a regular boy.

Reuben's heart twisted at the memory.

He should be laughing with his friends, not committing murder.

Reuben dropped Lloyd to the deck where he lay panting and coughing. Mira's glare darkened by the second, blazing in a cold heat. "I'm sorry. I'm sorry," Reuben sighed. "I can't. I'm sorry."

Mira started towards him. A halo of oppressive energy radiated from her in every angle. "Coward," she hissed, her eyes deep pools of nothingness ringed by a ghoulish smile.

Reuben's arms instinctively raised to shield himself, retreating until his back slammed into the railing. In so many ways he *was* a coward. A liar. A lunatic. A sham. He refused to be a murderer too. Even when not two minutes before he would have gladly embraced it.

That's the funny thing about time, he told Charles. *It always changes things.*

And that thought was imprinted on his mind as he fell thirty feet into the icy water below.

FORTY-SEVEN

MAGGIE WATCHED WITH PARALYZED horror as Reuben pitched over the railing and disappeared beneath the water.

Her brain couldn't even form words. *Please come up*, she thought, frantically scanning the darkness. *Please be alive.*

The last two minutes were reduced to a terrifying blur. Reuben would have killed Lloyd. She didn't understand what stopped him, but she knew it hadn't been her. His aggression disappeared without reason; he apologized to and retreated from something she couldn't see. The way his limbs seized, as though he'd thrown himself over the rail and yet didn't ... the same glossy look she'd seen on Florence Radford's face in the Winchesters' garden seconds before slapping her son.

Maggie began a frantic search of the deck. By her best estimation, it was now after midnight. No one was awake, or not on deck at any rate. Any officers on duty would be stationed on the bridge at this hour. And the bridge was on the other end of the ship. Too far.

Unrestrained shouting sounded like a good alternative. "Man overboard! Man over—"

A stiff backhand collided with her cheek and the blow sent her to her knees. Lloyd's rough hands dragged her back into a standing position against the rail. "How are you even standing?" Maggie gasped. She was no expert, but she assumed nearly being strangled should take more out of a person.

"Shut up!" Lloyd rasped, breaking shrilly on the second word. His palm pressed on the back of her neck, jerking her head forward so her vision saw only black ocean.

Reuben floated on his back about forty feet off the stern. He was alive, but not for long in such frigid waters.

"Let me go!" she screamed. "He'll drown, Lloyd! Or freeze!"

"Like I care." Lloyd's grip tightened on her wrist. Maggie twisted in vain, her skin rubbing raw under the strain.

"Don't be a murderer, Lloyd!"

"You mean like he was to do to me?"

"Killing him will not win me over!"

"Grah! Fine!"

The pressure on her arm disappeared. Maggie rubbed her sore wrist, her narrowed eyes on Lloyd's every movement. He stalked around the exterior wall of the smoking room, exiting the other side with a life ring in hand. "Happy, my dear?" he asked, and tossed it over the side without bothering to judge where it landed.

Maggie didn't hesitate. She sprinted towards the smoking room door, praying Ulrich hadn't left his usual post of cards, cigarettes, and cheap liquor. Why hadn't she thought of him before? If she could only get inside—

"Ah, ah, I'm not through with you yet." Lloyd's arm stole around her waist in the time it took for her to even think Ulrich's name twice. She dug her heels into the deck, only succeeding in tracing thin black sole marks from the door around the corner of the exterior wall. It was perfectly hidden. No one would notice them unless someone was searching.

Every minute wasted was another minute Reuben slowly froze to death.

"It was you all along!" she spat. "I should have trusted Reuben. Now let me go!"

Lloyd matched her sneer. "Who do you think you're going to?

He tried to kill me! Twice!"

"He told me what you did to Mira!"

Lloyd paused, and his grip slackened minutely before clenching with renewed vigor. She winced as fingernails dug half-moon grooves into her already bruised skin.

I'm going to die, she thought. Lloyd would throw her overboard after Reuben. Their bodies would sink to the bottom of the sea to join Tena and Charles and the rest of them. Or, if by some miracle, Tena *was* alive, she would believe Maggie and Reuben ran off together. Tena would think her sister abandoned her again. A fear was written in Maggie's eyes she could no longer hide.

"Oh, my dear," Lloyd soothed. "Why are you so afraid? I was never your enemy. It was you who made me the villain." Lloyd seized her chin, thrusting her lips upward for a rough kiss. When he pulled away, his smile was as cold as his eyes. "Did you honestly think I didn't know what you were playing at, my pretty temptress? I bet you bed him as well just to find out our secret."

Maggie returned his hostile expression stare for stare, drowning her fears within her determination. He may have recognized her endgame from the beginning, but she wouldn't allow him the satisfaction of winning.

"I warned you, Miss Archer," Lloyd breathed against her ear. "Rejecting me is a foolish endeavor. This is your final chance—return to Fontaine with me. You will regret it if you say no."

Maggie turned her head, allowing her lips to flutter over his. In that moment, she knew he hung on her very word. She only needed one.

"No."

If it was possible for Lloyd's expression to become any darker, it did. "Fine," he spat. "You had your chance."

Gripping her arm like a vice, Lloyd tossed her mercilessly onto the wooden planks. He wiped his mouth on the back of his hand, turning to face her one final time. "I hope your decision leaves you bruised and bloody, clinging to the pieces of your broken heart."

Maggie sat in silence as his retreating back disappeared around the corner. She managed to draw in a single shuddering breath, then in a single fluid motion, leapt to her feet and peered over the railing. Reuben's torso stretched flat over the life ring, his legs half-submerged behind him. In the dark it was impossible to decipher if he was awake or even breathing.

She flew towards the bridge, her heels ringing out in the silent night air. Bruises puckered down her vertebrae where Lloyd had slammed the door into her back; knots dotted her shins from repeated falls. Blood pounded under her skin with each fallen step. This was her fault, entirely her fault. If only she could have left well enough alone ...

Maggie laughed out loud. The sound escaped from somewhere deep in her throat, bitter against her lips as it emerged. Florence Radford once called her a harlot ... well, harlots was paid for flaunting their wares, were they not? She had received every payment she requested. The irony was she certainly had now lost everyone she held dear. Even herself.

Meanwhile, her maiden sister was most likely dead in the water below her ... Tena would find her repugnant.

What Maggie detested most wasn't that she regretted her actions. What she hated was that she couldn't. She must be cold and callous inside; it was how she would survive.

Lloyd desired her a broken heart as her punishment? Well, the joke was on him. She didn't have enough of a heart left to break.

FORTY-EIGHT

REUBEN NOTICED THE GLOW before his eyes recognized it as sunlight filtered red behind his closed lids. He raised them a cautious sliver, heaved a great sigh, and opened them fully. He was lying in his upstairs bedroom, third door on the right, the morning sun rippling upon his face through the open window.

Everything was as it should be. His mother's hand stitched quilt enveloped his curled body. His father's boyhood stack of worn magazines sat on the floor in the corner, the latest issue dog eared to mark Reuben's place. Atop his dresser was their only family photograph, over thirteen years old now, but still Reuben's favorite. Mira's locket held the same one in miniature.

Florence smiled for the camera, lovely as always, ever a woman able to light up a room with her presence. Harris was more serious, although the hint of a smile raised his lips. His hand held his wife's, their fingers ever so slightly entwined. Seven-year-old Reuben stood behind his father, smiling jubilantly, while five-year-old Mira sat on their mother's lap, tight spun curls and pinafore askew, captured in the midst of a laugh.

Reuben threw off the blankets, his bare feet savoring the warmth of the sun-heated floor on what should be an otherwise cool morning. Or should it?

What day is it? he wondered. *What month?* A series of unusual and horrible nightmares flooded back in incredible detail, conflicting his mind with competing memories. For a moment he sat in shock, two fingers measuring his thumping pulse. In his dream, everyone died. And he must have died too? It made sense. When you die in a dream, you wake up. He'd been killed before in dreams: stabbed, burned in fires, swept away in turbulent winds. But falling off a steamship? Now that was a new one.

A door slammed in the hall followed by light-footed skipping past his room and down the stairs. His heart slammed against his ribcage with the overwhelming need to see his family and lay his fears to rest.

Reuben leapt to his feet, hastily retrieving his trousers from the floor and a clean shirt and shoes from the wardrobe. As he descended the stairs, cheerful voices wafted back to him from the drawing room. MacDowell's *To a Wild Rose* crackled on the gramophone. And there ... A lump the size of England wedged in his throat.

Florence looked exactly like her photograph with dark hair wound atop her head and brown eyes shining as she sipped her tea. Harris circled the room with the morning *Gazette*. If Reuben's memory served him well, his father was usually on a daily quest to find mistakes in the columns, a search-and-destroy mission to fire someone. Today, he was his old self—only coy smiles at his wife over the top of the newspaper.

Their housemaid, Mrs. Butaine, bustled in carrying a tray laden with scones, strawberry marmalade, sliced ham, and several varieties of fruit. She left once more and returned with a second tray containing china plates, silverware, and a stack of folded napkins.

"Anything else, Mrs. Radford?" the older woman asked.

"No, thank you, Mrs. Butaine." The maid bustled back to the kitchen as Florence reached for the tray, glancing up at Reuben still glued in the doorway. "Reuben? I hope you don't mind eating breakfast in here this morning. Mira requested it, and this room does have the best morning light."

Reuben found it suddenly difficult to remain upright. He sank into the armchair closest to his mother before his legs forgot how to stand.

"Heavens, Reuben, are you ill?" Florence rested the back of her hand against his forehead. "No fever, thank goodness. Here." She poured a cup of tea, adding a dash of milk while she stirred. Handing it over to her son, Florence waved at her husband. "Harris, do open a window, will you?"

Crossing before the unlit fireplace, Harris threw open both sets of windows overlooking the front garden. A voluptuous breeze billowed the curtains causing the sunbeams to dance waves of light across the room. The ethereal quality of the whirling dust in the air settled Reuben, and he was left to wonder why he panicked at all. A dream, no matter how vivid, was only a fleeting illusion.

Reuben sipped his tea, his mother's perfectly proportioned pour flavorful against his tongue. Harris claimed a seat on the couch across from them and returned to the newspaper. "Reuben, have you completed the piece on the improvements to the courthouse?" Harris asked.

Reuben lowered his cup, wracking his brain for the article his father meant. He couldn't recall being assigned a piece about the courthouse, although his brain was probably still addled from his restless night. The notes were sure to be buried on his desk at the *Gazette*. "No, not yet. I'll finish it up first thing today."

Harris waved him off, then turned back to the paper. "If you haven't begun, all the better. They made more changes—I know, I know, why can't anyone stick to a decision?—that's the way they are. They're not happy unless they're spending more than the town can afford. Would you mind stopping in to record the new information?"

"Of course. Right after breakfast."

Delicate fingers covered Reuben's eyes, satiny white arms pressed close against his ears from above the chair. And then the lightest smile of a girl's voice. "Good morning, big brother."

Reuben's chest heaved. His fingers locked, the tea cup falling to the rug where he envisioned a deep brown stain cascading across the worn threads. Distress returned like an angry mother. He couldn't breathe. He couldn't think. He was two parts panic to one part rationality.

He staggered to his feet, suppressing the urge to black out across the coffee table. He clung to his sister, observing her every feature in order to convince himself she was alive. Mira's hair fell across her shoulders in shining russet curls, a portion twisted and pinned against the back of her scalp. Her prized locket glimmered against her dress's mint green chiffon bodice. Reuben met her eyes last, afraid of which version he would find hidden there.

Her eyes glimmered back as dazzling as her smile. Her childish features had disappeared along with any hatred or misunderstanding that may have wedged between them. She was beautiful, grown up in the time between sleep and waking.

Mira laughed. "You should see your face, Reuben. Close your mouth or you'll catch a fly."

Reuben swallowed. His hallucinations were part of a terrible world he'd invented in his head. Another nightmare. He was awake now and everything was as it should be.

Mira drifted over to the gramophone. She shifted through the choices, and the music cut out with a squeak as she switched records. Reuben sank to his knees, dabbing a napkin over his spilled tea as empty static transitioned to the airy strains of Stephen Foster's *Beautiful Dreamer*. Mira danced on her toes, turning with drawn eyes to the soft melody. Her movements glided her towards him like a ship on the water. Icebergs danced across his vision darker than sunspots.

Reuben placed the soiled napkin and empty teacup on the table. He had never been on a ship, or seen an iceberg, so why could he describe every jagged edge of the North Atlantic? Mira circled back to the tea tray; her hips swayed with the rhythm as she served herself a cup and poured more sugar than there was liquid to catch it. The crystals littered the table as soft as snowflakes.

Dainty shoes buried beneath drifts of white. Dancing beside a Christmas tree adorned with colored baubles. Two sisters, one with golden eyes, one with blue.

Reuben shook his head, the dream swept away with the swipe of Mira's hand across the fallen sugar. Reuben only had one sister. She was the one who mattered. She was here. She was real.

His nightmare could return to the depths it came from.

Shaking the last sugar crystals into the cup, Mira accepted Reuben's hand when he offered it to her. He turned her about in perfect form, rounding their parents until Mira's pleas convinced them to join in. Harris held his wife close, his hand on her back where social convention brushed the edge of impropriety.

Reuben smiled. Some things never changed.

"Do you think we should leave them alone?" Mira giggled. "We could take breakfast out back?"

Reuben twirled her in a circle so her gown billowed out in mint swirls. "That's a brilliant idea."

After loading their plates with food, they lounged on the porch settee, the gramophone's music muffled through the exterior door, and the breeze kicking the scent of the garden towards them. Mira babbled about everything and nothing while Reuben could only listen, silently eating his breakfast. Her animated chatter reminded him of the night he stayed out until dawn talking with Tena, and realized he still didn't know what happened to her. Was she alive? He stood with the intention to find out.

"Are you headed to the courthouse already?" Mira asked.

Reuben looked back at her, startled. She popped another berry in her mouth and cocked her head at him in inquiry. *Of course,* Reuben thought. *Tena isn't real either. I made her up in my head.* Of all the people he'd encountered in his dreams, she was one of the few he wouldn't have minded continuing into wakefulness.

"Reuben?" Mira set her plate on the seat and stood beside him. "If you're leaving now, I suppose I'll be off to school as well. Mr. Hartford said he would bring me home on his lumber wagon with the boys."

"No!" Reuben cried. "No wagons. I'll walk you home. Wait for me. And, whatever you do, don't go near the railroad tracks."

Mira's nose wrinkled. "Why ever not?"

"Because I would never forgive myself if something happened." Reuben stopped short. "Who built that house?"

At the bottom of the porch stairs, in the land normally housing their vast garden, now lay a single long stone-laden pathway. The trail's end contained little more than a gated fence and beyond that a house. Its appearance was unimposing by all respects and would not garner a second glance if it had not appeared at random in their own back garden. The pale grey brick of the two story structure was in contrast to the ebony iron rails of its fence, and the double covered porch over the entrance wasn't even noteworthy. It stood out simply because it didn't fit in.

Reuben halted at the edge of the porch, a hand above his brow to block the sun. The strange residence tugged at him. The longer he stared at it, the more troublesome the feeling of deja vu became.

"Who lives in that house?" Reuben asked. Mira narrowed her eyes in the direction he pointed, squinting in the distance.

"You see a house?"

"You don't? Right there!" He waved wildly. "Past the gate. I— *What are those?*" Gigantic evergreens rose along the path from the edge of the Radford property to the iron fence. They towered stories above the siblings, monstrous trees threatening to block out the sun.

Mira extended a hand to his forehead as their mother had done. "I see the gate, except no house and no trees. Beyond the gate is nothing. There's always been nothing there."

Reuben studied the house. Growing up, he didn't remember

there ever being a gate. His brain hurt. "We should find out what's in there."

Mira seized his hand. Her fingers burned like ice against his skin. "I don't think we should. What if it leads somewhere bad?" Her voice became meager, more akin of the girl he remembered.

Reuben eased her into the crook of his arm and kissed her curls. Her mass seemed fragile again beneath his grasp. Watery doe eyes searched his. "You can't change it," she whispered.

"Change what?"

One tear escaped her brown eye and sketched it's way down her cheek. "The past."

The vision sliced through him then, penetrating every inch of his suppressed memories.

"Which day would you redo?" Laurence asked.

"There are so many," Reuben replied. "How could I only choose one?"

"You must."

But Reuben was the time traveler. And he wanted to right every wrong.

His throat constricted Everything in his dream—the sisters, the ship, Mira's death—it was all true.

Reuben turned on Mira with wild eyes. "Which one are you?" he demanded. "Are you my sister or the other one?" She hadn't changed in the prior ten seconds. Her eyes weren't dark, her face remained unscathed by malice. She wasn't clawing his eyes out, which he supposed he should take as a point to the positive. But if he was awake and Mira was really Mira then ... His voice crackled low in his throat. "Am I dead?"

Mira didn't reply. She wrapped her arms around Reuben's waist and nestled her cheek against his chest like she had when they were little. "It could be worse."

"I'm dead." The words tasted sour. "I'm dead," he repeated as if saying it again would make it better. It didn't. "What could be worse than dying?"

"Don't you remember? It's why you're here."

Reuben latched onto the fading memories of his meager life. There had been so much joy to their family once, overwhelming love, and security even, and he'd allowed a series of stupid decisions to destroy them forever. He should have tried harder, fought stronger, been more determined to keep his family alive. Mira's death may have dug the hole, and his father's may have nailed shut the lid, but Lloyd gave them the materials for the coffin, and Reuben chose to construct it with his own hands. Where he should have built a home, he instead built gallows. He created artificial ghosts so he could never forget.

That was how he died—one last attempt to absolve his mistakes only to die by them. In every space he ever lived, whether real or illusionary, Mira was always right. There was always something worse than death.

Wherever he stood now, the sun soothed his skin, the wind gently brushed across his face, and Mira was secure in his arms— the combination of perfection.

The gentle patter of his mother's voice floated through the kitchen window. She was Florence again, returned to her right mind, no longer tortured by her little girl's memory. He witnessed her exchange the luncheon platter for her husband's sturdy kiss. Harris laughed, finally consumed by his family instead of his work.

Wasn't this what Reuben wanted? To be free of his demons and his family made whole again? His arms tightened around his sister. A mere week ago when he pressed a pistol to his skull, he had by no means expected God to be so gracious. Reuben never asked Him for paradise, only peace.

Nevertheless, it appeared paradise was what Reuben had been offered. He could accept death if it meant heaven with his family.

A shrill whistle strained, and a seven car passenger train ground to a halt before the porch, steam billowing from the engine's undercarriage. From the first class compartment stepped none other than Charles Kisch, oddly done up in top hat and tails.

He tossed his hat over Reuben's head with a flourish and grinned. "Oh, this is not heaven, Radford."

"What are you doing here?" Reuben called over the whooshing steam. "Where did this train come from?"

Charles beckoned him forward. "Come find out."

Reuben started off the porch and collided with a previously non-existent herd of mahogany dining chairs. He stumbled over the first, drove his knee into the second, flipped backward over the third, and landed painfully across the arm of the fourth. Rubbing the knot already rising across his patella, he gaped at the sea of magically formed furniture.

"What the...?" The immediate area between the porch and the train now contained no less than fifty closely packed chairs, each identical to those surrounding the inside dining table. There wasn't even enough room to maneuver his way out of the mess without causing further damage to himself. To make matters worse, Mira had vanished. Reuben began hoisting chairs over his head and chucking them across the porch. The move was surprisingly rewarding.

"Cigar?" Charles asked, offering one already lit when Reuben finally tunneled his way through. The train blew another low blast and rolled away in a whoosh of steam as mysteriously as it had arrived.

Reuben took a long draw from the cigar and released the smoke in one long wisp. "So, the train?"

Charles grinned and lit his own. "I had to get here somehow, did I not? Why not first class?"

A normal man would find more than a few things odd about this situation. With Charles there now, however, nothing seemed out of the ordinary. The appearance of a mass of chairs or trains without tracks wasn't strange. The worries of Reuben's life were suddenly insignificant.

Then again, perhaps accepting death changes a man.

Charles puffed on his cigar as he analyzed the house. The stonework path lay darkened now from the evergreens which blocked the sun. He started at a brisk pace towards it, leaving Reuben to match Charles's longer gait. "I do not remember this house. Who lives there?"

Reuben halted mid-stride. "You can see it?"

"Of course I can see it." Charles gave a tap to his cigar, loosing ashes from the end and continued walking. "You do understand you only see what you want to see here."

Reuben ran to catch up, thrusting his hand out for Charles's arm. "This isn't real?"

Charles tossed his cigar away. Another appeared in his hand. "Who said that? Just because it is not heaven, that does not make it imaginary."

"So if this place is real then ..." Reuben blanched. "Is this like a holding cell before I'm sent to hell?" This had suddenly taken a dark turn.

Charles glanced upward and shook his head. "I would doubt it."

"But I *am* dead?"

"I never said that."

"So I'm *not* dead?"

"I never said that either."

Reuben threw up his hands, releasing his cigar into the firmament. "Stop with the riddles, Charles, which is it?"

Charles offered him a smirk liken to Emil. "It is up to you."

Reuben pressed his hands to his temples. If he wasn't already dead, he was probably having an aneurism that would quickly lead to his demise. The trees streaked by in a blur of sap and pine needles only to release them at the house's iron gate. Thunder rumbled across the ever darkening sky.

He tapped his fingers on the fence, just as he had tapped out his frustrations on deck with Maggie. The structure loomed above him, nothing short of foreboding. He understood now where this house would lead. A doorway back to a life full of uncertainty. A choice. For all Reuben knew, he would wake up a helpless cripple, frostbitten legs lopped of by a doctor's scalpel. Would Maggie marry him then, only to resent him later? Would his hallucinations still haunt him?

Here in this weird and wonderful other world—he would call it limbo ... perhaps even purgatory if such a thing existed—this place offered everything he wanted. Charles told him this wasn't heaven. But to a boy fleeing reality, escaping himself, this was close enough.

"You need to go back to your life," Charles said firmly. "It is important you do."

Leave it to his best friend to read his mind. "Why?"

"Because I cannot." Charles ground his heel into his cigar stub, streaking the black ash across the paving stones. His expression was tight and determined. "I know that is selfish, and I am not sorry for asking it."

Of course, thought Reuben. How had he been so ignorant? How else would Charles know this wasn't heaven unless he himself had already been there? How could Reuben leave behind the only person to ever truly understand him?

Reuben was ten years old again, staring down at a little blond haired boy who chose to sit alone in the school yard. The boy stared up at him with those lonely eyes, knowing his words were sure to drive Reuben away like all the other boys. "*Hallo. Ich spreche kein Englisch.*"

"Hello." Reuben extended his hand. It was a full minute before the other boy took it and struggled to his feet. "I don't speak that language," he laughed. "We'll learn together, yes?"

"What if I stay here?" Reuben asked Charles.

Charles nodded towards Reuben's home. "You could. Stay with your family. You would be healed. But before you do, there is someone else you should consider."

Reuben strained to divine anything from the weathered house before him. The windows were too dark to make out the largest piece of furniture, let alone who might be inside. "Who?" he asked.

"The only one who can convince you to go back."

Reuben's fingers were on the gate's latch before he could contemplate he'd made a decision. Only Charles's voice stopped him from opening it fully.

"Radford?" The word lay more definitive than a slamming door. They were parting ways, not just to board a ship or say goodnight, but forever.

Reuben stepped back. "Couldn't you come with me?"

With a wane smile, Charles pulled Reuben to his chest. The two men clutched each other tighter than was socially acceptable, however in times like this it was the only way that felt right. "*Nein*, Reuben."

Reuben laughed though his tears. "Careful, Kisch. Your German is showing."

"I figured you can have the final word."

"Not this time. This time it's your turn." Reuben managed to unwrap himself from Charles. "*Freunden für das Leben*."

Charles grinned. "Agreed. Mates for life."

"And after that?" Reuben asked, his voice breaking on the final word.

Charles held the gate open for Reuben to pass. "Even then."

He turned for one final look at his friend, his brother, only everything behind him was gone. His childhood home and all the people in it vanished into inky blackness. The only place to go was inside the house ... It was time to wake up from this dream.

Reuben closed his eyes and prayed. *Just three seconds and you'll wake up*, he told himself. *Just like last time. Three seconds and you'll see if it was worth it.* Reuben breathed in the acrid scent of pine, filling his sinuses with their bitter odor.

Please, God, he prayed. *Let it be worth it.*

One. The gate clicked into place behind him and Reuben opened his eyes.

"Well, I wouldn't have expected that."

If the grass was always greener on the other side, this was nothing short of vibrant viridian. Glittering evergreens lined the walk up to the house, transformed with golden garland and flickering candlelight, sending a warm glow across the pathway. Snow fell softly above him, although never quite reaching his skin. Reuben ascended the stairs in a trance, unable to resist the young woman who appeared before him. Her iridescent eyes beckoned him forward, swallowing him into their depths, while her lithe fingers fiddled with an evergreen sprig, carefully plucking each needle only to toss them aside. As Reuben drew nearer, he drank in every line of her facade, every angle of her figure. Reuben swallowed. Enchanting—no other word was enough.

Charles's words echoed in his head. *You are only seeing what you want to see.*

So many abominations had taken residence in his brain at one time or another; out of all of the horrors, how had such a vision broken through? Who was she?

Time melted around them like watercolors on a canvas, drifting in and out to blur the line between dreams and consciousness.

Two.

Reuben reached for her hands, laced their fingers to keep a hold on this place awhile longer. The warmth of her touch felt real enough beneath his skin even as her essence waned. What color was her hair? Were her eyes blue or brown? He was already losing her, and he didn't even know who she was.

"I need to go back," Reuben told her with more certainty than he felt. His voice sounded surprisingly steady despite the wrench inside his gut. "Will you be there?"

She smiled and all hesitation evaporated. He knew her smile. He loved that smile more than any other. "If you still want me to be."

His hands moved to her jawline, drawing her to him, holding her gaze and praying he would never need to look away again. Every breath drew them closer until it seemed not even time could separate them. The atmosphere came alive with color, glowing in candlelight, about to burst. A fire burned somewhere deep inside him, intensifying until there was no differentiation between angst and desire. "How could I not want you?" Reuben breathed. "You remind me that even in my darkest hour one thing always remains."

She leaned into his touch. "What is that?"

"Hope."

~~~

Three.

Reuben opened his eyes to pain. His body screamed as though he had been attacked from all sides by a thousand hammers. Every muscle in him ached for relief, his nerves on edge. The overhead light seared his eyes from too long in darkness, nevertheless pain meant he was alive.

Alive.

As the thought seeped back into his bones, slowly the terror also subsided. He thanked God he wasn't dead. It was incredible how only a week ago he wanted to be.

He remembered a place in his dream limbo, so warm and beautiful. His parents were there. And Mira. She'd been exactly how she should be. And Charles ... and someone else. There was a vague recollection of a woman ... and a house. Evergreens and candlelight. But little else.

Reuben came back for her. For the woman in his dreams, for a face he couldn't recall, and a name he didn't remember.

You are only seeing what you want to see, Charles had told him. There was only one woman he wanted to see right now.

That was when the other memories hit, colder than the excruciating bite of the ocean he fell into. He squeezed his eyes closed until kaleidoscope formations danced behind the lids, but he could never again blind himself to what happened. He'd left Maggie with Lloyd. Was she safe? Lloyd had bested him again, taken control of what was most precious in his life, and once again Reuben failed to stop it.

He dragged air through his lungs, trying to send oxygen back to his brain. His hands clenched so tightly that only the fabric beneath them saved his nails from slicing into the skin. Blood pulsed through him in a deafening roar.

Reuben blinked furiously, bringing a hand up to his eyes so he could make out where he was. Whitewashed walls and six squat metal beds stared back at him. Two beds down from him, a young woman in a starched nurse's outfit checked another man's pulse. Running a hand over the crisp white sheets pulled tightly over his own bed, Reuben realized somehow he had been rescued from the water and taken to the ship's hospital.

He threw his legs off the side of the bed, ignoring the pain searing down his right leg into his bandaged ankle. He must have injured it during the fight, but right now he didn't care how. He needed to find Maggie.

The moment he placed weight on it, however, it buckled, sending him face first to the cold floor. The young nurse gasped, her heels clicking on the tile. She said something in concerned German his brain was too groggy to decipher before wrapping an arm under his. Reuben knocked her hands away and managed to push himself to his knees on his own.

"I don't need help," he breathed, and was shocked by how rough his voice sounded. How long was he asleep? The curtains were drawn on every porthole, making it impossible to tell day from night. "Did I sleep all day?"

She replied in English with a thin frown. "Why, sir, you have slept for three days. It is the afternoon of the nineteenth."

Reuben fell back against the bed frame. Three days. How could he have lost three days?

"Did they say what happened to me?" he asked. This time he

accepted her help up when it was offered to him, but still refused to lie down. Instead, he hovered on the edge of the bed, ready to commit murder the second she told him Maggie was a corpse in the morgue.

Perhaps sensing his agitation, the nurse sat beside him and offered a comforting smile. "This must be difficult to hear. Missing three days and all. Your lady saved you. Ran all the way to the bridge she did, found Officer Schmidt to pull you from the ocean. You should thank the heavens that the ship were stopped. You was quite barmy, climbing the rail the way you did."

"She told you I climbed the railing and fell? Was that all she said?"

"Yes." The nurse rested a hand on his arm. "You might feel ashamed as you should. Those bruises best remind you not to try something so foolhardy again."

Reuben splayed his hands on his thighs. The skin puckered on every surface with dark red scabs and ugly purple bruises. It would take a complete simpleton to not understand those injuries couldn't happen from a fall. Only well-intended blows would create such damage. But the nurse didn't ask and Maggie hadn't told them. She'd invented a story rather than see Lloyd punished. But why? To protect Reuben? Or was there something more?

The nurse rose, smoothing the creases from her apron. "Shall I request some food then, sir? You must be starved."

Reuben nodded, unable to pull his eyes from his battered hands until he heard the click of heels return with the tray. As he ate, the vengeful Mira emerged from his wounds, breaking them open to seep over him inch by inch. Still, Reuben held on to his reason for a little longer. Until day turned into night, and he could fight it no longer. Only then did sleep overtake him again and Mira's ugly voice filled his head like an incurable disease.

FORTY-NINE

AFTER DAYS OF CLOSED QUARTERS, mounting tension, and general morose, Maggie determined *Höllenfeuer* was in the running for the world's most depressing ocean voyage. As if news of *Titanic* and the possible impending demise of their own ship weren't enough to send everyone into a panic, they now had impulsive fellow passengers to contend with. Gossip spread like wildfire and soon everyone knew about "that foolish Englishman who tried to climb the railings like monkeys climb trees."

Maggie's explanation had sounded so absurd from her own mouth, she was shocked Officer Schmidt believed it when she ran onto the bridge begging him to lower an inflatable. Hearing the rest of the passengers believe it too made her head spin. No one asked about the extensive bruises Reuben sustained from the fall. Neither had Lloyd called on her or apparently mentioned the incident in first class. Thanks to Maggie's extensive talents of deception—or exceedingly stupid luck—it seemed they would arrive in America without anyone being the wiser.

The clock chimed, claiming Maggie's eyes from her breakfast plate. "Nine o'clock," she told Amara. "Time to collect Mr. Radford."

Amara offered to wait outside the hospital door, leaving Maggie to face Reuben alone. As relieved as she was that he would make a full recovery, she was also nervous. Physically, he would recover, but mentally? In the minutes before he plunged over the railing, he had flickered from ferocious violence to cowering from some unknown force. She'd heard him apologize, but not to her. Had such an act cracked his mind? Would things be the same between them? Would he abandon her before they reached St. Louis?

Reuben stood between two metal beds, leaning into the looking glass to adjust his tie. At the same time he struggled to prop a wooden crutch under his left arm. His face swelled under dark bruises while an unsightly mauve line ran across his neck and a swollen cut forced up the right corner of his lip. Even broken as he was, he was still one of the most attractive men she'd ever seen.

Reuben limped his way towards her, and pulled her to him with his free arm. Maggie folded her arms around him and her cheek found the place where his heart beat beneath his wrinkled shirt. A mix of laundry starch and sea salt wafted across her nostrils, a reminder of why he was here.

It was because of her. And a lie that very nearly cost him his life.

"You're safe," Reuben whispered against her hair. "The nurse told me you were, but I was worried. I was afraid Lloyd—"

"Lloyd won't bother us anymore." Maggie stood on tiptoe to cancel his arguments with a kiss. Reuben's hand found the curve of her back, pressing her to him while his mouth explored hers.

"I'd like to take you back to my cabin," Reuben murmured. His fingers ran up her spine to wrap around the chignon at the base. He kissed her cheek. "Yes, I think I would enjoy that very much."

Maggie flushed hot and cold all at once and pulled away. He'd never been so forward. "Your ankle—"

"I don't need to stand for that." Reuben shifted his crutch. "Last time was a disaster. I want to do it right."

"That'll be enough of that," piped up a nurse Maggie hadn't noticed before, hidden behind a desk in the corner. "This experience should keep you away from poor decisions, not towards them. Remember that."

"Yes, ma'am." Reuben succumbed to Maggie's arm as the little woman's frown followed them from the room.

Ulrich rested against the far wall in the corridor, engulfing the hall in cigarette smoke, while Amara stood ten feet away, unsuccessfully waving her arms to clear the air. "Completely unsanitary," she bickered to Maggie. "This is the hospital for goodness sakes! What would his mother say?"

"Meine Mutter ist hier nicht," Ulrich laughed and flicked ashes in her direction.

"Ugh!" Amara shrieked. "You are disgusting!"

"He's been awful since you fell overboard," Maggie sighed to Reuben. "He will not leave us alone. I can't understand a word he says, and I told him we do not need escorts—" She pointed at Ulrich's cigarette. "Amara's right. You shouldn't have that in here."

Ulrich shrugged at Reuben. "Blackjack?"

Of course, thought Maggie, *he can say that word in English. If only he could apologize for stalking us around the ship, making lewd comments, and eying us like roast lamb for four days. Nevertheless, he also didn't pry for details after Reuben fell overboard, so that's something, I suppose.*

Reuben turned his standard debonair smile in Maggie's direction and reached for her. "I thank you for keeping watch over the ladies, Ulrich. We, however, dock tomorrow, and I've barely spent any time with my fiancé."

Ulrich's cigarette hung in his lips. Amara squealed and lunged at Maggie to topple them both into the wall. "Why did you not tell me?" she exclaimed, jumping about like a child. "We will have many things to write to each other! Weddings and then—oh!" Amara danced in tight circles until Maggie restrained her arms to stop her. Alas, it only ceased her spinning, not her excitement. "Babies!" Amara finished. "Maybe as early as next year? Do you think? Oh, Reuben, you will be a handsome father!"

Reuben went as pale as Maggie felt. "I'm only twenty," he managed, and Maggie breathed an inward sigh of relief. On a long list of differences, thank heavens they agreed on something.

An unexpected glimmer of optimism surged in her chest for the first time since she'd left Fontaine. A wedding would be a chance for her to set things right. Maybe marrying, even if for the wrong reasons now, would be the right choice in the end.

Her eyes met Reuben's in the kind of rare moment Bianca and Edith had giggled about for years. Even the rainbow of bruises and eventual scars couldn't hide what was written there. Yes, Maggie decided, if she could do only one good deed in a lifetime of ill repute, she would do it for the only person left who loved her.

She had always believed herself far-distanced from the woman who shared her dark hair and stormy blue-grey eyes when all along she was destined to share her mother's life. Maggie would marry Reuben as Laurence Archer had married Beatrix, not for love like her father, but for loyalty. Because it was the honorable thing to do.

"We need to celebrate!" Amara declared. She swept them away from the sterile hospital up to the promenade where the ship's band performed the strains of an unfamiliar rag. Even her annoyance at Ulrich vanished with the news of impending nuptials, and she insisted he prance her around the deck in a surprisingly well-manicured partnership.

Collectively deciding it was high time to save what was left of this miserable crossing, the other passengers quickly caught Amara's enthusiasm. Pretty soon couples littered the deck in their own versions of the dance steps, first the rag then a waltz, followed by a two step. Unable to participate, Reuben and Maggie claimed a bench to watch the merriment hand in hand.

Reuben tapped his crutch in the direction of the ocean. The number of icebergs had diminished considerably as *Höllenfeuer* drew closer to the coast. "I promised to take you to Iceland, didn't I?"

Maggie rolled her eyes. "This isn't exactly what I had in mind."

"I think this is just as good." Reuben tipped his head to brush his lips across her temple. When he leaned back, he was smiling.

With the slightest squeeze to his injured fingers, Maggie beckoned her features to mirror his satisfied expression. "It's our last day at sea," she murmured. "In a few days, we'll be reunited with Tena and Charles. We'll all start a new life together."

Reuben's smile wavered, the wounds on his face tugging at his skin before his lip managed to rise again. "I hope that's so."

She knew it was foolish thinking. The reality was both Charles and Tena were dead. Sometime last night she had accepted it when she woke drenched in sweat, Tena's name falling from her lips, and could barely find her way back into sleep. But every time she acknowledged it in the daylight, she came a little bit closer to her ultimate breaking point. She'd held it together this long; she wasn't about to buckle now.

At least she had Reuben.

And so the day passed hour by hour in pleasant accord—dancing, merriment, and light-hearted conversation at dinner. Reuben's eyes danced mischievously whenever he glanced her way, and Maggie would blush, remembering his promise to compensate for their first night together.

The distraction was so nice she finally stopped mulling over how she'd sold herself out to Lloyd four nights ago. It was one of those things—it happened; it was bad. Let's move on.

And never ever tell Reuben the truth.

FIFTY

Which is to say he woke a thousand times from nightmares that made him want to bawl and wet himself. Only, unlike an infant, no one was going to comfort him.

Dreams swirled him in and out of consciousness, ripping open memories he'd long since stifled.

Twelve-year-old Reuben absently flipped the pages of his penny dreadful, rereading an issue he'd already read four times. Across the school yard, ten-year-old Mira double dutched with her friends while they waited for the carriage home, her braids swinging with her rhythm. Being twelve, Reuben refused to join such a childish game, but he would still smack anyone who dared tease his sister for it.

"Excuse me, mate?"

Reuben glanced over the booklet at a boy around his same age, although unfamiliar in appearance, with tousled tan hair and a smooth smile. He gestured to a second issue peeking out of Reuben's open satchel. "Mind if I borrow that?"

"Sure." Reuben tossed it over.

"Thanks! Should have brought mine." He gave another winning grin and settled himself on the pavement. "They say these things

327

will turn you degenerate. Utter rubbish." He stuck out his hand. "Lloyd Halverson."

"Sounds like the name of a bank manager." Reuben extended his own arm to grip the new boy's hand. "Reuben Radford."

Lloyd chuckled. "Sounds like the name of a factory worker. And my father's not a banker. He runs a shipping firm."

"Reuben!" Mira called. "Did you see? I almost made forty turns!" She skidded to a stop beside them and gave Lloyd a shy smile. "Oh, hello."

"Why, hello," said Lloyd. "Who are you?"

Reuben shrugged. "My sister, Mira."

"I'm Lloyd, Mira. I was watching you jump. I thought you were brilliant." Lloyd grinned the same smile Reuben now knew could win over women from far and wide. At the time, he'd assumed nothing of it.

Mira dipped her head, said a quick "thank you," and rushed back to her friends, although she didn't attempt any more double dutch winning streaks.

"You embarrassed her," Reuben reproached.

"It was a compliment." Lloyd thumbed through the magazine. "She'd better get used to it. Such a pretty girl will have more than compliments to contend with."

Tremors coursed through Reuben's body, the memory raising him to consciousness. He smothered the pillow over his face to muffle the wracking sobs that heaved his chest. Tears soaked the material and, try as he might, he couldn't cease his limbs from shaking. Anguish flooded him like a swirling hurricane ripping across the coast. It had been years since he'd cried in this way, not since he met Maggie.

Ulrich grunted, the creaking bed enough to calm Reuben to a manageable level. Throughout the previous day, he had convinced himself he was stable, only everything felt off. He couldn't forget what happened. And he couldn't stop asking why.

Reuben threw the covers off and somehow managed to dress himself in the dark. The pain in his ankle had at least subsided to a tolerable level he could limp on without a crutch. He stumbled out of the room, limped down the corridor, and tripped up the stairs into the unforgiving cold. He lit the last of his cigars, allowing the smoke to plume in his mouth before releasing it into the still atmosphere. The hour was too late to procure liquid courage; tobacco would have to do.

He took his time getting there, partly because his brain was screaming, "It's three a.m.! No good decisions are made at three a.m.!" and partly because his ankle regulated him to a snail's pace. But even the wisdom of his brain and a sluggish ankle couldn't steer him from cabin 223 tonight.

After a shout, a piece of furniture falling, and a flurry of cursing, the door opened.

"Well how about that Lady Luck? You're still alive."

Lloyd looked bad. Like "How are you standing?" bad. Thin scratches littered his face, deep navy bruises surrounding both eye sockets, one lid nearly too swollen to open fully. Thick maroon lines banded his neck like tiger stripes. Even a high collar couldn't hide all of the damage. He must be receiving meals in his room; it was too obvious his injuries weren't due to his own clumsiness.

Reuben pressed a hand to the door as much to elicit entrance as to afford his now throbbing ankle a rest. "Sorry to disappoint. Can I come in?"

"You have a self-destructive streak, don't you?" Lloyd sneered. "Come in here and you're not leaving."

Reuben shot Lloyd a dubious glare. "You plan to murder me in your own stateroom? I'm too large to fit through the porthole and it'll be difficult to carry me outside to throw me overboard. Won't it be a bit obvious who did it when they find my body in your room?"

Lloyd's jaw clenched. "I loathe you."

"You're not winning any awards in my favor either."

After a full minute of silent mutual disgust, Lloyd glanced down the corridor in both directions and thumbed at Reuben. "Get in here."

Reuben stumbled into the room and fell across the couch to elevate his foot. He had been incredibly stupid by not bringing the crutch.

Lloyd tied his dressing gown and sat across from Reuben. "What would possess you to ever come here?"

Reuben rubbed his ankle where pain spidered under his touch. "I needed to ask you something."

"It'd better be important to wake me in the middle of the night. I stubbed my toe on the chair."

"Are you serious?" Reuben gestured to his leg eliciting a mighty laugh from Lloyd.

"Yeah, I guess you're about as bad as me, eh? Do you like the necklace you gave me? My father will think I was in a fight over some broad."

"That's about right, isn't it?" Reuben muttered.

"True enough." Lloyd squinted at the clock on the dressing table, and sat up in what could only be construed as anticipation. It was difficult to make out facial expressions between the bruises. "Maggie doesn't know you're here, does she? You *are* grinding her, aren't you?"

Lloyd would have received a third black eye if Reuben's ankle had allowed it. "That's not your concern," he snarled.

Lloyd nodded in overt approval. "My, oh my, you *are*! Well, I'll be! I'd never have thought you capable. Reuben Radford finally managed to snag a woman."

"Why couldn't you let me have her?" Reuben spat. "You could have any other woman you want."

Lloyd smirked. "Ain't that the truth."

Reuben was losing his patience. "But you picked *her*. Why?"

Lloyd shrugged. "I had my reasons."

"You'll have a missing appendage if you don't tell me what they are."

Lloyd laughed. "Now there's the Reuben I love to mess with. I was afraid taking a lover had made you go all soft. Or maybe it did which is why she needed me to satisfy her."

Reuben pushed himself into a sitting position. "Screw you."

"Nah, mate, you're not really my type. Listen, if you're looking for me to cry and moan, begging your forgiveness, I won't. I would however like to thank you for making this such a delightful little game. It's almost a shame to end it."

Reuben tested his foot, pressing weight until he could stand. The pain was still considerable, except his desire to leave was stronger. He winced slightly with the first step, then took another, fighting his way to the door.

"She's lying to you."

Reuben paused, breathing heavily against the closed door. Lloyd's voice had lost its edge. No irony, no mocking, just straight fact.

He pressed his forehead against the door. "Who?"

"Maggie," Lloyd affirmed. "She came to me rummaging for information about you."

"She told me that."

Lloyd's steps shuffled up behind Reuben. "Did she tell you how she divined said information?

Reuben's hands clenched the front of Lloyd's shirt faster than his brain could process how he'd arrived there. "You told her after you did the same thing to her you did to Mira!"

Lloyd stood still. Confusion clouded his face. He didn't even try to push Reuben away. "You think I raped her? That's a pretty foul accusation for someone who can't even say the word."

"Don't even deny it!"

"I will deny it, because it isn't true. Maggie was free to walk away. She chose to stay."

"Liar!"

"No. I may not always toe the line of honor, but I am also not a liar. There are some hard facts you need to hear. Will you please release me?"

Reuben ached to wring his already damaged neck. "No. Talk."

Lloyd nodded. "Very well. I hate you, Reuben."

"That much has always been clear."

"Yes, but you don't understand why. I didn't force myself on Mira. Not exactly."

Forget punching him, thought Reuben. *I'll gouge his eyes out.* "Yes, you did!"

"Ugh, please." Lloyd held up a hand. "Shut up and listen. I liked your sister. But I was fourteen and an idiot."

"You still are."

Lloyd gave a cursory stare. "I thought fourteen made me a man, and making love was something men did with women they liked. I thought Mira was simply nervous and needed me to push her through her fear. My father assured me I'd done nothing wrong, and you convinced Mira to make up lies to ruin us. Eventually I realized I had been too aggressive with my feelings, but I still loathed you for perpetuating Mira's hatred for me. At least when she died, all the talk ceased. I could finally move on."

Reuben released Lloyd's shirt. Everything inside him burned. Lloyd was no less a scoundrel in his eyes. He had still raped Mira in Reuben's opinion. But Lloyd had also in some twisted way felt actual affection for her. Reuben always believed he only had true affection for himself. Maybe if Lloyd was raised differently or if Reuben had been a better friend ... maybe everything would have ended differently.

"Why go after Maggie then?"

Lloyd's usual arrogant cockiness resurfaced from between his mottled contusions. "Haven't we established that I hate you? I liked Mira; you turned her against me. Then I wanted Maggie." Lloyd rubbed his hands together. "She was beautiful and oh, so tempting. Her mother found me exquisitely charming. Everyone told me she didn't want to marry. What a challenge *that* presented!"

"Maggie *didn't* want to marry," Reuben slapped his hands against his thighs. "You didn't have a chance."

"Only because *you* scandalized her. Even if Mr. Archer accepted my proposal, my father would have insisted I sever all ties. What good was she to me after you'd had her?"

"Then why couldn't you leave it alone!?"

"Oh, Reuben, isn't it obvious? I had an entirely new reason for loathing you now," Lloyd leered, each word profanely articulated. "You stole Maggie from me. Just. Like. Mira." Lloyd's lip curled, the glint in his eyes unmistakable. "Maggie offered herself to me on a platter. All she wanted was information. And she was willing to do *anything* for it."

Reuben leapt with precision on his good ankle where his fist leveled above Lloyd's face. Perfect striking position. "Why should I believe you?" he snarled.

Lloyd shrugged. "You don't have to. It makes little difference to me. I already got what I wanted."

Reuben clocked Lloyd in the shoulder as hard as he could, feeling the scabs break open across his knuckles. Lloyd sprawled backward on the carpet, gripping his arm as he went down. He kneaded the tender muscle and glared up at Reuben. "You really don't believe me?"

"I do." Reuben turned his back on Lloyd. He threw the door open, catching the edge with his outstretched palm as it rebounded against the wall. Splinters wedged into the skin beneath his fingernails and a low growl formed deep in his throat. "I believe you," he repeated. "But that sure doesn't mean I have to forgive you."

FIFTY-ONE

REUBEN WALKED UNTIL THERE were no boards left to walk. He hobbled to the stern where the black sea met the darkness of the sky. In time the stars faded, and the glow of the sun rose to meet him. The ocean lightened to an inky green, waves churning from beneath the hull. And still, he waited. He knew one of them would find him eventually.

Mira arrived first. She perched atop the rail, ankles linked through the rungs, a slight snigger escaping her lips. She gripped the top rung in both hands and leaned back to view the water below. "Why don't you throw yourself over? No one to save you this time."

"Shut up. I'm not doing that again." His interrogation with Lloyd was supposed to bring him closure. *The truth shall set you free?* Instead of liberating him, Mira remained as clearly visible as the surrounding ocean. Reuben wanted to shut the door to his past; unfortunately the past had her small black boot wedged in the opening.

He had desired more from Lloyd than what he received. More than wanting to make Lloyd pay, he had wanted an apology. For Lloyd to admit he was a worthless excuse for a human and guilt ate his insides like it tore up Reuben's. He wanted vindication for his sister and for Maggie and for ruining his life.

The dream limbo nagged at the corners of his mind like a flame licking the edges of a photograph. He remembered everything until he walked through that gate, then it went fuzzy as if he'd been forced to watch through a frosted window. There was a woman there he couldn't recognize ... his own personal Pandora's box ... someone who reminded him to have hope in the midst of the chaos.

A violent laugh escaped Reuben's throat. Hope for what? Hope Lloyd was actually lying? Hope Maggie hadn't chosen to be with someone else less than twenty-four hours after she'd been with him? Hope she would marry him? Hope that she actually loved him?

Why did it have to be Lloyd? As if it wasn't injustice enough for the man to have violated Reuben's sister, he had also seduced Reuben's ... what exactly was she to him? More importantly, what was he to her? For pity's sake, *she* made love to *him*! She'd thrown herself at him that night, not the other way around. Why did she have to throw herself in with Lloyd's lot too? Why wasn't Reuben bloody good enough for anyone?

Like a specter floating in on the rising sun, Maggie appeared beside him. Wisps of brunette hair broke loose in the wind, winding around her heather blue irises. Reuben held her cheeks between his trembling hands to prove she was the same cemetery girl he knew before. She was still with him, something physical he could touch and hold in a mind full of illusions. Despite the hollow pit within him, Reuben's lips found hers.

Was this how his mother felt before she died? Alone and abandoned, trapped within her own mind, lost to despair?

No, not alone.

She may have been imprisoned in her own thoughts, but she hadn't been alone.

And Reuben wasn't either. Even in an empty room, there was one person he could never escape fully.

He closed his eyes, clutched Maggie's hand, and breathed in the salty ocean air. He could almost pretend they were back on the Southampton pier joking about going to Iceland together. Reuben concentrated on that single thought and poured all his willpower into what he wanted. Or didn't want.

He threw his most colorfully worded demand into the universe and opened his eyes.

"You honestly thought you could be rid of me so easily?" Mira sneered. Her fingers ran over a black shoe mark on the rail, the only evidence of a late night scuffle, and released a mirthless laugh. "Since you're clearly not intelligent enough to decipher this on your own—or maybe you are, I *am* in *your* head after all—I'm going to spell it out for you."

She raised her hands as if this was the simplest thing to comprehend. "I'm a manifestation of your guilt, Reuben. Why do you think our mother went batty? She blamed herself, just like you blame yourself for not protecting me, for not being able to keep our parents alive, for your inability to make Maggie love you."

Don't listen to her, Reuben thought. *She'll go away if you just - don't - listen.*

"No, I won't. And you don't want me to. Charles said so. I'm as real as anything else. You only see what you want to see."

Reuben shook his head, swatting his hands and hitting only empty air. "You're not real. I created you and I can be rid of you."

"Maggie will leave you before I will." Mira smirked. "It just kills you inside, doesn't it? To look at her and know you're *still* not enough for her. You're a deranged madman exactly like our mother. It's no wonder she doesn't want you. You're worthless."

"Liar!" Reuben yelled, sending his voice out like shock waves. He pressed his nose an inch from hers, seething. "You're not Mira," he hissed. "I saw my sister. I know who she was. And she wasn't *this*. She wasn't you. And I won't be the man you think I am. Not anymore."

Mira's face went blank, all emotion lost. Her eyes stared empty into his. "Then who are you, Reuben? Who are you now?" The hallucination released her grip on the rail and dropped backward, her skirt fluttering around her. She dissolved in the air even before the sea could claim her. Water churned against the hull, propelling frothy waves behind them, the ship unaware this moment had significance above any other.

Reuben stepped away from the rail, trembling. "Mira?" he whispered. The wind whistled back. It was only empty air, barely more than a breeze, but it settled inside him like a screaming gale.

A warm fire lit in his gut slowly burning upwards through his chest. For once he couldn't decipher if it was trepidation or exhilaration coursing through him. Had it worked? Had it been so very simple to free himself of her? Was his madness finally at an end?

Who are you, Reuben? Who are you?

For five years, Mira's memory had haunted him. Her loss triggered an avalanche in his soul, accumulating with every step, deeper and heavier, crushing him from within. She became a part of him, more entwined with his paces than his own skin. If she was truly gone, would he even recognize himself without her?

His fingers jolted as Maggie's hand slipped against his. Such a normal gesture. She chewed her lip and said nothing, and she didn't need to. Her expression mirrored the way Reuben looked on his mother every day for the last two years of her life. He didn't need to worry anymore how Maggie would react if she discovered this hidden side of him. She'd seen his mother in the Winchesters' garden. She knew.

Reuben ran his free hand over his eyes as pain crept up his weak ankle, no longer numbed by adrenaline. Maggie cast a cursory glance at the offending leg. "You should rest."

"It's nothing. I'm fine." He released her hand to bury his own in the pockets of his coat. "I hate this bloody boat."

"Me too." Maggie folded her arms around herself, fully releasing her lip from the confines of her teeth. "They posted a list of survivors."

"Charles is dead."

"Yes." Maggie squeezed her arms tighter, her gaze firmly set upon the deck boards.

"And Tena?"

The rising sun played across Maggie's hair in honey highlights—the same stunning shade as her sister's. She raised her eyes to his, and Reuben sucked in a breath.

"Tena's alive."

FIFTY-TWO

ELEVEN HOURS LATER, REUBEN, Maggie, Ulrich, and Amara disembarked at the piers in Hoboken, New Jersey, before boarding a train to New York City's Grand Central station. Ulrich departed the second they announced the upcoming station, claiming to hate weepy women at goodbyes.

"We won't weep, Mr. Klassen," Amara said. "Perhaps you will miss us a little though?"

"*Nein, fräulein.*" Ulrich handed Reuben a scrap of torn newspaper with an address written across the print. "I'm staying at this boarding house. If you're ever in New York ..." Ulrich vanished before the train even rolled into the station.

As they entered the main terminal, Amara pointed out a slender young man waiting on the platform. "There's my Siegfried!" She clasped Maggie's hands. "I am happy to have met you, Maggie." She nodded to Reuben. "Both of you."

"And I, you," Reuben replied. "Best wishes on your marriage."

"And on yours." She pressed a folded paper into Maggie's hand then embraced her like a sister. "Write to me. *Auf Wiedersehen,* my first American friend."

"It was quite a crossing." Maggie squeezed the younger girl. "Farewell, Amara."

Amara skipped off, ashen plait bouncing down her back and,

without a thought, threw herself into Siegfried's waiting arms. A laugh threw his head back then drew her close for a quick embrace. Amara handed him her case, gave one last wave goodbye, and disappeared into the crowd.

"What now?" Maggie asked.

What now, indeed? Reuben wondered. They were simply two people in a railway station, two among hundreds of travelers from all corners of the world. Every belonging they now possessed fit in two cases and a measly satchel, none of which could prepare them for an unknown world outside the station's doors.

Reuben focused on Maggie. She focused on him. They locked sights in a rare moment when neither of them turned away.

He pressed her hand to his, and softly circled her left ring finger with his thumb. "Let's get married. Today if we can."

"You're not serious?" Maggie tried to wrench her hand away. Reuben refused to let her. They *were* having this conversation.

"Maggie, you said you wanted to marry me. Let's not wait. We'll surprise them all with the announcement."

"I want Tena at my wedding."

"Maggie, I don't have any family. And a big affair would only remind Tena of what she should have had with Charles."

"But we don't have a home."

"We'll find a place. Does it matter where if we're together?"

Maggie stared fixedly at her fingers, still tense inside his grip. "We've only been engaged a few days. People will assume we're about to fill another bedroom." She yanked at her hands again and Reuben released her.

"Why should it matter?" he asked, suppressing his desire to demand answers outright, despite the gnawing in his gut to do so immediately. "You want to be with me, don't you, Maggie? When you look into my eyes, you understand you can trust me and I can trust you. Because we would never lie to each other about how we truly feel. Am I right?"

He tilted her chin to face him, only this time, Maggie wouldn't look into his eyes. She looked everywhere but at his face.

He lowered his lips to hers, only the instant his hands wrapped her waist, every muscle tightened beneath his fingers. "Maggie," Reuben breathed against her lips. "You do want to marry me, don't you? If Tena being there is what matters to you, we can wait."

Maggie instantly relaxed. She pressed her lips against his with a soft smile. "Thank you for understanding. After everything we've been through, there's no one I'd rather suffer through life with."

Reuben straightened up, and retreated a full five feet before turning a circle, his fingers wrapped in his hair. Another train raced into the station, streaking across the platform towards them. One line down, porters pushed trolleys stacked high with cases, others assisting passengers to their correct compartments. People with destinations. People with lives. People like Amara, who tossed herself in Siegfried's hands as if to say, *In every country, in every way, I'm yours.*

"No," Reuben said firmly. "I don't want life to be something we *suffer through.* I want a life we celebrate, even in the most menial things, even in the worst moments, because we're so thankful to have each other."

Maggie frowned. "That's what I meant."

"Did you?" Reuben retrieved his pocket watch, carefully opening the face. The hands stood still at 11:53, the time they were overcome with sea water. He tried to rewind it, but salt had rendered the timepiece useless. "When I was unconscious, I ended up someplace not quite heaven, but not quite alive either. I saw Mira, my parents ... and Charles. And there was a woman I can't recall—I think she must have been you—waiting to take me home. I had to choose between death with them or life with you."

"But why—"

"Why would I come back?" Reuben snapped the watch shut. "I'm not a fool, Maggie. I know nine out of ten days are awful, but that means one is still good. Maybe it's only another May Day, just another fantasy, but I chose to live for it all the same. One moment of happiness, Maggie ... the hope for that moment is what saved my life."

Maggie frowned. "Careful, Reuben, you're starting to sound like my sister. Tena believes suffering is only temporary. But look at life, Reuben. Look at what happened to her and Charles. This isn't some storybook. Life doesn't have happy endings."

"What about the girl I met in the cemetery? *She* believed we all deserved a happy ending."

Maggie threw her hands up. "That isn't me anymore! I grew up. Do you know what happens at the end of *our* story, Reuben? We die. And everyone else is left alone."

"But, Maggie—" Reuben reached for her and she sidestepped him the same way she'd danced around her feelings for two years. Only now she was an animal trapped in a cage, and Reuben had just opened the door.

"My father spent his entire life with a woman who hated him. Your father watched his wife go completely mental. You almost killed Lloyd after he forced himself upon your sister. Then again when I slept with him. You were thrown off a ship! My mother disowned us, my father's dead, and my sister lost her fiancé. A ship full of innocent people sank to the bottom of the ocean!" Maggie's shoulders shook. "Now, Reuben, tell me again how I should believe there's hope for the world."

Realization flashed upon her face as she understood what she'd said. "Forgive me, Reuben. I will marry you, but so much has happened to us. I'm overwhelmed for a way to survive it."

And just like that Reuben understood exactly what he had to do. And he also knew there would never be a way to change it.

"I know Lloyd didn't force you. You agreed."

Maggie paled. She took a breath, and in that silence, the answer sounded loud and clear. "You asked him, didn't you?"

Reuben's heart clenched. He finally had the proof he wanted, and it didn't make it any easier to say what came next. He captured her hand between both of his and sighed, memorizing the shape of her fingers, and wishing he didn't need to let them go.

"I can't marry you, Maggie. I don't want to be with someone who will do anything to survive. I need someone who wants to *live*. The good, the bad, and the really *really* horrible days. The ones so trying they feel like an ocean we can never cross. And in the midst of it all, she smiles because she believes I'm worth it." Reuben raised his gaze back to hers. "You were worth it to me."

"Reuben, I never wanted to hurt you." She blinked once slowly, the only indication that some small part of her truly meant what she said.

He smiled sadly. "Someday you'll meet someone who not only makes you face your fears, but helps you embrace them. And him?" Reuben pointed out the doors. "Him you won't want to deceive."

"But, Reuben, I ..." She paused, took a deep breath, then tried again. "I really care about you." There was a desperation in her tone that revealed the truth far louder than if she'd screamed it at him. And it pained Reuben to finally acknowledge it.

"But you don't love me."

"Reuben, please ..." Maggie pleaded.

"No, Maggie, you don't. When you do fall in love, you'll know this wasn't it."

Admitting to himself that she didn't love him, had never loved him, soiled all the emotions he had lain at her feet. He'd offered her his heart like a diamond and, not only had she rejected his gift, but she'd thrown it back at him with the force of a stone. Maggie didn't even know all the thoughts crowded in his mind, didn't know by half, yet the secrets she did know Reuben wished he could snatch back.

Grand Central Station bustled with activity, and the sun shone through the raised windows like any other afternoon. Reuben released Maggie's hand with finality. It seemed such a feeble way to end things after all they had been through.

Maggie's eyes sank, as empty as the ocean's darkest depths.

"What now?" she asked.

"Now," Reuben handed Maggie her case. "You find your sister. Tell Tena I'll see her soon."

Maggie nodded. It appeared she wanted to say more, but Reuben didn't want to hear false apologies. He shuffled away before she could utter a word.

FIFTY-THREE

AFTER THREE DAYS ON A PACKED TRAIN, Maggie arrived alone in St. Louis, her attire pitifully distressed, lugging her single small case down the street without a clue where she was or where she should be. She figured she would be used to city life after her time in London, only this wasn't London. Buildings appeared taller, their individual girths wider, set upon a neat grid of streets with unfamiliar names, the mechanism for which a bustle of motorcars, horse-drawn carriages, and trolleys made their way. In time, she might find it beautiful; however, today she was standing back in the dining saloon that first night on *Höllenfeuer*, lost in a city of foreigners even when this city spoke her native tongue.

Closing her mind to the bustle, she fell to the memory of her simple walks through London, sometimes on Derby's arm, more often alone. She remembered the scent of the flower sellers' baskets, and the little girls who held them, each one tugging on her skirt to ask for a farthing. Then bringing the stems back to her tiny upstairs room to dry on the window ledge, their sweet perfume drifting her to sleep, reminding her of May Day.

Of her sister.

Of home.

~ ~ ~

Two hours and many wrong turns later, Maggie finally received directions from a street vendor to the city postal office. The desk clerk, who sported an accent Maggie couldn't place and barely understood, jotted down the Kischs' address and outlined the quickest path.

Now she stood on the walk before a narrow, three-story, red-brick home, with white lace curtains in the windows, and a spattering of pale purple and yellow flowers under the ledge, the likes of which Maggie had never seen before. This cobbled street was one of many she'd passed, each lined with homes of a similar fashion, all closely situated together with thin yards stretching behind them. Common, demure. Nothing resembling where she came from.

It was exactly the kind of place Tena and Charles would have made a perfect home in. For a few misbegotten days, Maggie had even planned it for herself.

A plump blond woman answered the door, brow wrinkled above gentle eyes as she wiped her hands on her apron. "Good afternoon. May I help you?" she asked in a noticeable German accent.

"Hello. I'm Maggie Archer. Is this the Kisch residence?"

"It is. She's been expecting you." The woman produced a warm smile and opened the door fully, revealing a narrow hallway straight through the home to another open exterior door. And there, in silhouette, stood Tena. She wore a lemon yellow apron over a simple black mourning dress, sleeves rolled to the elbows and hands starched with flour. Her hair, once so pristinely pinned, now hung loose, tied back in a single scrap of blue fabric. The golden band on her fourth finger completed the picture of a married life she was no longer destined for.

Maggie set her case inside the doorway and ran the short distance to her sister, where they met with outstretched arms. Not a word was spoken for the longest time, for what really could be said? Tears slid down Maggie's cheeks and for the first time since their father's death, she didn't fight them back. Eventually, the plump blond woman edged past them, and Tena released Maggie, swiping her palm over her own damp cheeks.

"Look at my manners," Tena sniffed. She took the arm of the other woman. "Mrs. Kisch, this is my sister, Maggie. Maggie, this is Charles's mother, Elsa."

Elsa pressed a kiss to Tena's brow. "There is no need for apology, dear. The house is empty. Spend time with your sister." Elsa extended her warm smile to Maggie. "You will stay with us as long as you like, dear." With a nod, she retrieved a bowl of unsnipped green beans from the kitchen and sidled out the back door.

"I'm so glad you're alive," Maggie said, not bothering to dry her tears.

Tena managed a lopsided smile. "I'm glad you are too. But I'm afraid that Charles ..." Her eyes dimmed, a single tear working its way along her cheekbone. "I miss him, Maggie."

"I know." She wiped her thumb across Tena's cheek and wrapped her arms once more around her sister's slender frame. "You meant everything to him, do you know that? He told me. He loved how modest you are, yet feisty enough to lie, steal, and enter taverns with abandon."

Tena released a gentle laugh. "*My* Charles? He complained most of the way home that night about my *feisty* behavior. Then Reuben heard an earful the next day."

She stepped back, her gaze locked on the front door as if someone else had joined them. But when Maggie turned to look, no one was there. "What is it?" she asked.

Tena slipped past her into the living room, brushing aside the window curtain. Her head swiveled from the front stoop down on end of the street, then the other. "Where's Reuben?"

Maggie froze in the doorway. Her heart tried to escape from her chest then began its ascent up her throat. She clasped her hands behind her back to hide their trembling. What should she say? She only came on this journey for her sister, and Tena was all she had left. If she told the truth, Tena would despise her. If she didn't, Tena would ask Reuben and still hate her. Thousands of miles away, in a little inn in Southampton, the sisters promised to have no more secrets. One way or another, Tena would finally see Maggie for who she was.

So Maggie talked. She sat Tena on the couch and poured out ten days' worth of ocean madness to her sister. She told her about her night with Reuben; she explained about the fight and Reuben nearly dying. She revealed the long debated secret between him and Lloyd, which shocked Tena, but not as much as learning what Maggie did to discover it. She gave her sister every distasteful detail, expecting Tena at each revelation to lose her temper and pitch Maggie from the house. Not that Maggie would have stopped her.

"That's why he's not with me now," she finished carefully. "He's probably still in New York."

Tena's expression remained passive. She rested her arm across the back of the sofa and peered through the window draperies with a gaze not quite focused. "He'll take you back," she said quietly. "Don't lose him like I lost Charles."

"Did you hear what I said?" Maggie spluttered. "I was terrible to him and, even now, I'm not sure I would have done it differently. I'm too much like Mother. Reuben deserves more than I could ever give him and he knows it. Aren't you even a bit upset about what I did?"

Tena stood abruptly, seizing the fireplace tongs to drop another log onto the low fire. "Oh, I most certainly am, but your sordid exploits are nothing compared to everything else raging through me." She fixed her gaze on the burning logs. "Today's my birthday, Maggie. Did you even remember?"

"I should have," Maggie said then added a weak, "I'm sorry. Happy birthday." She was making this day go from worse to exceptionally awful.

"I'm nineteen," Tena continued. "Nineteen and essentially a widow. Basically homeless. The dress I'm wearing doesn't even belong to me."

"You haven't lost everything," Maggie argued. "You still have me. May Day is our day. This year, there's no one else I want to spend it with." A morsel of genuine remorse filled her, the first she'd felt all week, and surprised her that she could feel it at all. "I've made mistakes, Tena. Too many to count. I made promises I intended to break. And I think if Father asked me now which day I would redo, it would be every day I left you to pick up the pieces."

Dropping the fireplace tongs back on their hook, Tena swept from the room and up the stairs without a word, leaving Maggie to watch her retreating back and choke down her rejection. It was exactly as she expected, only more civilized—no screaming, crying, or household eviction. Tena was grieving; she probably couldn't wrap her mind around one more upset right now. Maggie should save them both the trouble of an inevitable row and move out now.

"You're not going anywhere, Maggie Archer," Tena's voice called from upstairs. "I know you're thinking it, and if you step out that door, so help me, I will lose the rest of my calm and bludgeon you with your traveling case."

Maggie stared at the empty staircase for a half-tick before the laughter began, edging up her throat until it reached full out maniacal proportions. She doubled over, clutching her stomach as her muscles strained against the relief that, at least for the moment, she seemed to be in something resembling her sister's good graces. For some inexplicable reason, Tena didn't hate her. If the world were upended and Maggie stood in Tena's shoes, she couldn't say she would have listened, much less invited her to stay. In fact, she *knew* she wouldn't have. She would have screamed and squawked, then walked—no, sprinted—from the house to take part in whatever idiotic notion came to her mind first. Maggie would have disowned her sister all over again in true Beatrix Archer style.

My, that was a sobering thought.

By the time Tena returned with an envelope in her hand and a troubled smile on her face, Maggie's own features had reverted to an expressionless mask. She pointed at the envelope. "What do you have?"

"It's from Father."

With three words, Maggie lost the ability to remain composed. She strode to the window, throwing it open to gulp fresh air. Heaven help her, she was having a swooning fit, and she was not the type to swoon over anything. Revealing dark secrets, admitting her fault in things, and now fainting over a scrap of parchment? A week with Reuben had changed her, and apparently not for the better. "I don't understand," she said weakly.

Tena crossed the room to join Maggie at the window. "That's what I said when Reuben handed it to me Easter night. Turns out Father trusted him with more than we knew."

She held out the envelope until Maggie finally took it. The red wax seal was still intact. "You didn't read it?"

"No, although I wanted to," Tena admitted. Her eyes nearly brimmed over again with the words. "I couldn't understand why Father would leave anything for you when you weren't even there. If anyone deserved his final words, shouldn't it be me? When it survived in my coat pocket when nothing else did, not even Charles, I nearly went mad. I began screaming on the rescue ship, and as such, can now tell you the quickest method to obtain copious sedatives." She unwrapped the ribbon from her hair, her fingers absently traveling through the curls as she spoke. "But after a few days passed, and a couple more obnoxious fits, I decided that if this letter could survive a shipwreck, I could too, and maybe you needed to read it more than I needed to hold a grudge."

Maggie ran her index finger over the raised "A" in the seal. Meant for their last name, it carried an entirely new meaning for her now. "Even after everything I told you? How can you not loathe me?"

A simple smile slid across Tena's lips, and a tiny spark flickered behind her eyes. "Not to worry. There will be a day when my brain understands fully that Charles is gone, and Reuben is gone, and reason will lose out to anger. I'll say a mess of words I know I'll feel, yet wish I never said. When that happens, I hope you'll forgive me too, because we're sisters and someday that might be all we have."

She rested her hand upon Maggie's, trapping the letter between their palms. "You're more like Father than you think. Mother wouldn't have told me the truth. And she certainly would never apologize for it."

FIFTY-FOUR

"WILL THIS DO, SIR?"

"Brilliantly," Reuben said as the taxi slowed to a stop at the cemetery's gate. He handed the cabbie his fare plus an extra quarter. "Wait for me, please."

The cabbie jangled the coins in his palm then pocketed them. He cocked an eyebrow at Reuben in the backseat. "Listen, I didn't ask before, seeing as the fare was so good, and it's not my intent to offend, but what is it you're up to this far out?"

"Nothing crass." Reuben swung open the vehicle door. "I think I'm finally ready to say goodbye."

Five years ago to the day, he shoveled a mound of dirt atop a little coffin, and watched his world be buried with it. Two years later, he met Maggie, and it ever so gradually reformed. Today restarted his life one more time. One more chance to get it right.

Would she try to meet him? He'd purposefully rode nearly four miles outside the city so she cwouldn't. He missed her and he couldn't pretend he didn't. But he missed Charles as well. And Tena. Fontaine. His home, his family, and Mira most of all. Every part of Mira, the good and the terrible—he missed the familiar.

He'd had his wits about him for a week. No voices screaming, no mocking laughter. Just his own thoughts, and the freedom to be himself again, whoever that might be now.

He roamed through the gravestones, searching for one that

352

might stand apart from the others and eventually settled on Lucia Hadden. Only sixteen years old, she'd been dead now fifty-two years. The adjoining plot listed a deceased Betty Kirkwood and the blank engraving for her still-living husband Gregory.

Bending to retrieve a fallen twig, Reuben bent to chip the packed dirt from Lucia's name. "We all deserve a good story, do we not, Lucia?" As he worked on the stone, picking the grime from its edges, fibers spun themselves into a tale that reminded him of his cemetery girl, the one from two years ago, the mask of a woman he wished existed. Before they leapt onto the same train traveling in different directions.

"Back then Maggie would have created a wonderful story for you, Lucia." He rubbed his palm over the stone, licking his thumb to wipe the edges of each letter. "She'd say you always found the good in people; you never turned your back on them. You met Gregory and your life had meaning. Even if it only lasted for a year, barely time enough to discover anything. Who can say, maybe lies and truth didn't matter to you. Then, you were gone, and like the rest of us, Gregory prayed one day it would all make sense, only never believing it would. Doubting his very existence without you."

Reuben wiped his hands, standing with a flip of his jacket to hook his thumbs in his pants pockets. His sister asked him who he was now without her. The simple fact was he didn't know. And that was enough for now. Accepting the unknown meant the very thing he'd wanted all along.

Freedom to start over. Freedom to make new mistakes. Freedom to love and live again. Navigating through uncharted waters, equal parts terror and exhilaration.

He kissed the tips of his fingers to Lucia's name, remembering how Mira's engraving once scratched his skin. "Gregory loved you, Lucia, just as any of us love another. Until one day, we meet someone, like he met Betty, who leave us in wonder how there was ever any doubt. So he buried you side by side, believing that together you would welcome him into paradise. What then, Lucia, could be a more beautiful story than that?"

The wind swept through the tree branches, whistling across the church's stone facade to caress his face. Almost like the touch of a hand, a gentle kiss to his cheek. As quiet as a whisper, as compelling as a sigh. "Goodbye, Mira."

The taxi's horn startled him back to existence. Reuben wiped the corners of his eyes with his sleeve and headed back to the waiting driver. "'Bout time," observed the cabbie. He thumbed behind him to a covered carriage Reuben hadn't noticed. "You familiar with that dame? She's been watching you about ten minutes now." Behind the driver of the other carriage sat a young woman too hidden in shadow to identify fully.

Reuben tugged at his hair and swore. Maggie. Of course. "Yes, sir, I know her. Wait two minutes. I'll take care of this." Slamming the vehicle door, he stalked down the road, yanked open the other carriage, and stopped dead when he saw Tena waiting on the other side.

"Hello, Reuben." Tena smiled and all Reuben could do was stare. She was here. She was alive. He had known it, but seeing her was like extracting pneumonia from his lungs, unaware how long he'd labored to breathe until the air returned.

"How'd you know where to find me?" He struggled through the words.

Tena shrugged. "Would you believe I simply know you that well?"

"You asked the driver to take you to the most remote cemetery outside the city?"

She blushed. "I did actually."

"Then you do know me that well." Reuben laughed, finally releasing his death grip from the door handle. "Wait one minute." He jogged back to relieve his own taxi then slid into the cramped backseat beside Tena. He tapped on the driver's seat. "1282 Lemp Avenue, please."

The carriage settled into a rhythmic jostle as the double team pulled them along the narrow dirt road. Tena relocated her handbag from the seat to her lap, affording them a few inches more room, and settled into the seat beside him. "How have you been?" Reuben asked.

Tena absently unfastened and refastened her jacket buttons. "I have been better," she said slowly. "There's so much I need to tell you. The newspapers only know part of it. And Charles—"

"Stop," interrupted Reuben. "Don't tell me."

"Don't you want to know?"

"Yes. I guess." Reuben glanced at the driver, aware he was listening, and probably eager to hear any intimate details of *Titanic*'s sinking he could pass to the newspapers. After writing for the *Fontaine Gazette*, Reuben knew even small town papers could be ruthless. "But shall we leave it alone for today? It's May Day; let's not ruin it."

Tena nodded, her gaze lingering upon him. Reuben's neck burned under her stare, as he realized his beaten appearance was surely not what she'd expected. Half-healed bruises painted his face like an impressionist canvas, splatters of dull ochre and vivid jade dabbed over buried maroon and navy blue contusions.

"Tena, I can explain this—"

"Quiet. I already know."

"You *do*? What do you know?"

"I know everything. You and Maggie. Maggie and Lloyd. Please, I'd rather not repeat it." She reached for one particularly ugly bruise near his left eye, the warmth of her fingers lingering an inch above the skin. "Do they hurt?"

Wrapping his fingers around hers, he lowered the backs to his lips. "Not so much anymore," he murmured against her knuckles where the scars on his own fingers stood out against her unblemished skin. Unintentionally, his thumb found the smooth edge of her engagement band, and he couldn't bear the weight of her watching him. "I'm so sorry, Tena. Charles should be with you, not me. What can I ever say to make it better?"

Tena shook her head. Those brazen eyes lay burnt at the edges, holding out against the flames and not entirely succeeding. "Say you're my friend whether Charles is here or not." Her fingertips traced the mauve scrapes across his skin, healed enough to conceal the pain but not the reason for their existence. "Tell me you can overlook what Maggie did. Please say you'll still be here. I want to hear that you'll stay."

Of course he would, Reuben thought. He would always stay for her. He would always come back. For *her*. He could see it so clearly now; she was the woman on the porch in his dream limbo, his amazing light of hope in the anarchy of midnight. His lifeline. And one day, when the moment was right, when the misery of Charles's death was safely tucked away in memory, then he would tell her.

Reuben molded Tena's hand in his, their fingers softly entwining. "I'm not leaving, Tena. For you, that much I can always promise."

Tena's enchanting smile in response, the little way her lip dipped when she tried to conceal her delight, the same look she'd had a thousand times before and it never meant anything ... today that look could have sustained him forever.

To Reuben, time had always appeared as a predicable element. Seconds into minutes. Minutes into hours. Hours into days, on into a lifetime until death swallowed him up. He couldn't stop it or slow it down, rewind it or influence its course. It was a simple fact: Life keeps moving and one must move with it.

Yet, that was also the incredible thing about time. If you wait but a day, an hour—one single unexpected moment—everything can change.

EPILOGUE

JUNE 8, 1912—
ONE MONTH LATER

"HAPPY BIRTHDAY, MAGGIE. YOU'RE TWENTY. Are you ready?" asked the reflection in the bedroom's looking glass, the face of a woman many years older than the tiny girl Maggie felt inside.

"I thought I was," she admitted. "Now I'm not so certain."

She stared at her father's letter, held so often over the last month, and never opened. A letter this meaningful deserved an equally important moment for reading, and the starting point to her twenties felt like the perfect one.

Only now she didn't want to open it. Breaking that seal could change the entire course of her life. Those words would either affirm everything she knew to be true or disintegrate them. Her father always believed in her. He encouraged her, protected her, loved her enough to let her go; he wrote this letter in his final moments—whatever he said had to mean something in an enormous way.

Releasing the breath she'd held for five weeks, Maggie stripped the envelope open.

Dearest Maggie,

It saddens me that my time grows short. I find myself with many fears these days, in particular I fear what type of life I leave for you to endure.

There is a secret your mother holds, and once I am gone, she will not hesitate to tell you. I am sorry I cannot explain myself. It is her secret to reveal, although I fear she will attempt to destroy you with the truth.

Know this, Maggie: I have cherished you and Tena all your lives. I loved you more than any father could. Your happiness was all I ever wanted above my own.

Claim your happiness, my little girl. Love will find you one day. Ensure it is with a man who understands your heart.

Love always,
Father

No, thought Maggie. *Not again.*

With a sweep across the room, she dragged her traveling case from underneath the bed, burying the letter within her few belongings. Shoving the case back from where it came, she fell across the bed, hot tears dripping upon the coverlet.

Their mother would not have power over her or Tena, to control their lives with whatever surreptitious admissions she might say. She couldn't find them here, and Maggie would never, *never*, ask for the truth. She wouldn't again ask anyone to divulge their past. Not after Reuben. Not after Lloyd. Not after the secret she herself now carried.

Both hands slid to her middle, her fingers splaying against the slight curve as she closed her eyes to the only truth she could, at least for today, still deny.

Some questions were better left unanswered. And others were best never asked at all.

AUTHOR'S NOTE

HISTORICAL FICTION IS THAT strange genre of literature that takes readers into a world of fantasy, while still maintaining reality. With this goal in mind, I researched online, scoured the library, reviewed my own family's details, and watched my fair share of period films. I strive to immerse readers in the time period while ensuring the story is ultimately about the characters—their personal growth and relationships with each other. That is the appeal of historical fiction for me—dates may change, technology may improve, and fashions alter, but at our core people are inherently similar in every era. The past can always teach us something about our present.

So where did I begin? With my own family of course. Shortly before beginning my journey with these characters, I took on the challenge of documenting our family's genealogy. In the process, I discovered some truly amazing ordinary people. The names Reuben, Maggie, Tena, Charles, Emil, Friedrich, Laurence, Archer, Kisch, and Radford were all pulled from our family tree, although their stories are completely of my imagination. The one exception is Mira's story, drawn directly from that of Mary Kollasch. Mary died May 2, 1911, at the age of twelve, when the lumber wagon she rode in with other school children was hit by a train. Mary had an older brother on that same lumber wagon who survived. I know little else about them beyond the news article I found, but that one story led to much of the imagined dynamic between Reuben and Mira. Also, while I knew that the surname Gietl was quite clearly of German origin, I was surprised to find so many other lines of German immigrants in our family. And from those origins, the fictional Kisch family was born.

Well, what about Fontaine? Is it a real town? No. The town of Fontaine is completely drawn from my imagination; however, its inspiration draws primarily from Alton, Hampshire and other surrounding towns. Likewise, Fontaine's traditions surrounding the imminent marriage of the May Queen are fictitious, however still based in fact. May Day is a real holiday celebrated on May the first. Originally descending from pagan tradition, it does place emphasis on fertility and romance. Historically, the May Queen was chosen from one of the young unmarried women of the town and was the center of the May Day parade. May Day baskets and the maypole were also popular traditions. The moment I learned about this romantic by-gone holiday, I knew it would be the perfect starting point for the series.

And finally, I'm sorry to say that, while *Titanic* is clearly a real ship, *Höllenfeuer* never sailed the seas. She was inspired by two German ships that sailed across the North Atlantic Ocean at the same time as *Titanic* and were witness to much of the aftermath: Norddeutscher-Lloyd line's *Bremen* and *Rhein*. After learning so much about *Titanic* from the passengers' perspective, I wanted to incorporate this familiar piece of history from an alternative viewpoint: that of the bystanders and the passengers' families.

I could list every interesting story I came across, but then this note would be two hundred pages long, and I would never finish the next book. That said, if you have a question, contact me and we'll talk history! I love learning from you as much as I enjoy sharing what I've learned.

To send me a line or for updates on future projects, visit: kelseygietl.com

ABOUT THE AUTHOR

BORN AND RAISED IN ST. LOUIS, Missouri, Kelsey Gietl grew up with a love of books and excessive use of her library card. She earned a Bachelor of Fine Arts in Theatre Design and Graphic Design from Stephens College in Columbia, Missouri, and has made a career in fields from event planning and proposal writing to product management and communications.

In her free time—when she's not writing, reading, or researching—she enjoys yoga, musical theatre, beach vacations, and gallivanting around St. Louis with her amazing husband and two beautiful children.

Across Oceans is her debut novel, to be followed by its second volume, *Between Rivers*.

You can connect with her online at:
kelseygietl.com

68197149R00221

Made in the USA
Lexington, KY
04 October 2017